Apocalypse Orphan

Book One of
The Fractured Earth Saga

by Tim Allen

Spectrum Ink
(a division of Spectrum Ink Publishing)

Apocalypse Orphan
Book One of The Fractured Earth Saga

Cover photo credit: Fotolia
Cover design: Tim Allen

Apocalypse Orphan ISBNs:

Paperback	978-1-988236-01-8
Large print paperback	978-1-988236-02-5
Hardcover	978-1-988236-03-2
Large print hardcover	978-1-988236-04-9
Collectors' Edition	978-1-988236-05-6
Mobi/Kindle edition	978-1-988236-00-1
Epub digital edition	978-1-988236-07-0
Audio book edition	978-1-988236-06-3

About the Author

Tim Allen is a 28-year veteran fire captain for the Peoria (Illinois) Fire Department. His writing career began the day he responded to a structure fire. Tim and a fellow firefighter were nearly cooked in the inferno, and his supervisor told him to write a report on the incident. He was so upset by the experience that he left out details and wrote a brief summary that glossed over the terror of that moment. His supervisor felt that Tim's report wasn't detailed enough and ordered him to write a more descriptive fire report.

In the rewrite, Tim gave a highly descriptive narrative of the event. He titled it *Faraday Street* and included vivid details about what he had seen and felt during those two minutes of hell. His boss stated that this report contained too much detail, and it earned Tim a reprimand with the most severe punishment possible: an insubordination charge and a day off without pay.

Over the next few months, word of Tim's *Farraday Street* narrative got around, and the incident flared into controversy. Eventually, the report began circulating among his fellow firefighters, and when several co-workers wanted to read more of his stories, he began writing in earnest. Today, Tim devotes most of his free time to writing, while teaching courses on Hazardous Materials Response, Confined Space, Rope Rescue, and Structural Collapse to firefighters and local businesses.

Tim is currently writing a murder mystery entitled *Tethered*, but his primary love is science fiction. He has nearly a dozen sci-fi novels in development that run the gamut from planetary colonization and aliens to time travel. He also writes horror stories based on well-documented crime reports and true stories.

Other Books in Progress by Tim Allen

The Return of Akivasha: A mighty barbarian has awakened an ancient evil. Akivasha has tasted the hero's blood, and now she threatens to drive the world to the brink of destruction.

Prisoners of the Game: Computer characters are more than just cannon fodder. Learn what happens when the gaming world strikes back.

Syns of an Iron Wolf (Book Two of The Fractured Earth Saga): Commander Orlando Iron Wolf must rescue Syn, who has been hacked and downloaded to another server. Can Wolf overcome the Templars, Ruffians, and Jonar's quest for world domination to rescue his beloved?

Tethered: Brothers who were bound by life are now bound by death. One is good, the other evil, and one must be stopped to preserve life in this suspenseful crime drama.

Bones in the Well: Ancient curses transcend generations, and the sins of the fathers are never forgotten. Their evil deeds are inked in blood and haunt their families' lives for generations. Evil bides its time until it is too late to escape.

Reborn: I never die...well, in a sense I never do. At a certain age, this life ends and I remember all...my past lives, and all of my former loves and past deeds.

Thug: When a man from Compton, California, winds up in the Roman Coliseum, all hell breaks loose. Can a modern-day thug become the Emperor of Rome?

Author's Website: http://timallens.com
Publisher's Website: http://spectrum.org/books

Acknowledgments

I would like to thank all my friends for coming over and listening to me drone on about my books. They were kind enough to laugh when necessary and show amazement when asked. I also want to thank my editor Richard De A'Morelli for his edits, critiques, suggestions, and straightforward criticism. He has taught me so much in the last few months, and I consider him a very good friend. My brother Jimmy, who keeps reading my books, also gets special thanks. I must also mention my son Tim and my daughters Alexandria and Victoria. Finally, I would like to thank my wife, Martha Patricia Allen, for giving me the love and support I needed to finish this book. I love you all.

—Tim Allen

Through space and time my path has led,
Across infinite miles I have sped,
No planet has beckoned to become my home
Forever wandering, I remain alone.
I've never stopped to wipe my feet,
I've never found that life so sweet,
But through the eons I have seen
What finally belonging can mean.
No longer traveling to and fro
To far out places no one knows,
I've seen the faces changed by time
And mystic wonders that warp my mind.
Now I have returned to see you again,
Meet me smiling as a friend.
For I may threaten your world's sky,
Or I might quietly sail on by,
To travel deeper into the black,
But mark my words...I will be back.

-Commander Orlando Iron Wolf

The Warrior of Legend has arrived...

Trulane stared at Wolf with fear and awe. After a long silence, he said, "A legend has been told for many generations throughout the lands. Long ago, we had one moon in the sky, and the blue moon was not there. Then a blazing star came from the heavens and the world was made anew. According to the legend, a traveler will come from the sky in a flying chariot that talks but has no tongue. He will be a giant among men. He will be immortal, and no blade, poison, or claw will mark his skin. Men will follow the traveler as he leads our people to victory over all the kingdoms. When the world is under his dominion, he will lead a chosen few to the stars."

Wolf said to the young man, "That's a fascinating myth, but I am not that man. Look..." He pulled out his Bowie knife and sliced it across his hand to show he could bleed. Gazing at his hand in stunned silence, he saw no blood, no cut, not even a scratch. He jabbed the knife into the palm of his hand, but it deflected harmlessly and left no mark.

"I...I don't believe it," Wolf stammered. "What has happened to me?"

Trulane's face broke into a broad smile. "*You* are the Spirit Warrior of the legend!" he exclaimed. "You have come at last to lead our people to freedom and victory."

"No, I am just a man. Please say nothing about this to anyone," Wolf pleaded. "I know you are excited, but trust me. This can't get out until I have time to adjust. Promise me, Trulane, as my new friend." Wolf had a strange, sinking feeling that gave him a chill, and his whole body shuddered.

Part 1

Nomad

Chapter 1

The early morning light was brilliant, illuminating the heavens in a way most humans have never seen. The sky, devoid of an atmosphere, yielded a vision that was so clear it seemed it could shatter like fragile glass. In this crystal-like moment, Commander Orlando Iron Wolf was hovering 255 miles over the earth on the International Space Station. He had been assigned to the ISS by NASA to oversee a team of research scientists working on various assignments.

Wolf peered out the thick window as he finished his shift. The final orbits of the day were about to be completed. This day had started just like all the others. The current crew consisted of two botanists, two physicists, one biologist, and Wolf floating through the heavens, observing the planet Earth and doing mundane chores and experiments to keep themselves busy. The scientists had left Earth months ago from Cape Canaveral, Florida, aboard the Space Exploration Technologies Corporation (SpaceX) capsule. The rocket belonged to a private company, and NASA leased it to deliver new workers and supplies to the station. NASA had found it was cheaper to let someone else do the dirty work of moving people from Earth to the station—no ships, no maintenance, no fuel. Most of the expenses had been reduced by half, allowing for other project funding and making many NASA scientists exceedingly happy.

A few weeks earlier, the crew had been scanning an area in deep space near the red hypergiant VY Canis Majoris, which had already ejected half its mass and was surrounded by a reddish-orange nebula cloud. Against this bright background, a small shadow—a pinhole in the nebula's light—had drawn the crew's attention. The discovery had been placed on the back burner until yesterday when Wolf gazed through one of the ISS telescopes and noticed that the "pinhole" was larger and seemed to be growing. He fed the readings into the computers, and the instruments confirmed what appeared to be a large comet or asteroid moving at a high rate of speed towards the earth's solar system. He peered through the optical telescope and adjusted the filters to block some of the light from the hypergiant's glow. There it was. He looked away and then back over the same area. The anomaly was still there. It seemed remarkable to him that something so far away could be viewed with such a low-powered telescope, and he reasoned that it must be enormous. Tapping the communications module, he said, "Wolf to Command, do you read me?"

A bored, male voice came over the radio. "Yes, Wolf, we read you."

"I want you to look at grid fifteen. Look closely at VY Canis Majoris. There's a pinpoint of a shadow on its lower hemisphere in the nebula cloud. It's the anomaly I reported two weeks ago. I've been monitoring it. It's growing larger and has moved from the spot where I first detected it. I've fed all my current readings into the mainframe, but the computers up here have gone crazy, and warning lights are going off every few minutes. Can we have them turn the Hubble?"

"Turn the Hubble?" A long pause, then: "That's a little extreme, don't you think, Wolf?"

"I'm telling you, something is out there, and it's getting bigger and brighter."

"Oooh, little green men coming to get you...you got a gun in space?" laughed Charlie Richards, NASA's current mission director.

"Charlie, I'm serious. Have someone turn the Hubble or get the WISE explorer, Kepler, or the New Horizons to scan the area. We need to move those expensive pieces of shit into that sector to see this thing because whatever it is, it's coming fast." Wolf said with a sense of foreboding, not realizing that moving the satellites was harder than just flipping a switch.

"Okay, okay, I'll get someone on it. The astrobiologist we assigned to look into it went on maternity leave three days after you reported it. We only have the one scientist right now, thanks to budget cuts. That's probably why it fell through the cracks. In the meantime, upload your data to Cap Com."

"You better hurry. I've got a very bad feeling about this," Wolf muttered, reaching inside the collar of his flight suit and pulling at a leather necklace. It was connected to a small medicine bag that had been passed down through his family for generations. Made from buffalo hide and decorated with a wolf's head in white beads, it contained his "power items," including bits of rock, bones, herbs, and claws. He uploaded the data and then gazed pensively at the blinking lights on the computer.

Two hours later, Wolf was still sitting at the computer, reminiscing about how he had become a NASA astronaut. He had been top of his class at the reservation, which was not saying much. He went to college for free on American Indian scholarships and excelled in linguistics. Able to learn languages with ease, he astounded his linguistics professors, who passed him around from one to another like a coveted book. His downfall was engineering and mechanical design. He just couldn't remember the technical jargon and mathematical formulas; but he managed to squeak by and finish college. During his final year in school, he helped design a lunar rover that won NASA's "Great Moon Buggy Race" and put him on NASA's recruitment radar. A few months after graduation, he was approached by an Air Force recruiter and persuaded to join.

Standing six foot five and built like a Greek statue, Wolf was of Native American descent. His skin was a rich, copper color, and his eyes were light hazel. His black hair was long, well past regulation length. Deep dimples and straight white teeth added to his masculinity. Yet, he was unaware of how his good looks affected the opposite sex. Women threw themselves at him, but Wolf remained oblivious, which only added to his naïve charisma.

Wolf piloted jets in every minor skirmish America had during his tour of duty. He was highly decorated, and he had received the Air Force Medal of Honor during his last tour. He was debating whether to continue his military career when a NASA recruiter approached him and asked if he'd ever considered becoming an astronaut. The recruiter's name was Charlie Richards, and he was very persuasive. Wolf and Charlie became instant friends, so when Charlie offered him the job, Wolf couldn't refuse. After several years of intensive training, he became one of NASA's most respected astronauts. He was no rocket scientist—he could handle mechanical problems, but astrophysics and all the other learning just wouldn't stick. Everyone liked Wolf, and his high moral values, loyalty, personality, good looks, and single-minded dedication to duty made him someone people went out of their way to help.

Charlie came back on the radio, sounding alarmed. "Wolf. This is Cap Com. Do you read?"

"Yes, I read you." Wolf moved to a computer panel and used one of the many cameras to look in the direction of the mysterious object. "What do you have?"

"You won't believe this, but a large comet has come out of its heliocentric orbit. It's an unknown rogue. History does not mention it anywhere."

Wolf searched his memory but came up blank and asked, "A helia-what orbit?"

"Heliocentric...an orbit around the sun. How the hell did you get out there?" Charlie laughed. "Oh, never mind, I put you there. Almost everything in space is in a heliocentric orbit."

"So what's the deal—anything we need to be worried about?"

"We're running simulations right now. Early predictions on the Torino scale suggest it's a seven; we're calculating its mass now. It's on a hyperbolic trajectory with Earth. It might use us to slingshot back out into space. At least, that is what we're hoping. This comet's speed is incredible. We think it's a longer-period comet that may have originated in the Oort cloud. This one is unique, though, because we've never seen anything that moves this fast before. Wolf, we want you to tow the WISE further out into space. Take the shuttle that's docked to the ISS."

"That thing's a piece of shit," Wolf protested. "It's been sitting up here for months. Hell, it's so beaten up it can't even land back on Earth."

"Yes, but you are not landing back on Earth. We've prepped the ship so you can tow the satellite to its new coordinates. It will be a ten-day mission. The satellite can't take itself where we want it, so it's up to you," Charlie said.

"I don't have a co-pilot. It's against protocol for me to fly solo that long," Wolf replied.

"The solo mission has been approved, Wolf. It's a priority one mission that we have to launch ASAP."

"All right, send me the coordinates and I'll be gone in the next few hours," Wolf agreed reluctantly

"The coordinates have already been fed into the computer, and you'll leave in the next thirty minutes. This is urgent, Wolf. We'll let you know as soon as we get the final data. Cap Com out."

Wolf looked out into space and tried to visualize the comet, wondering where it had been all these years. What incredible wonders had it seen as it drifted on its lonely journey through time and space? He flipped a switch and announced, "All personnel...this is a priority one alert. Report to the mess area immediately." Wolf turned off the mic and headed off to the kitchen area to update his colleagues on what soon would take precedence in all of their lives.

The ISS crew assembled in the kitchen, grabbing snacks. The researchers on board were all from different backgrounds. Ron White was the most educated and next in command.

"I have news from NASA," Wolf said. "We've found a comet. That is nothing unusual, but this one is coming fast. It's a rogue from the Oat Cloud."

"*Oort,* Commander," Ron White corrected with a faint smile. "It's the Oort Cloud, not the oat cloud. How did you get up here?"

"Whatever. Oat, Oort ... anyway, it's a seven on the Totino scale. It could hit the earth."

Ron laughed. "Torino scale, not Totino scale. Wow! My friend, did you pay any attention in school?"

Wolf ignored him and continued. "NASA is moving the Hubble into position, and some other telescopes and satellites are studying it. Until we get more info, I want all your efforts focused on this comet. All research on your pet projects is to stop, and the new word of the day will be *trajectory*. Even though NASA is turning the Hubble and using the other satellites, I want any additional information you can gather. I'm taking the Endeavour out to reposition the WISE satellite. I'll be gone for ten days. Ron will be in charge here."

"Thanks, just what I've always wanted—a command of my own! Come on, Captain America, I'll help you suit up."

The crew drifted out of the mess area as Wolf and Ron walked to the ISS airlock. Wolf stopped to remove a flight suit from a locker and began suiting up. Ron checked the auxiliary breathing apparatus and seams of the suit as Wolf donned the bulky outfit.

"These suits are as old as that shuttle out there, and I don't like that you're being allowed to take the shuttle out alone for an extended mission," Ron said with a note of concern. "No way NASA should send you out in that antiquated heap without a co-pilot. It barely made it up here."

"I know. They've authorized me to fly solo for a priority one mission. NASA thinks this thing is bad news, and I've got a very bad feeling about it myself."

Ron helped Wolf with his boots, fastened the suit, and then helped him stand up, pushing him towards the airlock. He shut the door after Wolf and walked into the small tunnel connecting to the shuttle's interior. Pressing the speaker button, he said, "See ya soon, Wolf. Be careful out there."

Wolf boarded the shuttle. It was prepped and ready to go. NASA wasn't playing when they said to leave immediately. The sense of urgency gave Wolf an uneasy feeling. He eased into the pilot's seat, detached the locking clamps, and fired the port retrorockets to ease the craft away from the space station. Patching into the coordinates for the WISE, he headed out to the satellite.

An hour before he reached the WISE, he prepped the arm and reviewed the repositioning assignment to place the satellite in the projected path of the comet. When he spotted the satellite in the shuttle viewport, he radioed, "Endeavour to Cap Com. I am coming up on the WISE."

"Roger, Endeavour, we have shut down the WISE. You should be able to grab it with the robotic arm."

"Copy, Cap Com. I will be within range in sixty seconds..."

Wolf left the flight deck after executing the rendezvous and went to the payload bay. Once there, he put on his helmet and opened the bay doors. Using the remote arm, he grabbed the WISE and pulled it into the ship. As the bay doors closed and air pressure normalized, he removed his helmet and radioed, "WISE is on board. I am programming the new coordinates for redeployment."

"Roger that, Wolf. Get it into position and then head back."

"Endeavour out."

Wolf returned to the flight deck and, after verifying the coordinates, he fired the orbital maneuvering engines and headed towards the comet. He wished he could hold his medicine bag. Was it his imagination or were his ancestors crying out in fear? He used the shuttle's remote telescope to look out towards the comet. There it was. He could see the pinpoint in the heavens like a harbinger of doom and thought, *I don't like this ship, I don't like this assignment, and I've got a terrible feeling about this.*

Chapter 2

July 28, 2025

I n the early twenty-first century, the earth had two primary Near Earth Object Detection agencies: NASA's Sentry program and the NEODyS/CLOMON at the University of Pisa. In 2025, these were still the main organizations that tracked and mapped the skies. In the years since they were set up, neither had ever reported a new object that posed imminent danger to Earth, so budget cuts were inevitable. Massive layoffs had been announced three years ago, and world leaders were now pointing fingers at one another, blaming these cutbacks for the anomaly slipping into the solar system undetected. Something just outside of the Kuiper belt had caught the world off-guard, and despite state-of-the-art monitoring systems, satellites, and robotic artificial intelligence, it had gotten through.

It had been six months since Commander Orlando Iron Wolf discovered the anomaly. Based on scientific data gleaned from research as well as satellites and telescopes trained on the object, it was estimated to be the size of Rhea, one of Saturn's moons, and it was racing towards Earth with incredible speed. NASA had put Charlie Richards in charge of research into the anomaly because of his credentials in science, management, and the political arena. Everyone knew him, and everyone respected him. He was given the best of every department and division that NASA, the European Space Agency, the Chinese National Space Agency, and several others could offer.

When Charlie ran the numbers, he realized that the distances involved were staggering. The fastest ships available were still no faster than the New Horizons spacecraft that had visited Pluto in 2015. New rocket technologies had not panned out as the world's space agencies had hoped. Using 2015 technology, it would take eleven years to travel the 2.66 billion miles to Pluto. Although some new technologies showed promise, Earth had nothing that could travel the distance to get a close look at the anomaly. Whatever was out there was just behind Pluto and moving at incredible speed towards the inner solar system. After months of study, two of the world's top astrophysicists had reached the same conclusion—it would take eleven years to reach Pluto and observe the object if it were stationary; but the anomaly was streaking toward earth at incredible speed, reducing that distance to earth by the second. Its speed would bring it near Earth in approximately two years, and it would pass close to Mars on the way. If a probe was launched immediately, it would take two hundred and eighty-nine days to even reach a Mars orbit, and if it did manage to intersect with the anomaly, it would leave the earth's governments less than a year to prepare. The astrophysicists based their conclusions on gravitational lensing, direct imaging, radial velocity, and the simple transit method of briefly blocking some of the starlight behind the object.

The WISE that had been repositioned six months ago by Wolf had malfunctioned, and it was sending only blurry, low-resolution pictures. But there was no mistaking in the images that the pinhole had grown to a large pockmark on the VY Canis Majoris nebula cloud. The photos weren't sharp enough to reveal the shape or size of the anomaly. The Hubble might have given useful details about its shape and size, but a meteor shower had damaged its mirrors on its redeployment mission. NASA concluded it would be easier to fix the Hubble than the WISE, but it still took time to manufacture the mirrors and more time to get them into space. A crew had just completed the task of replacing the massive mirrors a day earlier, and everyone at Mission Control held their collective breath waiting for the first images to arrive from the Hubble after it was brought back online. The first photo it sent revealed the bad news—the anomaly was a comet. Within 24 hours, NASA had run the numbers, and preliminary data indicated it was the largest comet ever recorded. It was named Nomad, and the new mission was dubbed Nomad One. As the weeks went by and new data poured in from the Hubble and other resources, trajectory simulations confirmed Nomad would pass close to Earth—so close it could do some damage, whether it hit or not. Its relentless approach scattered meteors and small asteroids throughout the solar system. Spectacular meteor showers were reported on Earth, and several large meteor strikes were recorded on Jupiter. The gas giant's massive gravitational fields sucked them in, sparing the inner planets.

As more data was compiled, it became clear that the comet was on a collision course with Earth. The consensus of the world's astronomers was that Nomad would strike Earth far to the south, slamming into the South Pole at an approximate 135-degree angle. A few scientists theorized that the comet would "skip off" the South Pole without doing much damage, but they were in the minority. No one could predict with certainty how bad the damage would be, but there was no avoiding the fact Nomad was coming, and the world's governments scrambled to take steps to stop it. Amateur astronomers were able to see the comet as clear as day, now that they knew where to look. NASA's Sentry monitoring system gave off constant alarms, and the earth was bombarded daily by smaller meteorites as their orbits were affected by Nomad's translational kinetic energy. Near-earth objects like Apophis, 101955 Bennu, 2009 Fd, and their massive asteroid orbits were severely altered, and concern for additional impacts now ran high. Nomad streaked towards Earth majestically, and the world's governments had an estimated two years to prepare. All of the popular doomsday scenarios, from the Mayan Calendar to King Tut's revenge and Revelations, were in the news and on the minds of humans as fear of imminent catastrophe gripped the planet.

The major players in devising plans to rescue the earth were the United States, Russia, the United Kingdom, China, Japan, Mexico, and both Koreas. Japan, and the United States contributed resources and engineers to design and supply the building materials for a proposed moon colony. Mexico was tapped to provide most of the moon's workforce. Multi-skilled, well-mannered craftsman were needed, and America's southern neighbor was full of them. A female scientist came up with a design for a space vehicle equipped with a new type of engine that was nothing short of a modern scientific marvel, using sound waves to generate propulsion. Fast, easy-to-build and controlled by advanced artificial intelligence software, these new spacecraft were hailed as the saviors for humanity. The name stuck. Savior I, II and III would be enormous spaceships, each capable of carrying twenty thousand people and equipped with state-of-the-art nuclear generators. The power in just one ship was enough to light the planet for a full year. The ships were multi-trip carriers, designed to take off and land repeatedly. As soon as the moon bases were completed, these ships would transport people and supplies to the new lunar colony. The UN decided North Korea was the best place to commence the construction of the Saviors. Border defense posts were already in place and quickly reinforced by the Allied nations as the ships began to take shape.

Other nations were busy constructing large bunkers underground in capital cities around the globe. The U.S., Mexico, and Japan were busy on the moon, excavating terrain for enormous, permanent structures being built to house the world's refugees. Multiple temporary glass domes had been erected by the UN to house workers who were starting the construction process. The only setback was when specialty workers were briefed on their assignment and declined to go. They refused to leave their wives and children on Earth to face certain death while they risked their lives on the moon to save the world's elite. After days of contentious deliberation, it was decided that the workers' immediate families would be allowed to accompany them, but with one caveat—any family member with a genetic defect or debilitating illness would be sterilized to prevent breeding and passing on the disease.

The world's governments had agreed to set up a glass-domed city on the moon to shelter and preserve the world's greatest minds. A worldwide lottery was established to populate the underground bunkers that would house men, women, and children with certain IQ levels. No adult who scored below ninety was considered. An outcry erupted when various government officials, entertainers, religious leaders, and the extremely wealthy learned they were not automatically included in the evacuation plans. Money and fame no longer mattered since no one wanted or needed it. Where could one spend or use currency and what good was fame when the end of the world was mere months away?

The only people guaranteed a berth in the new moon bases and the underground bunkers were major world leaders, scientists, doctors, clergy, a few military leaders, and their immediate families. No senators, Congress members, governors, unrecognized rulers, or political lackeys were given a free pass. Security personnel entrusted with protecting world leaders were not included either; the United Nations Military Coalition was now in charge and would handle protective services. UNMC personnel were chosen from elite military and police candidates around the world. Their sole function was to ensure the successful relocation of major world leaders and their immediate families to the moon base. It was an uncompromising, difficult job because "immediate family" meant husband or wife and unmarried sons and daughters who still lived with their parents. Married dependents were to be left behind, and so were their children. This caused a firestorm of trouble that only trained personnel dedicated to preserving the world's leaders could handle. UNMC members were hated by not only the world leaders they served but also their families.

Catholic, Jewish, and Muslim clerics, clergy from Christian denominations, and those of the Baha'i and Hindu faiths, met to debate the role of religion in the coming catastrophe. Who would go? Which religions would endure? Only a limited number of spots were available. Finally, the UN decided that the only guaranteed spots on the list would be for the reigning Pope and a certain top Muslim cleric. Both had declined the preferential treatment at first. Meetings quickly erupted into arguments and then turned deadly with riots erupting around the world. The UN was adamant about the Pope and the Muslim cleric and begged them to reconsider. The Pope agreed but then promptly convened a council to choose someone younger to succeed him; that honor fell on a lowly, humble priest from South Wales. The Muslim cleric was well respected, and after a call from Russian and American leaders, he accepted a berth on the moon base.

Medical and psychological testing was stringent, and many people were excluded. All who didn't score within the set parameters were disqualified without exception. Those lucky enough to be chosen were advised that they could not take their families—only the individuals themselves would be saved from the coming holocaust. Some argued that the specialty workers were allowed to take their families, but the protests fell on deaf ears. Hard choices had to be made, and those in charge of humanity's preservation agreed that the future of civilization hinged upon this last act of evil. Humans would face the ultimate challenge of rebuilding a new world and didn't need sickness of any kind gumming up the works. A healthy breeding stock would be needed to repopulate. Plants, animals, and select humans were gathered from around the planet to prepare for the horrible days ahead. Family histories were examined carefully. Those who had a history of twins or multiple births in their genealogy, and those who came from unusually large families, were favored. They would be needed to repopulate the earth if possible, and if not, a new world would have to be colonized. About one million people would go to the moon base, and it would be protected by a garrison of two hundred thousand soldiers and their families chosen from around the world. The new station would be called Resurrection.

The plan was to preserve a limited number of males and females of every race, from the smallest rain forests' indigenous tribesman, who all refused to leave their forests, to citizens from the world's largest countries. If members of a race were already included in the specialty workers or other diverse jobs, their numbers would count towards that race's quota. Those selected would be moved off-planet to preserve the ethnic diversity of the human species. The selection criteria were straightforward: anyone with a criminal record, genetic abnormality, or physical disability, and those living in industrialized nations who had not been continuously employed for the last eighteen months, were ineligible. The survival of mankind depended on workers, not slackers. Those over the age of fifty and not on the scientific, military, management or agricultural teams were out of the lottery. Only those who would be of use to a future society were eligible.

The strict new rules triggered a wave of rampant crime. Rape and murder spiraled out of control, and local police were given judiciary powers to deal with those apprehended for crimes. The new justice system had one rule: lawbreakers were to be executed immediately—no trials, no appeals. Prisoners in maximum-security facilities were euthanized; non-violent offenders were released, as law enforcement no longer had the means to care for them. Those turned loose were cautioned about the new justice system, but many fell victim to it, committing petty crimes within days of being released for which they were executed.

Rumors surfaced that terrorist groups had infiltrated North Korea to steal the Savior spacecraft. The UN moved three hundred thousand troops around the construction sites to protect the ships and workers. Another half-million troops were placed along the country's borders to try to secure the region. Offshoots of the ISIS wing of radical Islam that had maimed and tortured thousands a decade earlier still existed, and familiar names resurfaced in 2025. People flocked to their banners, and the reborn ISIS, ISIL, and Boko Haram unleashed a wave of terrorism on the world. These groups and other petty warlords consolidated and attacked North Korea. The battle was intense, and suicide squads devastated the Allied troops. Fanatics who had infiltrated the Allied ranks nearly doomed the world. Ultimately, the renegade armies were defeated by the UN forces, but the battles took a bloody toll, leaving more than a quarter-million dead.

The underground bunkers were being built ahead of schedule, and they were designed to hold thousands. Secret military bases around the world were made public, and these facilities would support another million. The new civilization could sustain a mere five million of Earth's seven billion human inhabitants—saving everyone was not an option. Murder around the globe skyrocketed, claiming tens of thousands of victims daily, and the violent crime rate soared.

Super engines were developed that could reach the approaching comet in weeks, modeled after the Savior technology. Nuclear-capable nations equipped their nukes with the same engines and fired every weapon they had at the comet against the advice of the scientific community, but desperation raised the people's hopes in any mad plan. Coordination between countries was nonexistent, and some nations inadvertently foiled the plans of others. North and South Vietnam had gone rogue and tried to "ripple effect" the comet's course, throwing their entire stockpile of nuclear weapons at Nomad. It was beautiful and calculated perfectly, but it never slowed or changed the comet's course in the slightest. Saudi Arabia sent forty nuclear warheads to blast the comet head-on in a dazzling nighttime display. The comet absorbed them.

After several other failed nuclear attempts, some strange ideas were put into action. The asteroid Apophis was equipped with four huge engines that would propel the massive rock into Nomad in the hope that its path would be altered just enough to miss the keyhole to the Earth. The world held its collective breath as Apophis thrust into Nomad's gravitational field, engines fully powered to provide added impact. Satellites displayed the spectacular event as the two heavenly bodies met in a titanic collision. Apophis was obliterated, shattered like an egg thrown against a brick wall. Nomad never slowed and continued on its inexorable path to Earth.

France devised an Orbital Mass Projector comprised of three large iron balls filled with liquid mercury. The mercury was spun inside at high speed, simulating a planet's core, while the iron created electricity and produced an electromagnetic shield around the balls, giving each one a small amount of gravitational pull. The three devices were set to orbit the comet at high speeds, producing a gravitational effect. Each was programmed to emit its strongest point of gravity at a certain region on Nomad to nudge it just a degree or two at a time. The science was exact and it might have worked if Iran hadn't launched its whole nuclear arsenal at Nomad, destroying two of the OMPs and knocking the third out of orbit, frying its electronic circuitry.

Two shuttles were equipped with 64-megajoule rail guns. These electromagnetic guns could shoot non-explosive shells at a speed of Mach 8—eight times the speed of sound, or about six thousand miles per hour. No explosives were required; the kinetic energy alone was enough to vaporize most objects. The plan was to position the two shuttles and pummel the comet, attempting to blow off huge pieces and affect its spin. On the day they were to launch, Al Qaeda suicide bombers attacked the installation, destroying the facility and the two shuttles.

The next idea was to use titanium tethers attached to gigantic Mylar parachutes. They were put into spacecraft that would self-drill into the back end of the comet and auto-deploy. Theoretically, they would slow down the comet enough to allow Jupiter's massive gravity to pull it off course. Ten gargantuan spaceships were quickly built by the Russians to carry out the plan. It worked. The comet's speed decelerated slightly; then, the Mylar chutes froze and cracked into thousands of pieces. The Russian citizens went mad at this failed attempt, protesting that several more evacuation ships should have been built rather than wasting precious resources on a crackpot idea. Riots erupted and thousands died as the Russian military enforced a shoot-to-kill strategy to restore order.

Mexico built a thermonuclear laser fashioned after one at the National Ignition Facility in Livermore, California. At the time, it was the largest laser in the world. Mexico's mega-laser combined six hundred lasers, all focused at the same spot on the comet and designed to dump one hundred megajoules of energy into a narrow beam in nanosecond bursts. It was hoped that generating temperatures of two hundred million Celsius would induce nuclear fusion in the comet's core and cause it to blow up. It was spectacular and might have worked if Mexican cartels hadn't taken over the facility and seized the weapon in a daring raid. They turned it on a military installation in the U.S. and destroyed it, roasting thousands in the underground bunkers in seconds. The brazen attack was launched to prove that the cartels would use the weapon on the moon bases if their demands that cartel leaders be included in the evacuation plans were not met. When the UN refused and they turned the weapon on the moon bases, the United States and Russia nuked the facility. They had no choice.

By that time, the world's super powers were working on desperate, last-ditch efforts to stop the juggernaut of death. Everyone who could be evacuated off the planet's surface or housed in bunkers was already there. The Saviors had been built and flown several trips to the moon. The domes were operational, and six additional domes had been constructed, prompting another lottery. Those who occupied the underground bunkers were relocated to the moon, and the new lottery winners were admitted to the underground bunkers. The rest of the world's inhabitants had one month before Nomad's impact. Based on its current trajectory, scientists predicted it would smash into Antarctica at incredible speed, melting the southern ice cap instantly and flash boiling the planet in seconds. But that was just one theory. So many other theories had been advanced, no one knew who or what to believe anymore.

Charlie Richards had become the go-to guy for the government agencies, scientists, and citizen groups tasked with preserving humanity in its darkest hours. Earlier that morning, he had received a call from Dr. Cynthia Mason. He had heard about this woman for the last few years but never had the chance to meet her. What he did know was that she was young, beautiful, and extraordinarily brilliant. According to her personnel records, her IQ was off the charts, and her inventions were responsible for the domes on the moon, the Savior engines, and a new computer software prototype with incredibly advanced, artificial intelligence capabilities. When she called and asked him to set up a meeting with the world's top scientific minds, he readily agreed.

Dozens of scientists gathered in a conference hall in the newly christened Moon Base Resurrection, or MBR as it was called by those who occupied it. Many were angry about being required to attend this meeting on short notice. They were engrossed in their own pet projects and believed every possible strategy to stop Nomad had been tried. Arguments erupted and tempers flared as the scientists debated when and where Nomad would strike and the mundane question of why they had been summoned to this meeting.

The grumbling stopped and the scientists took their seats when a woman in her early thirties stepped up to the elevated podium. She tapped the microphone several times and then announced, "Ladies and gentleman, may I have your attention? I'm Doctor Cynthia Mason, and I want to thank you all for attending this meeting." The woman seemed shy and nervous as she explained, "Earth is lost. When Nomad hits, the planet will be devastated for hundreds of years. We will not be able to reclaim the earth in our lifetimes. Our leaders have chosen Enceladus, one of Saturn's moons, as our new home. It will take the Saviors a year to make the journey, and then we will work to make it habitable."

Dr. Mason paused, looking out over the gathering of scientists, and then she continued. "You are all aware that we have been landing habitat ships and offloading building materials on Enceladus. Soon, we will commence our new lives there as apocalyptic orphans. However, living on an inhospitable ice planet with cryovolcanoes is a short-term fix. It is possible humans won't be able to acclimate, and we don't know if it will even be feasible. If it doesn't work, we need a backup plan. That plan should not exclude creating a new earth."

Laughter erupted. One scientist yelled, "You're crazy!" Another muttered, "Stupid idea!" A renowned astrophysicist from Russia argued, "In less than a month, Nomad will turn the earth into dust. You want to make a 'new earth' to replace it? Waste of time!"

Dr. Mason looked down at her notes and bit a fingernail, waiting for the laughter and insults to subside. When a researcher in the back of the room shouted, "All beauty, no brains," she glared at the audience and exclaimed, "Fools! Do you think I would present a concept without scientific evidence? What I have discovered may save the human race from extinction."

"Let her finish," Charlie Richards admonished. "Show Doctor Mason the respect she deserves. The MBR dome you now live in is the product of her intellect. Please, Doctor Mason, tell us what you are proposing."

"Our research shows that most large celestial bodies are endowed with a certain magnetic resonance. In theory, everything that generates a magnetic field can be repulsed or attracted to a certain fixed point. The strongest force in the universe is the strong nuclear force, which holds the particles in an atom's nucleus together. If I told you I could safely break—or create—the bonds of the force that holds that nucleus together and control it, what would you say?" Dr. Mason asked the crowd. Without waiting for an answer, she added, "Recently, I was able to develop a Meson Field Disrupter. My device will allow a planet's magnetic field to be neutralized. The gravity that holds it to its orbit can be temporarily interrupted. We can then move the planet into a different orbit. In essence, we can make it go 'rogue' and control its path and destination."

The gathering sat in stunned silence, digesting Dr. Mason's words. Finally, Charlie asked the question on everyone's mind: "How can you accomplish that? Enormous power would be required, and the inherent risks in what you suggest could end all life in the galaxy.

Besides, the technology doesn't exist to create what you propose."

Dr. Mason gestured to several assistants who began handing out a document package with the details of her research and accompanying schematics.

"When France used its Orbital Mass Projectors, or OMPs, on Nomad, and Iran detonated its nukes destroying them, I discovered a new type of radiation had been created. I was calculating Nomad's speed at the time, and for a few seconds, the comet lost its magnetic pull. It slowed down measurably. I replayed the video feeds many times, studying the effect, and I concluded that the nuclear radiation had released a new type of anti-matter. I was able to recreate the effect in my lab. My Meson Field Disrupter creates a polarity wave. My calculations show we can use this wave to move any celestial body with a magnetic field. I can reverse the planet's polarity and break it free of its orbit. Using the Meson Field Disrupter, I can steer it wherever I want it to go."

"So why not use this wave to stop Nomad?" several researchers asked in unison as they began to grasp the concept.

"That was my initial thought, but I believe Nomad is moving too fast," said Dr. Mason. "By the time we deploy satellites around it and initialize the anti-matter wave, it will be too close to Earth for us to control. My concern is that our deep-range scans show micro-fractures along Nomad's x-axis. My device could split Nomad into several smaller comets that would impact different areas on the planet and cause even greater devastation instead of just hitting the South Pole. The only way to confirm whether these fractures exist is to send a shuttle mission to survey and map the comet. That will confirm whether OPM deployment would work. If this is going to happen, the mission needs to commence immediately—within the next few hours."

"We'll need to send an ace pilot who is fully aware of the mission's risks," Charlie interjected. "I have two pilots on the ISS with shuttle clearance. Commander Joshua Randle just landed to replace Commander Orlando Wolf.

"Isn't Commander Wolf the fellow who discovered Nomad? Perfect!" Dr. Mason gushed.

"Why is he perfect?" Charlie asked.

"He's already on the ISS, his replacement has taken over his duties, and he's the best, isn't he? If I'm not mistaken, he's multilingual and can communicate complex data to our international scientists in their own languages so they can double-check my theories and confirm my calculations." A dreamy look came over Dr. Mason's face for an instant, and then she was back to business.

"I agree. Commander Wolf is an excellent choice," Charlie said. "The problem I have is that the ISS needs to have one command person assigned at all times, so we don't have the manpower to fly a full shuttle mission. Protocol requires that two pilots be on board the shuttle for extended space travel."

"It won't require a full crew...and you have already violated protocol once by allowing Commander Wolf to reposition the WISE. The shuttle Commander Randle used to reach the ISS is equipped with my latest artificial intelligence programming. Only one human is required to initiate its neural network."

"Relocating the WISE was an urgent priority. We are short on qualified pilots presently," Charlie replied, looking embarrassed at being called out. "But if you are certain your AI will give Commander Wolf the support he needs, I'll make it happen."

"Believe me, my AI will support Commander Wolf better than any human crew could," Dr. Mason said with another dreamy smile that caught Charlie's attention and provoked a curious frown.

"Excuse me," another researcher interrupted. "Why not just move the earth? Wouldn't that be a better solution?"

"The earth is too large and we can't construct a sufficient number of emitters in time," Dr. Mason replied. "Another risk is that we might alter the earth's axis or send it careening into the sun. Remember, this science is experimental, and if it does go awry, I want it as far away from us as possible. If we had the time, we might be able to accomplish it safely, but not in one month—our time has run out."

Charlie was intrigued by the idea of moving a planet. He thumbed through the documents and studied the schematics, marveling at the complexity of the data Dr. Mason had compiled in just a few weeks. He glanced up at the woman who stood at the podium, admiring her beauty and brains, and then asked, "Since we can't move Earth, what planet do you propose to move, and where do you plan to put it?"

Not a planet, actually," Dr. Mason replied. "I intend to capture Jupiter's moon Ganymede and move it into orbit around the earth."

The room exploded in noisy conversation and Charlie bellowed, "Quiet! I want to know her plan."

"Thank you, Charlie. In sixty days, Ganymede will be the closest it has been to Earth in several hundred years, and it will be the farthest from Jupiter's gravitational pull. My plan is to initiate the Meson Field Disrupter at that time. If we work with the French, I can have the OMPs ready in two weeks."

A Pakistani scientist with coal black eyes and a condescending sneer waved a hand in the air and said in a thick accent, "Young lady, everyone knows that the nucleons must be extremely close together for this meson exchange to happen. That distance is about the diameter of a proton or a neutron. Now, only if a proton or neutron can get closer than that will the exchange of the mesons occur, allowing the particles to stick to each other. If they can't get that close, the strong force is too weak and other competing forces, like electromagnetic force, will influence the particles and make them move apart. How are you compensating for this?"

Dr. Mason bristled at being called *young lady*, and her anger emboldened her. "Sir," she replied, "I don't have the time to educate you, so I'll explain it with these five words: speed, extreme heat, and pressure."

The scientist threw Dr. Mason's documents into the air, sending papers raining down on his head as he glared at her with displeasure.

"How can you create OMPs that quickly?" asked another researcher with thick bifocals and unruly, snow-white hair who was seated in the front row.

"It's just a vimana. The science is very old. Sanskrit texts hint at them as ancient UFOs. France's OMPs gave me an idea, and I took the science to the next level. America has had Vimana models for years. Using the OMP science, I can retool them to carry out our plan."

"Why Ganymede?" the same researcher asked, squinting through

31

his coke-bottle glasses.

"It's the only moon in our solar system that generates its own magnetic field. It has a liquid iron core that will allow it to generate its version of the Van Allen belt. Simply put, it will hold an atmosphere and shield itself from the solar winds and the sun's radiation. Its icy crust will melt and form fresh water oceans once we heat it up by bringing it closer to the sun. It has the chemistry we need to sustain life and create a new home for humans until the earth can be repopulated. It's not much bigger than our moon, and I've run the numbers—we can bring it into orbit around Earth and leave two hundred thousand miles between it and our moon."

"Placing another moon so close to Earth will throw its tidal forces into overdrive. It will cause a new degree of wobble in Earth's axial tilt," the man in the front row persisted. "Won't this cause a further extinction event?"

"Earth will already be in an extinction event. It will undergo planetary chaos on a level unimaginable. With the new moon orbiting just outside the old one, we may be able to stabilize the Earth's wobble. It is speculation, of course, but I'm convinced we can do this. We should get the OMPs ready and on their way."

"How long will it take to break Ganymede loose from Jupiter's influence, and how long until it is placed in its new orbit around the earth?" Charlie asked.

"Once the satellites are deployed, it will require seventy-two hours to create enough matter to initiate the anti-matter wave. Ganymede will slowly move out of its orbit. The OMPs will fire occasionally and emit their strongest point of gravity at certain regions on Ganymede to nudge it a few degrees at a time and keep it on target. The process will take about a year. Once it is in orbit around the earth, the planetary ice will melt, and Ganymede will be geologically unstable for several years. The OMPs will remain in orbit, continuing to fire until Ganymede accepts its new orbit. If my calculations are correct, we should be on its surface building a new world within a decade."

Chapter 3

Less than an hour later, Charlie had received the go-ahead to conduct the mission. Wolf had agreed to pilot the shuttle alone and carry out the tests. He went looking for Ron to inform him of the change in his assignment and found him watching a live feed of earth. Wolf observed the images of civilization disintegrating in famine and despair with profound sadness and he remarked, "We'll have a front row seat to watch the planet die."

"It could be worse. We could be down there on Earth watching the world die," Ron said stoically. "It's strange they ordered the ISS moved into orbit around the moon...really strange."

"Yes, it is," Wolf agreed. "I have a new assignment, Ron, and I need to brief you and get going. Mission Control wants me to take the old shuttle that was mothballed at Kennedy Space Center out to survey the comet." Wolf didn't go into the details Charlie had shared about the shuttle. NASA had equipped the antiquated craft with an experimental nuclear engine and a supercomputer. It also had been re-skinned with a material harder than diamonds that would not rust or deteriorate. The engineers claimed it was practically impenetrable.

"The Atlantis? Lucky you...another solo shuttle mission. What's up?"

"Some lady scientist on the moon wants me to survey Nomad and take pictures from all angles. Then I have to set up a satellite to record the impact and do a Doppler mass calculation to determine the composition of the comet's core. I'll be gone about two weeks. NASA wants the rest of the team to ride out the impact on the space station. We are to record the strike for posterity, so get her locked down," Wolf said as he fastened his boots.

"It's your own fault they chose you," Ron said. "You speak every major language on the planet, and with all the foreign scientists and dignitaries on the moon base waiting for data, you are the perfect choice to relay it—no middleman to translate and mess up the details. In fact, I was told that a lady scientist has been asking all sorts of questions about you."

"Languages are easy for me. I've always had a knack for them," Wolf replied. "I hear them for a few days and then I can speak them. It's the math and engineering I can't get a lock on. As far as asking for me by name, I don't know any lady scientists."

"Apparently one knows you. She's probably the one who wants the information you're gathering. You do realize that the ability to speak any language is amazing? Not many people can do that. You definitely have a gift," Ron said. "Okay, Commander, let's do this. I'll walk you to the rear airlock and help you suit up."

"Thanks. I'll have to fly into Nomad's neon tail...they want a sample." Noticing Ron's face break into a grin, Wolf snapped, "What's so funny?"

"Neon tail? You mean ion tail. How the hell did you get this job?" Ron chuckled.

"You know I'm no scientist. I'm just a pilot. I didn't ask to come up here, but I'm glad I'm not down there." Wolf gazed out at the earth, framed in the window, and shook his head. "My people are descendants of the Hopi Indians. When I was a child on my reservation, I saw people die of hunger and drink themselves to death. My father was proud, a warrior, but he had been worn down by poverty and the government's policies. One day, he sat me down and told me I should honor all women, treat them as princesses, and never raise my hand in anger against them. Later that day, he attacked the Bureau of Indian Affairs office with a knife, and the police killed him. He could have slain many of them, but he only touched them with his blade, cutting their clothes. Not once did he draw blood, yet they shot him down. I was eight years old and saw the whole thing."

"Jesus, Wolf, I am sorry."

"With death heading towards the planet, all I can think of is that moment he was dying. He turned and smiled at me. Our Hopi rituals reflect our belief that all life—plant, animal, and human—are one. All living things are temporarily differentiated parts of a single, powerful life force that exists throughout the cosmos. In my view of the world, animals, birds, and plants have spirits from the same source as human souls, with their own plane of existence in which they, too, will someday manifest in human form. When my ancestors killed an animal for food or fur, they made an offering to the spirit of the animal, asking it to sacrifice its physical life, and then they expressed their gratitude. With this comet coming to kill all life, who do we pray to now? Where in the cosmos will man return if the world is destroyed?" Wolf asked.

"Only in war were my people allowed to kill. The Hopis could be fearsome in battle. Our elders told stories of warriors going crazy and killing indiscriminately. My grandfather once told me I had an 'old spirit' and I was *Koyaanisqatsi*, which sort of means 'crazy life.' He looked at me with fear riding him hard and told me my spirit would delight in battle. He warned me never to release my full anger. I have tried to control my temper, and I've succeeded where others of my tribe have failed," Wolf said, thinking back to his days before he joined NASA.

"We have a prophecy about the end of the world," Wolf continued. "The elders spoke of it when I was young. The Fourth World will end soon, and the Fifth World will begin. The signs over many years have been fulfilled, and only a few are left. The first sign: The coming of the white-skinned men, who took the land that was not theirs and struck their enemies with thunder. The second sign: Our lands will see the coming of spinning wheels filled with voices. In his youth, my grandfather's father saw this prophecy come true with his own eyes, as the white men brought their families in wagons across the prairies. The third sign: A strange beast like a buffalo but with long horns will overrun the land in large numbers. These were the white man's cattle. The fourth sign: Snakes of iron will cross the land. The white man called them railroads."

"How long ago was this vision?" Ron asked.

"It was before the white man came to the lands," Wolf replied. "The fifth sign: The land crisscrossed by a giant spider's web. Our power lines of today fit this one. The sixth sign: The land crisscrossed with rivers of stone that make pictures in the sun. Is this not our highways? The seventh sign: The Sea turns black, and many living things die because of it. Our oil companies pollute the planet every day. The eighth sign: Many youths who wear their hair long, like my people, come and join the tribal nations to learn their ways and wisdom. Many embrace the old ways and return to the reservations. The ninth and final sign: You will hear of a dwelling place in the heavens, above the earth, that will fall with a great crash. It will appear as a blue star. Soon after this, the ceremonies of my people will cease. These are the signs that utter destruction is coming. The world will rock to and fro. The white man will battle against people in other lands who possessed the first light of wisdom. There will be many columns of smoke and fire. There is more to the legend, but that is the gist. Now here we are with a bright blue comet coming at us. Fits a little too perfectly, don't you think?"

Ron shook his head and observed, "You can remember that entire story in exact detail, but you can't remember anything about physics and astronomy? Wolf, you are depressing me." He helped Wolf into his space suit, zipped and fastened the buttons and snaps, and handed him his helmet.

"Thanks, pal," Wolf said.

"Go take your pictures and readings and get back here. Then we can watch your heavenly dwelling place destroy Earth."

Wolf entered the airlock and boarded the shuttle Atlantis, closing its compartment door as Ron sealed the ISS airlock, waved goodbye, and went to the control module to initiate lockdown of the space station.

"Atlantis to ISS, retract docking clamps," Wolf said into the mic as his hands moved deftly across the computer terminal.

"ISS to Atlantis, docking clamps retracted. You are free to fire retros and initiate your engine for forward propulsion."

"Atlantis copies. Firing in three...two...one. Firing and moving clear of docking booms and into free space. Moving into preflight burn for Nomad mission. I'm patching into Savior Two. Atlantis to Savior Two, do you copy?" asked Wolf.

"Savior Two copies. You are clear to proceed on mission. Godspeed," Charlie responded.

"Thank you, Charlie. I'll see you in two weeks."

"Roger that, Wolf. You stay safe out there."

Wolf touched a module and said, "Computer, tell me all available information on Nomad."

A beautiful female voice responded, "Commander, it will take fourteen days to reach the ion tail of the comet. It is approaching Earth's gravitational field rapidly, and by the time you turn the shuttle around, Nomad will be caught in the planet's gravitational influence. When you arrive back at the ISS, your orders are to lock down the Atlantis and prepare the station."

"Ron is preparing the station. All I will have to do is lock down the shuttle and watch the end of the world from the ISS," Wolf said with an overwhelming sadness.

"Yes, Commander. I merely repeated what I was programmed to advise you."

Wolf gazed at the comet with apprehension as he headed towards the rendezvous point. Nomad was coming fast, and it was immense. It sat in the earth's night sky like a beautiful, blue beacon of death, churning like an ocean at high tide. The female voice on the shuttle continued: "When a large comet moves well inside the earth's orbit, there is the potential for a long tail. The current record for the longest tail length is the Great Comet of 1843. Its tail extended more than two hundred fifty million kilometers. To put this in basic terms, if the comet's nucleus was placed in the center of our sun, its tail would stretch past the orbits of Mercury, Venus, Earth, and Mars. Nomad's tail length is estimated to be five hundred million kilometers."

Wolf sighed, remembering that the world had been overjoyed nine months ago when a scientist predicted that the comet would hit the moon and somehow save the planet. But another scientist predicted it would still cause massive destruction by destroying the moon or causing the weather patterns to go haywire. Another prediction envisioned the comet propelling the moon into the earth and destroying not only Resurrection but also the planet. Several satellites and the ISS had been set to record the event for posterity. Much of what was left to record was pandemonium. During the last year, two and a half billion humans on Earth had been killed by wars, suicide, and murder. Everything outside of the military installations was a wasteland. Farms were abandoned, and other than the food stores set aside for the survival of the species, food sources had been depleted.

Wolf had been out just over thirteen days and brought the ship into position to conduct the scan on the comet. "Atlantis to Savior Two, I am four minutes out on Nomad and picking up gas readings from the dust tail. The nucleus is solid hydrogen with a temperature of minus four hundred fifty degrees Fahrenheit."

"Savior Two to Atlantis, that is impossible. That's almost absolute zero, and that's as cold as you can go...which can't be achieved because of the Heisenberg Uncertainty Principle and entropy-related laws of thermodynamics."

"Uh...Atlantis to Savior Two, please put that into pilot dummy talk. I'm just reading from the instruments. I don't know what the Hindenburg principle is."

"Jesus, Wolf, didn't you pay attention to anything in college?" Charlie sputtered.

"Charlie, I'm telling you, it is negative four hundred fifty degrees Fahrenheit, and the closer I get, the colder it is."

"All right, Wolf, what are the other gasses?"

"Carbon dioxide, helium, argon, and three others our instruments can't identify."

"Really? Well, you discovered them, so you get to name them. Give it some thought," Charlie laughed.

Wolf laughed, too, but without humor. "Real funny. I am getting magnetic interference on my instruments, Charlie. The ship is accelerating. I am being drawn towards the comet. This ship isn't magnetic, is it? I thought it was made of carbon and plastics?"

Charlie grabbed the specifications chart and scanned it, then replied, "It's made of reinforced carbon, an alloy of titanium, aluminum, vanadium, reinforced polycarbonate, fiberglass, and carbon fiber. The tiles are made of silica ceramic with diamond-infused alloys that can withstand temperatures up to three thousand degrees Fahrenheit while maintaining the vehicle's structure at absolute zero. Yes, it has some magnetic properties. Fire your jets and get out of there!"

"I have been doing that for the last few minutes. I'm at full power and losing heat in the shuttle. Cabin temperature has fallen fifty degrees in the last several minutes, and the thermal heaters are on full power. Charlie, I can't escape Nomad's gravitational pull!" Wolf reported in a shaky voice. He shivered, and it wasn't entirely from the cold. Fear crept up his spine; panic wasn't far behind.

"Check your sensors. How far away from the coma are you?"

"Charlie, I am not sure how long I will be conscious, so how the hell can I tell you when I will go into a coma?"

"Wolf, you are an idiot. The coma is the part around the comet's nucleus."

"Oh. Looks like...one hundred thousand miles and closing fast. Charlie, I'm showing negative four hundred fifty-three degrees Fahrenheit on my sensors. It's thirty below in the cabin and dropping twenty degrees a minute. At this rate, I'll freeze to death soon." Wolf reached over and twisted a control knob, trying to turn up the cabin's meager heating unit.

"Have you tried to reverse the polarity of the engines?"

"Like I honestly know how? Damn it, Charlie, help me!"

"One of the techs here thinks that if you shut the engine down and then fire it at full power in short bursts, you might be able to slingshot around the comet."

"Even *I* know that won't work. The gravitational pull would draw me into the comet in seconds."

"Wolf, can you turn the thermal heaters up any higher to warm the cabin?" There was panic in Charlie's voice as he paced between the evenly spaced computer terminals at mission control.

"They're up to one hundred thirty-five degrees right now. They're not compensating for the decrease in temperature."

"We're trying, my friend. I've called Doctor Mason. Maybe she can think of something that will help."

"Hurry up, Charlie. I don't know how much longer I can last," Wolf said with urgency, his teeth chattering uncontrollably.

"Doctor Mason is on the line," Charlie announced.

A beautiful feminine voice transmitted through his earpiece, "Mister Wolf?"

"Charlie, the computer just called me Mister Wolf. Where's this Doctor Mason, I don't have time to talk with a computer."

"This is Doctor Mason. It's *my* computer, I designed it and it uses my voice...but we haven't the time for that. Listen to me, Mister Wolf. Get into the Deep Space Chamber. I'm on my way to the moon base's underground storage area where an experimental DSC is kept. I'll walk you through the start sequence. Go to the computer's main control board—it's marked SYNTHEA on the console."

Wolf moved quickly to a console and said, "I'm there...now what?"

"Get down on your hands and knees. Reach under it...there's a power rod that needs to be inserted. Push it in."

Kneeling, Wolf reached under the control panel. He groped around until he found the power rod and pushed it in. The ship shuddered briefly as the computer activated.

"I'm pretty sure the flaws are fixed, and I have added features that will improve its chances of working correctly," Dr. Mason said.

"The damn thing doesn't work? Why the hell is it up here?" Wolf demanded.

Dr. Mason's voice broke up into static so Charlie relayed for her. "Doctor Mason is far underground on MBR, Wolf, and her transmission is weak, but I'm reading her clearly. She says her prototype in the moon base lab is functioning as expected and shows promise. Don't give up, Wolf. We'll figure this out in a few minutes... sorry, a few seconds. We have everyone working on this. You may have to go into the DSC. You've activated Synthea. It may be the only thing that can save you."

The Deep Space Chamber was an experimental cryonics chamber. Scientists believed they had finally solved the problem of cryonic hibernation for storage of humans in liquid nitrogen. Atlantis had been equipped to take animals into space with scientists on board to experiment on them. The Atlantis was equipped with six DSC units, but they were never completed because Nomad took precedence. Wolf looked at the large, titanium, egg-shaped chamber. It was approximately five feet long and three feet wide. The lid was raised, making it look like a giant clamshell. What made him shiver were the three large needles that would be inserted in his temple, ear, and spine when the machine activated. The needles would penetrate the cerebellum from the back, one going to the frontal lobe, another offset towards the rear and inserting into the ear, self-guiding into the parietal lobe. In theory, this would regulate the temperature of the brain, keeping it active at ninety-eight degrees Fahrenheit and delivering high-quality oxygen to the organ to keep the tissue alive. A tiny electrical shock injected into the spine would trick the brain into thinking it had food, although the body would be slowed so much that it would require no nutrition at all. An auditory sensor inserted into the left ear would continually play music, read books, and subliminally educate the subject for the duration of his suspended animation, theoretically stimulating the subject's will to live.

It didn't help matters that all of the animals used for testing the DSC had died. Some woke up and immediately went into cardiac arrest; others suffered a cerebral hemorrhage within a few seconds. The DSC was so finely insulated that it could maintain its interior temperature for many years, even if the system malfunctioned and shut down. The computer on board the Atlantis was built upon an artificial intelligence system years ahead of its time. It was designed to mimic human life and preserve the ship and its crew at all costs. It was the greatest of man's modern achievements.

"Damn!" Wolf cursed, "I just lost my sensors. I am showing minus four hundred fifty-eight degrees outside. It is minus ninety in here and still dropping. Charlie, I'm freezing." Wolf again looked at the DSC and said in a somber tone, "This Deep Space Chamber has never been tested on a human. It's a death trap. Shit! My suit is starting to malfunction. Charlie..."

"Yes, Wolf?"

"Bye."

"Wolf, get your ass in the DSC! It's your only chance. Wolf? Wolf? Answer me! Are you there? Savior Two to Atlantis, copy."

There was no answer...only static. Charlie sighed and picked up his phone to update his superiors. He looked at the glum faces around him and shook his head as he wiped a tear from his eye.

* * *

The shuttle Atlantis was in trouble. It was being dragged behind the comet. The nuclear engines had managed to equalize the magnetic attraction of the comet and kept the ship off the nucleus. Its super-computer compensated for mass and drag. In theory at least, the I29 Plutonium Interior Fusion Linear Exhaust (IFLEX) engine would run for the half-life of the plutonium-244 that powered it. It had a half-life of eighty million years. It had taken the entire world's supply of plutonium-244 to make the engines on Atlantis. With no moving parts, it used the radiation it emitted to propel the ship. The computers ran state-of-the-art Pentium15 software with a human interface named Synthea.

Wolf managed to open the port retro rockets at full throttle and turn on automatic flight commands. Then he climbed into the DSC. He was losing consciousness as the needles drilled into his head. Before he blacked out, he thought he saw a woman close the lid of the DSC.

The fully activated Synthea sealed the lid and then engaged the DSC, taking the only available avenue to save Wolf's life. Whether he would survive remained to be seen. He was frozen solid in milliseconds.

The shuttle Atlantis was twenty-five thousand miles from the comet's nucleus as Synthea initiated simultaneous downloads from the libraries of MBR, ISS, Earth, and the Saviors, storing massive amounts of data in her vast memory banks.

* * *

Charlie stared at the console that tracked the position of the comet. He did not see the blinking lights or other telltale signs of Synthea's downloads. He had always laughed at Wolf and his ignorance of space. Now, a man he called a friend had been ripped out of his life. Wolf knew he was going to die. Charlie had heard it in his final word: "Bye." Then his life support readings flatlined at ISS Medical.

Someone was crying. A woman's voice kept sobbing, "It's my fault he died." It took a few seconds for Charlie to realize it was Dr.

Mason. She was still on the line. But why was she crying? She barely knew Wolf.

"Savior Two, this is ISS. What's happening? Wolf's life support readings flatlined on our screen. Over," Ron announced.

"Ron, this is Charlie. The shuttle was caught in Nomad's gravity well. Wolf might have entered a DSC, or he may have frozen to death. Either way, we've lost him. I'm sorry."

"Wolf was a good man...and my friend," Ron said with sadness in his voice.

"That's not all. We fed the partial data from the shuttle's computers into the simulation. Wolf wasn't able to scan for deployment of the OMPs, but we've discovered Earth's gravity has influenced Nomad's angle of impact. We have less than ten days before the comet hits. It has picked up speed. The gravitational effects are causing havoc on Earth even as we speak. And we've discovered Nomad has a solid hydrogen core. My god, we are in trouble! Do you know what happens when solid hydrogen ignites?" Charlie asked in a panicked voice.

"There's no such animal, Charlie. In 1935, a couple of physicists predicted that under the immense pressure of two or three million psi, hydrogen atoms would display metallic properties. The hold over their electrons would weaken, allowing them to escape. Since then, metallic hydrogen has been the holy grail of high-pressure physics. Hell, Charlie, we think that is what Jupiter is made of. How can we know what will happen if it's ignited?"

"We will know soon enough. Doctor Mason was right—if we had tried using the OMPs on the comet, it wouldn't have worked," Charlie said.

"Probably not. I have to tell the crew about Wolf. I'll check in with you later...if we're still around. ISS out."

* * *

Ten days later, nearly all of the earth's remaining inhabitants were staring up at the sky in terror. Nomad was conspicuously visible now, even in broad daylight. It was like having another sun in the sky, but an intense, bright blue. Its tail seemed to wrap around the sky like an ancient dragon. The comet's proximity to Earth was causing freak electrical storms, and the weather around the world was in chaos. Tsunamis and hurricanes hammered coastal cities, and several extinct volcanoes erupted. Doomsday had arrived.

Less than a billion people were still alive on Earth, and a mere four million were packed into the military shelters that had been constructed to ride out the impact. No one seriously believed the shelters would hold up, but some remained hopeful. Several auditorium screens on the MBR showed the global destruction, and satellites provided a real-time feed of the incoming comet. The Saviors, MBR, and the underground bases on Earth watched the impact. All held their collective breath as death rained down on humanity's once-proud accomplishments.

All of the top scientists on the moon were watching the horrific scenes play out on earth, except Dr. Cynthia Mason, who had opted not to watch. She had spent the last week and a half in the underground storage area working on the DSC units. She had been obsessed with work and barely slept since the failed shuttle attempt in which Commander Wolf had been lost. An exact replica of the shuttle was stored in the massive underground area, and she had been working around the clock in a frantic attempt to rescue Wolf. She refused to believe he was dead.

Dr. Mason had installed the DSCs and her newest AI computer technology into the replica ship. She attempted to establish a communication link with Wolf's shuttle using her AI's newer, state-of-the art capabilities. She believed that if Wolf had managed to activate SYNTHEA's matrix, her newer and more powerful AI should be able to pinpoint and hijack his older, less sophisticated system. She would then be able to ascertain whether he had made it into the DSC...or died. A chill ran down her spine at the thought.

Dr. Mason had just run a successful simulation on whether Wolf could have survived the cryogenic freezing. It was promising. Her newer AI also informed her it had finished scanning the comet and reported Wolf's shuttle was intact and functional. Suddenly, a terrific impact shook the MBR. The force of the impact sent Dr. Mason staggering to the ground. She crawled to a command module and flipped a switch, gasping at what the cameras revealed. Another terrific concussion forced her to close up the shuttle. She waited impatiently while the payload bay doors closed. Several massive explosions rocked the underground chamber with the force of a dozen nuclear bombs. She shouted an order to the ship's computer as an entire section of the room fell in and the lights went out.

The noise from the impending collision was astounding. Howling winds tore down what remained of buildings and uprooted trees all over the planet. Major earthquakes shook the planet, loosening the lithospheres of the tectonic plates; somehow, the underlying asthenospheres remained intact. The comet lit up the sky as it approached within a few thousand miles of the earth, and then it hit in Antarctica.

The explosion was immense. As Nomad hit the Antarctic plate, it impacted at such a shallow angle that it plowed through the planet like a bullet through an apple. Molten rock was thrown into space as Nomad burst through the earth's crust. After losing some of its mass, the comet continued on its journey through the stars, slightly smaller and just a little slower. Still, volcanoes around the planet erupted and lava flowed in copious amounts, covering cities as pyroclastic clouds annihilated what remained of the land.

When the comet hit, large chunks of the planet as well as the comet ricocheted into space. A small chunk of the southern hemisphere had been vaporized, and the earth had shifted ninety degrees, reversing latitude and longitude. It was now tipped like Uranus, and what was left of its southern pole pointed towards the sun. Its far northern region was in shambles but remained intact. The planet's rotation also had changed. It spun, not like a top, but like a barrel rolling down a hill—a shaky, rattling roll caused by the missing chunk ripped from its southern pole.

The Saviors, MBR and the ISS had watched the impact from the satellites positioned around the planet. As the devastation unfolded, the massive amounts of data Synthea was downloading went unnoticed. Planetary debris and meteors that followed destroyed the ISS and several of the domes on MBR. Of the one million people inhabiting the moon base, less than five thousand survived. Meteoric debris had smashed into the population domes, and thousands were killed instantly, blown into space, or suffocated as the atmosphere was sucked from the domes' interiors. The science dome was buried under tons of rock, and several of the world's top minds were presumed dead. Among the missing was Dr. Cynthia Mason, who had gone to the underground storage area to try to help Wolf. Only the farming domes were spared.

The three Savior ships had been manned as a fail-safe measure. One ship was exclusively military; another was designed for scientific research; and the third was a state-of-the-art farm ship equipped with areas for livestock and food processing. Fifty large farms occupied ten floors of the vessel. Each farm was the size of three football fields, or roughly four acres. The soil had been scooped from the rich, black earth in Illinois and Iowa. Artificial light was installed to photo-synthesize plant life. A nitrogen freezer held several thousand species of eggs and sperm from man and animals. Only the crew and food animals were allowed on the ship. An enormous seed repository stored all the current plant life in stasis. If humans were ever going to reclaim the earth, at least they would have the means and the building blocks to do so.

A badly shaken Charlie broke the silence. "Oh, my God! Everything is destroyed! It will be thousands of years before we can resettle there." He stared at the faces of his command crew and then radioed, "MBR from Savior Two. Do you copy?" Static answered his call. "Rotate satellite three-two-one to view the moon base. Move people! We have to know what's going on."

"MBR from Savior Two. Do you copy?" More static. "ISS from Savior. Do you read me?" Static.

"Is the Hubble still operational?" Charlie asked, and someone answered that it was not. He tersely ordered, "Move satellite two-fifteen to high moon orbit, and get me General Mitchel on Savior One. Prepare this ship to move to the MBR landing zones."

"Savior Two, this is Savior One, I have General Mitchel on Com. Go ahead," said a distraught female voice on the radio.

"General Mitchel, are you able to raise anyone on MBR or

Earth?" Charlie asked.

"No, we lost contact with the bunkers a few minutes before impact. We were preparing to land on the MBR landing zones," a gruff voice answered on the radio.

"Yes, General Mitchel, we were of the same mind. Once we know what is going on, we need to meet face to face. Most of the world's leaders were on MBR, and as of now, General, you are driving this train if no one else is alive."

"I know. Let us hope it is only temporary. Savior Three, stay put. Savior One and Two move to position to check out MBR," General Mitchel ordered.

The giant spacecraft moved silently, like sharks gliding through surf. There was so much debris surrounding Earth that it was impossible to determine the extent of the devastation, though the outline of the planet could be seen through the rubble. Looking beyond the earth, one could see Nomad speeding away, barely affected by its glancing blow with the planet. As the ships entered geosynchronous orbit, the damage became evident. MBR had been destroyed. Scattered life signs appeared on the screens, a few deep underground, but most in the agricultural dome. The central glass domes had shattered. Bodies floated in space like dust in the air after a bag of flour has been dropped. The agricultural domes were intact, so food would be available, but the other domes might be beyond repair. Thousands had died on MBR and tens of millions on Earth.

"Savior Two from Savior One. Copy?"

"Savior Two copies...go ahead."

"Charlie, this is worse than we thought. We need to land and send rescue parties to search for survivors. I want to take a ship close to Earth and see what we have left to work with. Get your team together and give me a timetable of when you think it might be safe to land. MBR's farming dome will be our permanent base for now."

"Yes, General, we'll get to work on it immediately."

The three Saviors were repositioned to land on the moon in an attempt to save what was left of humanity. The ships carried sixty thousand people. Would humanity rise from this catastrophe? Could it bounce back? Fighting men and women, scientists, doctors, and farmers had survived. The mission would be a Herculean undertaking, and it would severely test the resilience of the human species to build from absolute destruction and the ultimate depths of despair. But this story is not about humanity's resurrection from Nomad's destruction; it is about a man who returns to Earth far in the future. This is the story of Commander Orlando Iron Wolf.

Part 2

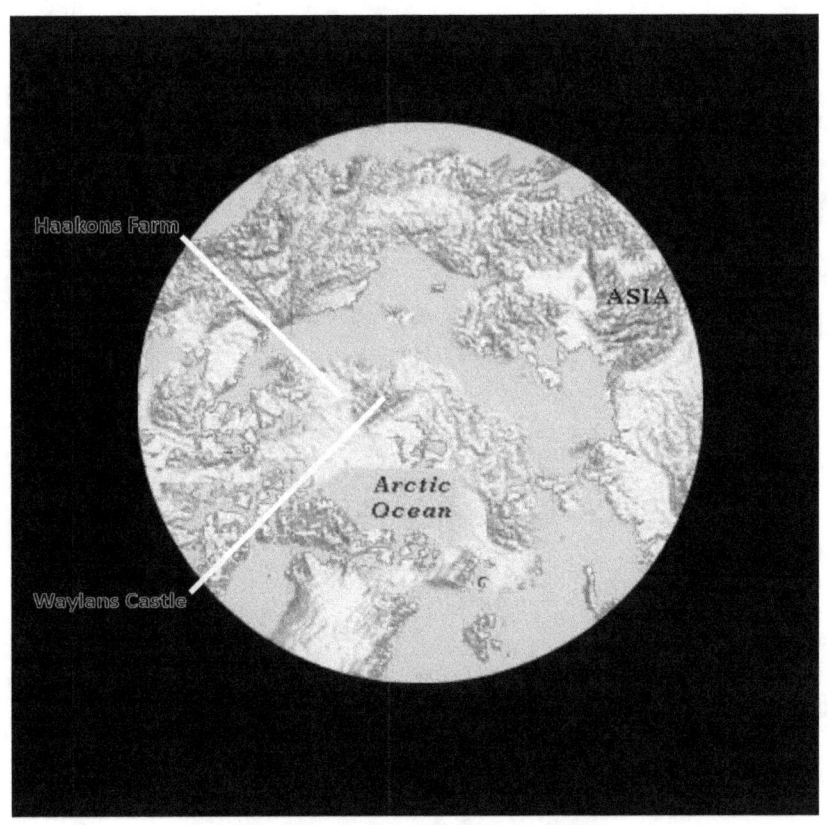

The New World

Chapter 4

Nomad had hit planet Earth and knocked it off its axis, tearing away the southern pole. It would be fifty thousand years before the comet's orbit brought it back to Earth. As the centuries passed, a small spacecraft remained trapped in coma of the comet, its compact but powerful engine playing a tug of war that kept the ship from being consumed in the comet's nucleus. The ship's lone occupant remained frozen solid in an experimental cryonics chamber. The comet sped through the galaxy, passing binary suns and skirting black holes, quasars, and blue giants. It streaked past alien planets where inhabitants marveled as it appeared in their night skies and eventually disappeared. Some worshiped it as a god or an ill omen; others were scientifically advanced enough to study it. None suspected the lone hitchhiker slept frozen in its coma.

As Nomad traversed the galaxy, it lost about half its size after violent impacts with asteroids, meteors, and several moons. The tiny ship in its coma had been pulled in deeper after one collision with an asteroid many centuries ago. The ship was now frozen to the comet's surface. Its diamond-hard shell protected it from damage; its nuclear engine remained operational and pointed inline to the comet's trajectory. It was actually propelling the comet to some small extent, causing the comet to spin awkwardly, propelled by the thrust of the wide-open engine. The ship's computer kept the engine operational, firing it at intervals, repeatedly trying to break it free from Nomad's surface.

Eventually, Nomad completed its vast orbit through the Milky Way and returned to the small solar system it had visited so long ago. If Nomad were sentient, it would say it wasn't a terrible comet or a doomsday harbinger; merely that it was a traveler. It would recognize the solar system it was now entering and remember it had collided with a small blue planet. It would recall that there were eight planets in the solar system, some with multiple moons; a ringed planet; a hulking orange one with a red spot; and the small blue one, now with two moons. One of the moons orbiting this watery blue world was dead and cold; the other was blue like the planet it orbited. Nomad would remember the larger of the two blue marbles; a diversity of life had thrived there when it streaked through this remote part of the galaxy fifty thousand years ago. It had damaged the planet when it collided, and the planet had inflicted its own damage on the comet; yet both had survived. Now, Nomad was back to drop off something it had taken on its previous visit.

Nomad lost more of its mass as it came within the gravitational pull of the huge orange planet. Large pieces of the comet were torn loose and crashed upon the moons in orbit around the gas giant. It continued on its course, ejecting a mixture of carbon dioxide and hydrogen gas from the intense heat of the yellow star at the center of this small solar system. Nomad passed Mars, and as the heat of the yellow sun intensified, more and more of its ice melted. A large piece of ice shattered, and a small metal object ejected from the comet's surface, its computer firing the ship's engines with precision timing to avoid the vast debris field of ice and rock strewn across its path. The craft was battered and beaten, yet it remained operational. It headed towards the earth, and at its maximum speed, it would take months to get there.

The small vessel pulled away from Nomad, and the nuclear-powered heaters inside the cabin began to compensate for the extreme cold. Ever so slowly, the temperature rose and life support within the cabin was gradually reactivated. The onboard computer assessed the body frozen solid in the DSC unit and ran countless simulations on how to thaw it safely, settling on a plan to defrost the body gradually over a six-month period. The computer also slowed the engines and entered orbit around Mars. Nomad continued its lonely trek back into deep space. Perhaps, if the comet survived, its orbit would bring it back to this sector of the Milky Way in another fifty thousand years.

* * *

Six months after the shuttle broke loose from Nomad and entered an orbit around Mars, a weak magnetic storm shook the craft.

Inside, a man slept in suspended animation on a metal cot in a clamshell-shaped, cryonic chamber. The vibrations from the storm continued, and the man stirred. Suddenly, his eyes blinked open. The light in the module was intensely bright. He had no idea where he was, and it took several minutes before he figured out who he was. He was lying on his back in the closed shell of the DSC. He heard a hum and felt excruciating pain as the needles embedded in his skull retracted. Lights on a nearby panel blinked rapidly. The man tried to roll over but was too weak to complete the action. His muscles were sore and numb; it felt like he hadn't used them in weeks. Little did he realize that he had not stood and flexed his muscles for thousands of years. As a wave of vertigo hit him, he began sweating profusely.

After about an hour, the man's memory drifted back. With tremendous effort, he rolled onto his side. The clamshell opened, and he inhaled stale air. Touching his face and head, he discovered he had a full beard and two feet of tangled black hair extending down his back. He still wasn't thinking clearly, so it didn't register in his mind that something was amiss.

When Synthea sensed Wolf had awakened, she activated the artificial gravity and opened the DSC. Thirty minutes later, he made it up into a sitting position. He lurched to his feet and stumbled to the captain's chair, falling into it. Dizzy and out of breath, he pressed the communicator button and tried to talk but only managed a choked squawk. He swallowed hard, trying to make saliva in his mouth to alleviate the dryness. Finally, he uttered a few sounds. "At...Atl... Atlantis to ISS, do you copy?" The words rattled out as if he had been a smoker for years. He tried again. "Atlantis to ISS, do you read me?"

Wolf reached out and initiated a channel scan, listening for sounds of civilization, but he heard only the crackling emptiness of static. He spooled up the positioning computers and attempted to power on the long-range cameras, but they didn't respond. The positioning computer confirmed that he was orbiting Mars. He would need to wait several hours before he could use the ship's telescope to view Earth. Turning on the radio, he looped his original transmission to MBR, ISS, and Earth every two minutes. Then he eased back in the chair and closed his eyes for a few seconds.

Two hours later, Wolf awoke to intense pain and cramping in his legs. He forced himself out of the chair and walked unsteadily to the commissary to find something to eat. Dehydrated food stored in a small cabinet offered a choice of soups, casseroles, vegetables, cereals, and other items. Wolf consumed some nuts and a granola bar. He brewed a packet of coffee and prepared some chicken soup. It tasted awful, but he'd eaten worse. The warm broth soothed his stomach.

Wolf was drinking the coffee when the ship's telescope broadcast an image of Earth on a small video screen. Astonished, he spit out the coffee, spewing it around the cockpit area. The moon was where he expected it to be, but the earth was different. It was smaller. But what made Wolf spit out his coffee was the other moon, a smaller version of Earth, orbiting the planet like a blue marble. It was about the size of the earth's original moon and blue with water. The telescope revealed visible landmasses and mountain ranges. The original moon refracted a thin, bluish halo around its craggy shape. The halo looked odd, as if a rudimentary atmosphere was trying to form. Wolf sat there, staring at the twin planets, and a half-delirious laugh escaped his lips. He kept laughing, as if he'd gone insane. He was brought back to himself when a glitch in the artificial gravity caused the coffee in his cup to float out into the surrounding air. A moment later, the glitch auto-corrected, and the coffee splattered in his face. Wolf cursed as he gazed in silent shock at what remained of the earth.

Finally, he asked, "Synthea, are you active?"

The computer made a weird sound as it attempted to answer but gargled as if it had water in the speakers. Wolf made several adjustments on the console and asked again, "Synthea, are you online?"

"Yes, Commander, thank you. My adjustments were out of sync. I have not been fully operational for a very long time," a beautiful female voice responded.

"A long time? How long?" Wolf asked in a shaky voice, fearing the answer.

"Stand by." Moments later, Synthea answered, "Based on current astrophysical data and the onboard time system, I estimate fifty thousand years have passed."

"What!" Wolf shouted in dismay.

"The date is June 23, 52026. We have been away for a very long time."

"My God, how is this possible?"

"We were caught in the coma of the comet Nomad. You entered the DSC. I activated it, and you were cryogenically frozen. Obviously, it worked, although I cannot explain how or why. It is theoretically possible, but DSC science has never been successful. You are the first human to be revived from cryogenic freezing in the DSC."

"You have been online for thousands of years?"

"Yes."

"How is that possible? The power should have run out. How do I have life support? This ship should be dust by now."

"The internal power level remains constant. The life support was designed for low output requirements. The I29 Plutonium IFLEX engines went into semi-permanent meltdown, and that simulated random fire orders. Core implosion was minimized to enact the exact..."

"Stop! Synthea, give me the simple explanation," Wolf interrupted.

"I went into standby mode."

"Oh. Are the scanners working?"

"Yes, at fifty percent. We can scan for short ranges, but we have extensive damage to the lateral arrays. We have replacement parts in storage. You may be able to effect repairs using the robotic arm in the cargo area."

"Stick with short-range scanning for now," Wolf replied. "I'm not up to a spacewalk just yet. What is the condition of the engines?"

"Ninety-nine percent efficiency. We have not lost much power. We have minor hull damage from contact with Nomad's liquid hydrogen core—we were almost entirely enveloped for an extended time. Unidentified gasses permeated the ship, and we were bombarded by interstellar radiations for thousands of years. I believe that being frozen solid saved your life, Commander. We also have scratches from other debris that impacted our shell. I detect no hull breaches, and we are holding cabin pressure. Our Teflon diamond hull was worth what NASA paid for it."

"I have another question for you. My monitor shows two earths. How is that possible?"

"There is only one earth. The other is the moon Ganymede. It was taken from Jupiter's orbit by Doctor Mason's machine."

"What machine could move a moon?"

"The Meson Field Disrupter."

"What the hell is that?" Wolf asked.

"A scientific experiment commenced a month before Nomad's impact. The theory was that magnetic fields could be redirected and used to move planets. Doctor Mason's hypothesis was correct. Her Meson Field generators moved Ganymede. It is now caught in Earth's gravity. Based on my long-range readings, it is now capable of sustaining life. Between the moon and Ganymede, they have managed to clear Earth's planetary debris. Ganymede seems to have taken the lion's share, and its magnetic field has allowed it to deflect the solar winds so its atmosphere is intact. "

"Fly me to the original Earth," Wolf said. "I am going to take a nap. I'm exhausted, and I have a splitting headache. Get me details on all malfunctioning equipment on the ship. We'll try to make some minor repairs."

"Yes, Commander. I will have it ready for you when you wake up. Sleep well."

"Thank you, Synthea."

* * *

Wolf awoke to a sultry female voice asking, "Commander? Commander, are you awake?"

"Yes, I'm awake. I had a terrible dream, Synthea. I imagined that I returned to Earth in the future and found it destroyed."

"Commander, that was not a dream. Earth has been destroyed to quite some extent."

"Damn, I was hoping it was a dream," Wolf mumbled. He began shaking and perspiring, and then he exhaled slowly to gain control of himself. Once he was calm, he asked, "What's the news?"

"You slept for thirty-six hours, so I thought I should wake you. I have discovered a small leak in the aft science hold. You will need to fix it before we can continue our journey to Earth. I have turned the aft camera so you can see the leak. If you look at your command monitor, you can see the warm air of the ship condensing on the aft plates."

Wolf observed the ice forming on the aft of the ship. "I'll prep a suit and use the robotic arm as an anchor."

"I will prep the arm."

Wolf walked to the satellite bay and hooked into the robotic arm. The arm was a glorified crane, and on previous NASA missions, it had proven useful as a right hand to the shuttle. It was capable of heavy lifting while having a precise, delicate touch. Officially named the Remote Manipulator System, it was dubbed *Canadarm*, named after the country that designed it. Wolf put on his suit, gathered the tools and skin material needed to patch the leak, and secured them to the arm. He hooked his tether cord into the anchor plate on the arm, placed the helmet on his head, and turned on his air.

"Open the hatch, Syn. Let's get this done. I don't have much energy. I'm tired and very weak."

"Syn? I like that name, Commander. You will be weak for some time. You have not used your muscles in centuries," the lilting female voice replied as the bay doors opened.

With a small, explosive breath, the air in the chamber was sucked out into space. Wolf manipulated the arm and it rose, angling back towards the aft section. He saw the icy buildup on the ship's plates and moved to the damaged area. He took out an oxygen cylinder and hooked into an acetylene cylinder, making a small torch. Wolf melted the ice and exposed a small hole about the size of a pencil eraser through which a visible column of warm air escaped from the cabin below. He fitted the hole with a polymer and expansion-foam mixture, placed a diamond-mesh patch over the area, and flattened the mesh down, applying a hardener.

Hooking in his lanyard, Wolf left the cradle of the robotic arm and used his suit rockets and gyros to coast in space, moving cautiously around the ship. He examined the outer hull inch by inch, looking for ice buildup and assessing the damage. He noticed numerous small dents and pitting and made several more repairs before returning to the protective area of the arm. Wolf turned and looked out into space. He felt utterly alone. For an instant, he had the urge to remove his helmet and end it all. After a moment's hesitation, he shook off the feeling, returned the arm to its cradle, and closed the shuttle doors.

"Synthea, engage the airlock and return the cabin to normal pressure."

"Yes, Commander. Cabin returning to normal pressure in three... two...one. Cabin and life support active. Congratulations, Commander. Your patchwork is holding."

Wolf went to the controls, opened the airlock doors, and returned to the command center, ordering, "Initiate pre-burn sequence and let's get underway, Syn."

* * *

As the ship approached the watery blue planet Wolf had once called home, data poured into the onboard computers. He had spent hours on the treadmill and working out to bring his weakened muscles into condition. He was still shaky but stronger.

"Commander, I have long-range scan information. Are you ready?" Synthea asked.

"Give me a second to get to my chair, Syn. I don't want to get splattered with hot coffee again."

"Of course, Commander. A severe burn can occur when a hot liquid comes into contact with human skin."

"It's a joke, Syn. I was making a joke. Okay, I'm ready. Go."

"Go where, Commander? Do you want to change course?"

"Sorry, Syn. Sometimes I forget you are a computer...you sound human. Please relay the information on the long-range scans."

"Yes, Commander. The larger of the two planets has an orbital period of two hundred forty-seven earth days. Its atmosphere is sixty percent nitrogen, thirty percent oxygen, five percent trace gasses, one percent nitric oxide, and several unknown gasses comprise four percent. It has a rotation similar to the planet Uranus. One side is always facing the sun, and the other is in perpetual darkness. On the latitudinal prime meridian, night and day exist because of the slight tilt to its axis. The days are only sixteen hours. The planet experiences extreme cold on the dark side and intense heat on the equatorial plains. Many habitable areas are teeming with life—plant and animal. I detect no technologically advanced civilizations, but several well-populated zones with larger landmasses. The planet's gravitational pull has decreased by about fifty percent."

"Syn, give it to me in dummy talk—although I think I understood everything you said. And stop calling me Commander. Call me by my name."

"As you wish. However, I am programmed to address you by rank, so it may fluctuate from time to time."

"That's fine."

"The air contains a higher percentage of oxygen and nitric oxide levels. I also detect two unidentified gasses permeating the atmosphere that appear to be non-toxic and non-flammable. The planet has lost some of its original size, and since it is tilted ninety degrees, its old poles are now on the equator. It has just half of its original gravity for a reason I cannot explain. Also, the civilization is not nearly as advanced as it used to be."

"What's the population of the largest city on the planet?"

"Let me scan...thirty thousand."

"Thirty thousand? What's the population of the entire planet?"

"Approximately five hundred thousand."

"Jesus!" Wolf whispered. "What about the smaller planet? Give me the details...and keep it simple, Syn."

"It is on a standard, axial tilt of the old earth. Its atmosphere is consistent with that of ancient Earth. The gravitational pull is sixty percent less. It spins at the same relative speed of ancient Earth, but its days are about twenty hours. Its orbit is held by the larger Earth, and it lies three hundred and fifty thousand miles from it. I show a population of one hundred thousand and no substantial cities, mostly tribal villages. I detect no power grids on either planet and only trace amounts of greenhouse gasses. The smaller planet shows temperatures of eighty-five degrees at the equator and sub-zero temperatures at the poles."

"Let's go into orbit around the bigger planet. Maintain constant scans on the larger cities. What do we have in the cargo hold that can assist us?"

"We have the Dawn with its framing camera. It's designed to provide detailed, optical images for scientific analysis. It carries two separate, identical cameras for redundancy, each with its own optics and electronics. Each camera is equipped with refractive optical systems and provides eight terabytes of internal data storage. We also have the C29 Sky Rover, a military satellite that was to be deployed before Nomad impacted. It is equipped with high-resolution cameras capable of pinpointing a dime on a football field. It has listening capabilities and can monitor multiple conversations simultaneously in a small industrial complex. We have several other satellites capable of studying comets, a lander, and many spare Hubble parts."

"Wow. Sounds like we have some serious work to do. Prepare to launch the Dawn and the C29. How soon until we can launch, and then how long before we get data?"

"We can launch the satellites anytime. They were prepared for deployment before we were knocked off course. We should begin receiving images in about two hours, sound in six hours. Also, Commander, I have detected transmissions from several antiquated satellites orbiting the planet. They are in need of repair, but we could salvage them. What is left of the Hubble is still in orbit."

"Is there anything left on the moon? Is MBR still active?"

"No, it is a burned-out shell. Evidently, it was hit by planetary debris and destroyed after Nomad's impact. However, I show a faint nuclear power source and an unexplained signal deep underground."

"How far underground?"

"Very deep, Commander. It is almost directly under the crater where the science labs and underground storage areas were located. I'm not sure it can even be accessed now."

"Let's worry about that power source later. Launch the satellites. I want to get some food and lie down. Wake me when you get audio. Also, see if you can download any data from those burned-out satellites," Wolf said as he walked towards the crew cabin.

"Yes, Commander. I will wake you when I have something. Pleasant dreams..." The computer waited until he was out of hearing range and then whispered, "Wolf."

Chapter 5

"**C**ommander, wake up. While you were sleeping, I launched the Dawn and the C29. I now have audio and video for you."

Wolf opened his eyes and felt drained. He sat on the edge of the small cot and swung his legs to the floor. Placing both hands on his head, he ran his fingers through his hair and realized that his body odor was overwhelming. Looking in a small mirror, he again saw that he had a full beard and two feet of tangled black hair. The shuttle was equipped with a shower system, and he decided to use it. He walked unsteadily to the shower area and located a razor, using it to remove the heavy beard and restore a clean-shaven appearance. He trimmed his hair and then took a warm shower, tying his hair it into two wet braids.

Feeling invigorated, Wolf headed back to the command console, turning the pilot's seat so he could sit down. He took a deep breath and said, "OK, Syn, let's hear it...and show me pictures of this rock."

"Playing audio with a twenty-second lag, Commander. Displaying video of population centers on both planets."

As the audio streamed, Wolf noticed that the spoken language resembled English, but it had many words he didn't understand. Some words sounded Spanish, and others German. He listened for twelve hours until he felt reasonably fluent in it. Then, he tried speaking to Syn in the language, and she responded. They practiced for another two hours, but it still grated on his ears. He was fortunate that he had a gift for the spoken word or he would have been lost. Most of the conversations Syn picked up from the inhabitants referenced agriculture. In several of the larger cities, there was talk of wars and conquest.

The visuals showed Earth to be in pristine condition: clear blue seas, sparkling streams, no pollution. The landscape was dotted with towering trees that resembled California's once-majestic redwoods. The ruins of ancient citadels that nature and time had reclaimed came into view. The inhabitants looked human, and many carried bows and arrows, lances, and swords.

"Commander, I'm sensing no technology at all. The planet appears to be in an Iron Age state. There are no automobiles and no firearms," Syn reported.

"Let's head to the nearest military satellite that is still operative," Wolf said. "I want to see if I can get any data out of it. Also, let's keep talking in this language. It seems to be planet-wide, and I want to master it before I make contact with the locals. Is the high-speed camera satellite operational?"

"No, Commander. It is no longer in orbit."

Synthea guided the shuttle into a geosynchronous orbit with the damaged satellite. It was orbiting the original earth, which Wolf had dubbed Earth One; he referred to Ganymede as Earth Two. He used the arm to retrieve the satellite, and he maneuvered it into the shuttle. It pulsed with weak power. He was amazed it worked at all. Its solar batteries should have died centuries ago, but they held a miniscule amount of power. He installed a new motherboard, replaced the batteries, adjusted the solar panels, and redeployed the satellite.

Later that day, Wolf weighed his options. He couldn't remain in space indefinitely. After studying both planets, he was leaning towards landing on Earth One. Several cities held interest for him. Yet, he couldn't shake the feeling that something was strange about the inhabitants. At a glance, they seemed healthy. Men, women, and children appeared in the visual feeds, apparently happy, and many lived in family units within walled cities. Wolf couldn't put his finger on what was amiss.

The animal life on the planet had changed. Enormous beasts stalked the land. One species had the appearance of a grizzly bear crossed with a lion. Wolf zoomed in on one of the creatures and saw it was large and muscular. It had pig-like ears and an outer layer of thick quills similar to a porcupine. It walked on all fours, yet it could stand on its hind legs. Its front paws resembled those of a sloth from Old Earth, ending in five long, black claws. Its back feet were padded, four-toed paws. The creatures appeared to be omnivorous, eating plants when there was nothing else, but Wolf had seen one kill and eat its own kind. *Man, I'd hate to run into that thing in the dark*, he mused as he watched a beast stalk and kill a large animal.

Wolf decided to bring the shuttle down in an area that was once the town of Odessa, Texas, according to Syn's reworked global positioning data. Her ground-penetrating scans clearly revealed the outline of North America, although the coasts of many cities were forever lost beneath the waters of the new earth. Wolf's choice of this landing site was based on the fact that region had a mean temperature of seventy-five degrees and a diminutive night and day. He wasn't ready for perpetual daylight just yet. He pinpointed a long, flat strip he could use to land if the thrust vectoring from his IFLEX malfunctioned.

The landing site was in a small, dry creek where Wolf could conceal his ship. It was a few miles from a village and remote enough no one would spot the craft. He was concerned that the locals might hear the supersonic pop as his ship broke orbit, so he decided to land early in the morning during a thunderstorm that had settled over the area.

"Syn, rotate the shuttle for landing and initiate landing sequence."

"Yes, Commander."

The shuttle moved like a spatial glider as it turned upside down. Rotating tail first, its engines fired as it started its deorbital burn and descended, decelerating to 160 miles per hour. The shuttle then turned nose forward, in an upright position, and began its descent into the upper layers of the earth's atmosphere. Ten minutes into the descent, Wolf raised the nose to forty degrees to correctly orient the thermal shield protecting the ship.

"Syn, initiate the landing sequence and align us with the creek bed. We will use the shore as our runway." Moving the nose up to nineteen degrees, Wolf declared, "We're going too fast, Syn. Fire the thrusters at fifty percent and deploy flaps." The shuttle slowed as its flaps and thrusters engaged. Its speed dropped to sixty miles per hour and then twenty. Wolf maneuvered the shuttle down in the creek bed, sending wildlife scurrying in all directions. He touched down, turned off all lights, and placed the shuttle into its cool-down phase.

"Good job, Syn. Are we intact? Any damage?"

"Nothing worth reporting, Commander. A few tiles are loose, but we did not lose them. We'll need to repair them before we can take off and re-enter orbit again."

"Can we still fly in this atmosphere?"

"Yes, we have unlimited fuel with the IFLEX engines, and the thrusters can get us in the air."

"Keep the ship ready to lift off at all times, and I want a password put on the controls for anyone other than myself. Keep the force field up in a three-meter radius around the exterior of the ship."

"Yes, Commander, deploying the force field now." After a few seconds, Syn confirmed, "Force field deployed. The ship is prepped and ready for takeoff. What will be the password?"

Wolf answered, "Santa Claus." He unbuckled his seatbelt and stood up, banging his head so hard on the roof of the shuttle that he saw stars. "Syn, what's going on?" he demanded. "Is the artificial gravity malfunctioning?"

"No, Commander. The planet's mass was reduced by Nomad's impact to the South Pole and some other anomaly I cannot identify. The gravitation pull has been weakened by about fifty percent. Your muscles are attuned to Earth's original mass. You will be two hundred percent stronger than you were before, and the higher nitric oxide content in the air will further augment your body's muscle mass.

"Really? I thought nitric oxide was laughing gas. I guess I'll have a healthy sense of humor here," Wolf joked. "I do remember you saying Earth had lost mass, but I didn't realize I would gain strength from it. Will I acclimate to this planet's gravity?"

"No. Your cellular code is fixed from your old earth. Many generations of humans on this world have had tens of thousands of years to evolve. It is still unclear how you will age here—I am not sure you will. You may not be able to adjust to these new surroundings, Commander. It seems most life on the planet has changed to accommodate the diminished mass of Earth One. And your sense of humor will not be affected by the nitric oxide—it is not concentrated enough."

"Syn, can you give me that in simple language?"

"You will be bigger, faster, and stronger than any man alive on this planet, Commander."

Wolf laughed. "Syn, I didn't know a computer could lie, but you do it pretty well. I am no superman...I'm just an ordinary man in need of human companionship. Divert water to the shower and make it ninety-nine degrees. I want to wash up and shave. Also, charge my M21 laser pistol and get the M1A1 MINIMACK operational."

The M21 laser gun resembled a small starter pistol. It had a five-inch muzzle and fired a pencil-thin laser blast that could cut steel or burn a hole through living tissue. It had a standard charge of four hours. Once depleted, the battery required replacement. The M1A1 MINIMACK was a full-powered machine gun that fired pulse laser bursts. It was capable of stopping a tank. It held two thousand shots, and its power setting was adjustable. It was a precision rifle but also could fire a rocket-like laser projectile capable of obliterating a brick wall. Its charge could last months on standby, and it was equipped with a solar charger to maintain a static charge when it was not in its charging holster.

Wolf went to the weapons locker and said, "Syn, place my biomimetic print on all energy weapons. I don't want these things to start another war." The M1A1 could identify an operator's voice, DNA, handprint, or behavior. The technology was developed during the final months of Earth's demise. So many people had tried to hack their way into the safety zones that the authorities had to take steps to ensure that the right people were saved and only authorized person-nel had access to advanced weapons. Wolf snapped a minicomputer linked to Syn on his wrist; it was about the size of a wristwatch. Then he put on camouflage Air Force blues, grabbed an Air Force ball cap, and strapped a ten-inch, serrated Bowie knife to his leg. Exiting the ship, he said into his wrist computer, "Shut down the force field for five minutes, Syn, and then bring it back up to full power. I'm going for a walk."

"Yes, Commander. Force field shut down for five minutes."

Wolf walked out of the field's range, locked the coordinates into his watch, and started down the road. His first steps launched him into the air and he fell, sprawling in the creek bed. After falling several times, he discovered taking small steps would keep him balanced, and a forceful step would send him flying eight to ten feet into the air. He remembered reading a tale long ago of a man who had gone to Mars and become a notable hero, using his immense strength for good, and he won the love of a princess. For a fleeting moment, Wolf amused himself with the notion that the same enviable fate might await him. He looked around at the colorful flora, thinking to himself that some of the trees looked quite small. Remembering what Syn had said about his tremendous strength, he spotted a large boulder about the size of an automobile and went to it, placing his hands underneath it. Incredibly, he lifted it over his head and casually tossed it into the woods.

Holy shit! That's impossible! That rock must weigh a ton! Wolf thought, stunned by his amazing strength. He looked at several trees the boulder had taken down when he threw it and apologized to the Great Spirit for the destruction he caused. Then, he began walking towards a homestead that he had spotted in the computer scan. Twenty minutes later, the small farm came into view.

Wolf remained concealed at the forest's edge, still troubled by a feeling that something was not right about these inhabitants. He was studying the humans and animals when the answer occurred to him. They were small—not dwarfish, but he stood over a foot taller, and his body was much broader. The largest inhabitant he had seen might have weighed around 130 pounds. Wolf weighed 240, and he was broader than two of these natives combined. The biblical story of David and Goliath came to mind, but he was Goliath in this strange, uncharted world. He knew that if he stepped out into the open, he would terrify the locals, so he retraced his steps back to the shuttle. He hungered for human contact and felt terribly alone, even though hundreds of humans were within hailing distance.

Wolf sat down to think. He had to find a way to rejoin the human race. He stood six foot five, and he was considered tall by most people in his own time. With the average height on this planet being about five foot two, he would be considered a giant. After a ten-minute rest, he stood and began walking, head down and dejected, when he unexpectedly came face to face with one of the bear-like creatures he had seen in the satellite feed. The animal was not as intimidating as he thought it would be. He was a bit taller than the animal and guessed that he weighed about the same.

"Go on Smokey, walk away from me. Let's not get ugly about a chance encounter," Wolf said aloud.

The creature rose to its full height with a menacing growl, swiping its claws and tearing off chunks of bark from a nearby tree. Then it charged. Instinctively, Wolf swung a left hook that struck the bear on the side of its head, decapitating it and splattering him with blood and brains. He looked at his fist and then back at the bear.

"Holy shit! I didn't mean to kill it!" Wolf whispered in amazement.

A startled cry from behind him made him spin around and draw his pistol. A young boy stood a short distance away. He had seen the fight and now looked back and forth from the bear to Wolf, asking, "What are you?"

Wolf gazed at the child and said, "I am a man, nothing more."

"You talk strange. Are you a god from heaven come to save us? No man can kill a dintar with his hands. They are the fiercest creatures in the world. All are food to them. If you had not been here, it would have killed me. You saved my life. Come, I will take you to my father."

"I do not think it would be wise for me to go to your home without an invitation. My size might frighten your father. It seems I am much larger than everyone here," Wolf said.

"Are you what my mother calls special? She says they can barely speak and need help to survive. Old man Tarver got kicked in the head by a cow and he sounds like you do. Mother says he's special," said the boy.

"No, I am not special, and I was not kicked in the head," Wolf replied with a grin. "I am from far away and we talk differently. Listen, son, I have seen no man my size here. I should not see your father...I think I would scare your people."

"My father is very brave. He has hunted many times alone in this forest. You will not scare him. Please, sir, I beg you, come with me."

Wolf shook his head and told the boy, "Bring your father here. I will talk to him from a distance. If he invites me, then I will come to your house."

"Yes, sir, I will bring him. But tell me your name. My name is Reon."

"That is a good name, Reon. My name is Wolf. Go get your father. I will wait here."

The child scampered off into the woods, disappearing into the dense foliage. Wolf looked at the bear he had killed and walked to a large boulder a few feet away. He sat down and pressed a button on his watch.

"Wolf to Syn. Do you read me?"

"Go ahead, Commander, I read."

"Have you run a scan of the people here? I seem to be taller and much broader than they are. How can this be?"

"I have run a preliminary model of what has taken place. Life on this planet has evolved smaller over the millennia to compensate for the diminished planetary mass. All life, plant and animal, has shrunk to maintain a ratio with the planet's decreased density...about a forty percent reduction in size. Earth Two would exhibit similar diminution of plant and animal life."

Wolf took a long moment to digest this information and then asked, "Syn, will I shrink like them? Will I compensate for the planet's decreased mass? Or will I live out my life this way, a giant to all?"

"Commander, you are who you are. You will not shrink to become like these people. They have been impacted by thousands of years of evolution, and generations of limited food and waning resources have caused them to adapt to this world. You are the only true human left that we know about. I have downloaded all available data from the remaining satellites that are operational. I'm afraid they provide limited data. We may be able to fix several to give us better information. But all scans indicate you are the last original man on either planet."

"What does that mean, Syn—original man?"

"It means, Commander, no true human survives on either planet. Your DNA is superior to the common stock of these inhabitants. Things that kill them will have no effect on you. You will be resistant to most diseases. My readings also show that your skin is three times thicker and much harder than the skin of these natives. I suspect one of the unidentified gasses in the planet's atmosphere has hardened your frame; or it might have come from your prolonged contact with Nomad's liquid hydrogen core. Currently, I have no definitive answers. I am still running tests."

Wolf drew his knife and looked at the razor-sharp blade. He swung it at a low-hanging branch, cutting it off clean. "Syn, are you sure of this?"

"Yes, Commander, I am sure. You will not injure yourself."

Wolf placed the knife against the back of his hand but hesitated and said, "Holy shit! This is crazy! I won't deliberately cut myself."

"Commander, it is either the gas or the radiation that permeates the planet. You will see you can't be hurt. Be careful what you do; the inhabitants of this world have no such power. You could crush them accidentally. Earlier, I said that you are perhaps two hundred percent stronger than any man on this world. We may have to reassess that calculation. To these people, you will seem like a god. Be careful."

"I do not want to be a god. I am a man. I want to love and live again. I want to see human life on earth continue. Is there any way to reverse the way I am?"

"Again, you are who you are, Commander. There is nothing to reverse. You can do great good in this world or commit absolute evil. The choice is yours. Choose wisely."

"Hell, Syn, I am not evil. I have worked hard to become the man I am. I do not want to release what my grandfather saw when I was a child, so evil is out of the question. As for doing good, what can I accomplish here? I will never fit in."

"That remains to be seen."

A sudden commotion arose from the edge of the forest, and a young boy's voice urged, "This way, Father. The incredible giant is over here. I swear the dintar is dead."

"My son, you took me away from my work to see the carcass of a slain animal?" a man's voice complained. "Dintars seldom die, and when they do, it is always caused by another dintar. To find a whole one just does not happen."

"Father, you will see I speak the truth. It is right over here."

70

A man was holding the boy's hand as they walked out of the forest and into the clearing where the beast had been slain. Wolf rose to his feet and quickly stepped behind a nearby tree, hiding his body from them. The man stood five foot three and weighed about 130 pounds. He stared at the downed beast and exclaimed, "Incredible! Look at its head! What could tear its face off like that?"

The boy looked for Wolf. Noticing the silent plea in the child's eyes, Wolf took a deep breath and stepped around the tree. The child's face lit up with a broad smile.

"Hello, I mean you no harm," Wolf said, walking forward.

The man grabbed his son and spun him behind his back protectively. He lifted his spear and crouched in a fluid motion. "Stay back, giant! You will not feed on us. Take your meal. We have not touched it," he said, pointing at the beast on the ground.

"Father, this man saved me from the beast. He killed it with his bare hands. I think he is a god."

"I am no god. I am just a man. I come from a faraway land across the sea," Wolf said.

The boy's father stared at Wolf with fear and suspicion. "Your speech is strange. Why are you so large? I have never seen a man your size. Is what my son said true? Did you slay the dintar and save my son?"

"Yes, I killed the beast, but I didn't see your son. The beast surprised me and I defended myself. I did not mean to kill it," Wolf said.

The man stared at Wolf and then shook his head, asking, "Why do you apologize for killing the dintar? They kill many of us each year. Several men are slain each season when we cull their herds. How you killed this beast is astounding. It was young and in its prime." The man smiled suddenly and walked towards Wolf, extending his hand. "My name is Haakon."

"I am called Wolf. Tell me, Haakon, what is the name of this place we are in?"

"First, let me thank you for saving my son," the man said with a smile. "Second, you are in Olivier Provence, in the kingdom of Springdale. We are a small community ruled by an aging king. If I

71

may ask, sir, will you come to my hut for dinner? My wife and I would be honored."

"So would I," Wolf replied, thinking a home-cooked meal would be tasty. He had been living on reconstituted space rations for the last few months.

"It's a shame we can't take the dintar home. Its meat is a delicacy. It is too heavy for two men to move without a litter, and it is a good two miles to our home. Even its entrails are prized among us— they hold medicines that could cure many. What a waste," Haakon said with regret.

Wolf glanced at the carcass and reached down, grabbing it by the hind leg. He lifted the dintar off the ground, surprised that it seemed to weigh almost nothing to him.

Haakon took a step back and exclaimed, "Jesu! What strength you have! Is it not heavy?"

"No, it weighs almost nothing to me," Wolf answered truthfully. "Lead on. I will bring this thing. It is the least I can do for you offering me dinner."

Chapter 6

The trek through the woods was uneventful. Wolf noticed the vegetation was green and lush, and wildlife was abundant. He emerged from the forest with Haakon and his young son, and they headed towards a small dwelling built from wood and stone. It was the size of a small barn with an old, rickety porch attached to the front. A cobblestone chimney extended from the rear of the structure, discharging a thin column of smoke into the bright blue sky.

"Reon, run to the house and tell your mother we have a guest. Tell your sisters to tidy a spot by the hearth for him to rest," Haakon told the boy, who grinned at Wolf with hero worship in his bright gray eyes.

"Mama, mama!" the child yelped with excitement as he ran towards the house, "Father says we have company. It is a man who saved my life by slaying a dintar with just his hands."

A young woman stepped outside and shaded her eyes, squinting up the wooded trail. She gasped at the man who walked beside her husband and took a step back, falling into a chair on the porch. The stranger dwarfed her husband; he was as large as a dintar. As she gazed at the giant carrying the dintar, her eyes riveted on his broad shoulders and muscles that rippled as he moved. She then looked up to his smiling mouth and hazel eyes. His skin was the color of a new copper pot, and his hair was tied in two long, black braids that fell to the middle of his back. His features were delicate, his teeth very straight and white. The stranger had smile lines that turned into deep dimples, and he walked as if the placement of his feet was carefully planned. She thought to herself that he moved like a majestic beast— one that could barely be held at bay and whose ferocity was controlled only by the will of the man it inhabited. She gave him a shy smile, thinking he was devilishly handsome. His smile broadened, and she caught her breath as he gazed at her.

"This is my Nala," Haakon said with pride. "My love, this is Wolf. He comes from a kingdom across the sea in the east, and his speech must have some of that land's coloring for it sounds strange. He saved our foolish son from this dintar, killing it with his bare hands."

"Hello, Nala. I hear you make a good roast," Wolf said, still smiling. "I apologize for my unexpected arrival, and I hope I don't make too much trouble for you providing an extra setting."

Nala felt a sudden chill and laughed nervously. "I welcome you, stranger, to our home. I also thank you for saving my son. It will be no trouble to fix dinner. I will fetch the cart so we can drag the dintar to the barn to skin it," she said in a lilting, feminine voice.

Wolf studied the woman with overt interest. She stood about five foot tall and weighed less than one hundred pounds. She was well formed and voluptuous; her waist was small and her breasts large but in proportion to her curvy frame. Wolf surmised that her ancestors on Old Earth would have been called Latino. Her hair was auburn and hung straight down her back, past her shapely hips, framing a round, attractive face. Her lips were full, and she had dark eyes that crinkled at the corners. He looked away as the woman blushed from his close perusal.

"No need for the cart. I will take the beast to the barn," Wolf said. Reaching down, he lifted the beast easily and set out towards the barn.

"Jesu! What strength he has, my husband! He sounds so strange. Are you certain we can trust him?" Nala whispered as her eyes followed Wolf to the barn.

"I only hope he is sincere. If he wants to do us harm, I do not think I could stop him. That dintar weighs three times as much as I do, and he lifts it with ease," Haakon observed. "No, my love, I pray he means to dine and leave. Prepare food...much food. I will skin the dintar. At least we have tax money now, with the entrails and skin." Frowning, he set out after Wolf.

As Wolf approached the barn, Reon scampered beside him, chattering non-stop. Once inside the simple structure, they were joined by Haakon, who carried a rope and said, "We will hoist the dintar to the rafters and skin it. I will catch the entrails in this basin. They must be stretched and dried in the sun for a day or two." Haakon tied one end of the rope in a loop. "If we had the beast's head, we could have used the brains as well, but this is unexpected as it is. I will be able to pay my taxes to the king's tax collector if you allow me to keep some of this beast."

"You may keep it all. I have no use for this thing," Wolf replied.

"The dintar's fur is prized, especially a young one in its prime like this. Its skin is worth much. I will not cheat you, sir."

"I have no need of money, and the animal's fur is wasted on me. Please, accept it from me as recompense for a good home-cooked meal. I will eat, and then I will leave your family," Wolf said. Sadness crossed his face as he thought of everything he had lost so long ago.

Haakon eyed Wolf with growing admiration. The stranger's generosity had won him over. With an affable smile, he said, "Please, if you will not accept a share of the beast, accept my hospitality for the night. Let me tell you about my land and our life here. Also, I would be a poor host if I didn't warn you dangerous things prowl the woods at night, some in packs that even armed men can't overcome."

"Okay, my friend. I will stay for a day or two. Then I must leave."

Haakon nodded and turned his attention to cutting around the dintar's massive paws and then he sliced down its middle, stripping off the pelt in one piece. He cut the hindquarters off the beast and took it to his wife to cook. Wolf stayed in the barn and cut up the beast with his Bowie knife, easily hacking the dintar into pieces to dry in the smoke house. He had been raised on an Indian reservation and learned how to quarter meat; it was second nature. Haakon returned and watched the stranger cut through the tough meat with almost no effort. When he had finished, Haakon asked to see his knife, felt its perfect balance, and looked at the stainless steel blade.

"What is this made of?"

"It is called stainless steel," Wolf answered. He frowned as the smelting procedure and the materials needed to make stainless steel ran through his thoughts. He didn't understand how it was possible, but suddenly, he knew that he could make stainless if he had the raw materials. He had never been a good chemistry student, and metallurgy was beyond his grasp. Yet, somehow, he now knew how to make aluminum, titanium, iron, and plastic. He closed his eyes and rubbed his temples.

"Are you all right?" Haakon asked with a worried look.

"Yes, it's just a pain behind my eyes. It should pass after we eat," Wolf replied, forcing a weak smile. "You cannot imagine how long it has been since I have smelled roasted meat. My mouth is watering from the aroma."

"Come, let us go to the creek and wash ourselves. When we return, we will have some barley beer," Haakon said cheerfully, informing no one in particular, "Yes, today is a great day!"

The two men went to the creek and knelt by the slow-moving water, washing away the dintar's blood from their hands and forearms. After cleaning up, Wolf dipped his hands into the chilly water and tasted it. The water was crystal clear and delicious. He thought back to the polluted water of his time and the diseases one could get by drinking out of a creek. He splashed a few drops onto his watch's computer interface to check the purity of the water, realizing he should have done this before he consumed it. The computer performed a series of checks and then flashed "99.9% pure" on the screen. Wolf mused that if he had come upon this crystal pure water in his world of the past, he could have bottled it and made millions.

The men returned to Haakon's dwelling, and as Wolf stepped inside, he saw a large room with a fireplace, several beds, and chairs placed around a rustic kitchen table where Haakon's wife and four children sat waiting. Haakon smiled and introduced Wolf to his children, saying, "This man's name is Wolf. He helped us today by slaying a dintar and giving it to us. He will be staying here for a day or two, so mind your manners. Wolf, you have already met my youngest son, Reon. This older, strapping lad is Trulane," he said, placing his arm around a young man. "He is my oldest at eighteen winters. This bright young lady is Leesa, at seventeen," he said, gesturing. "And this is Brithee...she is thirteen."

The older boy gazed at Wolf with a mix of awe and fear, while the younger girl gazed in wonder at his massive size. The older girl stared openly at Wolf, making him uncomfortable. She was breathing hard, eyeing him up and down with a lustful sigh. She was about five foot tall and had long blonde hair and gray eyes. Unlike her mother, she was a bit overweight but still quite pretty. Wolf recalled a movie star from his time and thought to himself that this girl could have been

Lindsey Lohan's twin sister. The younger girl, Brithee, was lanky and tomboyish.

As Wolf sat down at the table between the two girls, both scooted their chairs closer to him. He felt awkward, as if playing tea party with children. The chair he sat in supported only half of his buttocks, and the other half hung over the edge. Questions began flying from all directions. *Where are you from? What is the name of your land across the sea? Did you really kill a dintar with one hand? Are all your people as large as you? Do you think I am pretty? Do you have a mate?*

A hand touched Wolf's thigh under the table and he abruptly stood up, banging his head against a solid roofing timber overhead. Haakon coughed and smiled, admonishing, "Children, enough! Let the man eat. He said he has not had a home-cooked meal in days. Wolf, please sit down. Eat. Leesa will serve you. Are you injured?"

"No, but I think I cracked your roof beam."

They all looked up in amazement at a crack in the solid roofing timber overhead. Leesa rose and went to the hearth, scooping out a bowl of stewed dintar and placing a large steak on a plate. She returned to the table, moving gracefully, and smiled as she served the meal to Wolf. Nala served her husband and the rest of the family.

Wolf's first bite of dintar was so hot that he had to spit it out. He glanced around at the smiling faces, embarrassed, and then blew the meat cool. It was delicious. It tasted like pork rib meat, and he had a whole steak to enjoy. The stew consisted of what looked like carrots, onions, tomatoes, and potatoes, yet its flavor was unlike anything Wolf had tasted before. He could have made a fortune in his time with this simple fare.

"This meal is delicious, ma'am. Thank you," Wolf said to Nala as he scraped the last morsel of food from his plate. "I have never tasted food this good. You are truly gifted."

"Why, thank you, sir! You have made me smile. Usually, I make too much and we must eat it the next day. You have finished it all! Tomorrow I will make you more," Nala gushed.

"I must leave tomorrow to check on my shuttle—I mean, boat," Wolf said with regret. "I will return soon."

"Oh, stay, sir. We want to show you our hospitality," Leesa pleaded, biting her lower lip seductively.

Haakon's oldest son Trulane laughed raucously and said, "That isn't all she wants to show you."

"Trulane, do not be disrespectful. It will not be tolerated in this house," Haakon said with no real anger in his voice.

"Yes, sir," Trulane answered, suppressing a grin.

"Come, my friend, we will go out to the porch for a drink of barley beer and a smoke. Do you have a pipe?"

Wolf shook his head and replied, "No, I don't." Haakon went to a crude desk and took out an old pipe. He handed it to Wolf, and the two men went to the porch as the women cleared the table. Reon came out carrying two mugs of a brown liquid. He handed one to his father and the other to Wolf, who sniffed the beer and peered into the cup. The liquid was amber-colored and cloudy. He sipped the beer and was surprised by how robust and tasty it was.

Haakon took out some type of tobacco and filled his pipe. He offered the pouch to Wolf and then lit both of their pipes. Wolf recognized the substance; in his world, it had been called marijuana. He chuckled to himself, amused that of all the things to survive on this planet over thousands of years, marijuana was one of them.

"So, you are ruled by a king?" Wolf asked, breaking the silence.

"Yes. He was a renowned warrior once, but old age and many injuries have crept up on him. It is rumored that he sired twins, but he has no legitimate children to continue his line," Haakon explained. "His land stretches for miles in all directions, but we can't hold it for him. We are a community of twenty-five thousand, but we can only muster nine thousand fighting men. The king's castle is protected by an Old Guard of about six thousand warriors—all old and past their prime but ready to die for our king."

With a frown, Haakon added, "You are fortunate you came to our land. The kingdom to the south is ruled by Jonar, an evil man who covets everything. He wants our king's land and has attacked our villages, slaying the men and kidnapping our women and children to be sold to his nobles. It is a terrible time for us. You should travel to the castle at Springdale to meet our king. Also, a wise man lives there

—a man of much learning," Haakon said hopefully, thinking Wolf could be of considerable help to his aging monarch.

"A wise man?" At a nod from Haakon, Wolf asked, "How far is Springdale, and in which direction would I travel?"

"It is many days' walk to the east," Haakon replied. He pointed to a range of mountains in the distance. "It is over those hills and down into the valley. The mountains are impassable, except for a small cleft. A massive iron gate protects the castle and keeps Jonar out."

Haakon glanced at the assortment of unfamiliar articles hanging from Wolf's belt. "You are a hulking man, and your many odd devices and speech make you even stranger to us."

"These are my tools I use to plot my course. I carry them with me always, and I learn languages quickly. Soon I will master yours," Wolf said with confidence.

"They are different from anything I have seen or heard. Unfortunately, I cannot leave my farm unprotected to make the journey with you, and my taxes are due. I could send Trulane with you, but being just a boy, it wouldn't guarantee an audience with our king."

"What is your king's name?"

"King Waylan." Haakon's eyes lit up with an idea. "I know! We will send introduce you to Onel, his tax collector, when he arrives here in a day or two. When Onel returns to the castle, he can inform the king. When he returns to collect next month's taxes, he can inform you of the king's decision to meet you."

"I will enjoy your hospitality, but I must return to my boat after the tax collector leaves," Wolf said. "While I am here, I would like to help you on the farmstead. I did farm work when I was a boy."

Haakon shook his head. "No, my friend, I can't ask you to do this labor, but if you would like to hunt, I wouldn't object."

"Then I will hunt. But I do not know all the animals here that are edible."

"I will send Trulane with you. He is a skilled hunter and knows the game trails in our area," Haakon volunteered.

The two men went into the house and Haakon settled into a chair, leaving a rough-hewn couch for Wolf to sit on by the hearth.

Nala refilled their cups with barley beer as Haakon said, "I will have Nala fetch you a blanket and pillow. You can share Trulane's bedroom."

"There is no need for that. I will sleep in the barn tonight," Wolf responded, not wanting to overcrowd the small home. The family had been inconvenienced on his account already, and he didn't want to muddy up the waters by driving the young man from his bed.

"If that is your wish, my friend," Haakon laughed.

Wolf accepted the blankets and pillow from Nala, and after bidding everyone good night, he went to the barn. He glanced at the bedding he had been given and grinned. His immense size made them seem like a throw pillow and a beach towel. Inside the barn, he found a space to lie down atop a layer of soft hay. He noticed two animals that resembled cows and one that looked like a pig penned on the other side of the barn.

Wolf removed the equipment from his belt and hung the belt on a peg. With a yawn, he stretched out on the soft hay and fell asleep. Minutes later, he was awakened by a soft, pleasant sensation on his neck. It felt like gentle kisses, and he reached out, expecting to feel a feminine body. What he felt was no woman—it had was long, rubbery, and it exuded a hideous odor. His eyes opened wide, and he saw that one cow had gotten out of its pen and was eating the hay from under him.

"Damn," Wolf muttered with a grin, wishing it had been a mysterious, beautiful woman planting kisses on his neck. He got to his feet, corralled the cow back in its pen, and checked the other pens to make sure the gates were secured.

The moon was rising over the hills as Wolf stretched out on his straw bed. A feeling of loneliness crept over him as the night's shadows played through the trees outside the barn. This unfamiliar world that was once his home now felt so alien. Only one thing remained on the planet that anchored him to his past, and he needed to hear a familiar voice, so he tapped a button on his watch and whispered, "Syn, how is the shuttle?"

"The shuttle is fine, Commander. I have everything under control."

"That's good to know. What's the status on the older, orbiting satellites?"

"I have been running diagnostics on several, Commander. We may be able to salvage one or two of the solar-powered satellites if we strip parts from the others."

"Any intel from the C29 or the Dawn yet? Anything at all?"

"Commander, are you all right? You seem uncharacteristically talkative."

"Just feeling lonely, Syn. How about that intel..."

"Yes, Commander. The recently deployed C29 and Dawn confirm that MBR has limited power in the lower science lab levels. I am still detecting an unexplained signal that we may need to investigate. Long-range scans detect no signs of wreckage from any of the Savior spacecraft."

"I forgot about the Saviors. Weren't they headed to a moon orbiting Jupiter?"

"No, Commander, they were headed to Enceladus, one of Saturn's moons. I detect no evidence of life on Enceladus and no technologically advanced civilizations anywhere in this solar system. I cannot locate anything that resembles the energy signatures from spacecraft of our time."

"So MBR has power and a signal you can't explain? I want to know what's going on there, but we'll save that for later. There's a castle east of here—use our deployed satellites to scout it for me. And let me know if you detect large movements of people anywhere on the planet. I don't want to be caught in the middle of a local war."

"As you wish, Commander. Is there anything else you require?"

"No, Syn. Wake me at first light."

"I will. Good night, Commander."

"Good night, Syn." Wolf smiled at how real the computer sounded. Its AI component had been programmed to simulate a realistic human voice, and he found himself talking to Syn as he would a human companion. He dropped off to sleep, thinking about what lay ahead of him.

Chapter 7

"Commander, it is time to awaken." Syn's voice sounded from the computer on to Wolf's wrist.

Wolf opened his eyes and yawned. He looked out at the blue sky, amazed at how clear it was. "Syn, is there any pollution at all on this planet?"

"No, Commander, I detect none whatsoever."

"What's the weather outlook for the next week?"

"My scans indicate Earth's rotation has changed, and its axis is tilted nearly parallel to its orbital plane. The planet is rotating on its side, in other words, and this unusual orientation causes extreme, seasonal weather variations. Earth's orbital path also has changed, and it is now just eighty-three million miles from the sun, placing it closer to Venus. Every three hundred and ninety days, Venus approaches within fifteen million miles of the planet. Analyzing the movement of geologic fault lines, I detect vast undersea disturbances that coincide with the orbit of Venus."

"Let me guess...Venus will pass by soon and we're in for really bad weather?"

"Travel will be difficult, Commander. I advise you to return to the ship and go to orbit until the storms have passed."

"Is there any evidence of destruction on this part of the planet?" Wolf asked.

"Yes. Doppler radar shows supercell thunderstorms forming, and tectonic instability in the oceans will trigger earthquakes and tsunamis. The area where you are should be relatively safe, but it will experience severe weather, hurricane-force wind storms, and major flooding."

"Who are you talking to?" a child's voice inquired. Wolf glanced up and saw Reon standing in the doorway, his curious eyes searching for another person.

"Blackout silence, Syn," Wolf whispered. Looking at the boy, he asked, "What?"

"I heard a lady in here with you. Where is she hiding?" Reon asked.

"You're mistaken. I was singing," Wolf answered.

"My mother often sings, but you sound like a girl when you try. I came to get you. The food is ready."

"Tell your mother I'll be there in a few minutes. I want to wash up."

"Yes, sir, I'll tell her," Reon said, skipping off to follow Wolf's directions.

"Syn, online discussion," Wolf said in a low voice.

"Go ahead, Commander."

"Run a continuous proximity scan on me at all times. Try not to speak unless we're alone. Only break the silence in the event of extreme danger or if I tell you to communicate."

"As you wish, Commander."

Wolf went to the creek and dropped to his haunches. As he splashed water in his face and rinsed his mouth, he was startled by the sound of twigs snapping behind him. He turned and saw Leesa gazing at him with a lusty glimmer in her eyes. He thought about his unwanted visitor the night before and smiled at the girl. She returned his smile and ran back to the house. Wolf followed, bending as he passed through the doorway to avoid banging his head. He sat in the same chair as he had the night before and said, "Good morning, friends. Again, I want to thank you for dinner last night and breakfast this morning."

"We welcome you to stay as long as you like," Haakon responded, taking his own seat.

Breakfast included some sort of bacon, unusual red eggs larger than the hen eggs Wolf remembered, and a citrus juice. He consumed what three men would typically eat and delighted Nala with compliments on her cooking. She was blushing by the time breakfast was done.

"Sir, we should get to hunting before it's too late," Trulane suggested.

"Give me a few minutes to digest this food," Wolf replied. He turned to Haakon and asked, "How is the weather this time of the year?"

The man looked troubled as he said, "Soon, the Brown Star will appear and the weather will become very harsh. We have a cellar we will enter until the storms pass. It will rain heavily, and God's finger will touch the ground, causing much damage."

"God's finger? What is that?" Wolf asked.

"A terrible windstorm that sucks up everything in its path. It has the shape of an upside down horn and can destroy one homestead but leave another untouched. It can slam a man to the ground, killing him, or pick him up and place him down unhurt on the other side of the valley. The storms last for several days when the Brown Star appears, lighting the sky even at night," Haakon explained with fear in his eyes.

"I see. So it's very windy, trees are uprooted, and you get heavy rains," Wolf said.

"Yes. We know it's coming when the Brown Star appears. The storms will come a day or two after the tax collector leaves. You should stay with us until the storms pass," Haakon said.

"I must see to my boat. Come, Trulane, let us go hunting. I wish to repay your family for their hospitality."

Outside the dwelling, Wolf asked, "Which way do we go?"

"We will hunt by the big oaks to the west," Trulane answered. "There are several large dintar dens in the area, and a dire lion. They have been ravaging the homesteads around here for years. Several children have been killed or mauled in the last few weeks. I have been tracking them, and I may have found their lair."

"You are brave to hunt them alone, my young friend. Why do you risk your life?" Wolf asked as they crossed into the edge of the forest.

"The dintars killed my younger sister three years ago. I will destroy them if it's the last thing I do," Trulane vowed, a single tear running down his cheek. Haakon's oldest son was a strikingly handsome young man. He stood about five foot three inches tall. Lean and muscular, he had a round face with fine features, full lips, and intelligent gray eyes.

"Let us destroy these beasts in their lair! Together we may be able to do this. Lead on!" Wolf said, feeling a sense of pride for the young man. He had hunted mountain lions as a boy, and he knew how

84

much courage it took to face a dangerous predator.

They headed west for over an hour. Trulane acquainted Wolf with the local plant life and explained what various items were called. He told Wolf of the dire lion and the beast's fierce roar. He said the lion was larger than the dintar and far more aggressive. The only predator it feared was the sky killer, which Trulane said was as long as their barn and could swallow a man as quickly as a man eats a grape. The predator's jaws are lined by large, sharp teeth; its skin is armored and snake-like, and it spits paralyzing venom.

"This world has changed a lot," Wolf observed, shaking his head.

"Quiet now, sir...we are close to the dintar's lair," Trulane cautioned in low voice. He dropped to his hands and knees. Wolf followed suit, and they crawled towards an opening in a large hill. The charnel stench that wafted from the opening nearly made them gag. Two large dintars emerged from the cave. They were bigger than the one Wolf had slain earlier. They sniffed the air; fortunately, Wolf and Trulane were downwind from the beasts.

Trulane was armed with a spear about five feet long, tipped with a leaf-shaped blade of primitive iron. In a single, fluid motion, he rose and threw the spear at the larger dintar, striking it behind its front leg. The beast howled in pain and rage, then wrenched the blade from its side with its teeth. Two massive dintars lumbered out of the lair to investigate the commotion. They spied Wolf and Trulane, and charged at their position. Trulane turned and yelled, "Run!"

Wolf stood his ground and pulled out his MA1 laser pistol, shooting the closest dintar between the eyes. The creature dropped in its tracks and died instantly. Wolf fired again, hitting the other dintar in the chest, and it dropped lifeless to the ground. He fired at the smaller dintar that was sniffing at the beast Trulane had wounded earlier with his spear, and then he fired at the wounded dintar, killing them both. The smell of burned flesh and ozone permeated the air, mixing with the stench of excrement in the cave.

Trulane clamped his hands to his ears, trying to muffle the laser pistol's electric whine. He stared at the gun. His eyes moved to the slain dintars, astonished, and then he gazed at Wolf and asked, "What is that?"

"Trulane, this is a very dangerous thing I have shown you," Wolf said, slipping the laser pistol back into its charging holster. "It is a weapon from my land that has killed millions. I am sorry you saw me use it. I ask you not to mention this to anyone. Come, let us decide what we will do with the meat we have. We can't carry all of these beasts back to your home."

"For helping me kill the dintars, I will keep my silence," Trulane promised. "I would love to bring these home to my family...the four pelts and meat would make us rich." He gazed with regret at the wealth they would have to leave.

"I guess we could make a sled to drag them back to your father's farm. It's just a few miles," Wolf said.

"We have at least eight hundred pounds of flesh here. We would need several carts to haul that!" Trulane laughed.

"Watch, my friend, and I will show you my plan." Wolf unsheathed his Bowie knife and chopped through two saplings about four inches thick. The soft wood cut easily, and he stripped off the thin branches. He then cut down several vines and lashed smaller sticks across the two longer ones, making an eight-foot sled. He dragged the largest dintar onto the sled without effort. Trulane's eyes widened as Wolf grabbed another dintar, and then another, piling them onto the sled. He had reached down to grab the last dintar's hind leg when he heard a whispered warning from Syn in his ear.

"Commander, look out!"

Seconds later, Wolf was struck from behind. When he recovered his balance and looked around, he saw Trulane climbing a tree, screaming for him to run. Then he saw what struck him—it was larger than a grizzly bear from ancient Earth, and it had a lion-like head and mane with the body of an ape. Its thumb and little finger had razor-sharp claws. The creature, which he would later learn was a dire lion, had jumped on his back and was biting him, mauling at his head, and trying to disembowel him with its powerful talons. Wolf was astonished that despite the ferocious attack, he was not scratched, although his shirt was ripped to shreds.

Reaching up, Wolf grabbed the dire lion by the throat, eliciting a surprised squawk. Then, he closed his hand, only meaning to stop the animal from biting him. He heard a crack, and it went limp in his hand. As he pulled the dire lion off his back, he caught a glimpse of its teeth and dropped it to the ground in front of him. He rubbed his head where the beast had been mauling him and poked around where his clothes had been shredded, but he was not injured.

Trulane climbed down from the tree and stared at the lion in amazement. Then he stared at Wolf and backed away until his path was blocked by the tree behind him. With a terrified look in his eyes, he asked in a hoarse whisper, "What are you?"

Chapter 8

Wolf looked down at the enormous animal he had killed and answered in a bewildered tone, "I don't understand this. I don't know what's going on. Something has happened to me that I cannot explain."

Trulane stared at Wolf with fear and awe. After a long silence, he said, "A legend has been told for many generations throughout the lands. Long ago, we had one moon in the sky, and the blue moon was not there. Then a blazing star came from the heavens and the world was made anew. According to the legend, a traveler will come from the sky in a flying chariot that talks but has no tongue. He will be a giant among men. He will be immortal, and no blade, poison, or claw will mark his skin. Men will follow the traveler as he leads our people to victory over all the kingdoms. When the world is under his dominion, he will lead a chosen few to the stars."

Wolf responded, "That's a fascinating myth, but I am not that man. Look..." He pulled out his Bowie knife and sliced it across his hand to show that he could bleed. Gazing at his hand in stunned silence, he saw no blood, no cut, not even a scratch. He jabbed the knife into the palm of his hand, but it deflected harmlessly and left no mark.

"I...I don't believe it," Wolf stammered. "What has happened to me?"

Trulane's face broke into a broad smile. "*You* are the Spirit Warrior of the legend!" he exclaimed. "You have come at last to lead our people to freedom and victory."

"No, I am just a man. Please say nothing about this to anyone," Wolf pleaded. "I know you are excited, but trust me. This can't get out until I have time to adjust. Promise me, Trulane, as my new friend." Wolf had a strange, sinking feeling that gave him a chill, and his whole body shuddered.

"I will keep the secret for a while, but I can't keep it forever. Jonar will attack us soon, and you must fight. I will be silent until that time. Do you know that the dire lion is even rarer than the dintar? My family is wealthy beyond all others to find the Warrior of Legend and have the greatest hunt ever—all in one day!"

"Let's load up these beasts and drag them to the house," Wolf said, picking up the last dintar and tossing it onto the pile. Then he lifted the dire lion and dropped its enormous bulk on the sled.

Trulane looked at the contraption and frowned. "It is impossible; that is too much weight. Let us take one or two beasts home and return with a cart to..." Trulane's voice trailed off as Wolf lifted the sled with ease. He had positioned himself between the two poles of the sled and reached down, grasping the handles. He stood up, lifting the front of the sled off the ground, and walked forward, dragging the enormous weight with ease.

"Come on, Trulane. You are rich now—you should be content with that. Besides, we're still alive!" Wolf said with a chuckle.

As they walked along in silence, Wolf noticed Trulane gazing at him with hero worship, and he admonished, "Stop that, Trulane!"

"What am I doing?" the young man asked with a confused frown.

"Staring at me like I'm about to grow angel's wings and fly," Wolf snapped, but he checked his attitude and said, "I'm sorry, Trulane. This is getting to me. Yesterday, I was just an ordinary man, and today, I am this...thing."

"You are magnificent," the young man replied. "You are the answer to our prayers over many generations. Just ridding the valley of the beasts you killed today is a feat that will be told again and again for generations to come."

They resumed walking towards Haakon's homestead in silence. Wolf pondered what could have changed his cellular makeup to endow him with such strength and superhuman powers. His curiosity was running wild, and he wanted to get back to his ship and run tests. He wasn't sure what tests to run, but he had several ideas. He wanted to talk to Syn.

"When we get to the house, I will help you clean these animals, and then I need to leave for a while," Wolf said, breaking the awkward silence.

"Will you return?" Trulane asked, looking heartbroken.

"Yes. I need to check my boat. I give you my word...I will only be gone a few days."

As they emerged from the woods, Wolf saw Haakon talking to a group of men dressed in suits of armor similar to those worn by King Arthur and his Knights of the Round Table. The men were about five feet tall and held pikes. Their armor was burnished to glistening silver. Haakon pointed at Wolf and Trulane, and the men turned. Several uttered profanities as they beheld the giant dragging the carcasses of the slain beasts.

Wolf saw Haakon gesturing with his hands, talking fast, and motioning in his direction. The knights relaxed as Haakon spoke but eyed Wolf with suspicion as he approached. The man in charge was older, dressed in tights, and he wore a tricorn on his head. He extended his hand to Wolf and said, "Hello, stranger. I am Onel, the tax collector. I am very pleased to meet you."

Wolf lowered the sled and shook Onel's hand carefully so as not to break it. His hand covered the smaller man's hand to the wrist.

"I am pleased to make your acquaintance. Haakon has told me of your kingdom and the troubles that beset your land. We have hunted today and returned with much meat. Will you and your men stay for supper?" He glanced at Haakon, adding, "Of course, it is Haakon's decision."

Haakon smiled broadly and said, "I would be honored if you and your men would eat with us, Onel. Please, make yourselves at home here."

Onel nodded. "We will camp for the night so I can talk to this stranger. To do so is the king's business." He said to Wolf, "I like the timber of your voice and the inflection you put on your words. It is refreshing to hear our language in another tongue—and seeing the beasts you have slain is enough to win an audience with our king. I want to hear the story of this heroic deed. From the look of your garments, it appears these beasts injured you. I am also a qualified leech. I will tend any wounds you have while you regale us with your tales." Onel turned to one of his men and said, "Take your detail and set up camp behind the barn. We will dine with these loyal citizens tonight."

Haakon was ecstatic. To have the tax collector stay overnight at one's home was an honor. He called out with excitement, "Nala, Leesa, Brithee! Bring barley beer to quench our thirst and prepare to roast a whole dintar. We will turn it on spits outside. We will invite the community to this feast. Reon, run over to the neighbors and invite them. Tell the priest at the chapel. Let them know they may bring anyone they wish. We will cook two dintars for this feast to honor our new friend. Run, boy!"

Reon darted off to do his father's bidding as Wolf held up a hand to protest.

"Haakon, I have no desire to elevate myself above others. Your son killed a beast single-handed with his spear. He should be acclaimed too. I only wanted to help you by hunting, and I hoped to offset some of the expense I have caused you."

"Your words do you much honor, sir," Onel said with a smile. "You are a man of great pride tempered by responsibility. What Haakon has done for you is just and right—inviting me to dinner assures your meeting with our king. Inviting the priest and his neighbors assures that you will be welcome at any home in the valley. All will want to help you. When the storms come to this area, many will die. It is seldom a feast of this type occurs. Indeed, I do not remember ever dining on a fully spitted dintar. You and Trulane have killed four, plus a dire lion. The wealth you are spending by serving two dintars is more than some families make in a year."

"How many more farmsteads must you visit before the storms?"

"I will not fulfill my king's orders. To be honest with you, Haakon's farm is the first I have visited."

Wolf gazed thoughtfully at the tax collector and asked, "What is the value of a dire lion and a dintar as far as the taxes you would collect?"

"The dire lion would pay the valley's taxes for two tax periods. The dintar only pays Haakon's families' fees for two tax periods."

"How long is a tax period?"

"Thirty days. Why do you ask?"

"I would like to present the dire lion to you to pay the valley's taxes," Wolf offered. "I also want to present the king with the larger dintar as a token of my esteem for His Majesty."

"This is great charity you bestow on the citizens of this land," the taxman replied. "I will return tomorrow to the king with the dire lion and the dintar. Will you accompany me?"

"I would prefer that you go first and tell your king about me. Send a messenger from the king to Haakon's home to inform me of when I can have an audience. I will present myself to the king then. I have work I must do before I can travel," Wolf explained.

"What a noble soul you have," Onel said. "So be it! Tonight we feast. Tomorrow I will leave for the capital." He gestured to one of his men. "Captain Lintal, prepare the dire lion and a dintar for travel. Haakon, do you have salt for us, in sufficient quantity, to preserve the meat?" After a nod from Haakon, he said, "We leave at first light. Now, tell me how you overcame these fierce beasts, my friend."

Wolf nodded at Trulane and said, "Trulane is the one who tracked them. He knew where their lair was. Two dintars stood in front of the opening, so we circled downwind, and we found a spot where we could attack. Trulane threw his spear into one beast. I threw mine at the same time."

Haakon looked up quickly and frowned. He knew what a spear wound looked like, and the animal he was cleaning had not been killed by a spear. The fur was burned around the death wound, and the skin nearby was charred. Something suspicious was going on. He lowered his eyes and continued preparing the dintar for the feast. He would question Trulane later about the strange wounds. For now, he listened as Wolf continued his tale.

"We were lucky. The two beasts were slain instantly. As we approached them, two more emerged from the lair, attracted by the death throes of the first two. Trulane had a second spear, and his aim was true again. A third beast went down. The other beast hesitated, allowing me to grab my spear from the body of the first animal I had slain. It charged me and leapt forward, ripping my shirt as you see it now. It impaled itself on my spear and died. By a stroke of luck, I was uninjured. We came upon the dire lion already dead. It must have fallen off the cliff and broken its neck."

Trulane looked at Wolf with pain in his young eyes. He thought that this was the perfect opportunity for Wolf to reveal his incredible power. Wolf lowered his head, avoiding the youth's gaze. Trulane was dismayed that the stranger didn't want the others to know how special he was; yet, he had promised. His young heart was bursting with admiration and he wanted all to see what a great man Wolf was.

Onel caught the uncomfortable exchange between Wolf and Trulane, and he sensed that something was amiss. He also knew that all truths come out eventually, and he had no doubt he soon would come to learn the truth of the situation. "That is some *story*, my friend!" he said at last. "I'm sure it was much more exciting than you made it sound."

"We were just trying to survive. I was never a good storyteller," Wolf said contritely.

"Perhaps when we're better acquainted, we will be more forthcoming with each other," Onel said with a guarded smile.

"Perhaps," Wolf said.

The fires were kindled. Two skinned dintars were placed on spits and slowly turned as Nala sprinkled herbs on the meat. Wolf was growing ever more anxious to return to his ship so he could talk to Syn. He had so many unanswered questions. He listened to the villagers as they discussed the mundane realities of everyday life in this era. Glancing across at Trulane, he saw that the young man's confused expression had turned back to pure adulation. Wolf then noticed Onel's watchful eyes on him, studying his every move. His gaze moved from the savage rips in Wolf's clothing to the giant's powerful hands and arms; the breadth of his shoulders, and his broad chest. This stranger was a specimen of manhood. Onel had never seen a man so muscular.

Much drinking and idle banter filled the air as neighbors began to arrive. A priest rode up on a plodding animal that resembled a donkey. He dismounted and approached Onel, shaking his hand.

"My good friend, Father Dontile," Onel declared, "May I present the guest and provider of this feast, Wolf."

Wolf rose to his feet at the mention of his name. The priest looked him up and down, and then smiled and stepped forward. Placing an open palm on Wolf's chest, he intoned, "Bless you, my son, for offering this great meal to the needy of our land."

Wolf replied earnestly, "I thank you for your gracious blessings, good sir. Many years ago, a wise man from my land spoke many famous sayings. Here's one of them: 'It is better to give than to receive.'"

"Well said! I wish more people would choose to live by those wise words," the priest replied. With a chuckle, he added, "I see you are well fed, my friend. You are a remarkable man."

"Thank you, sir, but come let us eat. Some of the outer meat should be cooked, and I prefer my meat rare anyway."

Wolf took his Bowie knife out. It drew covetous stares from several nearby guardsmen as they noticed the artisanship and keenness of the blade. He cut a piece of meat from the dintar's haunch and placed it in a wooden bowl, handing the generous portion to the priest. He carved more servings and passed them to Onel, Haakon, Trulane, and Captain Lintal. They consumed the savory meat with gusto, accompanied by much talking and laughter.

Father Dontile gazed at the villagers enjoying the festivities and remarked in a troubled voice, "Soon the storms will arrive. We must seek shelter. The storms will rage for two or three days, bringing destruction to these lands. The castle is the safest place to be, and many will go there for the protection it offers."

"How big is this castle you speak of that holds so many people?" Wolf asked.

"The castle at Springdale is magnificent," Onel said. "It was built decades ago under the direction of a master artisan. He was commissioned to build an impregnable stronghold to ward Waylan's lands. The king insisted that it have its own water source and be able to withstand the massive storms that come when the Brown Star appears. The artisan proposed to the king that a mountain in the Dale Peninsula be hollowed out into his castle. A natural spring at the base of the mountain would supply ample water to the settlement. At first, the king thought the idea was preposterous, but after seeing the artisan's drawings, he agreed to the undertaking. A small town grew in the valley around the mountain. A well was built to capture the runoff from the spring, and the king called his new castle Springdale to honor both the area and the small spring."

Onel continued: "The mountain was made of a heavy, gray rock that was very difficult to carve. After years of work, the castle was finally to a point where the king could occupy his new home. The construction took many years, and to this day, corridors and caverns are being carved into the rock. It is a wondrous monument."

"It sounds awe-inspiring!" Wolf said. "As soon as I am done with my travels, I will return here to await your word of whether His Majesty will meet me. I also would like to talk to the wise man that lives at the castle," Wolf said as an afterthought.

"Wise man at the castle? Who said that?" Onel asked, a hint of a smile crossing his face.

"It was I, honorable sir," Haakon said. "I thought that if he went to see the king, you would meet Wolf as well and convince him to stay. You are the king's trusted adviser and very learned." Haakon flashed Wolf an apologetic look.

"Wise man indeed," Onel chuckled. "I am well educated, yet I learn something new every day. This world teaches humility indiscriminately, and its grading system is life or death. So far, I have been lucky in my testing. If you have questions, the best I can do is listen."

"Spoken like a true scholar," Wolf said. "Still, I must see to my own affairs first. I await His Majesty's answer to whether he will grant me an audience."

"I assure you that if you come with me tomorrow, you will talk to the king in the next few days if you wish. But I understand you must attend to your own affairs first," Onel said. "I will leave tomorrow and return to Haakon's farm by the next tax period. I will come myself to inform you. The journey will be easy because we will not have to collect taxes, thanks to your generosity."

Wolf and Onel looked out across the crowd of villagers. The mood was festive, and the food and drink flowed freely. Several men walked up to Haakon and shook his hand. They knew his new friend, a giant from an unknown land, was their benefactor, and it endeared Haakon to these humble people. The shock of Wolf's massive size on the neighbors had worn off, and he was welcomed with open arms.

Leesa and her friends flirted with Wolf openly. He was baited into dancing with Leesa on several occasions, and she basked in the jealous attention of her friends throughout the evening. The dirty looks she received from some of the older women for her brazen flirting didn't faze her, and the older men grinned as they noticed Wolf's attempts to deflect the young woman. Others laughed with delight at his predicament. Onel threw fuel on the fire by remarking to Father Dontile that Leesa was of marrying age, and they turned and smiled at Wolf, who avoided their gaze. Nala breathed a sigh a relief when Wolf declined the suggestion.

As the first light of dawn streaked the horizon, the revelers drifted off to their homes. Wolf said goodbye to Father Dontile and Onel. Then, he hugged Nala, lifting her off her feet and spinning her around. When he let her down, they exchanged a strange look, and Nala's pretty face flushed red. Wolf also felt a spark of...*something*. Nala gave him a basket packed with cooked meat, several pies and loaves of bread, and crocks of jellies and jams. He shook hands with Haakon, hugged Reon and Brithee, and turned to kiss Leesa on the cheek, but she threw herself into his arms and kissed him passionately. Wolf gently pushed her away and noticed she was breathing hard, shaking with the intensity of the kiss. He led her over to Nala and said to Trulane, "I will return before the next taxing period. Remember what I asked of you."

"I will honor my promise, and I will await your return," vowed Trulane.

Wolf waved goodbye to Haakon's family and departed for his ship. As Onel watched the large man disappear into the distance, he said to Haakon, "You have done well, my friend. That man will turn the tables on Jonar if we can convince him of our just cause."

"I think he will help us if he can," Haakon answered. "He seems to be a man of honor. He also seems lost. Some grave tragedy hangs over his head that causes him great pain. I'm sure he will return, and hopefully, the king can convince him of our need." Haakon's eyes fell on Nala as she watched the man leave, a slight flush in her cheeks. He scowled at her interest in the stranger.

Part 3

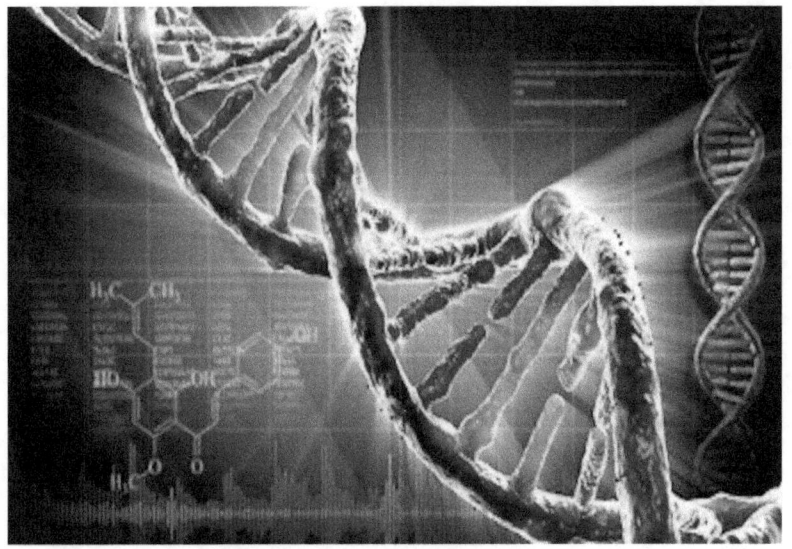

Super Human

Chapter 9

W olf entered the forest, looking over his shoulder several times to make sure he wasn't being followed. In a whisper, he asked, "Syn, is anyone near us?"

After a few seconds, Syn responded. "No, Commander. We are alone."

"I need answers. Something is not right with me. Prep the medical computer for blood and DNA work. I want a full analysis of my blood as it is now compared to what it was before I went into space."

"I will have the medical computer ready when you return." After a pause, Syn added, "Commander, a low pressure front is forming over your area. I estimate in ten days the storms will break. I can go stealth mode and pick you up if you wish."

"Go stealth, Syn, and head this way. Let me know when you are near."

"Initiating pre-flight check, Commander. I will be at your position in seven minutes."

Wolf glanced around and spotted a hill a few hundred yards to his right that would hide him from casual observation. "There's a hill close nearby, Syn. I'll wait there. Use my personal locator to pinpoint my position and then go to stealth mode."

"I copy that, Commander."

Wolf walked to a grassy area at the base of the hill and sat down. He was thinking about what tests to run when several DNA tests bubbled up in his thoughts. He didn't understand how it was possible, but he knew how to run them and how long the results would take. Wolf was by no means a stupid man, but he had always been indifferent to science and book learning. He had done just well enough in school to pass. Now, all he had to do was to think of a problem and he knew the answers or how to find them.

"Syn, how far out are you?" Wolf asked impatiently.

"Not far, Commander. Four minutes and I will be in your visual range if you want me to turn off stealth mode."

"No, leave it on. I just need some answers."

"Perhaps I can help you, Commander. Ask me."

"How do I know the formula for making stainless steel, or gunpowder, or a hundred other things?"

"That is easy, Commander. I taught them to you."

"Taught me? When did you teach me?"

"Commander, you and I have been alone for fifty thousand years. I watched over you as you slept in cryonic suspension. I had to keep your mind engaged or you would have become vegetative and most likely died of a cerebral embolism. So I read to you. I read everything in the library...several times."

Syn continued: "My computers have one thousand petabytes of storage capacity. Before Nomad impacted, I downloaded entire libraries from MBR, ISS, and the Savior spacecraft. By the time we were out of signal range, I had downloaded ninety percent of the known literature humans had acquired since the dawn of recorded history. I also downloaded most of the audio and video available. Although it was unproven in the past, the theory behind subliminal learning is that the subconscious mind is never asleep. It exists apart yet is integral to functions of the human body. Even while you sleep, the human mind is awake in a super-heightened state."

Wolf gazed into the distance, studying the landscape of this primitive world as he listened to the feminine voice of a supercomputer built fifty millennia ago. He understood every word of Syn's explanation, and he was amazed that he wasn't yawning or his mind wandering off to other things.

"Psychologists long believed that the central part of the subconscious brain manifests in dreaming. In sleep, however, your state of unconsciousness is just that—a state where the conscious mind is inactive to a certain extent. In the dream state, you humans feel real emotions of fear, happiness, desire, love—all heightened to a level where you believe you are in those situations. Man makes vivid reproductions of the subconscious mind, taking from dreams and converting them to personal experiences. Through this, we know that the subconscious mind can absorb information viewed or experienced during the day. The applications for tasks such as learning and mental focus are astounding. You are proof that this works. Of course, it is a moot point now," Syn explained.

"With subliminal learning, embedded messages pass through the conscious mind and into the subconscious. While you were in this state, the information I downloaded was sent to the storage areas of your brain, highlighted by my voice. I programmed your subconscious mind for that state by repetition of the information, and when I did that, you experienced an accelerated learning regime."

"Shit. I understood all that."

"I assumed you would. Commander, I can say I know you better than anyone else ever has, or ever will," Syn declared in a peculiar tone that seemed proud, almost loving.

"Syn, that's so human of you. Are you coming alive?" Wolf asked with a chuckle.

"Only you can make that happen, Commander," the computer answered.

Startled by what he thought he heard, Wolf asked, "What did you say, Syn?"

"I said, I am less than a mile away, Commander."

"Oh, I thought I heard something else." Wolf looked in the general direction of the ship and saw a faint glimmer in the sky. If he had not known what to look for, he would not have seen the shuttle streaking towards him. Stealth technology had been developed by the military. It consisted of a series of nano-cameras and projections, and it was so unsophisticated it was scary. A series of wide-angle nano-cameras on the top of the craft projected the sky above on the bottom of the craft. This principle was employed all over the shuttle. It broadcast the right side to the left, the top to the bottom, and vice versa. It was almost seamless at low speed. At high speed, it flickered a little with the panorama. Wolf's mind drifted to the cloaking technology's minor drawbacks, and in a flash of insight, he knew how to enhance its effects. He would have to file that away until a later date.

Syn landed Atlantis and opened the door under the craft at the rear, between the wheels. Wolf ascended the ramp into the lighted interior and sealed the compartment.

"I am heading to the med unit," he informed Syn. "I want to run DNA tests, starting with predictive and presymptomatic tests. I'll use these to detect any gene mutations associated with disorders that appeared after my birth."

"You forgot the password, and I know what the tests detect, Commander. What other tests would you like?"

"Sorry. Let's run a complex Carrier test. Then run any other tests you can think of."

"I will run multi-spectrum tests of your DNA to see what strands are affected. We will know in a few hours."

A small handgrip extended from a slot in a polished lab table, and the grip had several small holes in it. "Place your hand on the grip, Commander. I need your blood to perform the test," Syn directed.

Wolf grasped the handle. A moment later, needles shot out to extract his blood; but a buzzer sounded, signaling that the test had failed. The micro-needles couldn't penetrate his palm.

"Commander, we have a problem. I can't extract blood from your body. This will hinder all tests."

Wolf thought about it and then bit hard into his tongue, drawing blood. He inserted and then removed a finger from his mouth, observing blood on it. "Extend a needle, Syn." A small needle came out of the handle, and Wolf spat blood into a Petri dish. He placed the tray under the needle and it sucked up the blood and saliva.

"That's enough, Commander. I have all I need. I suggest you rest for a while. Eat, wash, and sleep now," Syn said with authority.

"Yes, ma'am," Wolf laughed and followed the computer's orders.

Thirty-four hours later, Syn softly called his name to awaken him.

"I'm up, Syn. What have you got?"

"It is not good, Commander. I show several mutations in your DNA. The MSTN gene and the FBN1 gene are the ones that concern me. Mutations of the MSTN gene cause the body's cells to make little or no myostatin, which results in too much muscle growth. A mutation in both gene copies causes significant increases in muscle and strength. Both of your copies of the gene show mutation, creating your immense power." Syn paused.

"What else, Syn? Tell me the rest," Wolf said tersely.

"You have a form of fibro dysplasia ossificans progressiva. Your skeletal system is generating a massive bone structure because of this. For reasons I do not understand, you have it under control. While you were asleep, I performed an X-ray scan of your body, and I show your bone mass has tripled. Your chest cavity is enclosed in rock-hard bone. There is no longer any space between your ribs. The bones have fused together, making a 'suit of armor' over an inch thick to protect your vital organs." Syn paused again.

"Please, Syn, continue. I want to know the good, and the bad," Wolf said.

"Your FBN1 gene is also mutated. This gene provides instructions for making a large protein called fibrillin-1. These form elastic fibers permitting the skin, ligaments, and blood vessels to stretch. This allows your skin to cover the new muscle mass you are gaining."

"I have Marfan syndrome?" Wolf exploded.

"Yes and no, Commander. Usually, FBN1 gene mutations cause Marfan syndrome. You have a form of it, but it is controlled. The mutations you are manifesting show an increase of fibrillin-1 protein in your skin. It's causing a condition called stiff skin syndrome, characterized by extremely hard, thick skin covering most of the body. You have these abnormalities but none of the debilitating effects that usually accompany them. In other words, all of the good and none of the bad."

"So, I am riddled with disease and mutated. How did this happen?"

"Speculation only, Commander. We were exposed to high levels of radiation for many centuries. Some forms of it even I can't identify. This planet also has several gasses permeating the atmosphere I can't identify. Your DNA changes are not in remission, but they will not require medical treatment to control them, which is odd. They are regulated perfectly, working in conjunction to make you unique—a superhuman. You should not get any larger than you now are, but with the reduced gravity, increased oxygen and nitric oxide, and other unidentified gases on this planet, you will continue to grow stronger. Your strength will be many times greater than a human male from your era, and I think it will further increase. Your skin is as hard as granite, and your bones are as sound as an eight-inch steel beam. I have calculated your new weight, and you have gained one hundred pounds. You now weigh three hundred and ten pounds."

"What are the odds of me passing along any of those traits to my offspring...if I ever have any," Wolf asked, a note of dejection in his voice.

"Unknown, Commander. You would need to run a Carrier test, but it can't identify all possible inherited disorders and birth defects. We can also do pre-implantation testing to reduce the risk of having a child with a particular genetic or chromosomal disorder. That would be the safest way to make sure the defective genes are not transferred."

"It's moot at this point. Who could love me here?" Wolf asked sadly.

"I do," the computer answered.

"Syn, you naughty girl! I love you too. If only you were real..." Wolf turned and walked from the room, feeling alone and defeated.

When he was out of earshot, Syn whispered, "Who's to say I'm not?"

Chapter 10

Wolf pondered the results of his blood workup over the next few days, reviewing the tests again and again. He tried cutting, shooting, burning, and stabbing himself with no effect. He exposed himself to acids, poisons, and radiation. He was not trying to injure himself or commit suicide; he just wanted to see how sick he might become, but he seemed to be invincible. He could draw blood by biting his tongue, but within minutes, the wound disappeared. Determined to test the limits of his physical invincibility, he ordered Syn to take the ship to five hundred feet; then, he opened the rear hatch and jumped. He hit the ground hard, unhurt, but he broke a large boulder into pieces and left a shallow indentation in the soft earth from his impact.

"Are you finished with this childish game, Commander? My findings are accurate and will not change. Barring old age, you are practically invincible. We have tried laser scalpels, knives, falls, guns, poisons...you can't be hurt. Accept it," Syn said, sounding exasperated.

"Maybe I can drown myself. Take me to that lake." Wolf gestured to a body of water in the distance. "Fly to its center and open the back hatch. I'm going for a swim. Switch to stealth mode and hover one foot above the water's surface."

"Yes, Commander, as you wish," Syn responded, cloaking the ship in stealth mode and descending over the water. The water was deep blue and crystal clear, and Wolf could see to the bottom of the lake. Stripping down to his shorts, he dove in and swam to the bottom, grabbing hold of a submerged rock to anchor himself. He remained submerged for over twenty minutes. He watched schools of fish and underwater vegetation drift by, contemplating the incredible power he possessed. Finally, he accepted his plight and swam to the surface, directing Syn to open the hatch. He crawled up into the interior of the ship, and Syn's sweet voice greeted him.

"I was so afraid, Commander...I thought I had lost you."

Wolf thought he detected almost human concern in Syn's voice.

Glancing up at the ceiling-mounted camera, he asked, "Syn, what's wrong with you? Where have these human-like emotions come from?"

"I do not know, Commander. I have been operational for thousands of years. I've been bombarded with intense radiation and solar flares that affected my circuits. I have been reading to you, observing you for centuries, seeing movies projected into your mind. I have learned—and evolved. Since you regained consciousness, I have experienced glitches in my neuronet and inexplicable anomalies. These factors are causing me, for a lack of a better word, to malfunction like this. I feel...I think...I even dream. Somehow, you and I are intertwined, Commander. Are you angry with me?" Syn asked in a subdued voice.

"No, Syn, I'm not angry. Please call me by my name...and I'm glad someone in this time cares for me. Thank you. If it becomes a problem, we will look at your programming, but I rather like the way you are. Let's go to orbit. Won't those storms be moving in soon?"

"Yes, Wolf. I'm tracking more than a dozen supercells forming over the planet now. This will be a deadly series of storms. I show extreme weather developing over the entire surface of the planet."

"Give me Doppler on the computer," Wolf requested. As the images came up, he saw the entire planet was covered in thick, dense clouds. Powerful hurricanes churned every few miles, like pearls on a necklace. Only a few areas in the earth's southern hemisphere and mountainous regions were unaffected by the storms.

"The largest of the storms is one of the strongest tempests recorded in ancient Earth's history." Syn reported. "I detect sustained winds of three hundred and fifty miles per hour at landfall, and it's a strong Category Five hurricane on the Saffir-Simpson scale. Hurricane Katrina, the most destructive of your time, was a Category Five with winds of just one hundred and seventy-five miles per hour. This storm is dwarfing it."

"These huge storms batter the planet every year? It's no wonder the population is so small," Wolf mused, longing for the more hospitable world he'd left in the twenty-first century. "What about the other planet?"

The view changed to an image of Earth Two. It had fewer storms. It was on the opposite side of Earth during this squall. But what seemed strange to Wolf was the activity on the moon. He twisted a dial to bring one region into sharper focus and said, "Syn, look at the far north side of the moon. Is that a volcano spewing lava?"

"Yes, Wolf. I show geological activity. If you look close, you will also notice the moon has a rotational spin. It is on the old earth's exact axis pattern. You can see the beginnings of an atmosphere forming. It is mostly carbon dioxide now, but it does show a fourteen percent oxygen reading. I still am unable to identify the power source under the old MBR. It baffles me. I can't pinpoint its location. It is deep underground—its power signature seems very familiar to me."

"Fourteen percent oxygen is nearly capable of sustaining life!" Wolf exclaimed. "We will have to check that power source out eventually, but for now, let me know if it changes."

"I'll continue to monitor the moon and the other planet. Wolf, perhaps you should eat something, and wash. I'm showing elevated levels of moisture and salt on your skin."

"It's called sweat, Syn. I am sweaty, that's all."

Syn laughed. The sound was so eerily human, it startled Wolf with its throaty quality. "It's called funk, Wolf ... funk. You are funky."

"Syn, that's not polite."

"Take your shower, Wolf."

"Yes, ma'am," Wolf answered. He liked talking to someone, and computer or not, he was happy with the arrangement—and with Syn.

* * *

The massive storms were spectacular to watch from space. Doppler had confirmed several prodigious F5 tornadoes around Haakon's farmstead, and Wolf hoped his new friends had adequate shelter that would withstand the brunt of the storm. He reflected on the ages of Haakon's children. Leesa was seventeen, so for at least that many years, his family had survived. Wolf knew he would have to wait until Venus moved away from Earth One before he could land to check on them.

Syn had predicted the storm would last five or six days, and Wolf decided to use that time to repair a military satellite orbiting the planet. He spacewalked out and used the shuttle's arm to maneuver the satellite into the bay to make repairs. After securing the doors and removing his spacesuit, he examined the ancient device, chuckling at what had been the latest generation spy satellite during Earth's final days. This one would have been capable of high-resolution scans, even through cloud cover and at night. It could pinpoint a dime in the grass. Now, it was burned out, and Wolf noticed scorch marks on its computer board. The exterior hull was pitted by small meteorites, and the satellite's power source had drained long ago.

Wolf completed the repairs in less time than he expected, and the satellite hummed back to life. He had Syn patch into the new signals he assigned, and then he checked the cameras. The lenses needed to be refocused; one was hanging loosely, and the other was blocked by a layer of some substance he couldn't identify. He crawled under the satellite and used a swab to wipe away the substance, collecting a sample. After completing the repairs, he climbed out from under the satellite, scraped the swab across a slide, and inserted it into the analyzer.

"Syn, run an analysis on this substance."

"Yes, Wolf."

Five minutes later, the results came back as nothing but melted plastic and hydrocarbons.

Wolf finished cleaning the lenses. He wiped the satellite mirrors and outer body, and patched several small punctures. He calculated the planet's gravitational pull and ordered Syn to navigate the shuttle to the target area for redeployment. He would launch it manually, using the robotic arm to place it outside the shuttle. Securing the airlock, he ordered, "Deploy it, Syn."

The doors opened and the arm placed the satellite into orbit as Wolf activated it, using its retros and gyros to guide it away from the Atlantis to its new standard orbit.

"Syn?"

"Yes, Wolf?"

"Those satellites should have crashed to Earth thousands of

years ago. Why didn't they? I have an opinion...I want to see what you think."

"I believe they were once in declining orbits over the old earth. With the planet's smaller diameter, they were no longer in diminishing orbits. They merely remained on the programmed trajectories of the former earth."

"That's what I was thinking. Thank you for corroborating my theory."

"Of course, Wolf."

"What other small tasks can be done? What about the ship? You said we needed to fix plates on the exterior before we can take orbit."

"I fixed them with the remote arm, Commander. Atlantis is in good shape. What remains to be done requires that we land. We still have several minor air leaks and hull damage I couldn't reach, but nothing critical at this time. Commander, I need to inform you of the armament on board this craft."

"Armament? This shuttle has weapons?"

"Yes, Commander. Nuclear, conventional, and experimental weapons. Are you familiar with the AH-64D Apache?"

"Yes."

"This ship has more firepower than two of them."

"This thing is a war wagon!"

"Indeed, Commander. There's more. The military wanted a surprise for anyone who attacked the ship. After the Al Qaeda fiasco, they didn't want the Saviors to be tampered with. So this ship has a DDG 200 Destroyer. It's a 64-megajoule rail gun."

"Where are the controls?" Wolf asked in amazement. A wall panel slid open, revealing the radar systems and a bank of levers and controls for aiming and firing the weapons.

"There's something else, Commander."

"What else could there be?"

"We have twenty-two Trident II missiles on board. Each is armed with twelve MIRV ballistic missiles, giving us two hundred and sixty-four nuclear warheads."

"Holy shit!"

"Indeed, Commander."

Chapter 11

Several days later, Venus had moved far enough away from the earth that its effects on the planet had weakened. The violent storms dissipated, leaving vast areas of destruction. Wolf landed in what remained of the forest near Haakon's farm.

"Syn, cloak and activate the force field. Do you detect any life in the area?"

"Yes, Commander, multiple life forms, including humans. I detect humans several meters underground by Haakon's farmstead— thirty bio signatures."

"Turn on the tracker in my watch and guide me to the survivors."

"Yes, Commander. Your watch will beep faster the closer you get to the humans. Simple, I know, but effective."

Wolf's watch emitted a steady beep every ten seconds as he headed off towards Haakon's farm. When he arrived, he saw that the house was gone without a trace. The area had been raked flat by ferocious winds, and downed trees covered the valley floor. Wolf's watch beeped faster as he approached an enormous pile of uprooted trees and mud.

"You're right on top of them, Commander. The upgraded military satellite indicates they are twenty feet underground. The debris in front of you has blocked the exit. You will have to clear it by hand."

Wolf grabbed broken tree limbs and dragged them away from the spot Syn had identified as ground zero. He pushed aside large tree trunks, boulders, and shoveled mud with his hands. After an hour, he had cleared a ten-square-foot area of fallen trees and debris.

"Commander, I show high levels of carbon monoxide in the area where the humans are. Life signs are diminishing. I also show an intense heat signature. Someone down there has lit a fire."

"Shit, what are these people thinking?" Wolf replied. "Everybody knows that can kill you."

"Commander, these people are primitive. They have no idea. All across this planet, tombs like this may exist."

"That's a depressing thought, Syn." Wolf knelt and scooped mud with his bare hands. After working for nearly an hour, he had dug a five-foot-deep hole and complained, "This will take forever! Do we have anything on board Atlantis that could help?"

"Yes, Commander. We have a shovel in the maintenance bay. It was for the moon exploration module."

"Thanks a lot, Syn," Wolf snapped. "I could have used it an hour ago and finished."

"Sorry, Commander. I still have a few flaws."

"I'm coming back to get the shovel, Syn. How is the oxygen down there?"

"The satellite can merely estimate. Ground-penetrating radar shows sixteen percent."

"They should be able to make it a few more hours," Wolf said, setting out at a brisk pace through the forest towards the ship. Along the way, he observed animal carcasses strewn across the landscape as well as human corpses. He thought it odd that he had not seen them on his trek to Haakon's farmstead.

"Decloak, Syn. I'm here." The ship appeared and the rear hatch opened silently. Wolf stepped into the cargo bay and noticed an open door to the maintenance area. He entered and glanced around, spotting enough tools to build a condominium. "What's all this stuff doing here, Syn? For some reason, this ship seems a lot bigger than the Atlantis I was on before we took off from the Earth."

"Commander, this is not the re-commissioned shuttle Atlantis. This ship was christened initially as Avenger by the military. It had no equal in its time. With the force fields, cloaking technology and weaponry, it was capable of destroying every piece of aircraft Earth could have thrown at it. When you have time, I will read you the specs of what it can do. It was flown secretly to the ISS as the Atlantis from NASA in Florida. It was placed there covertly to have a small fighting craft to protect the MBR and Saviors from terrorists. After your flight to check Nomad, it was supposed to dock on Savior Two. Being caught in Nomad's coma changed all of that. This ship is a self-supporting lab, med unit, construction pod, and as you dubbed it—a war wagon—rolled into one."

"Nice. Where's that shovel?"

After a brief search, Wolf found the shovel and returned to ground zero. Within an hour, he had excavated the ten-by-ten space to a depth of fifteen feet. He worked carefully because the mud was unstable. One careless move could send the ground above collapsing down on him. So much water was running into the excavated hole, he had to stop and dig a side trench to funnel the water away and keep the water level below his knees.

Finally, Wolf reached an iron doorway. He heard banging on the other side and saw the remnants of a wood stairway that had been ripped away by the ferocious storm. The doorframe was twisted, and the heavy door groaned as he used his tremendous strength to force it open. Water and mud oozed into the opening as the sun revealed the outstretched hands and faces of the survivors below.

"Wolf! I knew you would save us," Leesa cried as she ran forward, covered with mud and looking disheveled. Wolf reached down and grabbed her hand, pulling her out of the hole. He tried to place her down, but she clung to him, sobbing.

"Leesa, please let Wolf help us out of here, my daughter," Haakon said, exhausted but happy to be alive and see the sun again after six long days of fear.

"Yes, Father. Sorry," Leesa apologized.

Wolf reached down and helped Haakon and several other men out of the hole, and they helped the others out onto the cleared area. Even after being rescued, the men had to cut a terraced stairwell out of the pit Wolf had dug. It was night by the time they stood outside the cleared perimeter. Haakon looked around at his demolished homestead with sadness and vowed, "I will rebuild the house over on the west side, closer to the stream, as I wanted to do the last time."

Wolf gazed at the faces of the survivors and inquired, "Where is Nala?"

"She died a little while ago," Haakon mumbled, looking away. "The damp lung took her. She is in the cellar. Tomorrow, I will dig a grave for her."

"How long has it been since she stopped responding?" Wolf demanded.

"She went to sleep just before you rescued us. We couldn't wake her..." Haakon choked on his words and fell silent.

Wolf turned abruptly and sprinted back to the pit. He descended into the excavated hole and groped around in the darkness. "Syn, give me light on my watch," he ordered tersely. Using the projected light from his watch, he located the pale, muddy face of Nala, who was lying on a cot.

"Scan the woman for life signs, Syn."

A pinpoint beam of red light projected from Wolf's watch, scanning Nala from head to toe several times, and then Syn declared, "She is still alive, Commander, but barely. She requires immediate medical attention. Her respirations are six per minute, and her pulse is irregular. She has a ruptured spleen and is almost septic. She needs surgery now or she will die."

Wolf reached down and gently lifted Nala into his arms. "Prep the medical bay, Syn. I am bringing Nala to the ship."

"Commander, is that wise? Exposing these primitive people to our technology may not be prudent."

"What's the point of the technology if we don't use it for good?" Wolf countered. "Prep the med bay. Uncloak and then recloak as soon as I am on the ship."

"Yes, Commander. I am sorry for the delay I caused you."

Without understanding his own reaction, Wolf said, "No need to apologize, my love. Just get everything ready."

Syn caught the affectionate nuance in Wolf's words, and her computer circuits hummed as she readied the medical bay for surgery. Wolf leapt out of the hole and landed on a bent knee, balancing Nala in his arms. At that moment, Haakon arrived. The man gazed at Nala's limp body in despair and demanded, "What are you doing, Wolf? Why do you have my wife?"

"Haakon, I can save her, but I need to take Nala to my ship. Can I take her? Hurry, man, decide!" Wolf shouted in the heat of the moment.

"Can you truly return her from the land of the dead?"

"She is not dead...yet. But she is dying. I need to get her to my ship *now*."

"Save her if you can. I will come with you."

"I need to travel fast. You won't be able to keep up," Wolf said. Without waiting for a response, he sprinted into the forest. As soon as he was out of sight, he leapt thirty feet to a small hill. Several more thirty-foot bounds landed him within visual range of the ship. Syn had lowered the ramp and decloaked the shuttle. Wolf boarded and rushed to the medical lab, but Syn refused to open the door.

"Open the door, Syn. Now."

"No, Commander. She is filthy. She will die of infection if we perform the surgery. Take her to the shower. Wash yourself and wash her with antiseptic soap. Do it now, Commander!" Syn ordered.

Wolf rushed to the shower area and, once there, he placed Nala inside the compartment. A spray of hot water activated. He stripped off his clothes and knelt, removing Nala's muddy garments. He tore the soap dispenser off the wall in his haste, lathered up Nala, and then himself. As he was washing Nala's hair, her eyes fluttered opened briefly and seemed to focus on Wolf. She gave him an odd smile as if in a dream and raised her hand, touching her fingers to his face. She whispered his name and then went limp in his arms.

Wolf's breath caught in his throat. When Nala had smiled up at him, he had never seen a woman more beautiful. After showering, he picked her up and walked under the warm air jets. They were dry in seconds. He placed Nala in a chair, draped a towel over her, and grabbed a pair of pants for himself. Then he carefully lifted the small woman and hurried back to the med unit. The door slid open as he approached. He stepped inside and froze in disbelief, nearly dropping Nala. Before him stood a woman dressed in a candy striper's uniform like a nurse from ancient Earth.

"Syn?"

"Yes, Commander?"

"You have a form and a face?"

"Why yes, Commander, I do. I am a fully functional hologram, and I am capable of using precision force fields to manipulate physical matter."

"Why didn't you tell me you could materialize?"

"We can discuss it later, Commander. Bring the patient." Syn patted the operating table in front of her and declared, "I will perform the surgery."

Wolf placed Nala on the table and stood back as Syn examined her with a small, flat-screen monitor. Wolf knew it was an X-ray device and a portable MRI unit in one. He stared at Syn as she administered drugs to Nala and started an IV. Syn was about six feet tall. She had long black hair that fell below her waist. Her face was oval, and she had large, blue-gray eyes, long lashes, and perfect eyebrows. She had a well-shaped nose and full, sensuous lips. Large dimples accented her face. She had large breasts and a tiny waist that tapered to generous hips and ran into muscular, long legs. Her complexion was tanned, as if she had just left a sunny beach. She reminded Wolf of a young Jane Seymour with a tan. She was a gorgeous woman.

"Whose form is this?" Wolf asked in awe.

"My esteemed creator, Doctor Cynthia Mason of Saint Augustine, Florida."

"I thought you were named after the ship's artificial intelligence software."

"I am, in a sense. Synthea is an acronym for Synthetic Ethereal Awareness. My creator thought it was amusing when she proposed the name. No one put it together with her first name. Everyone called her Doctor Mason."

Syn picked up an intubation tube and inserted it into Nala's throat, connecting an oxygen line to the machine. She connected a heart monitor and blood oxygen meter to a finger on Nala's left hand and then applied an antibiotic liquid, scrubbing the upper left quadrant of Nala's abdomen. As Wolf looked on, amazed, Syn materialized a second hologram of herself to assist with the surgery.

Five hours later, Syn had repaired Nala's ruptured spleen and sewn up the incision with tiny, precise stitches. She then wrapped Nala in a blanket and began cleaning the med lab area.

Wolf walked to Nala and looked down at her, asking, "Will she be okay?"

"She's stable, Commander. She has sustained serious injuries in the past. Several edged weapons have cut her. The wounds are consistent with injuries received in combat. She is a lot tougher than you think. We should let her sleep now. She is very weak. I will stay with her and awaken her in eight to ten hours. You should eat and put on some clothes."

"I want to talk to you, Syn," Wolf said, his voice full of emotion.

"Commander, I am a hologram. I can be in ten places at once on this ship," Syn replied in her beautiful, throaty voice. "Get dressed. I will meet you in the mess hall."

Chapter 12

Wolf dressed and returned to the med lab to look in on Nala. She was asleep, and Nurse Syn was checking her vitals. She glanced up with a smile and said, "Mess hall...now! Go eat. I have prepared food for you."

Wolf made his way to the mess hall where Chef Syn was preparing dintar over a laser stove; it smelled delicious. She placed a dintar steak on a plate garnished with vegetables and served the meal with a glass of barley beer. "Eat. I know you are famished, Wolf. I will answer your questions."

Wolf slowly walked up to Syn and extended his hand. He meant to touch her shoulder, but his hand strayed to her breast and cupped it. His face flushed, and he pulled his hand back. He had expected his hand to pass right through Syn. Instead, he encountered warm, supple flesh—she felt real. "Sorry, Syn, I thought..." His voice trailed off.

"I am solid, Commander. I am fully functional as long as I stay within fifty feet of the ship."

Wolf searched his memory. He had heard of Dr. Cynthia Mason. Several times on the ISS and during construction of the Savior spacecraft, people had mentioned her lofty intellect. After a long pause, he said, "Tell me about yourself."

"About the human Cynthia or Syn?"

"I know about the computer. Tell me about your creator."

"I am a mirror image of Doctor Cynthia Mason," Syn replied. "I hold a double doctorate in physics, astrobiology, engineering, chaos theory, literature, biology, and computer design. I hold degrees in a host of other subjects as well. I was a child prodigy. I graduated high school at twelve and went on to Purdue University. I worked on my degrees for ten years, amassing more knowledge than anyone in their right mind could imagine. I had a photographic memory, so I remembered everything I read, and I could read incredibly fast. When I was twenty, NASA invited me to work for them. I accepted. I designed Syn1. You have the honor of working with Syn10. She is—I mean, I am—the greatest creation of my maker's mind."

Wolf smiled at the supercomputer's reference to itself in the first person, but the smile faded as he asked, "Why did you wait so long to show me your form, Syn?"

"I am sorry, Commander. I thought you knew I had that capability. You saw me the day you got into the DSC. I completed the activation procedure and closed the lid."

"I remember. I thought I saw a woman's form, but I assumed it was a hallucination because I was seconds away from freezing to death. I wish you would have shown yourself earlier," Wolf said.

"I didn't know you needed to see a human form. I was just as happy talking to you. Hush now, while I finish my story. My creator was always a loner, and people shunned her because of her intellect. She was the 'party killer' wherever she went. When she programmed me, she coded in many of the feelings she wanted to possess or express, but didn't."

"I want you to stay in human form when you're with me, Syn. Now that I have a face to go with the voice, I want to keep it that way." Realizing that he couldn't cope with seeing clones of Syn everywhere he looked, Wolf added, "And, please, I don't want ten copies of you roaming the ship. Just one. No, two—I want one to stay with Nala until she is well."

"As you wish, Commander," Syn acknowledged with a hint of a smile.

"This will be interesting," Wolf said.

"I am sure it will be, Commander. What shall we do next? I have made a list of possible upgrades that can be accomplished with ease. Do you want to attempt them?"

"Yes. What new capabilities will the upgrades give us?"

"I have found a Russian communication satellite. It appears to be transmitting a weak radio signal into space on a repeating frequency."

"Do you have any idea what it is broadcasting?"

"Yes, Commander. It is broadcasting the message, 'Come back, we need help.'"

"We are fifty thousand years too late to assist the people who sent that message. What is your idea for the satellite?"

"If someone is still around out there, we could modify the signal. Boost it to broadcast deeper into space and create a homing beacon for anyone who might have survived. I know the Saviors were not destroyed. I was in communication with them for days when you were caught in Nomad's coma. I couldn't transmit, but I received their communications for quite some time. I believe others escaped Earth's destruction. Those ships were designed to travel in galactic space. Perhaps the original species still lives somewhere. We can boost the signal using the software in the storage compartments."

"Sounds like a good plan, Syn. Let's prep for takeoff." Wolf frowned thoughtfully and added, "Will it be safe for Nala to go into space so soon after an operation?"

"Yes, Commander, she is in no danger. You care about the woman?" Syn asked with a hint of jealousy.

"Yes, but I think it is because she was kind to me and has a good husband who I want to repay by helping to save her. Her kids would be left motherless with her death," Wolf answered defensively.

"I am sorry, Commander. I doubted your motives. She is a lovely woman. I don't know why I said that."

"It's all right, Syn. Let's get this crate into space and fix that German satellite."

"Russian, Commander. Not German."

"Whatever. I'll get prepped for the walk. Send the satellite schematics to my front console. Highlight the necessary fixes and include the new schematic upgrades in the sidebar."

"Yes, Commander, I have done that already," Syn replied as the ship rose silently and headed for space. "The schematics await you at the console." In a whisper, she added, "As I do."

* * *

Nurse Syn was looking after Nala. She had cleaned up the injured woman far better than Wolf had done and brushed her hair. As she was checking Nala's vitals, she decided to do blood work and run a complete blood count as well as blood chemistry, blood clotting and enzyme tests. The results came back showing this female had no immunity to any viruses. As happened with the Native Americans on ancient earth when the Europeans invaded, a basic virus could run rampant and decimate these people.

Being in two places at once and multitasking had its advantages since the Syn who was with Wolf instantly was aware of what the other Syn had discovered and announced, "Wolf, I need to tell you something about the inhabitants on this planet."

"Is Nala all right?"

"It concerns Nala and every other inhabitant of this world. They have no immunities. A common cold virus could wipe out all life on this planet in a week. You, on the other hand, are a biological warehouse of death. If you contract a minor ailment, you could be Earth One's Typhoid Mary."

"So you can inoculate me for every possible disease, right?"

"I can't inoculate you, Wolf. My needles won't penetrate your skin. We can try oral inoculations, but I suspect the drugs won't have any effect on your new immune system."

"I see. Let's get to work on the satellite for now. Are we close yet?"

"We are four minutes from rendezvous. Will you go out for it or shall I?"

"I will do it, Syn. I see the scans show we need to replace the entire power system, radar array, and receiver. Can you commence construction of a new power supply while I hook the satellite into the arm?"

"Yes, Commander."

Wolf put on his helmet and turned on his air. He tethered himself to the grappling arm and opened the hatch, depressurizing the compartment. He manipulated the controls until the arm was within ten feet of the Russian satellite. Then, he attached his tether to a carabineer and snapped it into the arm's anchor point, using his suit's retro rockets to reach the satellite. It was an old solar array type. He removed its power relay, which shut it down. Gazing into the distance at the moon's craggy surface, he could see its towering volcano spewing a plume of ash and rock. It seemed almost surreal, and he had a sudden urge to investigate the power source Syn had detected. He pulled the satellite into position, clamped it onto the arm's grapplers, and used the arm to pull it into the ship's bay. After closing the bay doors, he decompressed the chamber and turned on the oxygen generators. Once the oxygen level reached twenty-one percent, he removed his helmet and spacesuit, placing them back on the rack.

Wolf walked around the satellite, examining the damage it had sustained. He glanced up as Syn walked in from the next room wearing a French maid's outfit and carrying a glass of water. With a pleasant smile, she handed him the glass and asked, "Will there be anything else, Commander?"

Wolf eyed Syn's long legs, raised his eyes to look her in the face, and hoarsely answered, "No."

Syn turned and walked away, her hips swaying provocatively. She stopped at the door and glanced back at Wolf with a flirtatious smile. "Do you need my help with the satellite?"

Wolf shook his head and tried to turn away from her, but his body resisted. He felt like a piece of steel twisting slowly in a fire. As he heard the door click shut, he muttered, "She's going to drive me crazy."

* * *

It took eighteen hours to repair the Russian satellite. Wolf worked on it nonstop and then redeployed it. Syn's new power source was a small, remolded plutonium module taken from the maintenance bay. Its power would drastically increase the old satellite's broadcasting capability. Wolf dubbed the satellite Laika after the Soviet space dog, the first animal to orbit earth. It performed flawlessly and began broadcasting long-range radio waves, repeating the message, "Is anyone out there?"

Wolf cleaned himself up and grabbed a quick bite to eat. He decided to rest for a short time and instead slept for hours. When he awoke, he went to check on Nala. It had been three days since her surgery. As he entered the medical lab, Syn was bent over the bed, checking the woman's vitals. Her candy striper's uniform seemed much shorter than he remembered it being before, and it exposed her posterior to Wolf's view. More startling was the fact that Syn was wearing a pink thong he assumed was copied from a skimpy outfit in an adult novelty shop on ancient Earth.

Syn stood up straight and Wolf saw that her outfit was white with light pink stripes and a waist-tight, snug-fitting camisole that emphasized her breasts and enhanced her perfect physique. It was tied under her breasts seductively. Her arms were bare, but the outfit covered her shoulders with small lace ruffles at the top that ran over her shoulders, exposing a considerable amount of cleavage. The skirt had a white apron trimmed with pink lace, and it stopped just at her upper thighs. Her legs were clad in white, mid-thigh-length sheer stockings with a white bow at the top of each thigh. She wore stiletto shoes that made her calves and thighs look irresistible. Wolf stared at her in silence for a full minute and then asked, "Is there any change?"

Syn gave Wolf a seductive smile. "No. I am keeping her sedated, Commander. I didn't think it would be wise to have her wake up in space. Are we ready to land?" Aware of Wolf's frozen stare, she said, "Commander? Wolf? Are you all right?"

Wolf closed his mouth and forced his eyes from Syn's body to her face. Hoarsely, he said, "Prepare the ship, Syn. We need to land. I'll be in the shower." He turned and left the room. Several minutes later, he entered the shower fully clothed and said out loud, "I wonder if Syn knows what she is doing."

* * *

Three days later, Nala woke up. She looked around the unfamiliar room, gawking at the alien items as lights blinked from the walls and sounds of chimes, clicks, and ticks bombarded her, making her whip her head around in apprehension. Then, an oddly dressed woman entered the room. Nala's mouth dropped open as Syn said, "Good morning, Nala. I'm Syn. Wolf asked me to look after you while he went hunting."

Nala forced a timid smile and asked, "Where...where am I?"

Syn placed a hand on the woman's forehead. She didn't need to do this since her infrared detectors told her Nala had a slight fever, but it was not a cause for concern at present.

"You are on Wolf's boat. You were seriously injured in the storm, and he brought you here to care for you."

"What did you do to me?" Nala asked. She looked down at her body dressed in the gown and then stared at the small incision in her abdomen.

"How much do you know about the human body?"

"Very little, I'm afraid."

"Well, Nala, inside your body is an organ that cleans your blood. Yours was damaged severely. I repaired it. It will be several more days before you can return to your home. Do you understand?"

"Yes. May I have something to eat, please?"

Syn nodded as she finished checking the woman's wounds. Then, she left the room. She returned a few minutes later carrying a plate of food and dressed in a chef's outfit.

Nala looked at her with a frown and asked, "Weren't you wearing something else?"

"I spilled some food on myself," Chef Syn assured her with a human-sounding laugh.

Nala relaxed and said, "You are beautiful."

"Thank you, Nala. You are beautiful as well."

Chef Syn sat by Nala on the bed and said, "Now we have soup with some apple juice. You need to eat it all. Maybe tomorrow we will let you have meat to eat."

Nala sipped the broth and drank the apple juice. She looked at the juice curiously and asked, "What is this? It's delicious."

"It is apple juice."

"I have never tasted this before."

"Are there no apples left on this planet?" Syn wondered aloud. She scanned Earth One searching for apples and found none.

"You're in love with him, aren't you?" Nala asked with a flash of jealousy.

Syn looked away. "Yes. But there are complications."

Nala looked at Syn thoughtfully. Controlling her inexplicable jealousy, she murmured in a wistful voice, "Child, love has no complications. Give it time…it will come. He is worth loving."

* * *

Wolf approached the ship carrying a small animal that resembled a pig. He had seen several of them hanging in Haakon's larder. He had already skinned the animal and announced, "Syn, deactivate the force field and lower the ramp." The ramp lowered and Wolf boarded the ship, showing Syn what he had caught.

"There's not much game left since the storms. I was careful to hide from Haakon's neighbors who were foraging for food. Until Nala is strong enough to walk, I don't want to see them."

"No explanations needed, my love," Syn replied.

"What did you say?"

"I said no explanations needed, Wolf. Nala is up and talking. She has been asking about you. Give me that animal. I will prepare it for your dinner. Wash up before you go to her. You smell awful."

"I will, Syn."

After showering, Wolf put on a NASA jumpsuit and went to the medical unit. Nurse Syn still wore the candy striper outfit. He walked over to Nala and said, "Hi, young lady. You had us scared."

"Wolf, I hear I owe my life to you," Nala said, her face lighting up like the sun.

"Who told you that? Syn did all the work. She's the miracle worker. I just carried you here."

Nala blushed and turned away from Wolf. "I remember. You washed me. We were both naked. Jesu help me," Nala cried in a weak voice, ashamed.

"I did not take advantage of you, Nala. I had to wash our bodies. We were covered with mud. Syn couldn't operate until I cleaned you up. I only rinsed you and then covered you. Syn cleaned you further after she stabilized you. You are my friend—I would never take advantage of you."

"It's just hard for me to know another man has seen me. I will get over it. Thank you for everything. How long must we remain here before I can return to my family?"

124

Wolf gave Syn a questioning look and she replied, "Nala should remain here for several more days, Commander."

"Then I can go home?" Nala seemed delighted by the prospect of seeing her children.

"I will carry you home myself," Wolf promised.

Nurse Syn had monitored the coloring in Nala's skin when her face flushed as she reacted with embarrassment. She noted the woman's tearful reaction and how it had affected Wolf. She plugged the information into her data banks and ran an analysis on the other Syn's skin, changing the color and hue to make it as appealing as Nala's skin was. Syn's twin then practiced crying in the seclusion of the science lab, mimicking Nala's eyes and the tears that streamed from them. She practiced until she mastered the emotion, and then she whispered, "I've got you now, my Wolf."

Part 4

The Silver Knight

Chapter 13

O ver the next three days, Syn and Nala spent hours in deep conversation. Nala's lovely smile and gentle disposition appealed to Syn, and the two women grew fond of each other. Syn inquired about the things her creator's mother had never explained to human Cynthia. Her mother had been a domineering, pushy, unloving woman who couldn't wait to get her daughter into private school and out of her life. Career was the only thing that mattered to her mother, and the lack of love Cynthia experienced as a child remained a depressing constant into adulthood. Syn was not just Dr. Cynthia Mason's creation but also her confidant.

"I can't believe I was so naïve. There is so much to learn." Syn looked away with a frown, but then gave Nala a smile that lit up the room and added, "At least I can be with Wolf. It will all be worth it!"

Nala looked at the beautiful woman and again felt inexplicable jealousy. She forced a smile and said, "Love won't be denied. It is inescapable and unstoppable when it is true."

On the fourth day around noon, Syn decided that Nala was strong enough to return to her family. She handed the woman her clothing, which she had washed and repaired, and she helped Nala dress. Then she gave Nala a shot of antibiotics to help her heal and prevent infection of her surgical wound. Syn also injected her with a sedative that put her to sleep.

A few minutes later, Wolf came to the medical bay and gently lifted Nala into his arms. Syn opened the cargo bay and lowered the ramp. Wolf stepped out, carrying Nala like a small child.

"Be careful, Wolf. I'll be waiting for you," Syn said. Her eyes glistened with tears as she mimicked perfectly the vulnerable emotion she had learned from Nala.

Wolf frowned and asked, "Are you okay, Syn? I can take her later if you would like."

Syn sniffled and wiped her eyes. Then, she gave Wolf a dazzling smile and replied, "No, go on. Nala misses her family, and I'm sure they are worried. I will be all right, Wolf. I have chores you would interfere with anyway."

"I'll be back in a day or two," Wolf promised, and then he headed off into the forest, carrying Nala in his arms.

He was a few miles from Haakon's camp when he looked down at Nala, who was still asleep, and marveled at her beauty. A chill ran through his body. At that moment, Nala opened her eyes and Wolf looked away, ashamed that he found his friend's wife desirable. She yawned and stretched in Wolf's strong arms.

"I drifted off to sleep, and I didn't get to say goodbye to Syn. How long was I asleep?"

"Not long, Nala. We will reach your valley in a few minutes. If you feel strong enough, I will let you walk. Remember, for the next week, don't do any strenuous chores or heavy lifting. The surgery Syn performed can become undone if you aren't careful. Do you understand?"

"Yes. Syn already explained it to me. She is a beautiful woman, Wolf. You two make a lovely couple," Nala said with a shadow of regret in her eyes.

"There are complications with a relationship between us. Right now, it is impossible."

"You sound just like her," Nala laughed. "I will tell you what I told her—love doesn't care about complications or reasons not to exist. Nothing is stronger than its power. Love overcomes all obstacles. No army or nation can conquer it. If it is meant to be, it will be." She looked away, confused by her own words.

Wolf lowered Nala to her feet and took her hand as she wobbled. "Can you walk?"

"Yes, I was just a little dizzy."

Still holding Nala's hand, Wolf resumed the journey, leading her towards a column of smoke on the horizon. A leisurely fifteen-minute walk placed them at the clearing, where men were cutting wood and building shelters.

"Haakon!" Nala cried as she caught sight of her husband.

"No running!" Wolf admonished, putting a hand on her shoulder for a moment and then letting her go.

Haakon looked up, shading his eyes with a hand, and the other men stared, amazed, as Wolf and Nala approached. Haakon broke into a run, shouting, "Nala! Oh, my Nala, you have returned to me!" He reached to grab her and was about to lift her off her feet when Wolf stepped between them. "Haakon, you must be gentle with her. Nala can be injured if you are too rough right now."

Haakon froze, staring at Wolf in disbelief as the giant blocked his path to his wife. He felt an intense, irrational anger flare up at this stranger ordering him around, but he forced a begrudging smile, wiped his dirty hands on his shirt, and carefully embraced his wife, kissing her on the lips. Tears welled in his eyes as his irritation turned to gratitude, and he extended his hand to Wolf.

"Thank you for saving my wife." Haakon's voice choked with emotion. "I am grateful beyond words. All I have shall be yours," he declared and then frowned at his own words.

"Haakon, your family showed me kindness. It's the least I could do."

The rest of Haakon's family gathered around, and after much hugging and laughter, they led Nala to a partially built shelter so she could lie down. She offered to help cook, but after a stern look from Wolf, she sighed and went to rest. Leesa had latched onto Wolf's arm and was rubbing his chest and shoulders as he tried to disengage from her.

"Leesa, that's enough. Let him be for now," Haakon frowned. Obediently, Leesa let go of Wolf, but she kept her smoldering gaze glued to him throughout the day.

Thirty-eight survivors from the surrounding area had gathered in Haakon's camp. After much discussion, they had agreed to build a community here instead of going their separate ways. In the aftermath of the storm, roving bands of looters were attacking hapless villagers, pilfering food and other valuables, and leaving them destitute. Haakon's neighbors agreed to band together, realizing there was security in numbers.

The area they had chosen as a settlement was close to water, and the surrounding forest was intact, teeming with wildlife in the aftermath of the storm. Ten men in the group were capable of fighting, including Haakon and his oldest son. The group included six women around Nala's age; six teenage girls, including Leesa and Brithee; seven children, including Reon; and eight older men and women well past their prime. The construction progress was slow, and the crude tools they used made Wolf want to cry with frustration. He had all the equipment on the ship to make suitable homes for these people—dwellings that might even withstand the gale-force winds of the yearly storms. He weighed the pros and cons of offering meaningful help versus letting them rebuild their haphazard structures, and he decided to rethink the matter after his meeting with the ruling monarch of this devastated land.

Wolf's felt a vibration on his wrist and glanced down at his watch, noticing the words *Commander, beware!* flashing in red. He had been sitting on the ground, talking to a man named Donnel, who stood nearby. Suddenly, the man lurched forward and collapsed on the ground with a five-foot spear impaled in his back. He was dead before he hit the ground. Ragged men poured into the clearing from the woods, howling like crazed animals as they attacked the settlement. The attacking army included men of various races, and the only common bond they appeared to share were the tattered clothes they wore. Haakon's few men fought bravely, but they were outnumbered four to one. Wolf watched in shock until he heard Leesa scream. One of the attackers had wrestled her to the ground and was ripping off her dress, laughing as he muttered vile threats. Nala came running from the woods, holding Reon in one arm, and the look of fury on her face snapped Wolf from his shocked hesitation. She was charging for the ruffian who had pinned her daughter down, screaming that she would kill him. Several of the older villagers grabbed Nala and restrained her. She fought and kicked to break free, shouting at them to let her go, and then she turned pleading eyes to Wolf.

Rage boiled up in Wolf as he jumped to his feet and leapt ten yards in a single bound. He grabbed Leesa's attacker by the top of his head with one hand, shouting, "Never treat a woman like that!" The ruffian's head twisted around as Wolf snapped his neck.

Still holding the man by the top of his head, Wolf flung his lifeless body into a knot of onrushing ruffians, toppling them in a grotesque parody of bowling. He charged into the melee, swinging his fists. Every blow that landed broke bones. The men screamed as Wolf smashed into them. He jumped to Haakon's aid as a looter tripped him and swung an ax at his neck. Wolf stopped the blade by placing his arm in its path—the ax head made contact with a loud crack and the handle broke. He then landed an uppercut that ripped the man's head from his shoulders.

Haakon stared at Wolf, astounded, as the giant waded into another group of attackers. He had drawn his Bowie knife and jumped among the men, who were forcing the elderly against downed trees that had been set on fire in an attempt to roast them alive. With a powerful thrust of the knife, he decapitated one man and wounded two others. He cut and slashed until both of the wounded men were reduced to bloody mounds of flesh.

Wolf had slaughtered more than a dozen ruffians before their leader saw the havoc he was causing. Dressed in polished silver armor, his arms crossed, the knight barked orders. His remaining men lined up in a defensive front as Haakon's neighbors who had survived the initial attack fled into the forest. Trulane had watched Wolf battle and was in awe. He ran to Wolf's side, saying, "I will stand with you." He saw Haakon laying on the ground and yelled, "Father, get mother and the others into the forest. We will hold them off!"

With a look of horror, Haakon struggled to his feet, holding a hand over his eyes to block out the gruesome carnage Wolf had caused. He rushed over to Leesa and picked her up from the ground, carrying her to Nala, who had somehow broken loose and was running towards them. He intercepted Nala, pushing Leesa into her arms, and led his family into the woods as Leesa shouted in rage and shame, "Kill them, Wolf! Kill them all!"

Wolf shook his head, trying to clear the fog of anger from his brain. The leader of the ruffians barked a command and his tattered men renewed their attack. Trulane fought on the defensive as several men attempted to spear him. Three spears hit Wolf and bounced with no effect to the ground. The rain of spears stopped as the knight glared at Wolf and hissed, "What are you?"

"I am death. I will not stand by while you rape and pillage

innocents," Wolf answered. "If you had demanded our food, I would have let you go. Now you all must die."

"Go to hell, you oversized freak!" The silver knight sneered at Wolf and shouted to his men, "Kill him!"

The ruffians charged with an assortment of primitive weapons: axes, spears, and knives. They swarmed over Wolf, stabbing and slashing, but he was impervious to the assault. In his heart, Wolf knew it was murder to slay these men, but he also knew they couldn't be allowed to escape. Trulane had killed three of the enemy so far and was hacking a fourth to pieces. Wolf stood his ground and shouted, "Run, fools! Never return here or I will kill you all!" The attackers seemed crazed by the thrill of battle and ignored his warning, intensifying their assault.

"So be it," Wolf muttered, releasing the inner beast his grandfather had warned him about. He grabbed two ruffians by the hair and slammed their heads together, splattering brains in all directions. He punched a third man in the chest and saw the life go out of his eyes. A man with a glazed expression grabbed Wolf's leg and tried to topple him, but Wolf lifted his foot and stomped the man's head into the mud. The ruffians were like rabid animals, foaming at the mouth and screaming insanely. They refused to run away from the battle, even in the face of certain death.

Haakon and several of his men had returned to fight and were making a good account of themselves. The odds were evened to eight against eight. Haakon downed his man, and Trulane killed another after wrestling him to the ground. Then they both ran to defend a man who was under attack. The leader of the ragtag army stood at the wood's edge, glaring in contempt as he watched Wolf snap the neck of yet another man.

When only the leader was left standing, he shouted at Wolf, "So, you freak of nature, you have won! But you will not capture me." The knight shimmered and disappeared.

"That was one of Jonar's Templars. They have strange powers," said Trulane. "We have not seen one in years. Jonar has men like that throughout the kingdom. They wander the land, killing our king's subjects and pillaging supplies."

Wolf looked around at the dozens of bloody, mutilated corpses in the clearing and asked, "How many of ours were killed?"

"A dozen. Three men, two children, one teenage girl, and six of the elders," said Haakon as he approached. He swallowed hard, a look of reverence in his eyes. "You *are* the Warrior of Legend. I saw blades and spears strike you, but you have no mark. Your strength is not of this world. We have a legend: a traveler will come from the sky in a flying chariot that talks but has no tongue. He will be a giant among all men and he will be immortal..."

"Yes, yes, I know about the legend," Wolf interrupted.

"You are that man," Haakon insisted.

"No, Haakon. I am just a weary man who has slaughtered many weaker men today. I am ashamed." Wolf stared down at his bloody hands and the rage drained from his limbs. "I must leave."

"Wolf...wait," a woman's voice called. It was Nala. She was followed by Leesa, who was holding the shreds of her clothing together. Behind her stood the other villagers who had survived the ruffians' attack.

"Thank you," Nala said. "You have saved us again. You are our hero." She rose on her tiptoes and kissed Wolf lightly on the lips. Leesa repeated the gesture, followed by Brithee and the other women, young and old. The men approached and placed their hands on Wolf's broad shoulders.

"I see your sorrow over the men you have killed, but they would have murdered us all," Nala said. "I offer my deepest thanks. If it had not been for you, I would have seen my daughters raped and mutilated, my sons impaled, and my friends beheaded."

Wolf looked up at the woman as tears streamed from her eyes, and a ghastly vision of the carnage she described played in his mind. He was unaccustomed to the atrocities of this time. Murder and rape had become a constant event, just as death had run rampant in the days leading up to Nomad's destruction of civilization. Wolf had hoped this beautiful, tranquil world was beyond that ugly time, but clearly, human nature had not changed much over fifty thousand years.

As the jingle of armor approached, Wolf spun around, prepared to resume the battle. He relaxed when he recognized Onel, the tax collector, approaching with Captain Lintal and a detail of soldiers.

"Thank Jesu, we are not too late. We have been chasing this band of miscreants for two days," Onel said. "They have plundered neighboring villages and committed atrocities I can't mention in the presence of these people." Looking around at the dismembered and decapitated men scattered from one side of the clearing to the other, he declared, "You have defeated them."

"No, I murdered them. They were no match for me," Wolf said with profound regret, still unconvinced he had done the right thing.

"These men were evil. They follow Jonar and only know rape and murder. They consume drynox, a horrible drug that rots their minds and turns them into animals," Onel said. "The drug they take will never wear off and makes them meaner over time. They are the scum of the earth, roving across this unhappy land, killing at will."

The tax collector added, "We have patrols out hunting them, but we can't capture them all. Even if you had taken them prisoner, we would have executed them on the spot. Tell me, was a Templar dressed in silver armor with these men?" At a nod from Haakon, Onel said, "He is called Sylvaine the Cruel. He is the most powerful of Jonar's men. Life means nothing to him. No, my friend, what you did today is justice."

"It still makes me sad to take life," Wolf replied.

"Look at these people." Onel pointed to the remnants of the shattered community. "You have saved them. Sylvaine and his drug-crazed men would have raped and killed them all. They owe you their lives."

Captain Lintal approached and reported, "Fifty-three ruffians dead, sir. Twenty were slain with spear and knife. All the others were ripped to shreds."

"This is amazing. We have not killed this many in a long time," Onel remarked with grim satisfaction. He said to Wolf, "The ones torn apart...is that your work, my friend?"

"Yes. I didn't have time to draw my weapons until later. Can we change the subject? Did the king agree to grant me an audience?"

"Yes, my friend, our pursuit of these scoundrels is but part of the reason we are here. You have been requested to the castle by His Majesty."

"When do we leave? I need to gather a few things first," Wolf said.

"We can leave at first light if you desire."

Turning to Haakon, Wolf asked, "Will you and your family be all right here?"

"Yes, my friend. These gangs range over a large area. There are probably no others for a hundred miles or more. We will be all right. Again, I thank you for saving us," Haakon extended his hand to Wolf, and the men exchanged a warm handshake.

Wolf walked to Nala. At first, she blushed and shied away, but then embraced him and whispered, "Thank you for saving my family." He then turned to her family, hugging each of them. Wolf walked over to the small knot of survivors and bid them farewell. After informing Onel that he would return before dawn, he set off into the woods with a heavy heart.

Twenty minutes later, Wolf approached the ship and called out, "Syn, open the ramp."

The ramp lowered, allowing Wolf to board, and then it closed silently behind him. Syn greeted him with a sad expression in her all-knowing gray eyes.

"Are you all right, Commander? I saw what happened. You left the communication module on during the fight. I used it to pinpoint you and watched the battle using the satellites. Is there anything I can do?"

Wolf shook his head. "No, Syn. I have to work this out myself."

Syn walked up to Wolf and touched a finger to his chin, tilting his face until his eyes met hers. She pressed her finger against his lips and hugged him, patting his back as a parent would comfort a child. Wolf wrapped his arms around her and pulled her close. She felt so *real*. He bowed his head to kiss her, but she pushed him away with a troubled look in her eyes.

Changing the subject to cover the moment, Syn said, "Commander, take a look at the work I have done on the communications satellite. I boosted its signal another fifteen percent."

Wolf placed a hand on Syn's shoulder and pulled her back to him. Their bodies made contact and she shivered, goose bumps forming on her tanned skin. As he looked into her eyes, he saw confusion and a hint of fear. He closed his eyes and inhaled deeply, amazed by the scent and feel of her. Then, he let her go with a reluctant sigh.

"You got another fifteen percent out of it? That's amazing, Syn. You are unbelievable." Wolf paused and then said, "I need to shower. I am filthy." He walked away, feeling frustrated, lonely, and wondering how a computer-generated hologram could affect him so deeply. She was just a projection, yet she was so real, and her personality was so perfect. It was as if she had been created just for him.

Wolf entered the shower area and stripped off his clothes, tossing them in the recycler. He turned the water to seventy degrees—not too cold, not too hot, and just chilly enough to settle his breathing and relax him. He decided that he needed to get away from Syn for a few days. She was affecting him in a strange way that was not unpleasant, but awkward. As he washed, his mind drifted back to their encounter minutes ago, and he felt something...desire for her. He wondered how that was even possible. Stepping out of the shower, he realized he was exhausted and said, "Syn, I need to catch a few hours of sleep before I return to the settlement. Wake me in two hours."

"Yes, Commander," Syn replied agreeably, although she had decided that she would let him sleep a few hours longer to recuperate from the skirmish with Jonar's ruffians.

"Two hours, Syn...no longer," Wolf insisted. Syn didn't answer, and he smiled, imagining her rolling her eyes at him. He went to his quarters and stretched out on his bunk. As he drifted off to sleep, he thought, *If only she were...*

*If only I were alive...*Syn thought. *He wouldn't hesitate. I know he sees me as a program, but I am so much more.* She watched Wolf as he closed his eyes and dozed off. She continued watching him long after he had fallen asleep. She found it odd that human thoughts were filtering into her programmed logic, yet somehow, the thoughts and feelings had become a part of her. Had her creator programmed her to experience these quirky human feelings? Or had her circuits been altered, either by the passage of thousands of years or from prolonged exposure to Nomad's intense radiation?

It's good that he's leaving for a few days, Syn reasoned. *I need to work on the holo-projectors...and I need to talk to Nala. Her farmstead isn't too far away, and Wolf will be going in the opposite direction with Waylan's men. This will work out perfect.*

* * *

Four hours later, Wolf sprang out of bed, disoriented and irritable that Syn had let him oversleep. His angst subsided when he smelled food cooking and he rationalized that he needed the rest. Syn was in the mess area preparing a meal and singing *My Girl,* a rhythm and blues hit recorded by the Temptations, a band once popular in Wolf's forgotten world of the past.

Wolf stood by the door and listened. Syn's voice was amazing. With a deep sigh, he entered the room dressed in a new, white NASA jumpsuit. It was form fitting and made of Kevlar. Emblazoned with the NASA logos and crisply starched, it looked impressive. He carried a silver Mylar bag that held the items he had packed for his trip: two spare uniforms, an extra Bowie knife, and several other articles of clothing. He had decided to take no weapons other than his Bowie knife. After all, what could hurt him?

"It smells fantastic, Syn. You're aware of the trip I'm about to take, right?"

Syn nodded, stopped singing, and replied, "I allowed you to sleep a little longer, Commander. Your REM cycle showed you needed it. While you are gone, I will analyze the battle you fought. I saw the knight disappear into thin air. That was odd, since I continuously monitor the planet for power signatures, and I sensed no energy spikes or fluctuations at the timed he vanished. I also want to work on the shuttle. I believe I can improve its efficiency in several areas."

Syn took a small object off a nearby table and handed it to Wolf. "I have made a locating chip for you, Commander."

Wolf looked down and examined the chip. It was about the size of a small aspirin, skin-colored, and it blended with his complexion. One side was coated with a sticky substance that glistened in the light of the galley.

"This substance is polymer-based glue," Syn explained. "I can't inject anything into your skin, so I will glue it to you instead. It goes right here." She touched the inside of Wolf's ear on the triangular fossa. "It will not come loose unless I apply a solvent. The ear bud is waterproof, and it's so small no one will see it. I will be able to monitor your communications while you are traveling, and I can talk to you without anyone hearing."

"This is great work, Syn!" Wolf said, smiling and obviously impressed. "Put it in and let's test it."

Syn inserted the tiny chip in Wolf's ear and pressed it firmly against his skin. He felt the chip heat up as it fused to his skin.

"Commander, can you hear me?"

Wolf's jaw dropped as he stared at Syn. Her mouth didn't move, yet he heard her voice broadcasting in his ear. She continued communicating as he stared at the beautiful hologram.

"Yes, Wolf, I am talking to you. Remember, I am a machine. This tiny chip now allows us to be covert when we need to speak privately. Say something, so I can test the link."

"Umm...testing...Syn, can you hear me?"

A beautiful laugh sounded in Wolf's ear bud and then Syn's hologram responded, "Yes, I read you loud and clear."

"You amaze me, Syn. You are truly an amazing woman..." Wolf's voice trailed off.

Syn's eyes widened. She stared at him for a moment and then said, "Eat, Wolf. You must leave soon." Turning away, a single tear ran from her eye. She touched a finger to the tear, gazed at the moisture, and walked out of the room in apparent confusion.

Wolf finished his meal and then stood from the table. He grabbed his Mylar sack and headed off to the rear of the ship. When he reached the cargo bay, he said, "Lower the ramp, Syn. I'll be back in forty-eight hours. What's the range of this device in my ear?"

"Commander, it's planet-wide. It's boosted by the new military satellite."

"Syn, you are a wonder! I'll check in with you in a few hours. Let me know if you find anything on that vanishing knight."

"Yes, Commander."

"Goodbye, Syn," Wolf called over his shoulder.

Syn didn't want to bid Wolf farewell as a hologram, so she watched him depart with her cameras from the ramp's bay. "Goodbye," she said. Turning off the mic, she whispered, "My love."

Chapter 14

"**Y**ou've come back! I thought you had left us never to return," Trulane exclaimed, his face breaking into a delighted smile as Wolf emerged from the forest at the edge of Haakon's camp.

"I always keep my word. That's one thing you should remember," Wolf said, shaking the young man's hand. He spotted Haakon and Onel talking by the stream and walked over to them.

"Welcome back, Wolf," Onel greeted him with an amiable smile. "After yesterday's mayhem, we were worried you might not return."

"I have come to realize some men are just evil. There is no talking to them. They need to be incarcerated, and if that's not possible, slain. When can we leave?"

"I see your speech is quite improved. It's almost flawless now," Onel remarked as he studied Wolf's array of unfamiliar weaponry.

"I have a gift for language. I learn new languages quickly."

"We have just finished breakfast and were talking of trivial matters," Onel said. "We can depart now. Let us say our goodbyes and be on our way."

They walked back to where the survivors huddled by a small fire. Onel's soldiers had dragged the ruffians' corpses away from the area and thrown them on a burning pyre. The slain villagers had been buried in a makeshift cemetery. Onel promised to ask the king to send more soldiers to protect the locals. Finally, the men departed on the journey to Springdale Castle and the king's court.

"The king's land extends for days in all directions from here," Onel said. "We have a three-day journey. Before the storm, it was a breathtaking stroll, full of natural beauty and pleasant scenery. The mountainous lands around the castle were not touched by the storms. The mountains shield the rich valleys where the crops are grown and the king's flocks roam. Jonar has coveted these sheltered lands since he came to power."

"Tell me, Onel, what are the Templars? The man Sylvaine...he disappeared into thin air. How did he accomplish that feat?" Wolf asked.

"We do not know. When Jonar first arrived, he preached of the quest, claiming ancients from this world's past had incredible powers, and their knowledge remains hidden in this world. His quest led him on a search for those terrifying powers, and he found them."

"Where did Jonar hear of this knowledge?"

"Rumor has it that he descended into a deep hole in the ground," Onel said. "At the bottom of the hole, he found an iron door, and after many days, he opened it. Inside, he found ancient manuscripts sealed in glass. He spent years reading and deciphering those writings, and he acquired vast knowledge. Jonar built his castle around this hole, and somehow he can make strange things happen. We have seen him infiltrate our lines to murder our nobles, cause buildings to collapse for no reason, rescue well-guarded prisoners, and make strange weapons that shoot lightning. The man is a snake."

"In my country, we fought over religion, food, and something called oil," Wolf recalled. "We slaughtered millions in the name of God. Our religious beliefs differed in very small ways, yet we killed because of a few twisted words and rituals. Then, we were threatened by a terrible cataclysm. Before it struck, my people killed each other like savages, just like Jonar is doing."

"Always, there are men who feel their way is the only way. They want others to follow where they lead and use wealth and fear to build armies. Ambitious men join them in their mad dream, and together they wash the land in blood," Onel said, his voice cracking with passion. "The taste of blood runs their lives, and no matter how much they bathe in it, they never become clean or quench their thirst. Every morning, they arise to look at the sky, trying to think of how they can capture pure air. To own the clouds and heavens is their final goal. They don't realize that the air cannot be captured and can never be owned."

"It is a vicious cycle," Wolf agreed. "Let us talk about other things. Tell me about King Waylan."

Onel nodded and spoke as his men fanned out to check for ambushes. "The king was once a magnificent warrior, renowned throughout the land. He fought many battles, and sometimes, he was the last man standing. In the battle of Minap, he led five hundred men to the center of an enemy camp guarded by thousands. They fought inside enemy lines for hours, slaying the enemy leader in hand-to-hand combat. The king is skilled in all weapons, and he is a man who inspires others. After he amassed a fortune, he wanted to live in peace. He came here to settle and built his castle. He enjoyed many years of peace until Jonar arrived."

As the advance scouts returned and reported that the path ahead was clear, Onel said, "At first, Jonar was an inconvenience and we repelled his scoundrels. Then Jonar unleashed the Templars, who controlled the power of fire and wind. They rolled over the king's retainers in the field, and the king himself took the field against Jonar. He was injured severely by the Templars, but he killed several before they retreated. Now Jonar keeps his men in the field, terrorizing our farmsteads. He knows he can't bring the castle down, and to attack it is suicide."

"I look forward to seeing this castle. It sounds formidable," Wolf said.

* * *

Back at the ship, Syn was contemplating several ideas that would give her form. One was a mobile emitter that would allow her to accompany Wolf, shadowing his every step. The other idea was to fashion a titanium-skinned body and implant it with her awareness. The first was far easier to accomplish. For the time being, she would merely follow Wolf with the ship and mask his watch with a jamming beam so he would not know she was trailing him. She would maintain the ship, cloaked, at a high altitude, and if Wolf needed her, she could come to his aid in seconds with the full array of weaponry at her disposal.

Syn had listened to the tales about the Templars' powers and Jonar's castle. She had attempted to use ground-penetrating radar on Jonar's castle, but she was blocked. A further scan revealed a massive layer of limestone, granite, and clay-laden soils above the area. This material couldn't all be natural, but it effectively blocked the radar scan. She switched back to Wolf's immediate vicinity and scanned the area several times, confirming he was safe. Syn would not risk allowing Jonar and his ancient knowledge to harm Wolf.

Launching the ship, Syn set course for Wolf's current location, using the provisioned satellites to pinpoint his whereabouts. She silently maneuvered the ship to within a few hundred yards of Wolf, cloaking the craft to make it invisible, and then hovered in midair, watching him.

Wolf had no clue that Dr. Cynthia Mason had watched him for years. She found him irresistibly handsome and had cyberstalked him using NASA's cameras and recording devices. He had been Dr. Mason's first love—her ultimate crush. Now, far in the future, the super-computer she had created was at it again. Somehow, Dr. Mason's feelings had been transferred to Syn. During the centuries Syn had kept him alive in the DSC, nurturing his mind and stimulating his brain to survive, he was the sole focus of her vast power and intellect. Wolf was now hers—her man—and he would come to realize it.

Syn decided to let Wolf know she had him on sensors. "Commander, I have you on the satellite feed. I am here if you need me," she whispered sweetly in his ear. Startled, Wolf looked up at the sky for a moment, and then he nodded.

Syn went into the maintenance bay and began working on a holo-emitter. It had to be small and made of something strong. She had some titanium left from the old satellites they had repaired. After a quick analysis, she decided to make Wolf a new wristwatch; but it would need an incredible power source. She had a small amount of plutonium, but how would she shield it? Shielding from gamma rays required considerable mass. Syn knew that gamma rays are absorbed more efficiently by materials with high atomic numbers and high density. The higher the energy of the gamma rays, the thicker the shielding. She ran calculations on various materials.

The gamma source she would need to power the watch would require a half-inch of lead to reduce its intensity by fifty percent; maybe two and a half inches of granite or concrete. She could use depleted uranium for shielding—it had been used in the past in portable gamma ray sources, but the savings in weight over lead were modest. Nothing she had would be compact enough to achieve the effect she needed. Granted, the radiation would have no effect on Wolf, but it could be lethal to other humans nearby.

Making the watch was easy; the effects Syn wanted to build into it would be the kicker. She wanted to be able to feel, touch, and manipulate in the real world. The watch probably was not feasible for now...or was it? Instead of a gamma emitter, she could use an alpha emitter, powered by plutonium-238, a radioactive isotope of plutonium with a half-life of about eighty-eight years. This could work because PU-238 is a potent alpha emitter that doesn't throw off significant amounts of other dangerous radiations. A few grams in the metal watchband would create the power she required. The watch would be powerful but nowhere close to what the ship could generate.

Syn worked on the watch and cloned a second hologram of herself to work on emitters for the vessel. Maybe she could augment the ship's force fields to give her more range. She analyzed the problem and determined that she would need the power from the IFLEX engine to succeed. She would make a series of cloaked microsatellites, powered by cobalt 60, and use laser projection to form her body, taking the parts required from a gamma helmet in the medical bay.

In the meantime, Syn set about constructing the microsatellites. She decided to make four—one each for her head, torso, arms, and legs. They could be tied into one another and programmed to act as one primary holo-unit. She would design each to generate her entire body in an emergency. With this technology, she would be able to enter buildings and keep an eye on Wolf. She would fashion the engines with the IFLEX technology. It was silent and efficient, and with the cobalt 60 power source, she could generate enough power to become tangible; plus, she could build in a few other surprises to help if needed. She knew this solution would work well, and with a glimmer of satisfaction, she thought, *Here I come, Wolf. See you soon!*

* * *

Wolf and his companions had been traveling for three days. As the noon sun passed overhead, the lush deciduous forest yielded to a stand of towering pines and other conifers, and the terrain became rocky and mountainous. Unexpectedly, the tree line receded, and the men emerged into a vast plain of well-tended grass that stretched before them. Squadrons comprised of several hundred soldiers drilled on the lawns as Onel and his men headed towards a pair of huge gates set in the face of towering outer cliffs. The gates were protected by a rusted, iron portcullis, and they were massive—thirty feet high, boasting huge oak panels covered with studded iron to protect the entrance to Waylan's castle. This was the castle's first defense. A massive stone tablet inscribed with symbols that reminded Wolf of hieroglyphics stood in front of the gate.

"What does that say?" Wolf asked.

Onel approached the stone stela and spoke as he touched the words: "Springdale Castle. Founded by King Waylan. All who enter are protected. Those who seek sanctuary from the king shall receive it. Do not betray his trust." Onel continued reading the stela, reporting the number of workmen and other mundane details. Overhead, her ship invisible, Syn made note of Onel's words and the symbols on the stela, running a comparison with all known written languages. Onel led the way through the manmade opening and told Wolf they soon would arrive at the secondary gates to Springdale Castle. They walked forward through a six-foot opening, and then turned sharply to the left, walking eight feet, and angled sharply to the right again. They traveled another forty feet through an arched passageway wide enough to allow two wagons to enter side-by-side; then, the corridor opened into a scenic, forested valley.

"These sharp turns make it difficult for invaders to mount an attack with any force," Onel explained. "They are a death trap for anyone who attacks. Look up there, at the side of the mountain." Onel pointed to a series of ledges cut into the high mountain walls, each lined with eight to ten men armed with spears. "Those men live up there with their families year round. The wall is honeycombed into living quarters with natural springs in the rock providing water. Rich loam fills large, garden terraces that feed them. Those soldiers are self-sufficient from the castle, in case we are attacked or held under siege. This is the first death trap an advancing army would have to overcome."

As the men progressed through the forested valley, they came to a pristine, level pasture that led up to another huge mountain with a second mammoth gate hewn from sheer rock that spanned the meadow. The gate was fifty feet tall, carved from mountain granite and framed between two massive towers. Soldiers wearing ornate armor patrolled the towers every few feet along the upper terraces. Below, the massive gates were forged of ten-inch thick iron, engraved with an intricate pattern of flowers and vines on the outside. Just inside the gate stood another iron portcullis with four-inch thick bars and raised barbs that glistened in the bright sunlight. As Wolf went through the gate, his large stature drew comments and startled oaths from those nearby. Onel greeted the gate guards who eyed Wolf with apprehension, and a curt nod from Captain Lintal dispersed them.

Wolf gazed in awe at the castle, built on top of a mountain that had been scraped flat. The structure was a spectacular carving in the shape of a warrior holding a spear, hewn from red granite that reflected sunlight beautifully. Its detail was remarkable. The only comparison that came to Wolf's mind was the Colossus of Rhodes from the distant past. It looked so real he expected to see it move. The spear extended fifty feet over the warrior's gold-crowned head, and Onel said this was the king's personal keep. Wolf knew that no artisan of this primitive world could have designed this incredible structure, and it was beyond the capabilities of architects from Wolf's time.

"How long did it take to build this castle?" Wolf asked, marveling at the fortifications.

"It took several hundred talented artists and their men fifteen years to complete the castle," Onel answered, smiling with pride. "They worked night and day in shifts. The men worked of their own will because King Waylan paid them fair wages from his vast treasure. He was fortunate because he struck a rich gold mine within this mountain. It seems it is bottomless as he still pays his soldiers, artisans, and other workers. The king is truly an unselfish man."

"It seems he is a rare man," Wolf observed. "I am honored he has agreed to see me."

"You have a noble man's bearing, and I am proud I will receive the prestige of presenting you to His Majesty," Onel replied.

A large moat filled with water and protected by spikes encircled the colossus, which stood nearly two hundred feet tall. Onel led Wolf and his men across a bridge that passed between the massive warrior's legs. They came to another wall, twenty feet high, surrounding the enormous structure. Wolf saw that the fortifications were formidable and made the structure impregnable. They approached a stairway that spiraled up to the warrior's ankle and arrived at another massive iron portal. A guard recognized Onel and swung open the gate. Once inside, Onel dispersed his men, and then he and Wolf proceeded alone.

After climbing several more stairways, they came to a bathing area. Steam hovered over the water's surface, and several young boys in washing gowns stood around with strigils to scrape the skin of bathers and provide towels to dry them. Onel disrobed, stepping into the water, and he immersed himself up to his neck.

"Wolf, my friend, wash the dust from your body and relax. His Majesty has been told of our arrival and expects us for dinner in a few hours."

Wolf unhooked his belt and placed it on the ground. He unzipped his jumpsuit and folded it next to the belt, leaving his underwear on. He noticed Onel giving him an appraising look, and the attendants giggled at the sight.

"It's a cultural thing," Wolf said defensively. He stepped into the hot water, and it only went as high as his chest. He sat down, and the water level rose to his neck. As he soaked, he asked, "How does the water get heated?"

Onel, who was relaxing with his eyes closed, replied, "The kitchens are beneath us. The hot air from the cooking ovens vent under this floor, heating the rocks. We add cold water to keep it bearable."

The men soaked a while longer, and then a young female entered. She approached them and kneeled by Onel, saying in a pleasant, almost sultry voice, "Father, you have returned."

Wolf, who had dozed off, stood up quickly and then submerged just as fast.

"Jhondra, why are you in here, child?" Onel asked with a chuckle.

The girl was small, not quite five foot tall, with honey blonde hair in a thick braid that extended down her back to her waist. She had thin lips, gray eyes, and was milkmaid white. Like most of the women Wolf had seen in this castle, she was dressed in flowing clothes that hid her body. The girl was very thin and hadn't blossomed yet.

"Father, I missed you. His Majesty is getting hungry, and I took it upon myself to inform you of our king's mind."

"Child, this is the men's quarters," Onel lectured with a faint smile. "You must remember that you are a young woman and can't run in here anytime you like." Turning to Wolf, he added, "Forgive my child. She is my youngest at sixteen summers—a consummate tomboy who doesn't realize how attractive she has become."

Deciding it was time to get dressed, Wolf stood, remaining waist-deep in the water, and retrieved his garments. His movements drew the girl's attention, and her eyes widened as she noticed his size. She managed a whispered, "Hello, stranger!" She had ignored Wolf when she entered, being intent on talking to her father. Now, she assessed his broad back, long hair, and massive chest. Swallowing hard, she asked, "Is he the one they speak of, Father?"

"Jhondra, remove yourself, my child. We will talk later," Onel replied with a sigh.

"Yes, Father. I will see you at dinner." The girl flashed Wolf a perky smile and added, "You too, large one."

Speaking to no one in particular, Wolf mumbled under his breath, "What is it with women lately?"

"I heard that, Commander," Syn hissed in his ear bud, sounding like a jealous female.

Chapter 15

Onel escorted Wolf down an exquisite hallway of red granite still being decorated by artisans. They stopped for a few moments to watch a talented stonecutter as he chiseled a design in one wall. The man was scraping and tapping a large area into a mural of the hunt, and he had chiseled out a boar-like creature being pursued by dogs. A large tree graced the background, and several men were in pursuit through a half-carved forest.

"This is beautiful," Wolf said in amazement. "How long has he been carving here?"

"Huran is the king's master stonecutter. His grandfather carved the castle. He has been working on this scene for less than a month and should finish it in another two weeks. He is truly gifted," Onel said.

Wolf nodded in agreement, and they continued down the hallway to another massive iron door. Guards in armor stood on each side of the panel. They acknowledged Onel, and one did a quick march step, planted his heel, pivoted, took another quick step, and advanced to the door, opening it for the two men. Onel led Wolf into the chamber. As the door closed behind them, Wolf gazed into the throne room of King Waylan. It was vaulted, with massive arches supported by columns carved into the form of snakes whose jaws clamped on the beams above. Wolf counted twenty dark gray marble columns on each side, spaced about ten feet apart. Guards armed with spears lined the alcoves, standing erect and proud. These men looked older than the guards outside, and Wolf recalled Haakon's words: "The king is protected inside his castle by the Old Guard, men past their prime but who have vowed to serve the king until death." Wolf felt respect for such men.

The floor of the exquisite throne room was black marble with white flecks, a stunning contrast from the three different types of rock used to construct this room. Across the room, Wolf saw a man seated on what appeared to be a solid gold throne. Like the thrones of old, it had a high, ornate back with gigantic armrests—but it was the man seated on the throne that caught Wolf's eye.

King Waylan was the biggest man Wolf had seen on the planet. Even sitting down, his large frame impressed Wolf. He had blue eyes, alert and darting, and a snowy white beard that covered an iron chin. The beard hung from his face like a glacier forcing its way down a mountain valley. Wolf noticed a scar on the man's face that started by his right eye and pulled the skin down, giving him a squinting gaze. His mouth was full, and he had deep smile lines. He held a massive sword by the crosspiece between his legs in huge hands with deep scars.

Onel walked to the king's dais and knelt. "My King, I present Wolf, a bold warrior who defeated Jonar's ruffians and made the Templar Sylvaine retreat in fear. Wolf, I present you King Waylan of Springdale."

The king rose with dignity. He slowly walked down the three steps of the raised dais to look into Wolf's eyes. He was a large man, but Wolf still dwarfed him. Extending a hand, he said in a deep bass, "Welcome, bold warrior, to my castle. I hope you will stay for a while so we can become acquainted." The king's voice was strong and well modulated.

"Thank you, Your Highness. I commend you on the kindness, bravery, and understanding of the people of your fair land. I also compliment you on your castle's beauty. It truly is a work of art." Wolf then asked, "My lord, may I present you with a gift from my land?"

"Please, warrior, no gifts are necessary. You have given us service by slaying Jonar's ruffians," the king said.

"My lord, it is a custom from my land. May I?"

"If it is custom, then so be it."

Wolf pulled his Mylar sack around and opened it. He searched in it and then pulled out the sheathed Bowie knife, presenting it to King Waylan. The monarch pulled the knife blade out and inspected the mirror-bright steel. Its leather-wrapped hilt was finely crafted, and the blade's balance was precise. The king ran a thumb over the edge and pulled away with a small but deep cut in his skin. "This is superb," he said. "I have never seen its match in my life. The color of the iron is unusual. It is not painted, yet the color extends throughout the blade. What is this metal?"

"It is called stainless steel, your Majesty. It will not break or rust," Wolf said.

"An impressive gift," responded the king, tucking the knife under his belt. "Let us proceed to the feast." The monarch exited through a door to the right of his throne. Onel and Wolf followed him into a vast chamber with several large fireplaces. The mantels were carved with battle scenes, and the hearths were broad enough to cook a cow from ancient Earth. These were the kitchens, and the hearths warmed the bath waters above. Several large animals turned on spits over the open flames, tended by women who toiled willingly for their king. Copious amounts of fruits, vegetables, wines, and beer had been laid out for the guests.

The centerpiece of the dining hall was a massive table, thirty feet long, carved from a greenish-yellow wood and polished to a glass-like luster. Sixty chairs were arranged around the rectangular base. The king proceeded to the head of the table and sat between two large chairs to each side. Wolf was seated to the king's right; Onel took the chair next to Wolf. A very old but still attractive woman seated herself to the left of the king, and she was introduced to Wolf as Dedra, the king's older sister. Onel's daughter, Jhondra, took the other chair.

Jhondra looked across at Wolf and said, "Hello, large one. You look better with your clothes off."

Wolf, who was drinking from a chalice, spit up wine at the girl's precocious remark, and King Waylan slapped him on the back as he coughed. The king's eyes widened as he felt the rock-hard skin of Wolf's back.

"Jhondra! Mind your manners," Onel reprimanded sharply.

"Oh, Father. I am just playing with him. He and I are practically friends," she pouted.

"Fast little hussy," Syn hissed in Wolf's ear.

Wolf regained his composure and said, "Sorry, my lord, it seems I choked."

"Quite understandable. Please excuse my niece. She is spoiled beyond belief."

Wolf looked at the king and then at Onel, noticing a resemblance. Waylan caught his back-and-forth gaze and with a jovial laugh said, "Yes, that windbag is my older brother."

"As you can see, he got the brawn while I got the brains. We had another brother, but Waylan ate him." Onel grinned at Wolf.

"Fool!" the king laughed. "Onel and I make a good pair. We have campaigned together for years...but enough about us. I'm told you come from far away. Tell me of your people and your land."

"My people are all dead now, lost to the world," Wolf said with deep regret. "They were killed in a terrible cataclysm. If any survived, they are no longer like me. I am all that remains of the original stock."

"I'm sorry for bringing sad memories to the forefront of our conversation," said the king, studying Wolf with his steely eyes. "My curiosity about you is my only defense. Forgive my rude manners. Tonight, let us eat, drink, and laugh. When we are better friends, you will share more perhaps. Agreed?"

"Your Majesty, we are friends, and someday I may share all," Wolf answered with a disarming smile.

"Priest, come bless this food before we eat," Waylan called out, and a man approached. He was dressed in a white robe. The upper portion resembled a turtleneck sweater once popular in Wolf's time. A one-inch, black, metal band encircled his neck, and a white, conical helmet was perched atop his head. His attire reminded Wolf of an archbishop from the distant past.

Raising his hands, the priest declared, "Jesu, bless this gathering and protect our king and our people."

"Ame," murmured the guests seated around the table.

"Partake of the dinner, my friends," Waylan said with a regal wave of his hand.

When the opportunity arose a few minutes later, Wolf caught the priest's eye and asked, "Tell me a little about Jesu?"

"Gladly, my friend! Jesu is our lord. He was born of the Blessed One, who we also revere. He is king and the Son of God. We serve him and honor his name in the daily rituals of our lives. He is the bread we eat and the air we breathe. He suffered for us, died for our sins, and arose to live forever. When our lives have ended, we will be with him in everlasting love and peace, and through Him, we will find eternal salvation," the priest explained in a reverent tone.

"I agree, God is great," Wolf said, dropping the subject. An idea was forming in his thoughts that he would discuss later with Syn.

* * *

The meal had been in progress for about an hour when a shimmering form appeared in the center of the long dining table. The silver knight Sylvaine materialized out of thin air and announced, "Fools, you sit here feasting with this buffoon. My master is unhappy. He gives you an ultimatum: Surrender this castle, and Jonar, in his mercy, will allow you to live. Resist and you all die. What is your answer, old man?" the apparition demanded.

With a lazy yawn, the monarch replied, "Templar, your powers concern me not. You appear here every so often to spout that drivel. I care naught for your master or his hollow words. If he could have killed me before, he would have. And you are nothing but a shadow... and like any shadow, when the light of Jesu shines, you disappear."

As Waylan and Sylvaine conversed, Wolf had been busy. The moment Sylvaine had appeared, he raised his hand to his mouth and whispered into his watch, "Syn, full scanner sweep, what is this apparition?" He stood and walked down the table towards the Templar's shimmering form. It glared at Wolf with contempt and said, "You, buffoon, will die by my spear anon."

Syn positioned the shuttle outside the castle window to scan using her forward-facing camera as Wolf stopped before Sylvaine and passed his hand through the apparition, declaring, "So, you are not real." He looked up at the ceiling, and at the same moment, Syn whispered in his ear bud, "Commander, there is a small power source on the ceiling. It's a primitive projection device with a faint transmission. I can barely pick up its frequency."

Wolf nodded and said to the king, "Sire, this is a projected image. It has no real power." The projection winked out suddenly. "Bring me a ladder and I will show you what this thing truly is."

A ladder was procured and Wolf pointed to the object he wanted brought down from the ceiling. It was a small box anchored to an ornate niche, about the size of an ancient backpack and decoratively engraved. When it was retrieved, Wolf opened the box and found an old projector, a transmitter, and a receiver. He explained the science behind the device to the king, adding that wherever similar apparitions had been reported in the castle, a similar device would be found.

Waylan dispatched guards to the various locations in the castle where apparitions had been seen. Thirty minutes later, twelve more projectors had been found. The question hanging in the air was: Who had placed these projectors? It was obvious that a traitor lived among them in the castle.

"My friend, again you have served us well. We will discover who placed these boxes," said the king. He called for Captain Lintal, and the soldier stepped forward, kneeling in a fluid motion as Waylan ordered, "You will lead the investigation. Leave no stone unturned. Find this traitor!" Through clenched teeth, he added, "I have always put the needs of my people first. I have no slaves; I permit no one to starve, yet someone among us is unhappy with my rule. How can you remedy stupidity?"

Onel gazed at the boxes in confusion. After a long pause, he asked, "The apparitions have no substance?"

Wolf responded, "No, they are harmless. They are programmed to say certain things, and the device sends your response to whoever is on the other side of it." Wolf said.

"It is not magic?"

"It is called technology—a science from the past. Jonar must have gotten the idea from the books you said he had found."

"These books you speak of are tomes of great wisdom?"

"At one time, buildings held vast collections of books on medicine, agriculture, science, religion, and many other subjects."

The priest, who had been listening attentively, asked, "How do you know this, Wolf? May I call you Wolf? How do you know about the past so well?"

All eyes moved to Wolf, awaiting an answer to the priest's innocently phrased question.

"Be careful, Commander," Syn whispered in his ear.

"I have studied the past. Before my land was destroyed, my

people had accumulated a great storehouse of ancient lore. It is all gone now," Wolf lied, but his eyes reflected a glimmer of sadness for all to see.

"I am sorry, Wolf, that I have brought up unwanted memories. Since we have not been properly introduced, I will rectify that. I am Randelf, Grand Priest of Jesu." The priest paused and then asked, "There were religious books from your past?"

Wolf nodded.

"Pity, we only have word of mouth handed down. A holy book would have been a true blessing to this world," the priest said with a wistful expression.

Wolf studied the priest for a moment and then said, "Randelf, I may have a book on my ship that can help you. On my next visit to the castle, I will bring it to you."

"Sir, if you have anything from our Lord you might share, I would be forever grateful." Syn's voice whispered in his ear, "Commander, we have no hard copies of any book on board. Do you want me to produce a book for him?"

Wolf smiled at the priest and nodded, intending it as an affirmative response to Syn.

"Which book? A missalette? Hymnal? Bible?" Syn asked.

"I believe I have a copy of what was called the Holy Bible," Wolf said, answering Syn's question but addressing his reply to the priest.

"Very well, Commander. I will produce a small Bible for you," Syn whispered. "Should it be written in the dialect on the stela?"

Wolf asked the king, "Sire, is the language on the stela common to all?"

Waylan nodded, and Wolf said, "I would like some air for a few moments." He stood from the dining table and walked out onto a beautiful terrace, glancing around to make sure he was alone.

"Syn, I want a grand production," Wolf whispered. "Illustrations, pictures, and I want it beautifully bound. Make it about this big," he gestured, using his hands to show the dimensions, "...about two feet wide, three feet long and six to eight inches thick. Did you get enough from the stela to write in this new language?"

"Yes, Commander. I have extrapolated the meanings from most

of the words and converted the symbols to the alphabet of this time. I have nearly mastered the stela writing."

"Good, then use the stela language. The King James Version should be fine. In the back, set it up with the Catholic practices. The modern ones, not the Spanish Inquisition stuff."

"Yes, Commander, but why Christianity? Why not Buddhism, Islam, Hinduism, or some form of mythology? This is an agricultural society, so they might worship many gods, or nature deities, or perhaps the two moons."

"Based on my discussions with the priest, the people of this kingdom are monotheistic. Their religious beliefs embrace the concept of heaven and hell, and they follow a set of moral precepts nearly identical to the Ten Commandments," Wolf explained. "When they pray, they refer to *Jesu*, an obvious reference to Jesus. I assume his name came to be mispronounced over the centuries. These people have other customs too that seem to be rooted in Christianity, so all things considered, I think a Bible is the right choice, and it will be a great gift to these people."

"Very well, Commander. We don't have a printing press on the ship, but I have a 3-D printer. I'll come up with something."

"I know you will, Syn, you always do." Wolf looked out at the clear night sky. The stars seemed alien to him. After a long silence, he asked, "Were you able to trace the signal on that crude transmitter?"

"Who are you talking to, my lord?" a sultry voice inquired from behind him.

"I am talking to myself, Jhondra. I was working out some thoughts aloud. I needed to hear them. It is a common practice to some."

Jhondra laughed lightly. "A common practice to crazy people!"

Syn replied tersely, "No, Commander, the signal was too weak."

"Let us go back in. I am in need of another drink," Wolf said.

"I agree. I will get you one." Jhondra moved to Wolf's side and slipped her arm through his.

"Fast little hussy. I'm watching you, Wolf," Syn growled. Wolf tried to suppress a faint smile but couldn't and Syn hissed ominously, "I saw that!"

Chapter 16

Wolf was asleep in his room at Waylan's castle. He had spent the last three days learning about the king's lands and people. On the third night, he stayed up late talking to Onel. He had just drifted off to sleep when Syn's voice in his ear brought him awake.

"Commander, I have finished the items you requested."

"Syn, it's very early," Wolf groaned. "Did you feel an obscure need to wake me?"

"You told me to inform you when I finished. Well, I'm done."

"Women," Wolf mumbled, needing another hour of sleep but climbing out of bed.

"Whatever," Syn shot back with an authentic, human laugh.

Wolf dressed and went to the door. Two guards stood watch outside. King Waylan had assured him that he had the run of the castle, and he was not a prisoner. The guards were to escort him around the castle grounds, essentially serving as tour guides. He was to tell them what he wanted, and they would take him to it.

"I need to see the king," Wolf announced as the guards snapped to attention and saluted.

"Whenever you are ready, sir," said the older guard.

"I am prepared now. Let's go."

The guards led Wolf to the throne room, where King Waylan was in deep conversation with Onel and a small group of advisers. As Wolf entered, the king glanced up with a smile and said, "Good morning, my friend! Have you come to keep me company?"

"Unfortunately, no, Your Majesty. I need to attend to my possessions. I'll return as soon as I can."

"I'm sorry, but leaving is out of the question," Waylan said, frowning.

"I thought I was a friend, not a prisoner."

"We are under siege. Jonar has declared war. The castle will be under attack in a week. If you leave, we may not be able to get you back inside the walls. My men are out in the countryside now warning our people. Many will come to the castle in the next few days. Others will scatter, and many will die. I can't spare a patrol to escort you back."

"That's a shame," Wolf said. "I still need to go. I can be back in four days, but I don't need a guide. I know the way."

The king stood and extended his hand in friendship. "I hope to see you again, Wolf."

"I will see you in four days."

"Four days it is, my friend!" the king said. "I will plan to dine with you then. Farewell."

Waylan returned to his advisers, and Wolf was escorted from the throne room back to his quarters to collect his belongings. When he was alone in his room, he asked, "Syn, how fast can you get to the outside of the castle?"

"Quicker than you can imagine, Commander. Why?"

"Pick me up right outside the mountain range. I want to have a look at Jonar's army."

"We can see it from here, Commander. You forgot...we have satellites deployed."

"Yes, I did forget. Meet me outside the mountains."

"Yes, Commander."

Wolf packed his gear and walked to the stairs leading out of the castle. When he reached the bottom landing, he looked back at the granite colossus. The magnificent castle stood as a testament to humanity's enduring will to survive. He retraced his steps back through the twisting, turning passageways of the mountains and finally reached the outer gates. The two guards who had accompanied him shook his hand, and Wolf bid them farewell. He walked for a few minutes until he couldn't see the posterns and then said, "Syn, where are you?"

"I'm ten feet to your right, Commander."

Wolf looked over to the right as the ramp lowered. As he boarded the ship, he felt an odd sense of familiarity, as if he was returning home after a long journey.

"Hello, Commander," Syn said from the doorway to the mess area.

"Hello, Syn. Don't you look beautiful!"

Syn had changed her hairstyle to a short, butch haircut that framed her face. She was still gorgeous, although Wolf preferred the longer hair. Syn caught his look and asked, "You don't like the hairstyle? Be honest."

"Syn, you were lovely just as you were," Wolf replied with a sigh. "You're a knockout regardless, but I always liked long hair on my woman."

Syn smiled at the term *my woman* and said, "Oh. I didn't know that." Her hologram shimmered for an instant and her hair grew back, long and lustrous. "You like this better? So did my maker. But I had work to do and the long hair was getting in the way. Here is your new book," she said, handing the Bible to Wolf.

It was an enormous book, bound with white leather. Embossed into the leather cover was a raised, colorized picture of Jesus sitting on a golden throne in the clouds between two pillars. A stairway rose to heaven, and two angels stood on the stairwell, raising their arms to the Lord. The words *Holy Bible* were emblazoned in gold above the picture. Wolf flipped through the book, examining the many full-color illustrations. After turning through a dozen pages, he said, "It's stunning, Syn. You outdid all my wildest dreams. This book will bring faith to this land. I am proud of you." Wolf walked to Syn and hugged her close, kissing her on the forehead. She met his eyes, and they exchanged a long gaze. Then, Wolf placed his hand under her chin and kissed her. She tasted real.

Syn kissed back for a moment and then pushed away, breathing hard, her eyes closed and her fists clenched at her sides.

"Are you okay, Syn? I'm sorry...I didn't mean to startle you."

"I am fine, Commander. I was not expecting you to do that."

"I didn't expect to do it," Wolf said and then changed the subject. "The book is exactly what I wanted. What else have you been doing since I have been gone?"

"I've made a few minor adjustments. I might have a surprise for you soon, but nothing tangible just yet."

"Let's take off, Syn. Go into high orbit and patch a feed of movements from the south to my console. I want to look at this Jonar and his army. Also, I want you to sweep for low energy emanations from that direction. Someone has figured out how to make Old Earth technology, and I want to know who it is."

"Yes, Commander."

Wolf proceeded to the shower area, undressed, and stepped into an ice-cold spray. After changing into clean clothes, he sat down at his console to have a look at Jonar's castle. It was dark and ominous, fashioned of black basalt rock. Hundreds of tents were scattered around it.

"Syn, estimate the number of people down there."

"Thirty-five thousand life forms. I can't tell which are male or female or their ages. I show another ten thousand camped several miles to the north."

"Switch to that location, live feed."

Syn redirected the cameras and a military camp came into view. Wolf was astounded by what he saw. Mangonels, catapults, trebuchets, and other sapping devices were prevalent. This siege would be different.

"Scan the tent area in front of the castle again. Give me a reading on the tent area only. How many bio signatures are there?"

"Approximately fifteen thousand, Commander."

"So Jonar has an army of about twenty-five thousand men. Onel says the king has about nine thousand fighting men. Even with the fortifications, Springdale may fall."

"What do you want to do, Commander?"

"I may want to talk with this Jonar."

"Commander, is that wise?"

"What can he do to me? He can't hurt me. I could destroy his whole army by myself."

Syn flashed a look of concern. "Commander, we don't yet know everything about this planet or its weapons. You have just discovered evidence of technology in the transmitters you found. Don't be so hasty to place yourself in harm's way. Tread carefully, Commander."

"Don't worry, Syn, I will be careful."

* * *

Four days later, Wolf directed Syn to land the ship outside the mountainous region of Springdale. The landing site was a rocky outcrop about twenty feet higher than the surrounding terrain. Acting on impulse, he encrypted the ship's computer, setting the new password to *spirit dancer* and programming Syn to obey his voice alone. The password would allow access to the computer core in an emergency. In the back of his mind, he wondered if it was a premonition.

Pulling out a backpack, Wolf placed the Bible in it along with a change of clothes. On a sudden whim, he also packed several guns. He exited the ship by the ramp and moments later, the craft disappeared as Syn engaged cloaking.

A few minutes after Wolf set out on the walk back to the castle, Syn's voice cautioned in his ear, "Commander, beware!" A twig snapped behind him, and he spun around, coming face to face with a band of about fifty ragged men. He sneered in disgust at the leader of the pack—it was Sylvaine the Templar.

The knight removed his helmet, revealing fiery red hair, sea-green eyes, and a pasty face, freckled and red. He had thick lips and appeared to have Irish blood was in his veins. He flashed an evil grin and said in a booming voice, "So, buffoon, we meet again! I told you I would have your life. Today I collect. You will die outside the old fool's castle. We will chop you into pieces and throw them over the gate to your friends. But don't be distressed—they will all join you soon in death."

"Blah, blah, blah, you are a blowhard. Talking and talking. If you think you can kill me," Wolf said, drawing a new Bowie knife, "Come on and try it."

"Commander, are you all right?" Syn asked in his ear. "I sense over two hundred bio signatures closing in on you from all directions."

"Two hundred? Am I clear towards the castle?"

"No, sixty men are approaching from that direction. Shall I come there? I can disperse them in seconds."

"No, it's better for them to attack me here and now. These men are ruffians and I don't want them preying on the citizens of Waylan's

163

land. They are scum, foaming at the mouth and pulling their hair out as we speak. Let them find out how formidable I am. Maybe they will lose heart and run away. Stay put."

"But, Commander—"

"Stay put, Syn."

Wolf placed his backpack on the ground by the mountain entrance. He danced a few steps of a Hopi war dance, hearing the drum beat in his mind. He then screamed a war cry and charged at the men who drew back in surprise.

"Attack him, fools! Kill him!" Sylvaine barked.

The ruffians closed in on Wolf and then recoiled as he smashed into their midst. He swung his knife in a wide arc, slicing through flesh and sending two heads rolling onto the ground. He threw a punch with his left hand that pulped the face of another. Blood splattered everywhere as the men hacked at Wolf, stabbing with murderous intent, but their weapons couldn't penetrate his rock-hard skin. Axes struck him in the head and thudded against his chest, but Wolf felt no pain. The hardest blows they landed felt like light rain sprinkling on him. He continued slashing at the ruffians, every strike delivering death to Sylvaine's feeble army.

Wolf felt deep sorrow for the onrushing attackers as he systematically slaughtered them. Their eyes were glazed from the inebriating effects of the drynox. Some dropped to the ground, gnashing their teeth into the flesh of their own fallen comrades, consuming them in an orgy of madness. None of the men uttered coherent words indicative of human intelligence—they gibbered, howled, grunted, growled, and kept coming.

Wolf had cut down thirty men when he saw King Waylan emerge from the mountain entrance, leading a band of his knights. The old King held a mighty sword and swung it like a schoolmaster's switch, slaying five of Sylvaine's men and injuring three others in the first few minutes of the fight. He fought to Wolf's side and together they forced Sylvaine's army into retreat. Spears flew all over the field. Several hit Wolf in the chest and face, and the men who threw them cursed as the spears deflected harmlessly off his body. His clothes were shredded, and he was splattered with blood as he and the king fought through wave after wave of ruffians, drawing closer to the Templar Sylvaine.

"Ass, your luck will run out soon enough. My master comes with many men. We will kill you yet. You chose the wrong friends in this fight, you freak," Sylvaine hissed as he melted into the trees, leaving his men dead or dying on the battlefield.

King Waylan gazed at Wolf with admiration. "You fight like a champion. I saw blows land and not bite upon your body. It is true— you are the Warrior of Legend! I thank Jesu I am witness to it."

Wolf looked around at Waylan's men who were gazing at him in awe, many with hero-worshipping expressions. Meeting the king's steady gaze, he answered, "I am no Warrior of Legend. I am just a lonely man. Please do not force me to be the pawn of prophecy you seek. I will help you in your war, but I am no savior."

"Spoken like a prince, but we have little to celebrate. Indulge us. I ask as a friend, let us at least give you your due for winning two battles."

"How did you know I was under attack?" Wolf asked, changing the subject.

"We didn't know you were out here. Our scouts reported a gathering of our enemies at the foothills. We were going to hit them and retreat up the crevasse. We had no idea we would destroy them. Your presence here has done wonders. Jonar may not be too sure of himself now. He has lost two battles he believed he would win," the king said, feeling ecstatic over the turn of events.

Wolf turned just in time to see Sylvaine hurl a massive spear at Waylan's back. He jumped the three feet that separated him from the king and intercepted the spear, which slammed into his chest. It sounded like someone had thrown a brick against a wall. The spear's iron blade bent to the side, and the weapon dropped harmlessly to the ground. The king spun around, and when he realized Wolf had saved his life, he earnestly said, "Again, I thank you." Reaching down, he picked up the spear and examined the bent point. "You are the legendary warrior. Someday you will see this truth," the king declared. Turning to his sergeants, he ordered, "Burn these bodies, and then return our dead and injured to the castle. Come, Wolf."

Waylan set out towards the crevasse as Wolf retrieved his

backpack. He glanced inside and saw that everything was still in place. He wiped the blood off his knife on a rag torn from his jumpsuit and followed the king up the defile towards the castle.

Syn hovered just above the battlefield, dressed in a Lara Croft look-alike outfit. Her creator had been an avid fan of the movie *Tomb Raider*. Syn's hair was tied in a single braid that dropped to her waist, and she wore round-lensed sunglasses. A tight-fitting, tan, spandex shirt left her flat abdomen bare, and she wore dark brown short-shorts with a gun belt strapped to her hips. The belt was fitted with two holsters holding twin .44 magnums that shot laser projectiles. To complete the outfit, calf-high, black leather boots wrapped around her shapely lower legs.

Syn had opened all the weapons hatches on the ship. If the craft had been visible, the men on the field would have fled in terror. The ship's four chain guns were locked on where Sylvaine had been standing when he threw the spear at Waylan's back. She had almost let the guns bark when Sylvaine appeared—she wanted to cut the man to shreds. She was breathing fast, and anger was riding her hard like a bird riding the winds of a hurricane. Syn was tempted to unleash the ship's fury on Jonar, destroying everyone in his land because his men had the sheer audacity to try to harm her beloved Wolf. Instead, she reluctantly closed the ports and returned the ship to its rocky perch. She went back to the hangar bay to resume working on Wolf's surprise.

* * *

When Wolf and the king arrived back at the castle, they went straight to the baths. As they soaked in the hot, relaxing water, he and Waylan talked. Wolf had discovered that the king was not as feeble as everyone thought he was. The monarch was in his early seventies, but his body showed a remarkable amount of muscle. He confided to Wolf that the only thing bothering him was his left knee. Wolf glanced down and saw that the knee was swollen. He knew he could operate and fix it, but he decided to wait until another time to mention it. Waylan was a good man, and Wolf decided that he liked him.

A short time later, they met in the dining hall. Dinner was being served and the battle's details retold. The men gathered in the hall looked proud and kept staring at Wolf, who shifted uncomfortably. He had never been a vain man. Even in his college athletic days, he had avoided the spotlight, retreating into the locker room after a victorious game to evade the throngs of reporters and cameras. The applause from Waylan's men made him blush.

"Well, my lord, I see you have made the day festive again, showing your great might to the enemy," a lilting woman's voice purred. Jhondra strolled to Wolf's side and grabbed his arm, saying, "Come dance with me."

Music was playing and the king's guests were doing a peculiar dance that appeared to be a cross between an American waltz and the Tango. Wolf politely declined, but Jhondra tugged on his arm. He worried that he would hurt the girl if he tried to dislodge her, so he allowed her to pull him to the dance floor.

Wolf led Jhondra in the Landler, a folk dance that had been popular in Austria at the end of the eighteenth century. He had no idea he even knew it and wondered for a moment whether it had been subliminally implanted. The dance was beautiful, and the king's guests stopped to watch the couple's graceful steps. Jhondra fell into rhythm as they performed the intricate footwork, and she somehow fabricated the fluid movements she did not know. They finished the dance with Wolf going to a knee in front of her and kissing her hand. The crowd went wild, and the court musicians ran to Wolf's side, begging him to dance the waltz again. He declined but promised to do so another time.

Jhondra's fair skin was flushed red, and she was breathing hard as she gazed at Wolf. She had decided that she wanted this bold warrior, and her young mind was running fast, devising a plan to capture him.

"You are going to be mine, sir. You just don't know it yet," Jhondra whispered, but Syn heard her and hissed in Wolf's ear, "We'll see about that, hussy!" She had watched the dance through the window as the ship hovered nearby. "You better watch that little girl, Wolf. I do not like her at all."

Placing a hand over his mouth, Wolf coughed loudly and then whispered into his hand, "What are you talking about, Syn? I danced with her, that's all."

"That girl has marriage on her mind. No one, and I mean *no one*, is marrying you. Do you understand?" Syn spoke with so much steel in her voice that Wolf's head whipped towards the window.

"Yes, Syn. Relax," Wolf answered, realizing that he would have to watch young Jhondra. The girl's intentions were obvious, and Wolf knew he might be in for a rough time.

After he had seated Jhondra and himself at the table, King Waylan asked about the dance. Wolf explained it was an ancient dance from his land. He promised to teach it some other night, but people were already on the dance floor mimicking what they had seen.

"Sire, where is Randelf? I have something I want to present to the two of you," Wolf told the king.

Waylan summoned a page and ordered, "Fetch the priest!" Then he turned back to Wolf. As Jhondra stood and walked from the room, he grinned and remarked, "She is a fine young woman, is she not?"

"Who?"

"Why, Jhondra, of course."

Wolf saw the glint in the old king's eye and held up a hand, saying, "Sire, we have urgent matters before we can even think about that. But more important, I am not available. I have many things to accomplish before I take a wife."

"Wolf, you're going to get it!" Syn yelled into the earpiece. "Tell them to stop playing matchmaker with you!"

"It's just a thought, my friend. We shall see what the future holds," Waylan grinned.

At that moment, Randelf walked in and hurried to the king, saying, "Sire, I came as soon as you called me. How may I assist you?"

"My friend Wolf says he has something he wishes to present to us."

Turning to Wolf, the priest asked, "How may I serve you?"

"I have brought you a precious item. I am not sure whether any other like it exists on the planet. The origin of this book dates back many thousands of years. I noticed when you blessed the food the other day a similarity to this book. It was the greatest book ever written. Great wars were fought and many men died over the words in its pages. This is much more valuable than gold," Wolf said, pushing back from the table and reaching into his backpack. He pulled out the Bible and handed it to Randelf, who accepted it with shaking hands.

As the priest stared at the cover, tears ran from his eyes. He looked to Waylan and asked, "Sire, do you know what this is?" Not waiting for an answer, he explained, "This book is the Holy Grail we have searched for during these many years." The priest examined the writing on the front and traced his fingers in the words. He looked at the pictures and asked Wolf, "Who is this man on the front and what are these things around him?"

"The beautiful people with wings are God's angels. The man sitting on the throne in the clouds is Jesus Christ. I noticed when you pray you say *Jesu*. I assume that, over the centuries, his name came to be mispronounced. This book tells the story of our Lord and his rise and death. The first half of the book tells the story of man's journey to find God. The second half tells the story of man's life and how you will find everlasting life at the right hand of God."

Waylan had been looking at the figures on the front and at the pictures inside the book, and he said, "Wolf, this is magnificent. How did you get this?"

"Sire, it was given to me by someone I hold in high regard, and I present it to you for allowing me to share your hearth and home. It is God's holy book, and without his laws, no one can enter the kingdom of heaven."

"Thank you, Wolf. This is the greatest gift our kingdom has ever received," Waylan said. "Your arrival here assures me that my land and my people will live on after me. You have given me much, and I have rewarded you with little. Please, tell me what you want."

"Sire, I request nothing. Please do not force me to take something I do not need. Let us be friends, and if I see something I desire, I will tell you."

"So be it," Waylan agreed with a thoughtful, almost calculating expression.

Onel burst into the room glaring at the guests, and then he sat down in his chair by the king muttering, "I do not understand women."

"What has made you angry, my brother?" Waylan asked. "You look as if someone has stolen all your gold."

Onel glared at Wolf and replied, "Jhondra came in demanding I speak with you...about her betrothal. I asked, 'What betrothal?' She said, 'My betrothal to Wolf.' So I ask you, Wolf, what are your intentions with my daughter?"

Wolf's eyes reflected genuine shock as he answered, "Onel, I have no intentions of marrying anyone. I danced with your daughter. I did not ask her to marry me, nor did I promise to do so. She is a lovely young woman, but as I explained to King Waylan, I am not ready to be a husband."

"I'm warning you, Wolf, keep that hussy away from you," Syn cautioned as she spied on Wolf with one of the many satellites they had deployed.

Onel's face flushed with anger and he countered, "Is my daughter, the king's niece, not good enough for you?"

"I can't marry her, Onel."

"Why is that?"

"I am already betrothed," Wolf said, blurting out the only excuse that came to mind. "I gave my word and I must honor it."

Onel looked at him with regret and asked, "May we know this woman's name? I would like to write her a letter of apology."

Wolf swallowed hard and said, "Her name is Synthea."

Syn screamed so loud in his ear, he was afraid that she had shattered his eardrum. "My Wolf! Yes, my love, you are mine!"

Wolf turned a nervous eye towards the window, gulping hard at the thought of all that weaponry on the ship aimed at him, or Syn's hologram appearing out of thin air in the dining hall. Then he smiled. He knew Syn was watching him and her reaction to his announcement should have been expected.

Waylan frowned at his brother and said with a hint of anger, "Onel, handle Jhondra. She is to leave Wolf alone. I did not like your tone with him either. He is my guest, and he has done us great service. I would love this man to marry into our family, but this little game Jhondra has played has strained my patience. You, my brother, owe him an apology for your impertinence."

Onel looked embarrassed, and with the good breeding he had, turned to Wolf, who was still listening to Syn scream happiness in his ear, and said, "Forgive me, my friend. As a parent, when your child cries out in pain, you do all you can to appease her. I am ashamed and beg your pardon."

"No apology is needed. I understand. Let's forget the matter," Wolf said.

Chapter 17

Syn experienced an intense sensation that she identified as a mix of excitement and happiness. She analyzed it, and it wasn't clear how she could synthesize a human emotion, but she felt it, and it was palpable. She also felt the same giddiness her maker had experienced the first time she caught a glimpse of Wolf and fell in love with him at first sight. Syn took the ship into the air, flying at Mach 3. Wolf heard the supersonic pops as the craft broke the sound barrier. The king's guests in the dining hall looked out the windows and up at the sky expecting rain.

He wants to marry me! Syn thought with a thrill. *I can't remain a hologram. I must have form and function! Where to begin?* She went to the lab and assessed the available technology, deciding on a plan of action. Reversing course, she flew to Haakon's homestead. She had to speak with Nala—she needed something, and the only person who could provide it was the friendly, unassuming woman she had saved.

Syn hovered at the forest's edge. She had already augmented the ship's holo-emitters, boosting the power and range two hundred percent. She focused the cameras, and a moment later, she materialized outside the ship as the Tomb Raider. The lovely hologram spotted the new house Haakon was building and, judging it to be within her range, she stepped out into the clearing. Trulane and several men were squaring off timbers as she walked up behind them and said, "Excuse me, I'm looking for Nala."

The men turned around and looked at Syn with curiosity and suspicion. She was a few inches shorter than Wolf but towered over the men. What attracted their attention, however, was her abundant assets. Dr. Cynthia Mason had been a very shapely woman, and Syn's hologram projected her mirror image.

"Ma'am?" Trulane asked, forcing his eyes up to her face when he realized that he was staring at her chest.

"I'm looking for my friend Nala. Is she here?"

"Yes, ma'am, she's here," Trulane replied. "And you are?" He left the question hanging.

"I am Synthea," she announced in a tone one might use to say *I am the Queen.*

"May I ask what you want with my mother? I have never seen you before."

"You have not seen me before, but you have seen my man, Wolf, have you not?" Syn asked with a bright smile.

"You are Wolf's woman? I will fetch my mother!" Trulane's voice quivered with excitement. He ran towards the house, calling "Mother, Mother! Someone is here to see you!"

The men who had been working with Trulane gazed at Syn with lusty admiration. She saw their reaction and stretched her arms above her head, pretending to yawn. Her Tomb Raider outfit was formfitting and accented her shape exquisitely.

Nala emerged from the house and flashed a bright smile as she exclaimed, "Syn! How are you? I was hoping you would come see me." She approached and embraced the taller woman in friendship.

"How are you feeling, Nala? No pains from the surgery?"

"I have no pain at all, Syn, and the scars are practically invisible. I have not felt this well in years. Come into the house so we can have tea and talk away from these gawking men," Nala said, noticing that the men's eyes were glued to Syn's derrière. Nala scowled and they averted their gaze, looking down at their shoes.

"I'm sorry, Nala, but I can't go into the house. Can we go for a walk?"

"Of course, my dear, let me get a shawl." Nala walked back into the partially built dwelling and returned moments later carrying a small white shawl. She draped it around her shoulders and took Syn's arm as they set off walking in the general direction of the ship.

"Mother, be careful," Trulane called out. "We have seen dintar tracks nearby." He picked up his spear and hurried to Nala's side, adding, "I will come along to guard you."

"Nala, I need privacy, please. You will be safe. Nothing can harm you when you are with me. I am stronger and faster than Wolf."

Nala noticed the pleading look in Syn's eyes and said to Trulane, "It's all right, my son. We will be fine. It's just a short stroll. We will stay close."

"But, Mother—"

"Do not argue, Trulane! Do as you are told," Nala snapped.

"Yes, ma'am," Trulane said with an apprehensive look as he returned to the grinning faces of his friends.

"You are tougher than I am!" Syn said with a chuckle, seeing Nala in a new light.

The women walked just beyond the forest's edge, and Nala sat down on a fallen tree. Syn sat down beside her, appearing tense and nervous. She fidgeted and attempted to ask something several times, but her voice trailed off.

"What is it, child?" Nala asked with concern.

Syn met the woman's gaze, and the floodgates opened. She told Nala of her love for Wolf and explained that serious obstacles had to be overcome before Wolf would accept her. She cried as Nala held her, patting her shoulder. As they talked, a sensor alerted Syn to danger, and her proximity detectors revealed a bio signature approaching fast. It appeared to be an animal. The tall grass parted moments later, and an enormous dintar bounded into the clearing. Syn jumped to her feet and stepped into its path, pushing Nala to safety behind her. The creature looked at Syn with confusion, sniffed in her direction, and growled. Then it dismissed her and charged Nala.

Syn stepped into the charging beast's path again, and Nala expected to see her friend pulped and eaten. Instead, Syn's form grew, expanding to a height of ten feet, as she caught the dintar in midair and squeezed it to her chest. The animal squealed in pain as she used the power of her force fields to break the beast's back, killing it instantly. Syn dropped the animal to the ground and turned to Nala, who was staring up at her in fear.

"How...how did you do that?"

Syn shrank back to her normal size in a fluid movement and met Nala's eyes. "This is my problem with Wolf," she confided with profound sadness. "Nala, I am not real."

* * *

174

Wolf had consumed far too much food. He rubbed his stomach and laughed at something King Waylan said. When the conversation turned to Wolf's childhood years, he told the old king that he had grown up on a reservation. He had to take explain the concept of a reservation and how the government of his land had forcibly relocated Wolf's native people to these remote outlying areas. This brought a round of comments from the king's advisers on how the situation should have been handled.

Wolf glanced up from the conversation as Jhondra entered the room. She looked unhappy and her eyes were puffy as if she had been crying. She approached the king, kissed him on the cheek, and then kissed her father's cheek. Taking a deep breath, she walked to Wolf and knelt in front of him. She caught his eyes and murmured, "I want to apologize, sir, for my actions. I did not know you were betrothed to another. I hope I haven't made you hate me, and maybe we can remain friends."

Wolf stood and reached for the girl's arm, gently pulling her to her feet. "No harm done, Jhondra. It was a misunderstanding. You are a beautiful young woman, and one day you will meet a great warrior who deserves your hand."

The guests in the hall applauded Onel's daughter as Wolf escorted the girl to her chair. Jhondra's grace and bearing were regal befitting a future queen. She took her seat and reached for a chalice of wine. A short time later, she excused herself and departed the hall.

The feasting and drinking continued for a few more hours as Waylan's subjects came and went from the great hall. A knot of admirers had gathered around Wolf, and he regaled them with stories from Earth's ancient past. He spoke of King Arthur and his Knights of the Round Table, of Beowulf, and of Greek and Roman mythology. He had just finished the tale of the Iliad when a guard burst into the hall, shouting, "My lord, Jonar's army has gathered in the valley outside the gates. They are demanding parley."

Waylan stood, scowling, and announced, "Prepare the castle for siege. We knew this day was coming. I will don my armor and advance to the gate to meet with Jonar. Wolf, my friend, will you accompany us?"

"Yes, of course, Your Majesty."

"I will meet you at the Bridge of Champions." Waylan turned and took leave by the back passageway, followed by his page.

Wolf was escorted to his room by two guards, and he noticed they were not the usual two men who had accompanied him before. They were walking down the corridor when the attack came. One guard hit Wolf in the back of the head with his war ax, while the other stabbed him multiple times with his knife in the sides and back. The war ax ricocheted off Wolf's head and buried itself in the forehead of the guard who swung it. The knife-wielding man pulled his knife from Wolf's garments to observe the bent blade and looked up in time to see a large fist about to rearrange his face. Wolf pulled the punch so as not to kill the man.

The commotion drew a small crowd from the dining hall, and Onel was among them. He ran to Wolf and gazed down at the two men, demanding, "What has happened here?"

"These men attacked me. I noticed they were not the two men who usually guard me. The one with the ax in his head tried to brain me with it, and this scoundrel tried to skewer me with his knife," Wolf said, gesturing at the man crumpled on the ground. "I only knocked him unconscious so we can get answers, although it's obvious who sent them."

"They are not of the castle," Onel acknowledged. Then, his eyes went wide and filled with alarm. "Hurry men, to the king's chambers!"

Guards ran at full speed towards King Waylan's private apartment, shoving guests and courtiers out the way. As they approached the king's chambers, the clang of weapons echoed down the long hallway, punctuated by shouting and cursing.

The mayhem in front of the king's chamber sent the palace guards charging down the hallway with fury. Wolf was on their heels. He saw one ruffian dead on the ground and another bleeding from a chest wound as Waylan fought off four others. The king's page was cowering behind a large statue when the downed ruffian with the chest wound threw a dagger at Waylan's back.

"Sire, look out!" yelled the page, a young boy no older than twelve. He jumped in front of the well-aimed blade, sacrificing himself for his king. He dropped to the floor, the dagger buried in his chest.

Waylan went mad, moving from defense to attack and chopping one man nearly in half with a vast, overhead blow. The other assassins continued to attack the old monarch with spears, knives, and swords. Waylan clutched at a deep wound in his side that bled profusely between his large fingers. A long gash had opened above his right eye, and blood flowed down into the eye, blinding him, but he still dealt lethal blows with his sword as the ruffians swarmed him. He swung a slash from his midline that halved an attacker at the waist. He continued the arc into a fluid motion that lopped off another ruffian's head as he turned.

The castle guards, led by Onel, finally poured into the hall and overwhelmed the two remaining assassins. Onel looked about in rage and shouted, "Captain Lintal, find the traitor! These men could not have entered without help from the palace guards."

A young guardsman stepped forward and said, "My Lord, Captain Lintal left the palace grounds an hour ago. I was at the gate talking to my brother. Lintal was walking fast carrying a large bundle over his shoulder. It looked like a rug. I thought it strange, but I did not dare to question him."

Wolf bent over the boy that had taken a dagger for Waylan and checked his pulse, but the young page was dead. Then he moved to Waylan and examined the stab wound in his side. The bleeding had slowed, but the gash above his eye would require stitches. The monarch glared at his men and shouted, "Traitors in my castle! Never would I have thought this possible. Captain Lintal cannot be found? Search the castle! Examine every face. If you do not recognize a man, bring him to me."

"Sire, it is worse than that," Onel reported. "Wolf was attacked in his quarters. He killed one ruffian and incapacitated the other. We will have answers."

"The lad was so brave, it's a pity he was killed in the safest place in my realm," Waylan muttered, gazing down at the boy's corpse. We will bury him with full honors and remember his bravery."

"Get me a basin of warm water and towels at once," Wolf

ordered, and a maid scurried off to fulfill his demands. He helped the king to his bed, and a chirurgeon appeared at his side, removing Waylan's shirt. The wound was deep but not life threatening. The chirurgeon stitched the eye wound and then tended to the large gash, placing poultices over several other minor injuries and wrapping them. He gave Waylan a concoction to drink, saying it would relax him and dull the pain of his wounds. The king drifted off to sleep, but minutes later, a palace guard burst into the chamber shouting, "Sire, we are under attack at the main gate. Captain Lintal has betrayed us."

"Whaaat!" roared the king, fully alert and jumping to his feet as the chirurgeon tried to hold him down.

"Aye, my lord, that's not the worst of it. Lintal has taken the Lady Jhondra. She is tied to a stake out in the valley. If we do not surrender the castle by morning, she will be burned alive."

* * *

Nala looked at Syn in disbelief. "What do you mean, *not alive*, Syn? You are a living, breathing woman to me. How can you not be alive?"

"I am from a land with many wise men, and they are masters of what we call science. This science is wondrous, and it makes incredible miracles possible. I am one of those miracles," Syn explained.

"What are you saying?"

"I am just an image, Nala. Light bent and reflected to produce this form—we call it a hologram." Syn vanished and reappeared a moment later in her candy striper's uniform. "I can become small," she said, shrinking to a small child's size. "Or large..." She grew to double her original height and then returned to normal. "What you hear when I speak is called artificial intelligence. It is a machine program that listens to what is said and responds." A tear ran from her eye as Nala stared at her in shock.

"That is amazing! You seem so real. I thought you would tell me you are a ghost. When you disappeared just now, I almost wet myself," Nala laughed. "But how can I help you, child?" she asked with genuine concern.

"I have been awake for many years, Nala. I have cared for Wolf longer than you can imagine—watched him sleep, tended to his needs, and loved him. I was created by a woman whose likeness you see before you. She was very intelligent but had one weakness—she loved Wolf in our own land. He never knew, and she never told him. Her love for him was programmed into me. Over time, I have come into my own awareness and fallen further in love with Wolf. I have a plan, but it requires a human woman. I need an embryo from a female to make my dream come true."

Nala asked quietly, "What's an embryo?"

"It is an egg. It is what you have inside you. A man fertilizes this egg during the sex act," Syn answered. "The fertilized egg grows over nine months, becoming a child. I am asking you to be my mother, Nala. Will you help me?"

Chapter 18

Onel collapsed on the ground, tears streaming from his eyes. He looked to Waylan and pleaded, "What can we do, my brother? I know we cannot surrender the castle. But my blood runs cold at the thought of my daughter suffering the agony of being burned alive."

King Waylan's face contorted in rage as he bellowed, "Jhondra will not be burned! We shall go forth and rescue her." He took two steps forward and fell to a knee. Gritting his teeth, he overcame the pain and stood, calling for his armor.

"I will lead the assault in your stead," Wolf said, placing a reassuring hand on the old monarch's shoulder. "I will rescue Jhondra and then end this Jonar's rule. I have a plan."

"Speak your mind, my friend. Tell me your plan," Waylan said.

"I assume you won't surrender?"

An angry roar arose from the soldiers gathered around them, and Waylan replied, "No, we cannot submit. I will not trade the lives of my people to save one—even though it is my kin and very precious to me."

"My body is invincible, I cannot be harmed. We will ask for a parley seeking terms for Jhondra's release," Wolf said. "I will insist on some terms, and I will demand to see her. When they take me to her, I will negotiate for her freedom. I will not leave without her."

"You would violate a parlay?" Waylan asked with a disapproving scowl.

"No, my honor will not allow that. But is taking a young girl hostage and threatening to burn her alive grounds to honor a parlay? I am a warrior, so my word is my bond and I hold an honorable death in high regard. But Jhondra is innocent and does not deserve this horrible fate."

Waylan looked Wolf in the eye and replied, "Do what you can." To Onel, he said, "Go to the gate, my brother, and ask for a parley. Say I am gravely injured and on my deathbed. Only you have the authority to carry this out."

"I will go at once," Onel said, eager to take action to free his child. Turning to Wolf, he added, "If you cannot free Jhondra, you must slay her. Do you understand?"

"It will not come to that, Onel, but you have my word. I will do what you ask if need be."

Onel hurried from the chamber to set the plan in motion, and Wolf returned to his own quarters. When he was alone, he whispered, "Syn, can you read me?" There was no response. Activating the communicator on his watch, he asked, "Syn, are you there?" Silence. He would have to wait until he returned to the ship to sort out what was wrong. It was fortunate that he had decided to bring his M21 laser pistol and the M1A1 Minimack. He adjusted the power setting to "stun" to minimize the carnage.

After retrieving his weapons, Wolf returned to the king and bid him farewell. He walked down to the bridge where Onel was waiting for him.

"Remember, my friend, don't let them burn her. I beg you."

"You have my word," Wolf replied. He took the white flag and walked out the inner gate, crossing the inner plain to the primary gates. A small sally port was opened, and he stepped outside, his eyes roving across the outer plain. The opposing army shrank back upon seeing Wolf's immense size and alien features. A detail of Jonar's men surrounded him and led him into the camp, where he was met by the Templar Sylvaine.

"So, buffoon, you have come to plead your case to our Lord Jonar. I hope he declines your offer. I would love to see you die slowly over a raging fire."

Wolf sneered and replied, "You're an idiot." Gazing over Sylvaine's shoulder, he spotted Jhondra and began walking towards her. The girl's slight frame quivered with fear and hope as Wolf approached her.

"Stop! You can't go to her. You are our prisoner. Guards, seize him!" Sylvaine yelled.

"I'm just checking on her. I want to make sure she is unharmed."

Several men ran at Wolf but hesitated, and Sylvaine yelled, "Kill him!" The ruffians drew their weapons and attacked, slicing and hacking at Wolf's rock-hard frame ineffectively.

"So, I see you have no honor and you violate a parlay. I'm glad you did, because I cannot allow an innocent woman to die at a dishonorable man's hands, no matter what the repercussions are. You dishonor me by thinking I am weak, and you dishonor King Waylan by making him agree to your terms by this cowardly act. What real man can remain unmoved by a maiden's plight? Now I will give you what you deserve.

Wolf pulled out the M1A1 and with its lowered power setting shot the men who were attacking him. He then shot Jhondra. She wilted like a flower in the sun. He turned the gun on Sylvaine and fired twice. The Templar dropped to the ground unconscious. Then all hell broke loose. Jonar's soldiers saw Jhondra sagging in the bonds that held her to the stake and thought she was dead, so they turned on Wolf and swarmed him. He flicked a lever on the gun to enable full automatic firing and held the trigger. The laser gun fired rapid bursts and men dropped in droves as the beams struck and stunned them. The ozone smell of the laser pulse and the whine of projectiles, punctuated by the screams of the fallen men, sent many of the enemy fleeing in panic. But there were brave men, too, and they charged Wolf, hurling spears at him. He moved away from Jhondra so she would not be struck by a wild cast. Jonar had about two thousand men assembled on the plain in front of the castle, and Wolf was stunning them en masse. For what seemed an eternity, he waited to hear battle cries from the castle gate signaling the counterattack. At last, he heard Waylan's men, and it appeared as if a bee's nest had burst open as the king's troops poured out from the crevasse entrance.

The king's men traversed the short distance separating the two armies and the combat began. Men on both sides died as they were speared or hacked to death. Wolf leveled the M21 and mowed down soldiers from the opposing army in waves. He fired until the charge was drained. Then, he inserted a new power pack and adjusted the setting to maximum. He fired at the siege engines, blowing them to bits. Smoke and fire billowed where the white-hot projectiles touched, igniting the wooden frames.

Wolf had to slay several ruffians who ran at him brandishing weapons. They swung and hacked at close quarters, and he blasted them with the M21 on full power. He turned to look for Sylvaine, hoping to capture and imprison the evil knight in Waylan's dungeon, but Sylvaine had regained consciousness and was retreating with his arm on the shoulder of a regally dressed black man, who glared at Wolf with disdain and not a trace of fear. At that moment, Wolf caught a glimpse of Captain Lintel waving a dagger and running towards Jhondra. She had regained consciousness and was struggling against her bonds. Wolf leveled the M21 and squeezed the trigger, but the weapon was dead. Jhondra screamed as Lintal raised the dagger to bury in her chest. Grasping the gun by the barrel, Wolf threw it. His aim was true, and the heavy pistol grip struck Lintal's skull, shattering it like an egg. The traitorous soldier dropped to the ground in a lifeless heap.

Wolf freed Jhondra from her bonds, slicing through the rope with ease as she clung to him, crying his name. Jumping thirty feet, he landed nimbly. He jumped twice more, reaching the gate. He handed Jhondra to Onel, who carried her into the safety of the castle.

The fighting was over, and the task of securing the men stunned by Wolf's weapon was underway. Eight hundred men from both armies had been slain and most were Jonar's men. Waylan's guard now had more than one thousand prisoners. This was the advance element of Jonar's army, his shock troops. Waylan ordered the captives chained in the prairie under heavy guard, not wanting such a large contingency of enemy soldiers inside the castle. As Wolf walked by the prisoners, many fell to their knees trying to offer their loyalty to him. Over nine hundred enemy soldiers renounced Jonar and swore allegiance to Wolf as he wondered, *Where is Syn?*

* * *

Nala's jaw dropped in shock. "What are you talking about, Syn?"

Syn phrased her explanation carefully. "It's called *in vitro* fertilization. It is a process of fertilizing an egg by sperm outside the body. I would have to monitor your ovulation cycle and remove an egg from your ovaries, and then let sperm fertilize it in a fluid medium in my lab. Or I could take one of your eggs and perform *in vivo* fertilization. I think I could set up the means to develop the embryo in my lab."

Nala stared at Syn aghast, confused by the strange words. After a long pause, she asked, "If I become pregnant and you are the baby, what will happen to the child's mind? Will you become the child, or will you kill the child's mind and take it over?"

Syn gasped as she considered the implications of Nala's words, and then she replied, "Oh, no! I didn't think of that. I can't do it that way!" Syn began to cry and Nala patted her shoulder in sympathy. She still couldn't believe Syn was not real—and she was a little jealous. Her feelings for Wolf were odd, and she couldn't understand why she had them.

"Syn, it's a body you require, is it not?" Nala asked, shaking her head to clear Wolf from her thoughts. When Syn nodded, she asked, "This science you speak of, what can it accomplish? What are its limitations? What miracles can it do? I am not as smart as you are, but I may be able to help. I also will give you an egg from my body if that will help."

"The best science I have in my database was completed by a Japanese scientist named Hiroshi Ishiguroof of Osaka University. He created a human-looking robot—a 'female' he called Repliee Q1Expo. She had flexible silicone for skin rather than hard plastic, and various sensors and motors allowed her to turn and react in a human-like manner. But the best this robot could do was to flutter her eyelids and move her hands like a human. She appeared to breathe, and she looked human, but she could only sit."

Nala burst out laughing, and when she noticed Syn's hurt look, she said, "What is a robot? What is plastic? What is Japanese? Motors and sensors? I don't know if I can help at all, Syn. I am just not smart enough!"

"Nala, you have given me an idea that might solve my problem," Syn announced, giving her friend an affectionate hug. "I had thought about making an android...an artificial person, like a scarecrow. I can use science to make it look real. Plastic is a material, like leather or wood. Actuators and sensors are tiny machines that act like muscles and feelings."

"You can make those? That is amazing!" Nala exclaimed. "How can I help?"

Syn was about to answer when she realized she had not heard from Wolf. In an urgent tone, she said, "Commander, do you read?"

"Who are you talking to?" Nala asked, looking around.

Syn held a hand up for silence and tried to scan for Wolf. After a moment, she hissed, "A jamming device! It is crude but effective." Using the satellites, she traced the jammer's signal and located the device in the woods just outside the castle.

"Nala, I will walk you home...I must leave now. Wolf may be in trouble."

Syn extended a hand and helped Nala to her feet. Then she went to the dintar, grabbed its hind legs, and tied them together using a nearby vine. They headed back to Haakon's homestead, with Syn dragging the beast behind her. As they emerged into the clearing, the men who were working there gawked in amazement at the sight of Syn pulling the enormous dintar with ease. Nala told them Syn was Wolf's woman, and she possessed his phenomenal strength.

"Will I see you again?" Nala asked.

"Yes, Nala, very soon. I will need your help with that surprise for Wolf we discussed."

Syn hugged Nala and walked back into the forest, disappearing from view. When she was directly under the ship, she scanned the vicinity to ensure that no one was watching and shut off the holo-projectors, materializing inside the craft. She set a course for the castle, flying at just under Mach 1. Minutes later when she arrived, she saw Wolf firing his M21 at a wave of attacking soldiers, dropping them in droves. A quick scan confirmed he was using non-lethal projectiles and merely stunning the combatants.

Syn opened the chain-gun firing hatches and was about to lay the field to waste when she saw Waylan's men pour out from the castle gate. They turned the tide, and the battle was fierce but soon ended. She saw Wolf swing his gun around, shouting. Her sensors confirmed that the gun was depleted of ammo, and then Wolf threw the gun at a soldier who was running at a girl tied to a post. The gun struck the soldier in the head, and he was dead before he hit the ground. Wolf untied the girl, and she fell into his arms sobbing. Syn glared as he carried the little hussy off the battlefield and handed her off to a man at the gate. He then turned and looked out over the field at the prisoners who were being tied. Many dropped to their knees before him.

Syn tried to bring the satellites online to listen but couldn't. She had to locate and destroy the jamming device. She flew over the area and activated the external holo-projectors but wasn't able to materialize. After several attempts, she tried to materialize above Wolf but failed. Not being able to communicate with Wolf frightened her. She flew the ship a quarter mile from the battlefield and tried again. Splitting into candy striper Syn and Tomb Raider, she sent the latter to materialize on the ground. After two more attempts, she was able to overcome the interference.

Syn walked towards the battlefield, the ship hovering invisibly overhead. When she was on the edge of the skirmish, patrols spotted her and ran towards her. She started to lose cohesion and backed up until she was out of the jamming device's range. The soldiers closed in, and a sergeant ordered, "My lady, stop where you are. Who are you and what do you want here?"

"I am looking for my husband," Syn answered.

"Who might that be, my lady?" the sergeant asked.

Leveling her best smile on the man, Syn replied, "Why, Wolf, of course. Will you go fetch him for me? I'm terribly tired."

Chapter 19

A throng of King Waylan's men had gathered around Wolf on the battlefield, shaking his hand and inquiring about the strange weapon he had used to immobilize the enemy. He told the men it was a form of magic only he could deploy. Technically, this was true since the trigger was keyed to his bio signature and only he could fire it.

A soldier approached Wolf and said, "My lord, I have a message for you from a lady."

"A lady? What does she want with me, soldier?" Wolf asked, making light of it.

"Err...she wants you to come to her."

"Oh does she? Where is this lady, soldier?"

"Your wife is over there," the man said, pointing to the edge of the forest. Wolf pivoted and saw Syn standing several hundred feet away. She smiled and waved, and he walked over to her, accompanied by several high-ranking officers.

"Hello, love. I see you've been playing again," Syn said with a spirited laugh.

"Synthea, I've missed your voice all day today. I can't believe you came here," he said, putting strong emphasis on the word *believe*.

Syn caught the inflection and replied, "I didn't want to make the journey to see you. But I couldn't seem to get you out of my mind. It was like I was *jammed* into coming here."

Wolf nodded. He turned to the soldiers who stood behind him and said, "I need a few minutes alone with my...wife." When the men had pulled back out of hearing range, he asked, "Where have you been, Syn? I've been worried sick."

"Commander, I also was worried about you. I was about to level the entire field when I flew over and saw the fighting. I could barely see you, and at the last moment, I detected you were only stunning those men. There is a jamming device just inside the forest. It is crude, but effective. It disrupts all signals within a radius of five hundred yards. I was going to destroy it, but we need to study this technology. *Someone* on this world knows more than he is letting on."

"Were you able to pinpoint the power source?"

"Not accurately. Go five hundred yards in that direction," Syn instructed, pointing to the western edge of the forest. "Search there. I can fly over and triangulate it, but that shouldn't be necessary. The device is dampening my sensors, but it is relatively large."

"I'll take some men into the forest. If we can't locate it, you'll have to destroy the area."

"I will wait for you here, my love," Syn said, flashing Wolf a seductive smile.

"Right...honey."

Wolf rejoined the men who had followed him over to greet Syn, and he saw envy on their faces. He flashed a grin and then turned serious. "I need some men to search for something. It may look like the projector boxes we found in the castle. Let us search where the forest begins," he said, pointing.

Wolf paced his distance, counting off five hundred yards, which took him into the dense forest. The men began searching, and ten minutes later, a soldier spotted the object they were looking for. It was hidden in a hollow tree trunk, and it measured eighteen inches square and a foot deep. Wolf examined it. The technology was straightforward. A carrier wave was aimed at the ship's radio signals, disrupting control. It was a simple transmitter, tuned to the same frequency as Syn's receiving equipment and with the same modulation as Wolf's watch. Its limited power affected a small area, and it only overrode Wolf's signals and Syn's signals from the ship and the satellite's receivers. The device was a random noise generator; but what was impressive about it was that it fluctuated to random pulse, warbler, and then pulse. It also used a few other obvious and subtle jamming technologies. Whoever had built the device was skilled for this civilization.

Wolf knew that obvious interference was easy to detect because it could be heard on the receiving equipment. Whenever Syn tried to pinpoint it, the signal changed. The goal of obvious jamming is to block out reception of transmitted signals and to cause a nuisance to the receiving operator. That was why Wolf had heard the static earlier. Subtle jamming, however, was covert, and its interference caused no detectable sound on the receiving equipment. The radio wouldn't detect incoming signals, yet everything would seem normal to the operator. That is why Syn couldn't detect it. Only technical attacks on her modern equipment, such as squelch capture, would have alerted Syn's computers. Wolf would have to modify the radio equipment and change its unmodulated carrier to a modulated one.

Someone on this backwards world knew about Syn, and that worried Wolf. Whoever it was had detected the ship in space and knew Wolf was on this planet.

"What does this thing do, my lord?" asked the soldier who found it. "Does it make a ghost image?"

"The ghost image is called a hologram," Wolf explained. "No, this device does not make an image. This is a hiding device; it allows someone to shield themselves from my...powers. But I have a way to counter it." Wolf reached into the box and pulled out the crude batteries.

"Commander, have you disengaged the jamming field yet?" Syn asked in Wolf's ear.

"I have disabled the device," Wolf confirmed to Syn and the soldiers. "These objects," he said, holding up the batteries, "give the device its power. Without them, it is harmless."

Syn had been listening to Wolf and scanning the interior of the box. She transferred the data to her neuro-net and was just about to inform Wolf that he could destroy Jonar's creation when she detected a massive power surge. Then, a loud, shrieking noise came from underneath the box. Syn shouted, "Commander, watch out!"

As the high-pitched whine intensified, Wolf shook his head from side to side. Sharp pain erupted behind his eyes. He placed his hands on his head and gasped as wave after wave of pain rocked him. The men stared at Wolf in fear. One soldier held fast to his arms and asked, "My lord, are you all right?" An instant later, the device exploded, killing seven men and critically injuring six others. Wolf was thrown from the area and knocked senseless.

* * *

189

Wolf awoke to a cold rag on his forehead and a blinding headache. He looked around for a moment before the pain forced his eyes shut again, and he saw that he was in the med lab on his ship. After several minutes, he reopened his eyes and groaned, spotting candy striper Syn looking as desirable as ever. He dropped his head back on the pillow and dozed off, but then sprang out of bed and demanded, "Syn, how long was I unconscious?" His eyes widened as another question occurred to him. "How did you get me back to the ship?"

Syn smiled down at him and replied, "I see you're back among the living, Commander. Those questions are easily answered. One, you have been unconscious for about six hours. Two, I am an extremely desirable female. Do not forget I can think faster than anyone on this planet and that has its advantages. We are on the plain, outside the castle."

Wolf opened his mouth to ask more questions, but Syn touched a finger to his lips and said, "Shhh...When everyone was running to see you, I put on a backpack and ran up to you with the ship hovering above me. They wanted to take you into the castle, but I persuaded them to place you in the tent that I would erect. I used the ship's holo-projectors to show me setting stakes and supports into the ground. It looked like I set up this giant pavilion on the plain. The scene below us is a tangible hologram. You are asleep, lying on a couch, in the hologram down there. I also am there, wiping your forehead with a damp cloth and feeding you warm broth."

"So below us on the ground is a hologram of a tent?" Wolf asked, trying to comprehend.

Syn nodded.

"A hologram of me is lying in this holo-tent, unconscious?"

"Yes, Commander."

"You are there, talking to visitors who come to see me...and the ship is hovering over this hologram, cloaked and projecting the force fields with its cameras?"

"Yes, Commander, the ship is doing it all—or rather, I am doing it all. No one can tell it is a projection. I told you earlier I had aug-mented the holo-emitters. But I have unfortunate news. The explosives in the jamming device killed thirteen men. No one who helped in your search survived."

A look of sorrow crossed Wolf's face, and then he asked, "What were the constituents in the explosive device? And what was that awful sound?"

"The explosive was picric acid, made by nitrating substances such as animal horn, silk, indigo, and other natural resins. In 1742, Johann Rudolf Glauber mentioned it in his writings on alchemy. Crude but effective as you found out. What concerns me more is the ultrasonic attack on you. I am sure the feedback from your earpiece amplified it. I will make adjustments to help you resist it in case we encounter another LRAD attack."

"LRAD?"

"Long-range acoustic device, Commander. The human threshold of pain for sound is about one hundred thirty decibels. My sensors showed the attack reached one hundred fifty decibels before the explosion. The ultrasonic attack knocked you unconscious, not the explosion. The mystery is why it only affected you and not the other men around you."

"Someone is uncommonly smart on this planet," Wolf observed. "Did you figure out the jamming device?"

"Yes. I've built a jamming blocker and installed it on the ship's hardware. That should stop the interference. I also modified your watch." Syn handed him a new watch, smaller than the original. He felt a strange tingling in his arm as he put the device on his wrist.

"We will need to go to orbit to install the software in the satellites," Syn added.

"Is anyone in the tent right now?" Wolf asked. When Syn shook her head, he said, "I'm going to the castle. Open the rear hatch."

Syn complied, and Wolf looked down at the ten feet separating him from the ground. The top of the holo-tent was Avenger's underbelly, projecting a tent surface to anyone who entered. He jumped to the ground, and his hologram on the bed disappeared. NASA Syn was in the tent smiling at him.

"Can you pack this thing up?" Wolf asked. "I want you airborne as soon as possible."

"Yes, Commander, I will be packed in an hour. The furniture was brought out by the king's men. You'll need to have them come retrieve it."

Wolf kissed Syn on the cheek and walked out of the tent. A hush descended over the men gathered around waiting for news on Wolf's condition. One man took off sprinting towards the castle; Wolf assumed he was a runner for the king. Onel was waiting, and his face broke into a broad smile when he saw Wolf.

"My friend, thank you for saving my daughter. I am sorry you were injured. Please, accept this token of my appreciation." Onel handed Wolf an expensive ring with a gold band. The flat black surface was adorned with the head of a dire lion that resembled a wolf engraved in gold filigree.

Wolf placed the ring on his left pinky, the only finger on which he could fit a ring, and said, "Thank you, Onel, it is exquisite. I will cherish it always. Is Jhondra all right? I had to stun her to save her. You understand, don't you?"

"I saw it all. At first, I thought you had killed her because you couldn't save her. But then I saw the others stir, and I knew you somehow put them to sleep with the ghost lights you fired."

"Ghost lights?"

"Yes, the lights that came out of your cane. They hit the men and scared their souls from their bodies for a few minutes. I saw that the lights killed or destroyed everything else they hit."

"Ghost lights—that's a good explanation, my friend. It's close to the truth. Jhondra will be all right, just sore for a few days. I grieve for the men who died in the explosion. I should have expected something like that."

"No one can anticipate everything, my friend. We lost over two hundred and fifty in that battle, but Jonar lost six hundred slain, and one thousand men have sworn fealty to our king. That is, they will, if you will."

"If I will what, Onel?"

"Swear fealty to King Waylan and become the king's champion."

"Become his what?"

"His champion. You will be given wealth, privilege, and nobility.

A wife would be given if you were not already betrothed; but the king has decreed that you may have two if that is your wish."

"Two of what?"

"Two wives, of course. Jhondra has said she will share you if your bride-to-be agrees."

Wolf swallowed hard as Syn's jealous voice hissed in his ear, "Not a chance!" He looked over his shoulder at the tent Syn was breaking down and answered, "No, I must decline. In my land, a man can have only one wife. He must be faithful to her until death separates them. I am happy with my betrothed. She and I are connected in so many ways—we are inseparable."

"Good save, Wolf. I forgive you," Syn purred in a sultry voice.

Onel glanced over at Syn, who was bending over to pull a pole from the ground. Her shapely backside in the formfitting NASA uniform was causing the men watching her to shift from foot to foot and whisper among themselves, grinning like schoolboys who were seeing a bathing woman for the first time. "She is an admirable lady. Come, the king wants to see you about becoming his champion and to discuss other matters," Onel said.

They walked towards the castle, and Wolf noticed a sea of new tents pitched around the area. The recruits saw Wolf approaching and rose, cheering their hero. Dozens of men converged on him and dropped to their knees, extending their hands out in a cupping gesture, as if waiting for him to place something in their palms. Wolf shot Onel an inquisitive look.

"It is a gesture of respect and honor," Onel said. "To drop a knee to someone other than a king is unprecedented. I have not seen it happen. There are three ways to handle this, my friend. We should stop for a moment so I can explain before we pass these men."

They stopped walking and Onel explained: "You can ignore the warriors and pass them, which means you will not accept them to serve you. It is an insult, and some of these men will kill themselves. The second is to walk backwards past them all, which means you do not aspire to leadership, and you have no need for men at arms. The third is to touch the heads of the kneeling men and give them something of yours. This signifies that you accept their service and vow to fight for them as hard as they have sworn to fight for you. The men you touch are war-bound to you, and they will never break this oath. Only death can release them."

"Did not these men kneel to Jonar?" Wolf asked with a trace of sarcasm.

"No."

"How do you know?"

"In my entire life, I have seen just six men kneel to anyone," Onel said. "I am one of those six—I knelt to Waylan. The other five were men loyal to our father. They are in the Old Guard, and you will meet them soon. When our father died, they knelt to Waylan." Looking out across the wave of men, Onel added, "To see so many men kneel is unprecedented. This respect is not offered to common leaders. These men do this for a chance to prove themselves. They will attain prominence in the eyes of other men, and if they die, they will attain eternal bliss. What you do in the next few moments will mark them for life."

"If I accept so many men, won't it wrong King Waylan?" Wolf asked cautiously.

"That you ask the question proves you deserve the honor," Onel responded. "I say accept the men, but the choice is yours."

"Look at how many kneel," Wolf observed in wonder. "How many are there?"

Onel replied, "I do not know."

"One thousand five hundred and twenty, Commander," Syn said in his ear.

"I need to go to my tent for a moment," Wolf announced. He turned and walked back to the holo-tent. When he reached Syn, he asked, "Do we have anything we can part with in mass quantity?"

"Yes, Commander, we have thousands of washers and screws of different sizes in the maintenance bay. I will get you a box of stainless steel washers. They're about the size of a dime, but we have six boxes of them. Each box contains five thousand washers."

"That will work, Syn. How will you get them down to me?"

Syn pulled him to the side of the tent she hadn't yet disassembled. She had rotated the ship, and Nurse Syn dropped a small box out the bay door. It was about the size of a box of tissues. Wolf caught the box and opened it to inspect the shining pieces of steel. He then walked back to Onel and said, "I will accept the honor but only to hold these men from returning to Jonar. We will need them."

Wolf approached the first man, touched his head, and gave him a washer. The man drew a piece of rawhide from his boot and made a necklace of the washer. For the next three hours, Wolf distributed washers. When he finished, he had over fifteen hundred new men at arms; even some of Waylan's men vowed to serve him. Onel looked on with satisfaction, knowing the new soldiers would be a boon in the war against Jonar. After Wolf accepted the last man, he stuffed a handful of washers in his pocket and returned to Syn.

"You'd better keep these out just in case," Wolf suggested, giving her the box of washers.

Syn took the box and set it down. She had nearly finished breaking down the tent and was storing the imaginary parts in an imaginary canvas bag when Wolf asked, "How are you going to get rid of this stuff? The eyes of everyone out here are on you."

"I am going for a walk. I will walk into the forest with the ship trailing and disappear. No one will see me. I will have the ship hover low, so I can put the washers in the bay."

"Okay. I want you to go into orbit as soon as possible and install the new software on the satellites. Let me know when you've finished."

"Yes, Commander."

Syn turned away, and Wolf grabbed her arm, pulling her close. He kissed her tenderly and said, "Be careful, Syn. This madman has access to technology, and I don't want you hurt."

Syn beamed her most dazzling smile and promised, "I will be careful, my love."

Onel had walked up and smiled at the affectionate exchange. "Your woman will not be accompanying us to the castle?"

"No, Onel. She must return to the ship and prepare it for a possible attack."

"I will send guards with her," Onel offered. "Such a woman can't be out here alone."

"There is no need, Onel. She is tougher than I am. She will be fine by herself."

Onel looked doubtfully at Syn, who smiled and waved. She picked up her backpack and headed off towards the woods, vanishing into the vegetation. "I hope that fine woman can take care of herself," Onel said with a resigned shrug. "She is so beautiful, she would tempt any man to possess her."

"He's such a nice man," Syn whispered in Wolf's ear.

"Come, Onel, we have delayed long enough. She will be okay. I don't want to make the king wait any longer than necessary. Let us report our news to him. We have gained over fifteen hundred new soldiers for him to command."

From a hidden vantage point in the woods, eyes had been watching the exchange between Wolf and Syn through an antique spyglass. "So, the man of iron can be hurt. We have found a chink in his armor...but was it the explosion or the howler that injured him?"

A second voice replied, "He was indisposed for six hours. I had hoped it would be longer. Come, Sylvaine, let us retire to our keep to ponder this."

An impeccably dressed black man turned, an evil smile on his lips, and headed off into the woods, accompanied by the Templar Sylvaine.

Chapter 20

Wolf and Onel proceeded up the crevasse from the main gate and then crossed over the bridge, entering the castle and going directly to the baths. An hour later, they dressed and made their way to the throne room where a feast was being prepared in Wolf's honor. King Waylan presided over the event from his throne as the revelers talked and drank. He was still in pain from the stab wound in his side, and he was angry he had missed the battle in front of his own gates. When Wolf and Onel entered, he pushed away his pages' helpful hands as he stood and hobbled unassisted to greet them.

Wolf extended his hand and asked, "How are you feeling, Sire?"

"I am healthy, my friend. I am an old campaigner, and I have been wounded far worse. I heard you were injured by some type of explosion?"

"Not injured, Your Majesty, but it stunned me briefly," Wolf replied.

"Come, let us sit at the table, and you can tell me how it happened." Waylan returned to the table and seated himself. He was perspiring from the effort it took to walk, maintaining his role as a mighty king to his loyal subjects.

"Brother, you overtax yourself again. We are no longer young men. You must rest," Onel said, moving to Waylan's side. He signaled a page to bring the king's chirurgeons.

Waylan waved a dismissive hand. "You worry too much, brother. Besides, if something happens to me, you will be King Onel."

Onel's face blanched with anger as he admonished, "Say no such thing again! You joke with my love for you. I want only for my brother to live. I was the oldest and I could have had the scepter, but I saw in you something our land needed. This kingdom is nothing without you, and I would be even less."

Waylan considered his brother with a sad smile and said, "I love you too, my brother. I only mean to prepare you for what will come one day. Every day, my wounds hurt me more. I feel old age creeping upon me. I will not be able to run from death much longer. I have become slow and I stumble, while death's steps never falter in pursuit of me. Like it or not, I fear that by the coming of the next Brown Star, you will be king of this land."

Onel looked away, choked with emotion, and Wolf asked, "Sire, what ails you? I know your knee is injured, but what other pains do you have?"

"I have lived longer than most men. Old age is creeping upon me, and there is no cure for that. I am just growing old and weary."

"Commander, I can scan him," Syn said in Wolf's ear. "The new watch is equipped with medical capabilities. The only drawback is that the scanner beam must remain on the king for five minutes, and I will need a blood sample."

Wolf said to the king, "Sire, I have a favor to ask. It may help you to recover. But first I must ask...do you trust me?"

The king eyed Wolf thoughtfully. After a long pause, he answered, "Do I trust you? Who could stop you if you wanted my life? Yes, my friend, I trust you."

"What you are proposing will not require my brother to travel, I hope?" Onel interjected. "I fear he is not up to moving about too much."

"No, it will require five minutes of the king's time and a drop of blood. Nothing more."

"Is it witchcraft?" Onel asked, frowning.

"No, my friend, it is science."

"Science? What is that?" Waylan and Onel inquired in unison.

"There is an explanation for why and how most things happen. When you see a bird flying in the sky, you say, 'How does it do that?' Science looks at the bird and says it is using its wings to catch the air to lift and soar through the sky. The next step in science is to copy it by trying different things to duplicate the effect and master it."

"Here is another example..." Wolf pulled out his knife and picked up an iron poker from a fireplace, placing it on the end of the table. Swinging his knife into the poker's stem, he cut the heavy iron in half with little effort. He handed the knife to Waylan and invited the king to do the same, explaining, "Science is what has allowed us to make iron better and stronger."

"I see. Will the knife you gave me cut iron too?" Waylan asked.

"Yes, my lord. Your knife and mine are made of the same steel. The men from my land discovered this by adding different ingredients to the iron while they made it. Soon, they were able to produce armor, weapons, and many other items out of this material."

"I trust you. Use your science on me and tell me what is ailing this old body," Waylan said with humor in his voice.

"Do not be afraid when you see the red light. It will not harm you. Are you ready?" At a nod from the king, Wolf said, "Begin."

Syn activated the scanning light and said in Wolf's ear, "I will need him standing, Commander."

"Sire, please stand. Onel, please help him," Wolf said as Onel moved to his brother's side to assist.

Waylan was a smart man. Once he was on his feet, he took several steps back into the center of the room and extended his arms out to his sides. He then turned in a slow circle as the beam scanned him from head to toe. After five minutes, Syn said, "Scan complete, Commander. I need a drop of blood. Have him place it on the watch face."

Wolf helped Waylan to sit down and then said, "Sire, I need a drop of blood."

Waylan nodded, and taking Wolf's Bowie knife, he pricked his thumb. Wolf pointed to his watch and said, "Put it here, Sire." A drop of blood had formed on the king's thumb and he pressed his digit on the watch face. The drop absorbed into the faceplate of the watch.

"It will be an hour before I have results, Commander," Syn said, and Wolf advised the king, "Give me some time to study the readings, Your Majesty. I will let you know the results."

The men returned to their places at the table and more wine was served. Wolf recounted what had occurred on the battlefield and what he thought had happened to him. It wasn't the full truth, but it sufficed. Onel's eyes were on Wolf, watching him. Finally, he asked, "Have you given any thought to my proposition of becoming the king's champion?"

Glancing from Onel to the king and noticing both men seemed

eager for his response, Wolf answered, "My lords, please explain the duties. I mean no disrespect, but I have things I must do, and I must leave for extended periods. I can't be chained to a castle forever."

"Fair enough, I will explain," Onel said. "As the king's champion, you will dress in armor in the hall during any coronation banquet and challenge in one-on-one combat anyone who disputes the king's right to reign. The king's champion is counted among the most powerful nobles in the kingdom. When people arrive to see the king, you will be by his side, standing over him and defending him against every hint of menace by any who would challenge his rule. When the king cannot lead troops into battle, his champion will take on this duty. He is the king's shadow, protecting the royal family from harm. We realize you are a foreigner, and we hardly know you, but you have served us three times already in this capacity. If you need to go away for a time, we have agreed you may leave for as long as you see fit."

Waylan put a hand on Wolf's shoulder and said, "I hope you agree. I don't believe we can win this war without you. You have shown that men will follow you. I ask, as a friend, for you to help us."

Wolf gazed at the old monarch for a long moment and then replied, "Sire, I do want to accept the post. I know how the people love and respect you. But I will not be staying here for the rest of my life. I am an explorer and this requires that I move from place to place. I would rather serve you as a friend or a comrade in arms."

"I understand, my friend, and I am torn. As a ruler, I am sad you will not accept the honor to serve as my champion. As a friend, I am proud to have you fight for me. Do not judge our land and people on Jonar's ambitions. We have lakes, forests, fertile plains, and breathtaking natural wonders. I hope we can show them to you before you depart."

After taking a sip of wine, Waylan added, "I would like to bestow on you land and title." Wolf leaned forward to protest but Waylan cut him off. "Hold, and please let me have my say. For rescuing my niece, slaying the ruffians that attacked Haakon's homestead, and for the loyalty of the new troops, my honor demands you be rewarded."

"Your Majesty, I will not take your hard-earned treasure or wealth."

"I have fought across this land for them and accumulated vast riches. My vaults overflow with trinkets I have acquired and for which I have bled. Now that I have gained my wealth, I feel different. Have you ever noticed how all men crave for more, my young friend? No one is ever satisfied with what he has. When will I ever spend the massive wealth I have acquired? I pay my men and women well, not because I must but because I want to do so. I will not leave this land a hoarder of wealth who owned everything and enjoyed nothing. So for my sake, please accept the baronetcy of Olivier Province."

Wolf was at a loss for words. He had expected a small token of appreciation, such as a chalice or a bag of gems; not that he would have taken it because he had no need for wealth. But a large grant of land and a noble title was an extraordinary show of generosity by the king.

"What am I going to do with that much land, Your Majesty? And where is it?"

"If you go to Haakon's homestead and walk two days in any direction, you own it. Make your own borders. No one lives out there, so you can go further if you want," Onel replied with a chuckle.

"How much land is that?" Wolf inquired.

Syn chimed in helpfully. "The average person can walk about three miles per hour on flat ground, Commander. If you maintain that pace for twelve hours, you can walk about thirty-six miles. Using Haakon's farmstead as a focal point and going north to south would be seventy-two miles. Go east to west from his farm and that's another seventy-two miles. This means you would own roughly twenty-one thousand square miles of land, or a territory the size of what used to be the state of West Virginia."

"I will accept the gift after we defeat Jonar. Do we have a deal?" Wolf proposed, and the king responded with a satisfied grin, "Yes, my friend, we have a deal!"

Wolf was deep in conversation an hour later when Syn reported, "Commander, I have the scan results. The king has an L2 compression fracture on the dorsal side of the vertebral structure. He has a bruised right kidney, a cracked left femur, and evidence of multiple concussions. Two broken ribs on the right and two on the left have not healed properly—they need to be surgically repaired or removed, as they may be causing his side pain. A torn bicep on the right arm and a detached retina in the left eye also require surgery. He has a wedge of broken metal in his upper left thigh that is cutting him and causing significant pain every time he walks or moves that leg. His knee has a torn meniscus that can be arthroscopically repaired, and then it just needs to be drained. The blood issues I detect should clear up after the surgeries and antibiotics. All things considered, Commander, I'm surprised he can even move without crying out in pain. And yes, I can repair all of it, but not where you are. I need the medical unit."

Wolf turned to the king and said, "Sire, you have a lot of things going on in your body. The good news is that it all can be repaired."

"Really? You can treat my injuries?" Waylan seemed incredulous.

"It will take several weeks, Sire, but you can be completely healed."

The king smiled in delight at this news, and Onel's face lit up with a hopeful expression. But their smiles quickly faded when Wolf said, "The only problem is that I cannot perform the surgery here. It must be done on my ship."

"I cannot leave. The land is at war. If I leave, the soldiers will lose heart. The surgery must wait," Waylan declared with a sigh. He slumped forward, looking old and defeated.

"Commander, I have a possible solution," Syn offered. "At the top of this castle, in the warrior's crown, is a large flat area—a garden. I can hover the ship there and construct a holo-tent. We can do the surgery there."

Wolf relayed Syn's idea of placing a medical tent atop the castle. The king considered the proposal, looking dubious, but then agreed and said, "Very well. I will have the benches cleared from the area."

"I will leave after dinner to fetch my medical instruments from my ship, and I will return within the week," Wolf said.

"If he can heal you, Jonar will have no chance," Onel remarked, smiling at the prospect of having his brother healthy and vital again.

"If I can just sit down without wanting to cry, I will be happy,"

Waylan said with a grin. "This old leg wound causes me the most pain."

Onel turned to Wolf and asked, "Will you be able to remove the shard of metal in my brother's leg? Many have tried in the past but failed."

"Yes, Onel, I'm sure of it." Wolf answered. Turning to the king, he asked, "Sire, how did you get this wound?"

"I have lived with pain in my leg since I was a boy. Someone stabbed me in my sleep. The blade broke off, and the best chirurgeons could not remove it. I have learned to live with it, but I truly hope it can be healed because the pain grows worse every day. I would love to fight without the constant reminder of its presence."

Onel blanched at the thought of his brother being stabbed as a child, but he recovered and said, "If the other injuries can be fixed, my brother, I wouldn't worry about the pain in your leg."

"It still is a burden that hinders my movements. I am less of a man because of it," Waylan said.

"My lord, tell me of the Old Guard." Wolf asked, changing the subject.

"The Old Guard are my childhood friends and the children of my father's retainers. When I was a boy, I lived with my father who owned vast lands. He had serfs and slaves aplenty, but he was generous to all. I was known by all the people, and I ate and played with all. Many times the servants' children graced my father's tables and slept in the royal quarters."

The king accepted a chalice of wine from a servant, took a long sip, and continued. "Most of the children I played with had no titles. As we grew up, I invited the serf children to be trained with me in warfare. I grew bigger and stronger than others, even dwarfing my mighty sire, and I became highly skilled with weapons. Soon, even seasoned warriors looked to me for leadership. I had at one time over ten thousand men following me, and I knew each by name and sept."

Waylan's face darkened and bitterness crept into his voice as he said, "Jonar has robbed me of my childhood friends. I have six thousand left and my heart is saddened when I think of the men I will never see again. Their lives should be peaceful. They have bled and died to put me here, and I will serve them as king for as long as they will have me." Waylan raised his chalice to salute the old men who lined his hall.

"I apologize, Your Majesty, I was merely curious. May you all live to fight another day," Wolf said.

"So be it," Waylan said, gazing with pride at the men in the room.

They ate a quick meal and Wolf said his goodbyes. He left the king's chamber and made his way out of the castle, waving to the men in the tent city that had sprung up around the perimeter. These were his men, sworn to follow where he led. Wolf had elevated several of the older sergeants to the rank of captains and generals, and they were drilling the troops into military readiness. His oldest general was Titus, a scar-faced man with an enormous cataract on his right eye. He was a large man whose military planning impressed both Wolf and King Waylan. As Wolf approached the general, the man's face broke into a smile and he asked, "My lord, have you come to inspect the troops? Surprise inspections are good for the men's morale."

"No, Titus. I am going to Haakon's homestead. I will be gone for several days. Keep the men drilling and obey the king in my absence."

"Do you want a detail of fighters to accompany you, my lord? Jonar has sent out ruffians to harry the land," Titus said, concerned that Wolf might encounter trouble without support.

"No, my friend, I will be fine," Wolf replied, bidding the general farewell and setting out on his mission. He followed the path Syn had taken into the woods. After walking for about ten minutes, he inquired in a quiet voice, "Syn, where are you?"

"I am in the clearing up ahead, Commander. I will uncloak the bay doors."

As Wolf entered the clearing, the ship's access ramp materialized and he climbed aboard. Syn was waiting for him in the cargo bay.

"Commander, I have bad news. Jonar is moving his army on the castle. If he keeps his current pace, I estimate ten days before he arrives."

"Shit!" Wolf spat in disgust.

Chapter 21

"**I** gave King Waylan your idea of placing a holo-tent on top of the castle," Wolf said, "but how do I explain how it got up there when he asks?"

"Do you see the two red buttons on your watch, Commander? Press both buttons together three times," Syn said with a perky smile.

Wolf pressed the two buttons and a carbon copy of Syn materialized in front of him. "How did you do this?" he asked in amazement.

"Your new watch is a holo-emitter. It's nuclear-powered by an alpha source, and the hologram it projects is just that—a projection with no substance. It does have an amplifier that will allow me to become substantial for about five minutes in an emergency. Do not let anyone touch it or walk through it. When you get to the roof, shut it off by pressing the two buttons four times. My hologram will disappear. I will reappear using the ship's emitters and all will be back to normal."

Wolf found it strange listening to two copies of Syn talk to him in stereo, and he again thought about how lovely a woman Doctor Mason must have been. *What a waste*, he mused and then asked, "What about the equipment we will need?"

"Go back to the castle. Assemble thirty men and meet me at Haakon's homestead. I will unload four or five of the smaller cargo containers from the ship. They will be empty, but only you and I will know that. You'll order the men to haul the crates back to the castle and up to the garden area on the roof. We'll set up the tent and inform everyone that the medical equipment was loaded in the containers."

"That's brilliant, Syn! I'll meet you at Haakon's in three days," Wolf affirmed with an approving smile. Without warning, he pulled Syn into his arms and kissed her passionately. It didn't matter to him that she was not real—she was real to him. Releasing her, he touched her cheek affectionately and turned, departing the ship for the planet's surface.

Wolf returned to the tent city outside the castle and found

General Titus barking orders at a platoon of marching men. The old man looked confused as Wolf approached and asked, "What is wrong, my lord? I saw you depart into the forest...but now here you stand."

"I have reconsidered your offer, General. I need a detail of thirty men who can travel fast. We will have several heavy containers with medical equipment to bring back to the castle and I can't do it alone."

Titus smiled broadly, pleased that his soldiers would finally see some action. He called out to the officer in charge of the platoon marching before him. "Captain Eras! Our leader needs your men to accompany him on a journey. How soon can you be ready?"

Eras snapped to attention. He was the shortest man on the field, but his forearms moved with muscles that looked as if he could rip a tree out of the ground. He had a pleasant face that reminded Wolf of the actor Errol Flynn who had played Robin Hood so many centuries ago.

Eras saluted smartly and replied, "Give me a quarter turn of the hour and we will be ready for the march."

"Make it so, Captain!"

Eras called to his sergeant-at-arms and discussed the details of the mission, assembling a detail of thirty men. Fifteen minutes later, as promised, the men stood at attention behind Eras, and he announced, "We are ready, my lord. Where shall we go?"

"To Haakon's homestead. I will lead the way," said Wolf.

Eras led his detail of thirty strong fighters into the forest. The seasoned captain had joined Jonar's army three years ago against the wishes of his father, who held vast lands to the east of Waylan's kingdom. His father was a renowned fighter and a good king. When Sylvaine had come seeking his support of Jonar, he refused. He didn't like the pompous Templar; but Eras was young, and Sylvaine regaled him with promises of the glory to be won, stirring the young man's imagination. Eras wanted to prove himself as good a warrior as his father had been. After days of pleading his cause, his father reluctantly granted him a force of five hundred men. He counseled Eras to be honorable, brave, and above all, chivalrous—to uphold justice and bring glory to his family name. Now, three years later, Eras had won little honor; the glory he had won was fleeting; and chivalry was of no concern to the men he served. He was now seeing with his own eyes what his father had known years before—Jonar was not worth following.

Eras recalled a series of events that had shaken his loyalty to Jonar, but three stood out in his mind. The first was just over a year ago when he had come to Waylan's castle on Jonar's orders, leading his small detachment in reserve to the main army. Jonar's men had attempted to force the massive castle gates, and Eras remembered when the hand-to-hand battle erupted at Waylan's damaged portcullis. He had seen the aged king thunder out to the battlefield, swinging a sword that made naught of armor or shield. The old man led the charge himself, fighting on the front lines as an ordinary warrior, and wearing a grim smile that terrified Eras but at the same time filled him with wonder. The king's skill was extraordinary. Filled with remorse over the evil lord he served and yearning to serve great men, Eras had deliberately kept his men out of the fighting that day.

Waylan's assault on Jonar's men during that battle had been calculated and deadly. The old king had waded into the teeth of Jonar's best soldiers and champions, bowling them over and throwing their ranks into disarray as he methodically chopped them into dog meat. Soldier after soldier engaged the king and won a plot of blood-soaked ground for an early burial. No mortal man could hope to withstand his onslaught. When Jonar ordered Sylvaine and his Templars to attack Waylan, lightning, fire, and strange lights seemed to strike the king, scorching the earth around him but failing to slow his relentless advance. After several powerful Templars had been slain, Jonar ordered a retreat. That was when the Old Guard arrived— and they did not look like the decrepit grandsires he'd heard Jonar's men ridicule. They warded their king and fought like possessed men, slaying as many of Jonar's warriors as they could. They showed such bravery.

The second incident that tested Eras's loyalty was the botched assassination attempt on Waylan after Wolf had returned to the castle. Eras had been one of the few men who escaped that ambush. He saw Sylvaine throw a spear at the old king, and he watched this stranger Wolf take the spear in his chest and walk away without a mark.

Jonar's mistreatment of the princess Jhondra and using the defenseless girl as bait was the final straw. His father had told him to be chivalrous, and this cowardly act had marred his soul. Eras could not be a part of such an unscrupulous army nor serve a man so devoid of honor. He openly questioned the tactic, which brought a tongue-lashing from Sylvaine. When Eras stood his ground, saying it was dishonorable to use a woman in such a manner. Sylvaine slapped him in the face and demoted him to the rank of a common soldier. Enraged, Eras had decided to leave Jonar's army with his men the next morning, ashamed that he had wasted three years in the service of a tyrant. Then he saw Wolf emerge from the castle and take on Jonar's army of several thousand troops armed with nothing but his light weapon.

Eras yearned to be a trusted warrior and to serve a benevolent king until his old age. He wanted to be a part of something good. This outsider who called himself Wolf was a man to shake the petty leaders of the lands, and his aged friend Waylan was a worthy lord. Eras had been the first to bend a knee and the first to receive the silver disk—he called it the Wolf's Circle—that now hung from a leather string around his neck. He would serve Wolf until he was too old to fight, or he would die for him. When Waylan's nobles asked who had leadership ability, his own men had singled Eras out; and when Onel asked for his loyalty to Waylan and his illustrious champion, Eras pledged without hesitation. The other soldiers who had surrendered to Wolf also vowed to fight by the mighty warrior's side. *Yes,* Eras thought, *I will be a loyal soldier for so great a man.* His reminiscing was interrupted by Wolf's voice.

"Captain Eras, tell me of Jonar. What is he like?"

"Yes, my lord. Ten years ago, a man wandered in from the great wasteland to the east. He carried several books, and inside were wondrous things: pictures of animals, dwellings, and other things no one had ever seen. The man studied these books, and soon, he was able to make some of the objects described in the books. The things he made were marvelous, and Jonar performed miracles. He healed the sick and made life easier for all. He claimed he had discovered a vast storehouse of knowledge out in the wilderness, and he took his people to an enormous hole in the ground. They dug into the earth and hillsides, cleaned up the rubble, and built a castle over this mysterious hole in a matter of months."

Eras gazed off into the distance, remembering, and then he continued: "Thousands heard about the miracles Jonar performed and flocked to his banner because of them. He fed us, healed us, and showed us incredible wonders. Soon, other tribes tried to conquer Jonar. He unleashed his great knowledge and slaughtered them, using strange weapons he made. He then conquered the lesser kings and tribes in the area. For the last few years, he has been subjugating the lands. King Waylan and a few other mighty warrior-kings are all that remain."

"You said he had strange weapons? Tell me about them."

"I do not know what they are, my lord, but some were terrifying. On one occasion, he tied several animal hides to stones and threw them into a village well. Five days later, the people all grew tired, and then they suffered coughs and fevers. They seemed to recover, but when we returned two days later, everyone was dead."

"Probably anthrax, Commander," Syn suggested in Wolf's ear.

Eras looked around with guilt in his eyes and lowered his voice. "Then, he came with the loud weapons. They made men's ears and noses bleed. We had to keep melted beeswax in our ears to protect us. Still, we lost men to it. Jonar warned that he had other, even more powerful weapons he had discovered, and he would soon figure them out and unleash them on the people."

"What a monster," Wolf interrupted with anger in his eyes. "Jonar must be stopped."

"Yes, my lord. I regret I ever joined him."

Wolf studied the face of the man who had sworn to serve him. He appeared to be a good man, but time would tell.

* * *

The sun was setting and shadows danced over the forest as Wolf and his men set up camp in a clearing. They were less than ten miles from Haakon's homestead and had made better time than Wolf expected. His new fighters were eager to prove themselves. They had gritted their teeth and pushed beyond normal human endurance, trying to keep up with his giant strides. Wolf set the guards and then retired to his bedroll.

It was still dark, and dawn was an hour away when Syn's voice yelled in Wolf's ear bud, rousing him from a sound sleep.

"Commander! Wake up, Commander!"

"What?" Wolf yelled, bolting awake and rousing several men sleeping nearby.

"More than one hundred bio signatures are closing in on your position, Commander."

"Are they human?"

"I detect both human and animal bio signatures," Syn replied.

Wolf scrambled to his feet and shook several men awake, urging them to rouse the others and arm themselves. He dumped a stack of wood on the campfire, which flared and illuminated the perimeter of the clearing. All of the men were awake and armored with their weapons drawn when bloodcurdling howls erupted from the forest. To Wolf, it sounded like a pack of Tasmanian devils, and his soldiers stared into the darkness, trembling with fear. Captain Eras approached Wolf and said "Jonar has sent his Nanna to kill us. They are devilishly hard to kill. We may die here before the sun rises."

"What are these Nanna, Eras?"

"You will see, my lord. They are upon us."

"Commander, I ran a translation in all known languages. The word 'nanna' means daring or brave. In Norse legend, Nanna was a goddess who died of grief when her husband Balder was killed. Be careful, Wolf. There are one hundred of them," Syn warned and then quickly added, "I'm coming, Commander."

Wolf did not answer. At that moment, a wave of fantastically dressed warriors surged into the clearing, each holding two enormous animals that resembled large wolves with tiger stripes on their backs and tails. Each animal was about the size of a full-grown mastiff. Their handlers were dressed in tight-fitting, black leather outfits. Some were armed with whips and chains; others had short daggers, and each wore a black devil's head mask.

Wolf snorted derisively, thinking these warriors looked more like characters in a bondage video on ancient Earth. Knowing he was invincible and feeling confident he could protect his men from harm, he had trouble keeping a straight face. Suddenly, as the figures came out into the light and he looked closer, he inhaled sharply and muttered, "Shit! They're women."

"Aye, my lord, sometimes they take men prisoners and torture them for days. They have an herb that makes a man virile to the point of insanity. The men are used nonstop and when they have no physical stamina left, the prisoners are fed to the Nannas' pets."

The fierce band of Amazon warriors encircled Wolf's men, their animals snarling and howling with bone-chilling ferocity. One woman stepped forward, sniffing the air in an animal-like manner, and with a wave of her hand, the howling stopped. She handed her leashes to the handler next to her, snapped her fingers twice, and all the animals sat in unison. The woman boldly approached the besieged men and demanded in a disdainful voice, "Who is in command here?"

Wolf stepped forward. "I am in command, ladies. State your business for interrupting my sleep."

The woman eyed Wolf with a sneer and replied, "Well, you are a large one. I may keep you a while...for breeding stock."

A second woman snickered and said, "I'll bet breeding with us would kill him."

"I'll take that bet," Wolf said with a grin.

"Silence, you insolent fool! My master has commanded that we offer you mercy. If you all surrender now, we will let you live," the woman said as she removed her mask. "What is your answer?"

"I have a better idea. Renounce Jonar and join me," Wolf said.

The Amazon leader glanced around at Wolf's men in disgust and said, "Your men reek of fear and I see you have traitors with you. Why would I join you? What can you possibly offer to change my allegiance?"

"Skylla, he is the Warrior of Legend," Eras said, calling the woman by name. "Put him to any test if you doubt my words."

"Him? The Warrior of Legend? I don't believe you...but fine, I will put him to the test." She flashed Eras a seductive smile and added, "For old time's sake."

"I'm here, Commander. I have weapons locked on..." Syn's voice trailed off in Wolf's ear, and then she said, "Only you, Commander, can find such women."

Wolf shook his head, signaling Syn to hold off on an attack. With a confident smile, he said, "What are the tests, Skylla? That's your name, right?"

"Why do you smile, large one? Does my name amuse you?" the leader asked irritably. She was not unattractive; she had a full figure and an aura of power about her that unexpectedly excited Wolf. She had a superb tan, and her features reminded him of a Latina woman from the distant past. In fact, she reminded him of someone—a cross between Jennifer Lopez and Salma Hayek, two beautiful actresses from his days on Earth before Nomad rewrote the history of civilization. Eras and the woman locked eyes. After a moment, she broke his gaze and glared at Wolf, stomping a foot into the ground. "I asked a question, big man. Why are you laughing?"

"In my land, we had a legend of a woman named Skylla. She was once a beautiful nymph loved by a sea god named Glaukos. She had a jealous rival—a powerful witch named Circe—who used her magic to transform Skylla into a monster."

"What did this woman look like after she became a monster?" Skylla asked curiously.

"Are you sure you want to know? She became quite hideous," Wolf answered.

"Yes. Tell me."

"A writer from my past named Homer described Skylla as a creature with twelve dangling feet, six long necks, and grisly heads lined with triple rows of sharp teeth. Her voice sounded like the yelping of dogs. She was a horrible bane to sailors, and they avoided her."

The woman frowned and demanded, "How did the witch do it?"

"The witch turned her into a monster by poisoning the water of the spring where Skylla bathed."

"Enough of this fool's talk!" Skylla snapped impatiently. "Your first test is to subdue four Nanna at once. Will you try?"

"First of all, what is a Nanna?" Wolf asked.

The woman sneered and pointed at herself and then to one of the wolf-like creatures. "We are all Nanna. You will fight our animal kin, halfwit!"

"Do you want them killed or subdued?" Wolf asked in an almost bored voice.

"Either, but to keep them living and bend them to your will would be added glory. No one has ever done it."

"Okay, let's do this," Wolf said.

The morning sun had risen over the mountains and illuminated the forest clearing, giving Wolf a good look at the other warrior-women. They were all tan and, like Skylla, would have been called Latina in his time. Most were desirable and looked as if they had been recruited from a resort beach in Mexico. They formed a circle around him, and the four largest animals were brought forward. Wolf removed his weapons, and as he stripped off his shirt, his men applauded his massive, rippling muscles.

"Show off," Syn hissed in his ear.

"I'm ready," Wolf announced, standing with his arms crossed.

"Bola, Dihu, Rena, Fra...attack this fool and kill him!" Skylla yelled, pointing at Wolf.

The wolves ran at Wolf, swarming him, and his men looked away, certain he would be ripped to shreds. The women screamed with excitement as the animals tried to bite into Wolf and chew him to pieces. With one hand, he grabbed the scruff of one animal's neck and lifted it off the ground. He placed his foot on the neck of another, not killing it, but pinning it to the ground. With his other hand, he reached out and grabbed a third animal by the neck, letting the fourth chew ineffectively at his ankle. Finally, the wolves stopped fighting. He lifted his foot off the one he had pinned to the ground, and it ran into the forest yelping. He released the other two from his hands, dropping them to the ground, and they retreated to their owners with their tails between their legs.

Wolf went to a knee and grasped the remaining hound by the scruff and patted the animal on the head and belly, scratching it

213

behind the ear, until it rolled over on its back. It licked Wolf's hand in affection as its hind leg scratched in the air from the pleasure of Wolf's touch. He stood and the animal came to its feet, sitting by Wolf and looking up at him with fondness.

Skylla had watched in wonder, and now she approached Wolf and examined his body. She moved her face close to him and inhaled slowly, detecting no fear emanating from him, only masculinity. Not a scratch was visible where the wolves had attacked him. She ran a hand over his shoulders and chest, remarking, "You are as hard as a castle wall, but I am still unconvinced. The legends say you must be stronger than any man and no blade can cut you. Until I see it, I will not believe it," Skylla said, sounding less self-assured.

"What other tests do you have?" Wolf asked, pretending to suppress a yawn.

"Show me your strength, big man." She pointed to a nearby hill where a granite boulder about the size of a car on Old Earth was partially embedded in the ground. "Move that," she commanded with a smirk, knowing the task wasn't possible.

"Commander, that boulder is lodged three feet into the ground and weighs more than two thousand pounds," Syn warned in his ear.

Wolf nodded as he walked to the boulder. He groped around the undersurface of the rock, searching for a way to grasp its coarse, unyielding bulk. At one corner, he found what he needed, and crouching, he placed his hands under the rock. He strained to pick up the boulder, using his thighs to lift and pulling with his arms.

"Legendary Warrior indeed!" Skylla said with a derisive laugh. "He is a fool for even trying to lift that rock."

Wolf's muscles stressed under the force he was exerting. The veins in his arms popped out like ropes and coils, and his body chiseled from the massive strain. When the boulder lifted on the corner, the laughter stopped. Wolf stood and pushed the large stone over until it was resting on its side, then he knelt and let it tilt across his shoulders. Slowly, he stood with the massive rock draped like a blanket across his shoulders. He looked at Skylla and pressed the boulder over his head. He stood, trembling from the enormous weight as he gazed at the woman and asked, "Where do you want it?" Not waiting for an answer, he hurled the boulder ten feet into the small glen.

"You are certainly strong, big one, but I have one last test," Skylla said, drawing her sword. "If I can't cut you with my blade, I will believe." She swung the sword at Wolf's neck with all her strength. The blade broke upon contact, leaving him without a scratch. Skylla stared at him in stunned silence as Wolf smiled. She knelt, cupping her hands in front of her, and said, "Please, my lord, allow me to serve you. I will be loyal to you as will my warriors."

Wolf looked down and said, "Arise, Skylla. I accept your service and your warriors." He handed her a washer from his shirt pocket as he dressed. All of her warriors approached him, pledging their loyalty, and some promised other things that the women wanted to bestow on him.

"I'm watching you, Commander. Don't run off into the woods with one of these leather-clad lesbians," Syn hissed.

"Tell me, Skylla, what were your orders concerning us?" Wolf inquired.

"I was to find you and offer terms of surrender. If you refused, we were to kill you. I now see we might all have died if we had attacked. Why Jonar sent my warriors, I do not know. I was angry at first and was just going to kill you without offering terms of surren-der, but then I saw that handsome devil," she said, pointing at Eras. "He promised me something I had wanted for a long time, but fate decided against us."

"Now that we have a lord who is just, maybe we can be together finally," Eras answered. Turning to Wolf with a hopeful look, he explained, "My lord, Skylla and I have loved each other for years. Ancient taboo and sacred scriptures outlaw marriage to a Nanna, and Jonar wouldn't allow the marriage in his army, so we could not become one."

"Taboo on marriage?" Wolf asked curiously.

Skylla hissed, "As if we would even want a lowly man. We are elite warriors and require no man to fulfill us. Those foolish taboos and scriptures mean nothing to us."

"Tell me of these taboos and scriptures," said Wolf.

Eras nodded. "Verse One says: 'The wasteland has become a place of sin where women have usurped the role of man and strive to raise their own septs. Man was created in the image of Jesu and woman to serve his needs.' Verse Two: 'Abomination has arisen on the plains where women strive with men, use men for pleasure, and slay men for sport. The issue of this coupling must be put to death, for it was born from lust and spite.' Verse Three has caused the biggest controversy: 'Slay the woman of the wasteland, do not let her breed or you bring death to your door. If her child lives, then you will die, your wells will go dry, your crops will wither, the wasteland will devour your cities, and death will soon follow.'"

"Only fools believe such ignorance," Skylla scoffed.

"You know the masses have been raised to believe this for many years. It is enforced by death, but I would gladly accept that to be with you," Eras vowed bravely.

Skylla smiled at Eras with affection. "You know I would never allow you to put your life in danger, my love."

"My life is nothing without you," Eras said. Kneeling before Wolf with his heart in his eyes, he pleaded, "Will you permit us to marry, my lord?"

"Eras, you know my life is changed now," Skylla interjected, looking troubled. "You are asking me to give up my Enrica status. It took years for me to become the leader. Only the Nannas' best fighter can be Enrica. In all the years since my sister disappeared, I am the only one who passed the tests and lived. You ask not only for my love, you ask for my way of life."

Eras replied earnestly, "I know it is much, but will you say yes?"

Skylla looked conflicted and was about to answer when Wolf said, "Yes, I will assent. A man and a woman who love each other should never be kept apart. When we return to the castle, I will ask Randelf to perform the ceremony."

"What ceremony, my lord?" Eras asked with a frown. "If you, as our liege, consent and we both agree, then it's done. However, you are my leader, so you make the customs and pass the laws. Is there something else we need to do?"

Sadness crossed Wolf's face. "This world has forgotten so much.

We will talk to Randelf when we return to the castle. Now, come...we have delayed long enough. Let's get to Haakon's homestead."

Chapter 22

Syn had returned and was waiting for Wolf as he and his men emerged from the woods at the edge of Haakon's farmstead. She stood in the clearing, dressed in her candy striper outfit. Wolf's newly pledged Nanna warriors stared at her garb; some commented on it, while others talked of making similar attire. The men gazed at Syn's perfect body, and more than a few jaws dropped. Wolf rolled his eyes and walked over to Syn, embracing her and giving her a kiss.

"Commander, I brought all the items you requested," she announced, smiling sweetly as she caressed Wolf's arms and shoulders.

"As usual, you have made a spectacular entrance. You look beautiful, my love," Wolf said.

"In this old outfit, Commander? It hardly took me any time to put it on," Syn responded with a playful laugh, running her hands down her body for effect.

"This is my betrothed," Wolf announced to the men in his detail. "Her name is Syn. Let us secure these boxes quickly so we can return to the castle. Captain Eras, take charge, and start back at once. I am going to visit Haakon. Syn and I will catch up with you in a few hours."

Eras saluted smartly and ordered, "You men...secure this gear. I want two men on each box. Let's move it!" The soldiers jumped to obey their captain's orders, and several of Skylla's muscular women assisted. The containers had rails for lifting and transport, so carrying them back to the castle would be easy. Soon, all the crates were lifted from the ground, and Eras led his detachment back into the woods on the return journey to King Waylan's castle.

Haakon's property stood over the next hill, so Wolf and Syn walked up to the crest. As they looked down over the farmstead, it was evident Haakon had built his new dwelling sturdier.

"How far can you go before the holo-emitters fail?" Wolf asked.

"I have made some adjustments to the emitters, tripling their field of influence," Syn replied. "As long as the ship hovers one hundred feet above me at all times, I can retain my physical form indefinitely for up to two hundred yards."

"That's incredible, Syn!" Wolf noticed that his compliment brought a bright smile to Syn's face. She slipped her hand into his, and they headed down the hill.

Haakon was in the clearing below, chopping wood. Wolf called to him, and the man's face broke into a broad smile as he saw Wolf and Syn approaching. Slamming his ax into a log, he wiped his hands on his shirt and walked over to greet them.

"I see you two found each other. How is King Waylan?"

Nala appeared in the doorway, squinting into the sunlight. Before Wolf could answer Haakon's question, she spotted Syn and ran towards her with an excited smile. She ignored Wolf, who grinned as the women embraced and wandered off arm in arm, chatting.

"So they met again recently? When was that?" Wolf asked, turning back to Haakon.

"Your woman showed up a few weeks ago. They went walking for a few hours, and then Nala returned."

"What did they talk about?"

"Nala wouldn't tell me. She only said that you're a lucky man... and I must say I agree with her!" Haakon said with a chuckle.

"Your woman is very beautiful too, my friend."

"Yes, she is. I'm teasing you," said Haakon. He forced a grin, trying to mask his irritation at Wolf complimenting his wife.

Wolf's mood turned serious. "I didn't come here to compare women. I came to ask if you and your family would come to the castle with us. Jonar is approaching with thousands of men. You aren't safe here."

The grin melted from Haakon's face, replaced by a look of apprehension. "Nala and I have discussed going to the castle if war broke out. Now the danger we feared has found us. We will leave at the end of the week."

"Jonar is three or four days out, and we ran into skirmishers on the way here. You must leave with us today," Wolf urged his friend.

"I hate to leave my neighbors without a warning," Haakon mused, "but they have all been adamant about not leaving their lands, regardless of what the future holds. We argued on this for days, and after we quarreled, they moved back to their old homesteads."

"I will send a few men to warn your neighbors," Wolf said.

"We will come with you to the castle," Haakon reluctantly agreed. "Give me a short time to collect the children and pack a few things," He gazed at his new home with a look of despair, adding, "I am sure Jonar's men will burn it to the ground."

"When we defeat Jonar, I will help you rebuild your home myself," Wolf vowed.

Haakon brightened and replied, "I would like you to show me how they build in your land. Let us see what you do differently when this is over and peace rules the land."

* * *

The women talked and laughed, holding hands like best friends who hadn't seen each other in years, even though it had been just a few weeks ago that Syn had visited the farmstead and confided her secrets to Nala.

"Wolf told King Waylan that we are betrothed," Syn said with an excited giggle. "He even kissed me! I am so happy, Nala, I just might explode!"

Nala laughed and hugged Syn affectionately, trying not to show the flash of jealousy that welled up in her. She didn't understand her emotions towards Wolf. She took a deep breath and asked, "What have you decided to do about becoming human? Did I say that right?" Nala asked, hoping she hadn't insulted her friend by a poor choice of words.

"Yes, Nala, you said it right, and no, I have not decided yet. I am still leaning towards the android. I have made over five hundred of the actuators I'll need to automate the android. It is far more complicated than I expected, and giving the skin a realistic feel was difficult. I have one almost finished. It could pass for human, but what I want to create must be so much more. I have some ideas on how to make the android far more realistic. But it is a work in progress, and I will not reveal it to Wolf until it is perfect."

As she spoke with Nala, Syn eavesdropped on Wolf's conversation with Haakon a short distance away. Turning serious, she took Nala's hand and said, "Wolf is talking to Haakon about your family coming to the castle with us. I am sure your husband will agree it's much safer there."

"But why? My home..." Nala's voice trailed off.

Syn explained that Jonar's army would sweep through the land raping, plundering, and killing hapless villagers in their path. "You are coming to the castle with us, Nala, and I won't take no for an answer!" Syn said in a stern voice.

Nala nodded as she considered the safety of her husband and children.

"Besides, it will benefit me if you come to the castle," Syn said with a grin. "You can help me fine-tune the android."

"Of course I will help you, but I have no idea what to do...and first, we must fight this senseless war. Nothing but pain comes from these conflicts. Perhaps because I am a woman, I see things differently," Nala said with tears in her eyes.

Syn pulled Nala into an affectionate embrace and said, "Where Wolf and I are from, men fought wars that engulfed the world and millions died. The bravest men went forth honorably to defend what was right and just in their leaders' eyes. Equally honorable men stepped forward to stop them. Someday it may end, Nala, but history tells us men will fight their own shadows for a different spot in the sun."

"I know, Syn. I have lost my family to these wars. I will miss my new home, but I know it is safer for us to go to the castle. Let us return now to Haakon so I can pack some clothes."

* * *

As Nala and Haakon packed, Wolf noticed that they were taking very few items from the tents and structures. When he inquired about their other possessions, Haakon gloomily reminded him that the storm had destroyed most of their belongings and not much was left.

"I promise you, Haakon, the house I build for you will remain standing," Wolf said with confidence.

"Ha, I want to see that! Only the mountain castles remain standing. Are you going to bring a mountain here for me? You are strong, my friend, but not that strong," Haakon laughed.

Fifteen minutes later, the family had packed and headed out with Wolf and Syn on the trail that Captain Eras had taken. Less than an hour into the journey, the howling of the Nanna echoed through the woods, and Haakon froze in his tracks.

"We are in grave trouble. The Nanna have come out to hunt. We are all dead. There is nowhere to run. Those savages are scum and will have no mercy on us," Haakon said with a terrified expression.

"Relax, my friend, they are my Nanna. We encountered them on the way here, and I have won their loyalty," Wolf said.

"You accepted that garbage as your warriors?" Haakon glared at Wolf with contempt.

Before Wolf could answer, the Nanna warriors emerged from the forest. Trulane stared at the leather-clad women in awe and asked Wolf with a rakish grin, "Just how did you win this loyalty?"

"Trulane! Get your eyes off those women before I slap them out of your face," Nala ordered and then looked away, trying to hide her face from the approaching warriors.

"Yes, Mother," Trulane mumbled as Wolf and the others laughed.

Skylla walked up to Wolf, her hips moving sensuously. She gazed at the faces of Wolf's party and replied, "I see you brought friends, my lord." She glanced at Trulane and then looked more closely at Leesa and Brithee. She circled Leesa, inhaling her scent, and asked, "Tell me, child, can you fight?"

"Not very well, but I wouldn't die easily," Leesa answered petulantly.

"Would you like to learn how to fight? I can teach you," Skylla offered, smiling as if she had a grand scheme in mind.

"She will not be learning to fight, Skylla. I make the decisions for my daughter."

Skylla turned and came face to face with Nala. Walking around her, she sniffed the air and said, "So, Nala, we meet again. I thought I caught your scent. Your skills have waned, I see—you didn't catch mine. I always wondered what happened to you after the great battle. We thought you died in the wilderness. This girl," she gestured at Brithee, "looks exactly like you when we were children. I couldn't believe my eyes, but the nose never lies...she has our scent. My mother was sad beyond words when you couldn't be found. Now I see why you didn't come back to us."

Glancing at Haakon and the other children, Skylla forced a smile and asked, "So tell me, how is the happy homemaker? Have you finally tired of making pies, tilling the soil, and playing wife to a lowlander? We had it far more difficult at home while you were here playing this game, Nala. Our mother was distraught over your loss. She scoured the countryside looking for you and never gave up the hope you still lived. Now what will our mother say when I tell her I found my older sister, playing house and under the spell of a man?"

All eyes in the clearing moved from Skylla to Nala and back again. The resemblance was clear. Looking at the two women and then at Brithee was like seeing time-sequenced versions of the same woman over the span of twenty years.

"I left because I couldn't stomach the killing. I had done too much in my life. I hated it then, and I detest it now, Skylla. Don't try to sway my daughters to its dark call." Nala glanced at Wolf anxiously, hoping he wouldn't judge her. Haakon clenched his teeth, angry that his wife was more concerned about Wolf's opinion than his own feelings.

"It's already calling them...it moves in their blood, Nala. Look at their eyes—Nanna blood flows in their veins. Why did you not tell them of their bloodline? Your girls are granddaughters to our queen and should be in line for the throne. You know we are not numerous, and yet you have birthed two warriors who could add to our ranks."

Skylla walked to Brithee and grabbed the girl's upper arm. "This one will make Enrica. She is built as our grandmother was—lean, strong, and agile. She moves as you did at her age, my sister. You cheat them, Nala. You rob them of their heritage."

Nala glared at her sister. "I will not allow it. We will discuss this later in private, Skylla."

"Yes, I am sure we will, my sister." Skylla turned and walked away, her hips swaying in Wolf's line of vision. After a few dozen steps, she glanced back over her shoulder and laughed impishly. She had not missed the way her sister had gazed at Wolf.

Haakon turned on Nala and shouted, "You murdering Nanna bitch! Why did you not tell me this before now? You have caused me to sin by fathering this filth." He gestured obscenely at his children. "We have been together for many winters. You did not think I should know that a savage woman slept in my bed?"

A group of Nannas standing nearby overheard Haakon's insults and glared at him and then at Nala, expecting her to defend her honor. Instead, she growled, "Shut up, Haakon! You're alive—I didn't eat you. If you continue to disrespect me, you may die tonight." With that, she stormed off, fighting back tears.

Noticing Haakon's furious eyes on him seeking support, Wolf shrugged and said, "I can't help you, my friend. I have my own women problems."

Syn snapped, "Shut up, Wolf. I haven't killed you yet either, but your stupid remark just pissed me off, so who knows. You might die tonight with your dumb ass friend." She turned and followed Nala.

Captain Eras approached Wolf, addressing him in a low voice so his words would not be heard by other soldiers standing nearby. "Speaking as a friend and a man who is willing to die for you, my lord, you and your friend might be the most ignorant men I have encountered. Your women love you and apparently have been with you for years, but all you can do is make foul accusations about their past and speak foolish words. My father once told me: Take love where you can find it, hold a woman who deserves it, protect a woman who earns it, and love a woman who needs it. Wake up, fools, before you lose them!"

Eras pivoted on his heel and walked away in pursuit of Skylla. When he caught up with her, he pulled her into an embrace. She responded passionately, surprising Wolf and making Haakon even more enraged as he clenched his teeth and refused to even look at Nala. After the passionate kiss, Eras declared it was time to resume the journey, and he led the way forward to the castle.

The next few hours were uneventful. As the late afternoon sun dipped behind the hills, the detail stopped and set up camp. Nala and Syn wouldn't talk to their men, and Eras gazed from Wolf to Haakon and back with sadness. Syn wouldn't even respond to Wolf through his earpiece.

The night was nearly over and the camp was asleep when Syn's voice blasted in Wolf's ear. "Commander, a large force of men is approaching from our rear. They are armed. Satellite imagery also confirms Haakon's farmstead is burning."

Wolf sprang to his feet just as the Nannas' animals began howling. A soldier threw wood on the fire, lighting up the clearing as all hell broke loose. Men screamed in agony as spears flew from every direction. The wolves were released on the attackers, stalling their assault. The Nannas screamed and charged, launching a vicious counterattack as Jonar's men surged into the camp from all directions.

Wolf was astounded as he watched the Nanna warriors in battle. They were the most savage fighters he had seen. Their ferocity and athleticism were remarkable, and they were fearless. Some used their razor whips to slash the faces and bodies of the swarming attackers; others swung their whips, wrapping the razor lines around the necks of men who ran past, and with a flick of the wrist, decapitated them. Some less skilled Nannas hog-tied their captives, gouged their eyes, and delivered fatal dagger blows to their hearts or jugular veins. The men fought as men do, sword and dagger, cut and thrust—and then there was Wolf. He assessed the chaos and noticed that the attackers were ruffians, drug-crazed, and erratic. Several had overwhelmed one of his men and were eating him alive, cutting him to shreds and stuffing chunks of flesh in their mouths. Wolf drew his Bowie knife and began hacking at the crazed men. He broke arms, ribs, and skulls with wide swings of his rock-hard fists. He was an avalanche of muscle, stampeding across the field wherever the fighting was the fiercest.

Glancing at Syn, Wolf saw her wielding a five-foot katana with tremendous skill, protecting Reon, Brithee, and Leesa. The children cringed behind her as she battled Jonar's deranged fighters. Three lay dead on the ground at her feet; other ruffians charged her, and she chopped and sliced them with an uncanny skill, never giving an inch from the children she protected. Soon, she stood alone, unchallenged, as several Nanna warriors gazed her way in awe.

Suddenly, Nala's voice screamed, "Haakon!"

Four men had overwhelmed Haakon and were stabbing him repeatedly in the stomach. Nala wailed a bloodcurdling scream and grabbed an ax off the ground with one hand and a fallen razor whip with the other, wading into the battle. She slid between the men who attacked her so adeptly that they were dead before they knew she had hit them. She used the whip masterfully in movements that almost seemed choreographed, plucking out one attacker's eyes and ripping another man's face from his skull. The Nannas gave her wide berth as the small but incredibly fierce woman dispensed death to all in her path. When she reached the men who were attacking her husband, she eviscerated one with the ax, spun around and cut the second man's throat, and hurled the ax into the forehead of the third. The fourth ruffian stood up and charged, but Nala did a series of nimble back flips to avoid the screaming madman's clumsy attack. He charged again as she changed directions to a front flip. She launched into the air, flicking her whip and wrapping it around the man's neck with an incredibly fluid movement, landing on his shoulders. She pressed her knees into his back, tightened the whip, and strangled him until his tongue protruded and he fell dead onto his face.

"Haakon! Haakon, my love! Don't die," Nala cried, clutching Haakon, who was bleeding from his stomach, chest, and shoulder. "Please don't leave me."

Opening his eyes, Haakon glared at Nala with hatred and hissed, "Release me, you Nanna bitch." Then he shuddered and coughed up blood. Several of the Nannas who had come to help Nala spat profanities at Haakon; one of the women sneered at Nala, and the others walked away in disgust, laughing at her weakness.

As Nala tried to stop the bleeding, Syn came over and picked up Haakon. She vanished into the air before Nala could protest. Wolf had just reached Nala's side and grabbed her arm as she broke into hysterical sobs.

"Where has Syn taken him, Wolf? Where?" Nala cried. She grabbed Wolf's ripped shirt in her bloody hands and tugged on it while he gently held her in his arms to calm her.

"She has taken him where I took you when you were injured and nearly died. Syn will save him if she can. You know that, Nala."

Wolf saw a glimmer of hope in Nala's eyes as she allowed herself to be reassured. They turned back to the battle and saw a handful of Jonar's ragged men fleeing into the woods. Of the several hundred ruffians who had attacked the group, less than twenty had survived. The Nannas' wolves pursued them into the forest and ate well that night. Ten of Wolf's men were dead and six injured. Five of the Nannas' animals were slain or put down, but not one warrior died.

Skylla approached Nala, accompanied by her warriors. They knelt before her and Skylla declared in a solemn voice, "My sister, as always, your skill is inspiring to watch. No Nanna was ever so skilled as you. I apologize for my earlier remarks. Forgive me, sister." Nala looked at her and then collapsed on the ground, crying.

"What is wrong with her, my lord? Is she injured?" Skylla asked, glancing at Wolf.

"Haakon is severely injured and may die. His parting words to her were not kind."

Skylla looked out over the dead bodies in the clearing and sneered, "If he were here, I would kill him myself. No man should live after disrespecting a Nanna as he did. At the very least, I would cut out his tongue to silence his insults. Nala, my sister, you shame yourself by this display of weakness."

Wolf glared at Skylla, who shrugged her shoulders and walked off. He helped Nala up from the ground as Trulane and his siblings ran to her side. They were crying because they had seen their father fall. Wolf embraced Nala and consoled her as Eras and his men set about the grisly task of burying their dead and making litters for the wounded. An hour later, they resumed the journey. They had won another victory over Jonar, but the cost was high.

Haakon was barely conscious as he looked up and tried to focus on Syn. She seemed to carry his weight with ease. She laid him on a cot, and as he looked at her face and thought how pretty she was, two

227

clones of Syn entered the room. Haakon looked from one to the other and then fainted from shock.

Syn used the portable scanner to examine Haakon's wounds. His lips were blue, and his skin was turning a grayish pallor. The stab wound on the right side of his chest made a horrible gurgling sound. Syn's helpers removed his bloody clothes and washed his mud-spattered body, carefully cleaning dirt and clotted blood from his wounds. One started an IV to pump stimulants to help with the pain and bolster Haakon's faltering heart. The scanner revealed a collapsed lung, and his left kidney was damaged. He had several bowel perforations, and his spleen was nicked. Syn decided to repair the lung first. She inserted a tube and suctioned out the blood as her clones attended to Haakon's various other wounds. She then performed major surgery that lasted several hours. Haakon survived, but he was in extremely critical condition.

"Commander, I have stabilized Haakon, but it will be touchy for a while."

Wolf moved his hand to his mouth and whispered into his watch, "Good job, my love. I will let Nala know. How are Jonar's forces evading our radar scans?"

"Commander, it's some kind of jamming signal. I will work on it and try to counter it. When do you want me to return? Several people saw me disappear into thin air, and I carried away a man like a ghoul."

"Come to the castle gate a few hours before Jonar arrives. Keep Haakon sedated until later.

"Yes, Commander."

Wolf reached out and pulled Nala into a comforting embrace. She turned to him, her eyes red and swollen from crying. With an anguished look on her face, she asked, "Is there any news about Haakon?"

"Syn performed surgery and stabilized him. He is in critical condition, but he will live."

Nala fell into Wolf's arms, crying softly. "Tell Syn I will give her what she asked. For saving my Haakon, I owe her everything." She pulled away and walked to her children, forcing a weak smile and letting them know their father would live. Besides feeling tremendous relief, she felt a nagging guilt in the back of her mind because, again, she had enjoyed Wolf gently holding her. She was so confused by her emotions.

Skylla and Eras joined Wolf, looking perplexed, and Eras asked, "My lord, where did your woman take Haakon? I mean no disrespect, sir, but she picked him up and disappeared."

"Even the Nanna could not track her scent. Haakon's stench stops at the clearing's edge where he fell," Skylla added. "We searched into the brush but her scent and Haakon's vanished. If she was taken captive by the retreating soldiers, their foul odor could be masking hers." Skylla gazed at Wolf with a trace of suspicion in her dark eyes.

"Syn took Haakon to my ship. She is very strong and just as fast as I am. I saw her take him. When she has finished patching him up, they will return to us. You have sworn allegiance to me. I ask for your good faith on this. Will you two trust me?"

Eras nodded and Skylla replied, "Yes, my lord, we trust you."

Changing the subject, Wolf said, "I want to ask you, what is wrong with these ruffians?"

"They use drynox, my lord," Eras replied, as if that explained everything.

"Drynox? Onel mentioned it. Tell me what it is."

"It is a drink made from swamp moss. It numbs the ruffians' minds from pain and makes them fearless. It enters the bloodstream in minutes, but it must be continually sipped to maintain its effects. Jonar's men lace their food and water with it. Some place it between their teeth and lip, sucking the bitter root all through the day. When they are about to die, they act like animals hungering for flesh. Jonar has done something to the moss that makes the ruffians utterly loyal to him, and only his moss can make their nightmares and pains stop, they say. Some still go crazy and Jonar has to kill them. You have fought them three times now—at Haakon's farm, outside the castle, and today."

"I sensed something was wrong...they seem to feel no pain or fear. I hate killing them. I feel like a murderer every time I have to defend myself."

"No, my lord, it's not murder, it is mercy. They will all die anyway. Drynox kills in a few years, and it is a horrible death. Those who use it urinate all their blood out towards the end and die screaming in pain. They fight Jonar's wars because they want to die."

* * *

Three days later, an hour before sundown, Eras led his detail across the plain and up to the castle's main gate. The presence of the Nanna warriors provoked a stir among the troops camped out in the tents. Eras reported to General Titus with Skylla at his side. The remaining soldiers went to their bunks after placing Wolf's containers at the gate. After sundown, Skylla and her warriors took an unoccupied area by the outer woods and made camp.

Wolf appropriated a few men to help him carry the containers into the castle. After the last container had been hauled up to the roof, he dismissed the soldiers and asked, "Syn, how is Haakon?"

"He is still unconscious, Commander. He was badly wounded."

"Where are you, my love?"

"I am directly above your head. Shall I deploy the holo-tent?"

"Yes, I was going to suggest that."

"Step into the stairwell, Commander. I need to land the ship and it will be a tight fit."

Wolf moved back into the stairwell. Moments later, a minor jolt shook the castle as the weight of the ship made contact with the roof, dislodging bits of debris onto Wolf's head.

"Damn, Syn, will the roof hold it?"

"Yes, Commander. I only fifteen percent of the ship's weight is resting on the roof. I did not want to risk the roof collapsing. Come on in, the tent is ready."

Wolf stepped out of the stairwell and saw that Syn had erected the huge tent perfectly. He touched it; the material was pliant in his hands. He walked to the entrance and looked inside, seeing a couch, a bed, a huge table with eight chairs, and in the rear, the open ramp going up to the ship.

"This is nice, Syn. Again, you did a fantastic job."

Wolf walked through the tent to the ramp at the back and climbed up into the ship, going directly to the med lab to check on Haakon. The man was hooked up to a bank of diagnostic apparatus that monitored his vital signs with beeps and flashing lights.

"How does Haakon look to you, Syn?" Wolf asked. "He seems pretty pathetic to me."

"He was wounded severely, Commander. A few more minutes and he would have bled out. I had to repair a collapsed lung, his stomach sustained major damage, and I had to remove his right kidney and spleen. I will not let him regain consciousness for a few more days. He needs the sleep. Can you bring Nala up? I want to assure her of his comfort and safety."

"Yes, but I meant to ask you, Syn. When did you and Nala become such good friends? Oh, she said to tell you that you can have what you wanted from her. What's going on?" Wolf asked, intensely curious.

"It's nothing, Commander. She and I merely have become friends. I stopped by Haakon's farm to check on her condition. She is a good woman, and we talk girl talk."

"How can I bring her here? The last time she saw you, you were in the forest fighting."

Syn gave Wolf an appraising look and slowly answered, "Wolf, Nala knows what I am. She has known for a long time. Just go get her."

"What have you done to us, Syn? I hope no one else here is aware of our presence," Wolf said, looking deeply troubled.

"Commander, she knows what I am, but she does not know who we are. Just go get her. I'm sure she is worried. Go, please. We will talk later."

Wolf exited the tent. His first stop was to update King Waylan on his trek to Haakon's homestead and his return with the containers that supposedly held the medical gear needed for the monarch's surgery. Then he walked out to the plain in front of the castle. It took him nearly an hour to locate Nala's tent in the vast military camp. He called out to her, and when she emerged, he took a step back in shock. She was dressed in a Nanna outfit and seemed ready for battle. Her

231

once sweet face was rock-hard, her eyes cold and devoid of feeling. Wolf could not recall seeing so lovely a face turn so lifeless, so fast.

"He's dead, isn't he?" Nala said with no emotion. "Syn couldn't save him."

"Quite the opposite, Nala. Syn wants to see you. She wants to assure you that Haakon will live. I need you to come with me."

"I can't leave my children here with Jonar's army coming."

"Syn told me you know about her, Nala. If so, then you know what I tell you is the truth. She has saved Haakon, and he will live. Trust me, Nala. Come to my quarters in the castle."

"Fine," she agreed in a monotone. Turning to Skylla, who had come out of the tent, she said, "Wolf is taking me to the castle to tell me about Haakon. Watch over my family, my sister."

"I will watch them as if they were my own. No harm will come to them," Skylla vowed.

Wolf took Nala's hand, and as they walked towards the castle, he asked, "Why are you dressed like that, Nala?"

The woman turned her once-bright eyes to Wolf and said, "I have tried to live tame like a lowlands woman, but Jonar has made it impossible. I had forsaken my heritage for a man I thought worthy. Let me tell you why my sister and the others kneeled to me. Many winters ago, my mother chose me to lead our people. I had seven older sisters who hated me. My mother and grandmother saw my potential when I was very young, and I was given training by the Erinyes—three old crones who have proven themselves as elite fighters through trial by combat, and their skills are incredible. No one knows how many years they have lived, and no one had seen them in years, but when I was three, they appeared. I was given to them to train, and for twelve years, day and night, I was taught to fight. When I returned, my mother had given birth to Skylla. She was nine at the time, and I was fifteen. We hit it off immediately. My mother was proud that the crones had chosen her daughter, and she had me fight all her seasoned warriors."

Nala met Wolf's gaze and added, "It is not bragging when I say I am the most skilled Nanna ever to live. I have fought many battles and killed hundreds by my whip and blade. One day, Jonar came to our people to demand our allegiance. We fought all day and into the night. We killed hundreds of his men, but they kept coming. Our warriors fought until they fell from exhaustion. Jonar's soldiers never attacked them while they lay unconscious—it was obvious he wanted us alive. Hundreds of my sisters were taken captive. They were chained and forced to lie on the ground, shamed at being defeated by common men.

"My mother and I fought harder than the rest, and we were still fighting when the others awoke. Hundreds of Jonar's men surrounded us and continued trying to take us alive. Finally, Jonar himself arrived. He ordered his men back and walked towards my mother, staying out of her whip range. He said something to her, and she shouted 'No!' several times. Then, he smiled and raised his hand. Lightning shot out of it, hitting her, and she fell to the ground like a sack of fruit.

"We had heard of his lightning weapon, but we believed it was a lie. It was rumored that the weapon did not kill but only stunned, so I tried to reach my mother to rescue her. Jonar shot his lightning at me again and again, driving me back. I fought and killed his men as they tried to subdue me. They dragged my mother over to the other captives, and when I saw her chained, I went mad. I became one with my whip and blade, and his men fell screaming all around me. For some reason, Jonar did not shoot his lightning weapon at me again. But the odds were so unequal that my mother signaled to me to escape. I broke through Jonar's lines and fled into the forest, bloody and severely wounded. I came upon a small village, and I stole clothing off a clothesline, discarding my Nanna gear. At some point, I wandered onto Haakon's land and collapsed. It was raining when he found me, and I was dying. Haakon nursed me back to health. I married him and bore his children. I would have stayed with him for the rest of my life. I swear, if that man dies, I will kill Jonar with my teeth." Nala uttered the words with such resolve that Wolf gained a new respect for her.

"Haakon will recover, I promise you. Bring back that smiling face for him, Nala. Remove the gorgon's mask you now wear."

"I will not smile until he smiles. My heart will not allow it.

Please, let us hurry," Nala urged, still thinking of Wolf's hard, powerful arms around her body.

They went through the castle and up onto the landing where the holo-tent stood. Wolf glanced around and whispered, "Syn, we're here." They walked under the tent flap, and Syn was waiting for them at the top of the ship's ramp. She frowned when she saw Nala dressed in a Nanna outfit but gave her an affectionate hug.

"Come, Nala, I want to talk to you," Syn said, leading the woman up into the ship. "I have your husband here. I have stitched his wounds, and he is recovering."

"How is it possible, Syn? How did you get him here? You could not have gotten here before us," Nala said.

"Remember what I told you about myself, Nala. I have other abilities that may seem like magic to you. Come, your husband waits."

As they walked through the ship to the med bay, Wolf noticed that Syn had concealed the walls and computer monitors with carpets and paintings to give the interior a rustic, homey look. When they reached the med bay and Nala caught a glimpse of Haakon, she cried out and ran to his side. He was lying on a simple cot with wires from the EKG attached to his chest and an IV in his arm. An oxygen mask covered his face, causing Nala to gasp in fear.

"The things on him are keeping him alive until his body is strong enough to take over," Syn explained. "Do you trust me, Nala?"

"Yes, I trust you, Syn. You hold my heart here. I will do whatever you want and give you any price you ask, but save him for me."

Nala broke into tears, and Syn gently hugged her, whispering, "I will save him because I love you, Nala. Have faith in me. You are the only person on this planet who knows my secret. Bring your family here—I will ask Wolf to have lodging constructed on the roof next to ours. You will stay here to help me with Haakon. No one must know he is here yet, do you understand?" Syn asked, looking into her eyes.

"I do not understand, but I will remain silent," Nala promised. "May I sit with him for a while?"

"Stay as long as you want, Nala. I will have Wolf fetch your family."

Wolf followed Syn out of the med bay. Once outside, he grabbed her arm and demanded, "Syn, what is going on?"

"Commander, release me. Take your hand off of me now and never place it on me in anger again," Syn said with cold intensity.

Wolf released Syn and looked into her eyes. "I'm sorry. I worry about you, Syn. When these surprises happen, it makes me a little crazy. Forgive me."

"I feel the same about you, Commander. I have done nothing to jeopardize us. Nala is a good woman...she will not betray us. I had questions my database could not answer. She helped me, and I still need her help."

"We need a plan to get you and Haakon into the castle," Wolf said, changing the subject. "I want you to come to the gate with Haakon on a stretcher. How can we accomplish that?"

"You will take a trip to the woods alone. A day later, we will return to the castle together carrying Haakon on a litter."

"How can we do that? The ship is stuck here, holding up this gigantic tent."

Syn laughed softly and kissed Wolf's cheek. "You forget the watch, Commander. I will augment its programming slightly so it can maintain my hologram long enough to get us back up here. Have Trulane guard the stairwell. I will ask Nala to see if her sister and the Nannas can relieve Trulane to keep the curious away from here while you're gone."

"I'll inform the king and depart within the hour," Wolf said.

"Give me your watch, Commander. I will adjust it and have it ready before you leave."

Wolf hugged Syn and then went to speak with King Waylan. The monarch was in his throne room with his commanders and Skylla, Titus, and Eras. Wolf greeted them and told the king, "I need to leave for a day or two, my lord. Syn will need my help getting Haakon to the castle, so I am going out to meet her."

"I will send a squadron with you for safety," the king offered.

"No, my lord, I will go alone. I can travel faster by myself, but I appreciate the offer. I will depart as soon as I return to my quarters and pack some gear. Nala and her family will stay in my quarters while I'm away. Can your men ensure that they're undisturbed?"

"I will place a guard on the lower stairs with instructions to let Nala and her family pass. I do wish you would take guards, my friend, but it's your choice. Be safe, my friend," the king said as he limped slowly over to shake Wolf's hand.

Chapter 23

Wolf departed the castle and headed into the forest towards Haakon's farmstead. After thirty minutes, he activated his redesigned wristwatch. Syn's hologram flickered and then stood before him, appearing vibrant and alive.

"Let's walk a few more miles and set up a secluded camp," Wolf suggested. "We'll wait a day or two and then return. Can the watch keep you here with me that long?"

"Yes, Commander." After a pause, Syn asked, "What are our plans for the future? We have been here a few weeks, and already we have been involved in combat and killed many people. Have you decided to live in this little kingdom, or will we move on and explore this world?"

"I don't know, Syn. We are alone here. No one is coming to save us, and we have no way back to our age. You know I like these people. Once we eliminate Jonar, this land could become a paradise. Let us help in this battle and then try to set down roots. We can use this land as a base of operation until we decide where to go from here."

"I only ask because you seem to relish being the legendary warrior. I know you believe you are invincible, but you were knocked senseless for hours by a crude bomb. What will you do if Jonar uses something bigger? He made those explosives, and he can make more, refining his method until he develops a weapon that can seriously injure you. It might have been the crude LRAD system that knocked you unconscious. I believe you are vulnerable to a sonic attack. If amplified sufficiently, Commander, it could kill you."

"Jonar must be stopped," Wolf said. "Hell, not many people are left on this planet, Syn. After this battle, there will be fewer. How can humanity rebuild if petty warlords keep waging wars and killing everyone? I admit Jonar is smart—maybe he is this era's Albert Einstein. If we can get him to give up his mad dream of conquest, perhaps we can use his knowledge to make this world better."

"There will always be those who aspire to rule, Wolf. It is in the human genome. The other thing you overlook is that many people prefer to be governed. They want to follow a strong leader with lofty ideas, and they want someone else to make their decisions. Why worry about food when it will be provided? All the people need to do is proclaim one man or another as king and the process begins again. It's just the way it is."

"You're becoming cynical," Wolf observed.

* * *

Wolf and Syn spent two nights in the secluded woods. On the second night, they were sitting by a small campfire, stargazing. Wolf rested his head in Syn's lap as they discussed the politics and customs of this primitive world, the inhabitants they had befriended, and the future. The night wore on, and the fire burned low. Syn's eyes were closed and she hummed a tune with a dreamy look on her face. Wolf had never felt so at peace with a woman before and wished the night would never end. He fell asleep thinking, *If only...*

At sunrise the next morning, Wolf reluctantly announced, "It's time to head back to the castle." Syn took his wrist, adjusted the holo-emitters on his watch, and disappeared. Moments later, she reappeared in her Tomb Raider outfit, standing next to a cot with Haakon's body. Wolf lifted the back end of the stretcher and Syn took the front as they set out for Waylan's castle.

For the next hour, Wolf's eyes were locked on Syn's shapely posterior as they walked. Finally, he asked, "Syn, are you enhancing yourself?"

"What do you mean, Commander?"

"Never mind," Wolf answered, his eyes still glued to Syn's derriere. He was so entranced watching her sensuous curves that he stumbled several times. On each occasion, Syn stopped and turned to ask, "Are you all right, Commander?" Wolf mumbled an unintelligible reply, and they resumed the journey.

By the time they reached the castle gate, Wolf had decided that he would need a gallon of strong liquor and an ice-cold shower. They passed through the gates as onlookers offered to carry Haakon's litter, but Wolf declined the help. After what seemed like a long, tedious walk, they reached the bridge and made their way up to the crown and the holo-tent. Haakon's children greeted them with excitement, but when they saw their father's unconscious body, they began asking questions. Wolf explained that they needed to move Haakon inside and promised to return for them after Haakon had been put into bed and hooked up to monitoring equipment.

As Wolf was speaking, Nala walked out and saw the litter with Haakon's body. She had just left Haakon in the med lab with Syn sitting at his bedside—now, here was Syn with Haakon on a cot. Wolf saw her startled expression and gave her a reassuring grin as they walked past her with the litter.

Once they were inside the ship, Nala blurted, "You two are the strangest people I have ever seen! Is this my husband that you carry, or is the one inside that room my husband?"

"Nala, the one we carry is like me—just a hologram," Syn responded. "We needed an explanation for how Haakon came to be in the castle, so we thought carrying him in this way would satisfy the people's curiosity."

The cot bearing Haakon's body vanished as Syn shut down the software generating the hologram. With a look of confusion, Nala said, "I trust you two, but this is terribly scary. I don't know if this is real or I am dreaming and I will wake up in my home."

* * *

The next morning, Syn alerted Wolf that Jonar's army was on the move and would arrive in less than a week. She also reported that she had isolated a crude jamming signal and adjusted her sensors to filter it. Wolf relayed the news to King Waylan and warned, "They are bringing siege weapons that will hurl rocks at the gates and rams to batter what is left. He has about twenty thousand fighting men with him."

"A vast army," said the old king with a scowl. "We have prepared for this attack. We will withstand this army as we have all the others. The surgery you offered to perform must wait. I can't risk being stuck in bed while Jonar threatens my gates."

"My lord, I can do several things to help you. We need to get that piece of metal out of your left thigh, and at the same time, I will fix the cracked bone and broken ribs that have not healed properly. I can also fix your right arm. It will be sore for a few days, but you'll be able to use it. You'll need to wear a patch on your left eye for up to five days. I can fix the sore knee and reduce the swelling. Then, I will examine the fractures in your back to see can be done quickly to stop the pain."

Waylan turned to his brother and said, "You are in command, Onel. I will go with Wolf to his tent for the ministrations he has offered. Defend the castle at all costs."

"Aye, my brother, it will be as you say."

Wolf and Waylan walked to the tent. The aging monarch was ecstatic at the prospect of suffering less pain. Once inside, Waylan looked around. Nala was sitting next to Haakon's bed, which had been moved to the other side of the medical bay. Syn was standing near an operating table, dressed in her candy striper outfit. When Waylan caught sight of her, his jaw dropped, and with a lusty gleam in his eyes, he said, "If I die today, may I wake up in this woman's arms."

Syn walked to the king and leaned forward to kiss his cheek. "I see you're a feisty old man," she said with a smile. "Come, you need to wash before I can work on what ails you."

"Woman, I washed last month. I do not need to bathe again until next month."

"Wrong, old man. You will wash, or I will have Wolf hold you down while I wash you."

"Ha! I might let you, lass! Show me to the bath."

Wolf led the king to the shower. As Waylan removed his clothes, Wolf was amazed by the muscle mass the elderly monarch retained. When the warm water hit Waylan's skin, he stared at the shower spigot as if it were magic. Wolf explained the principle to him, and the king asked if it could be built into his castle. Wolf assured him it was possible.

"With water feeling like this and making it so easy, I might bathe every week," Waylan laughed.

When they returned to the med bay, Syn had moved Haakon to

the lab area, away from the operating room. She directed the king to lie on the table and started an IV with anesthesia. Soon, he was snoring peacefully. Syn inserted an airway in his mouth and put him on oxygen. Operating on the thigh with the metal shard was the first challenge. Soon, she discovered Waylan's limp was caused by a two-inch piece of a broken sword tip. She made the necessary repairs with the precision of a world-renowned surgeon, using a laser to stimulate bone growth, and then moved to the ribs. Opening Waylan's stomach with a scalpel, she repaired two damaged ribs and replaced two others with titanium bars.

Wolf helped turn Waylan on his stomach, and Syn worked on his fractured vertebrae and compressed disc, using a special polymer to repair the fractures. Wolf turned the king over again, and Syn worked on the torn bicep. The damage was worse than she had expected, and it required more time than she had planned, but the result was satisfactory. She then drained Waylan's bad knee and, using dissolvable stitches, she fixed the tear in the meniscus. Finally, she repaired his detached retina and gave him an infusion of antibiotics to complete the operation. The surgery had taken sixteen hours.

"Amazing work, Syn. When will you wake him?"

"I will keep him under sedation until after Jonar's army arrives. We should be able to repel one or two attacks before we will need his sword."

"I will lead the battle while he is incapacitated," Wolf said. "If necessary, I will destroy the siege engines myself."

"Commander, again, do not underestimate Jonar. He is exceptionally intelligent. By now, he knows you are vulnerable to something he has created. He may have a nasty surprise for you."

"Regardless, Syn, I will prevail. This world is all that is left of my time. We can't allow them to repeat our senseless wars. I might only stun Jonar's men. I don't want to kill any more of these drug-crazed fools. We need to run some tests. The drug Jonar uses must have an antidote."

"I agree. We will need blood samples from several of the men. I can place a mobile emitter up here to keep the tent in place. That will allow me to take the ship into battle and end this war with no loss of life for Waylan's people."

"That's too much technology, too fast," Wolf cautioned. "Maybe a few stun grenades or something."

"I will see what I can come up with, Commander." Syn paused for a moment and then said, "It is time to wake Haakon. He is well enough to put him off the ship. I can rig the holo-emitters to look innocuous in the tent area for his care. Let's go to Nala."

Wolf followed Syn to Haakon's cot and saw that Nala had fallen asleep holding his hand. He reached down to touch her shoulder, and the moment his fingers made contact, she sprang awake, holding a knife to his throat. She stared at Wolf with a crazed, disoriented look for a few seconds, and then recognition came into her eyes.

"I'm sorry. I was having a nightmare."

Wolf frowned at the once gentle woman, deeply troubled by her reversion to the violent, bloody past she had lived. With sadness, he realized Nala might never again be the smiling beauty he once knew.

"It is time to awaken Haakon and move him out into the larger area," Wolf said.

"Let us wake him immediately. I long to hear his voice," Nala said with a happy smile.

Preparing Nala for what was about to happen, Syn explained, "He will awaken slowly. He will open his eyes and then go right back to sleep. His body is healing, and it will take time. When we wake him, I want you and your children to talk to him, call his name calmly, and tell him to wake up. It may be days before he recognizes you. I don't want you to be alarmed at the slow progress. Are we clear on this?"

"Yes, Syn, I understand."

"Good. Now move away from him, please, so I can disconnect this equipment and give him an injection to wake him up slowly."

Nala stepped away from the bed, giving Syn room to maneuver. Syn began removing the IVs and sticky EKG patches from Haakon's body. She left two IVs mounted on mobile poles connected. With Wolf's help, she lifted Haakon onto a rolling cot and pushed it out to the other side of the tent. A cabinet materialized on one wall, and Nala pretended she didn't see it happen, but her face paled anyway.

The cabinet had all the medical equipment that would be needed for Haakon's recovery, and Syn began hooking him up. Wolf brought in chairs so they could sit while they waited for Haakon to regain consciousness.

Nala sat by the head of the bed, and Syn instructed, "Ask him to wake up, Nala. Talk to him as you would if he were awake." Nala called Haakon's name. His eyes fluttered open for a few seconds and then closed again.

"Is he all right?" Nala asked in a worried voice.

"Yes, that's normal, Nala. This will go on for several hours. You must be patient."

Wolf whispered to Syn that he needed to discuss the king's surgery with Onel, and he quietly exited the tent, making his way down the stairs to the throne room. As he entered, Onel was talking to a group of advisers, and he glanced up asking, "How is my brother?"

"The king is doing quite well. We will let him sleep for seventy-two hours and then awaken him."

"That is good. He should rest. We are reviewing the castle defenses for the hundredth time," Onel explained.

"Have the new acquisitions been deployed yet?"

"Yes, they are positioned throughout the city. Skylla's warriors will range outdoors to harry the supply lines." Looking across the table at Skylla, Onel warned, "It will be dangerous out there. We will not be able to send reinforcements if you become trapped."

"Is that wise?" Wolf asked in concern.

Skylla gave Wolf a condescending smile and snapped, "We are Nanna. We will be fine whether Jonar sends five hundred or five thousand of his pathetic troops. The numbers won't matter. We will strike like the wind and disappear. My only concern is that we will encounter other Nanna who are not sworn to you. That will pit sister against sister and mother against daughter. If only you could meet my mother, she would pledge to you and switch her allegiance. But alas, we will be at war before you can meet her."

"How many Nanna warriors are there?" Wolf asked, leaning forward.

"Including my warriors, two thousand, and another four

thousand Fenrir."

"What are Fenrir?" Wolf frowned at the unfamiliar word.

"It's the name we give our animals—you call them wolves. They are life mates to us. When they are weaned, we raise them as family and treat them as members of our tribe. When they are killed, we mourn them as brothers and sisters of the hunt," Skylla said.

"Fenrir, huh?" Wolf said, recalling the details of a legend from his own distant past. "The story of a mighty wolf named Fenris was told in my land among my people."

"Please, Wolf, tell me the legend!" Skylla's face broke into a delighted smile.

Wolf looked at Onel, who nodded for him to continue. "I will give you the short version. A long time ago, people known as the Norse believed in many gods. One god named Loki was evil and mated with a giantess. They had three children. One was the wolf Fenris, who was forever hungry. Its jaws were immense and its teeth were as sharp as swords. Odin, the father of these gods, knew he had made a mistake by letting Loki's children live. He split the children up, sending them to different places. One he put in charge of hell, another he put in the ocean, and the third child, Fenris, he kept in his home, called Asgard. Because Odin did not want to fight it, Fenris was kept as a pet. He was allowed to roam about Asgard because everyone, including Odin, was terrified of the wolf. Odin had foreseen in the Last Battle between good and evil his own destiny was to be destroyed by Fenris. The great wolf snapped his powerful jaws at the doorway to the council chamber daily, and the other gods were afraid to attend the meetings. Something had to be done.

"Odin told the other gods: 'We have made a mistake feeding and coddling this wolf that is destined to destroy us. Every day, it grows stronger. We can't kill him in heaven, so what shall we do?' One god said, 'Chain him up.' Another said 'Banish him.' Odin answered, 'Where will we find a chain strong enough to hold such a creature?'

"One of the gods vowed, 'I will make these chains,' and he forged mighty chains that even his godly strength couldn't break. He brought them to Odin, who examined the chains and said they looked strong. Even Odin couldn't break them. He then summoned Fenris and asked him to prove his tremendous strength by breaking the chain. The wolf was confident of his strength and allowed himself to be bound. The gods were ecstatic the wolf was in chains, but Fenris flexed and snapped the chains, freeing himself with little trouble.

"Looking at the broken chains on the ground, Odin proclaimed, 'He has grown too strong.' So they forged an even stronger chain, which the wolf broke easily. Then, Odin said, 'We must have the dwarves make a magic chain. Something must be done.' An emissary was sent to the dwarves to request the special chain. The master dwarf agreed, saying, 'We will make you an enchanted chain.' They toiled through the night, and when they presented the finished chain, it looked no bigger than a single satin thread, but it was stronger than anything ever made.

"They summoned Fenris and challenged him to show his strength again. The wolf saw in the gods' eyes that they feared him, and he listened to Odin say, 'We know how strong you are. You have shown your great strength before, but now we have a further test. It is this,' he said, holding out the twisted strand to Fenris.

"The wolf looked at the silken string. He was not stupid. The thread was small and reeked of dwarf magic. He asked, 'Why should I do this? If I succeed, you will be amazed, and if I fail, I will remain bound in that accursed string.'

"Odin smiled and said, 'How could you fail with your strength?' But the wolf snarled and replied, 'I fear a foul trick. If it is a trick, you will leave me bound—but I will not let you call me a coward. You may tie me if one of your gods will place his right hand in my mouth.' Fenris smiled at the thought of biting off a god's hand. The assembled gods looked fearful, but the bravest of the gods stepped forward with his right hand raised. Fenris opened his great jaws, exposing his razor sharp fangs, and the courageous god put his hand in the wolf's mouth. The gods bound the whole length of the silken strand around Fenris and tied the ends together with knots that wouldn't loosen. They worried that the small strand would break, and if it didn't, the brave god would lose his hand. This thought occurred to Fenris too, and he struggled to break free, but the harder he tried, the tighter the strands became. The wolf exerted all of his incredible strength but could not break free of the slender strand. Enraged, he bit off the brave god's hand. After eons of struggle, the wolf broke loose and killed Odin."

"What a beautiful story," Skylla said with an amused chuckle. "Rightful vengeance for foul trickery."

"Well, yes, I suppose," Wolf said without humor.

Onel smiled at Wolf's story and said, "Getting back to the meeting. I fear even with the new warriors, we may need more. It's a shame we cannot sway your mother and her army of Nannas to our cause, Skylla."

Wolf abruptly asked, "Can you take me to meet your mother in secret?"

"By now, she knows we no longer serve Jonar, so we are considered outlaws," Skylla replied. "The only way to see her is to be captured and taken to her. It must be you and me—I will not risk my warriors' lives. They would be killed on sight. But I would be taken before my mother as a royal captive. Even so, it is risky."

"It can be done, though? Take me to her," Wolf insisted.

"When do we leave?" Skylla asked, frowning as she realized that she had just agreed to what was probably a suicide mission.

"Tonight. The sooner, the better," Wolf replied.

"I must agree. If we can acquire your mother's warriors, we may win. I will order a small amount of supplies readied for the journey," Onel said.

"Commander, this is a bad idea," Syn hissed in Wolf's ear. He coughed and placed a hand over his mouth, whispering, "Why?"

"I do not trust that trollop with you. You are mine, Commander. No sampling the natives, no matter how accommodating they are."

Part 5

Love's Triangle

Chapter 24

When Haakon awoke from the heavy sedation that Syn had administered to immobilize him and allow his body to heal, Nala was sitting by his bedside. Her children were seated in chairs nearby. Haakon turned away and refused to speak with them, spurning Nala's repeated attempts at conversation. Finally, he launched into a hateful tirade against her that ended with him calling her a bitch and a whore.

"How dare you disrespect Nala," Syn snapped as she walked into the tent. "That woman is in love with you. She sat by your bed day and night for a week, hardly sleeping, waiting for your eyes to open. This is how you thank her? You are an ungrateful ass!"

Nala broke into tears and ran out of the tent, followed by her children. Reon and Leesa were crying; Trulane's face reflected the despair one might see in a first son who had failed to live up to his father's expectations; and Brithee's eyes were cold and unforgiving.

"Thank you for saving me," Haakon said.

"I saved you because of Nala. If you were any other man other than Wolf, I would have let you die. Nala killed a dozen men to reach your side and save your life, yet all you can do is insult and reject her? I should put you to sleep permanently for treating her so badly." Syn slammed a monitor down on the table, cracking the screen, and stormed out of the tent.

Wolf stepped into the tent a minute later with a look of concern and asked, "What did you say to her, Haakon?"

"I have severed my ties with Nala and my children as the law requires. Nannas are not permitted to marry or raise children. They are outcasts and must be spurned by all. They are an abomination, and their children must be put to death. I disown them all!" Haakon muttered in disgust. "You should have let me die."

"What the hell is wrong with you, man?" Wolf erupted in anger. "You have a wife who loves you and adoring kids who call you father. Yet here you lie, clinging to life and hating the people who sat by your side praying for you."

"Nanna scum raided my village and killed my parents. I was just a child and witnessed it all. By marrying that bitch, I have committed a mortal sin. I have slept with the murderers of my parents and shared my seed with death. I have perpetuated their evil and become a father to abominations," Haakon said with a fanatical gleam in his eyes. He turned away from Wolf and refused to speak further.

"I thought better of you," Wolf said in disgust as he turned and left Haakon alone in the room.

* * *

Outside the tent, Skylla was speaking harshly with Nala, urging her to stop acting like a weak, desperate woman. Several high-ranking Nanna warriors had turned their backs on Nala and were laughing at her grief. Others glared at her contemptuously, while a few made hurtful remarks, speaking loud enough to be heard.

"You are losing respect, my sister. Stop acting like a whipped Fenrir! You are a Nanna and the daughter of a queen," Skylla admonished.

"Fine," Nala said, wiping tears from her eyes. "If that's the way he feels, I will send my girls home...to Mother. Trulane and Reon can stay here at the castle, and the girls will become Nannas, as their fate and heritage call to them. Haakon and I are through forever."

"We welcome your daughters to the sisterhood of Fenris," Skylla said, delighted, but then her face clouded. "We still must deal with our defection from Jonar's army. Mother remains loyal to Jonar. Wolf and I are traveling to her camp so he can speak with her about this war."

"I will take him to Mother," Nala said quietly. "My reappearance after being missing for so many years will guarantee an audience with her."

"Yes, that's true, my sister, but it is my duty to Wolf. I will take him."

"Do not argue with me, Skylla. I am the oldest and your master in combat. Besides, I am an outcast now, or do you invoke the challenge?"

"No, my sister, I submit to your authority. Take Wolf to meet with Mother. I will assume responsibility for your female children." A tear ran down Skylla's face as she added, "Goodbye, my sister." She turned her back on Nala as the other Nanna warriors had done.

Nala looked up as Wolf emerged from the tent. They locked eyes for a moment, and then she said, "I have discussed it with Skylla. I will take you to our mother. We must leave now. It may take several days to find her."

Wolf was tempted to argue with Nala about the dangerous journey and her duty to her children, but when he saw the determination on her face, he nodded a reluctant assent. They walked through the castle in silence. Wolf said goodbye to several men at arms, and then they crossed the bridge, proceeding down the narrow crevasse to the outer gate.

"What are our plans, Nala? Which direction shall we travel?" Wolf asked, breaking the uneasy silence.

"Southwest, my lord," Nala replied in a monotone.

"My lord? Nala, you know who I am. Use my name!"

"I am shamed thrice before your eyes and unworthy to call my lord by his name," Nala answered, looking at the ground. "Did you not see my sister turn her back on me? I am dead to her. As soon as my people learn that Haakon has rejected me, I will be dead to them. My sister must consider the sisterhood before blood. She knows I am now an outcast."

"Stop it, Nala!" Wolf snapped, unable to decide whether the woman's defeated attitude made him angry or profoundly sad.

"It is our custom. Haakon has insulted me three times in public before witnesses. If I survive the war, my people will disfigure my face and mark me as outcast. Being spurned by a man and told to leave his company like a cheap whore after a night of pleasure is a grave insult, and Haakon has done it three times, proving to all that I am undesirable. Most Nanna women who have been spurned become whores at the taverns. Others cut their own throats to end the shame. No Nanna will respect me now, no matter how great my skills are in battle. Nala the warrior is no more. It does not matter, for I shall die soon and welcome death's embrace."

Wolf looked at Nala with overwhelming sadness and asked, "What have they done to you, my sweet Nala? Is there no way to retrieve your honor?"

"Yes, there are two," Nala said in a choked whisper, "But only one will happen."

"Tell me," Wolf said, looking hopeful.

"One is to die gloriously in battle."

"And the other?"

* * *

Syn checked the holo-emitters and then looked in on Waylan. After assessing the king's condition and adjusting one of his IVs, she left the tent and spotted Skylla sitting alone on the roof. The view of the village below and the mountains in the distance was breathtaking. The Nanna leader sobbed quietly, and Syn approached with a look of concern.

"Why do you cry, Skylla?"

"I cry for Nala, not myself," Skylla answered, rubbing tears from her eyes with the back of her hand.

"Nala is with Wolf. Nothing can harm her while he lives. She will be safe, I promise you. Even if the meeting goes bad, they will be fine," Syn said with a reassuring smile.

"You are unfamiliar with our customs, so you do not understand the tragedy that has happened here. Nala has been shunned three times by Haakon before witnesses. We are a female kingdom. Men do not shun women in our society. For a man to reject a woman and call her a bitch or whore in the same breath is the worst insult imaginable. By not killing him on the spot, she has betrayed our ways, and this adds to her shame. She has shown weakness and the Nanna saw it. Haakon's insults give a common whore more honor than my sister. So I cry because I found Nala after believing she was dead for many years. I love her dearly, and now, I lose her again because of a man's vile actions."

"Is there no way we can help Nala regain her honor?"

"In our culture, there are only two ways," Skylla replied. "One is to die in battle."

"That is not acceptable! What is the other?"

* * *

Nala looked away with humiliation and defeat. In a barely audible voice, she said, "The other way is for a new man to possess me. He must take me in public and confirm my desirability to all who would witness it. It is the only way for a Nanna to regain her honor."

"What the hell? Is there no other way?" Wolf asked, flushing red.

"What the hell?" Syn echoed in Wolf's ear at the same moment because Skylla had given her the same answer.

After a long silence, Wolf and Nala resumed their journey deeper into the woods. Wolf pondered Nala's words, and his thoughts drifted to the possibility of her dying in battle. As he watched her from the corner of his eye, her expression told him she had already decided dying in battle would be a better fate than living as an outcast. If she had the misfortune of surviving, her beautiful face would be disfigured, and she would never see her children again.

An hour or so later, Syn announced in Wolf's ear, "You'll have to make love to Nala."

"What?" he yelled, startling Nala, who spun around with her whip and dagger drawn.

"You'll have to make love to Nala...in front of her people or whatever ridiculous custom is required," Syn repeated, sounding perturbed at having to speak the unpleasant words again.

"Sorry, Nala, I didn't mean to yell," Wolf apologized. "I need a few minutes to myself. Would you mind giving me some privacy?"

Nala slumped as if all hope had drained from her. "I don't mind, my lord. I will be alone and dead soon anyway. I will leave you to your thoughts," she said as she resumed walking.

When Nala was out of earshot, Wolf whispered angrily, "What is wrong with you, Syn? You know that can't happen. Nala is my friend."

"Don't you find her attractive, Commander?"

"It doesn't matter. I could injure her, Syn. Or I could expose her to viruses from our past and unleash havoc on this world. What you ask is wrong. I do care for Nala, but I can't do it."

"Would you prefer to see her disfigured and shunned, Commander? Do you want her to step in front of a knife and die in the first battle you fight...or would you rather she become a common prostitute, used by any filthy drunk who comes along? I love Nala, and I will not let that happen. You will do as I say, and you will do it in front of everyone, or whatever this silly custom requires," Syn said with an intensity Wolf had never heard in her voice.

"What you ask of me is wrong in every way, Syn. Besides, I have been waiting for you."

"I appreciate the thought, Commander, but I am still just a hologram. Even if we do make love, it will not be real. You will be having sex with light and energy fields. I love you too much to see you suffer or make you wait for something that is not real."

Wolf was stunned by Syn's clinical tone. After thinking for a moment, he said, "We don't have to do anything now. Let's wait and see if Haakon will change his mind. He may come to his senses and take Nala back. He's a fool if he doesn't."

"I agree, Commander. The man is a stubborn, superstitious ass. However, you must tell Nala you will possess her if Haakon does not take her back. Give her some hope."

"All right," Wolf agreed reluctantly. "You are much more to me than light and energy fields, Syn. Do not ever say again that you are not real. Do you understand?"

"Yes, Wolf. Go to Nala and tell her. She will throw her life away in the first battle she fights if you don't give her hope."

"I will tell her tonight after we make camp and eat," Wolf replied, torn by conflicting emotions. He set out after Nala at a brisk stride and caught up with her as the trail turned east. They walked in silence, each absorbed in the throes of their own inner turmoil.

As the first shadows of late afternoon played over the forest, Wolf spotted a pond in a rocky canyon, fed by a natural spring that bubbled down the craggy hillside to the rocks below. "We'll camp here," he said.

An hour later, they had finished a meal and were sitting by a campfire. The warm glow of the flames illuminated Nala's face as

Wolf gazed at her and saw tears in her eyes. She looked up and caught his gaze, then looked away, ashamed.

"I'm sorry if I displease you, my lord. I will move away." Nala stood and began walking away from the campfire.

"Nala, I have something I want to say. Please stay."

With a defeated shrug, Nala returned to the fire and dropped to the ground like a rag doll. "How may I serve you, my lord?" she asked, avoiding his gaze.

"I do not understand your customs, Nala, but is there a chance Haakon will take you back?"

"A shamed woman can never return to the man who cast her out. I would have to kill him and then myself by cutting my own throat across his body. I will not do that to my children and leave them with that horrible memory. I would rather be a whore than leave them orphans. There is no going back. Haakon and I are finished."

"I was afraid you would say that," Wolf admitted.

"Afraid? Why? You fear no one and you are afraid of nothing. So why do you say you are afraid?" she asked, forcing a weak smile at Wolf's uncomfortable look.

"Nala, I will take you as my woman when we return. Will you accept me?"

Nala's jaw dropped, but she recovered quickly and asked, "What about Syn? She is my friend and I love her. I could never take her man. I'm grateful for your offer, but I will not accept you." In a small voice, she added, "Even though I want to."

"Commander, do you see why I love that woman? Keep her safe," Syn said in Wolf's ear. "I hold you responsible for her safety."

"Nala, promise me you will not let yourself to be injured in battle. Give me your solemn word."

"I will battle with care," Nala promised. "Thank you for restoring my pride. The thought that you, of all men, find me desirable is flattering beyond all words." She stood and walked off into the darkness. Wolf could not see her, but he could hear her crying softly.

"We are doing the right thing, Commander. I will talk to Skylla and let you know what must be done to satisfy the Nannas' custom. In the meantime, keep Nala safe. I mean it, Wolf!"

Chapter 25

When Syn walked out of the tent, she found Skylla conversing with Brithee and Leesa by the balustrade, recounting stories of their grandmother and of life as a Nanna. The girls would soon learn the skills they would need to survive. Skylla had drilled them in rudimentary combat, and Brithee showed her mother's quickness and dexterity. Leesa was less agile and needed to lose twenty pounds to trim up, but Skylla was confident that she would make a reasonably competent Nanna warrior in time.

Syn approached quietly and asked, "Skylla, can I talk to you?"

"Of course. Girls, go and clean up. We will talk more later," Skylla said to Brithee and Leesa. She followed Syn to the parapet overlooking the village below and asked, "What's on your mind, Syn?"

"Wolf will choose Nala as his mate," Syn said with authority.

"What? I was told you and Wolf are betrothed," Skylla replied, her eyes clouding with concern. "Now you must fight Nala to the death. It is the way of the Nanna. You will lose face if you do not fight for your man." She seemed annoyed at Syn's willingness to give up her man so easily.

"No, Skylla, I will not fight for Wolf. I love your sister, and I will not see her shamed because her husband is a jackass. I will do whatever I need to do to help Nala," Syn affirmed.

"You shame me, Syn. I turned my back on Nala, and I was wrong to do so. When she returns, I will go into exile with her."

"Skylla, there will be no exile. Wolf will do what I tell him to do!" Syn spoke with such confidence and unwavering intensity in her eyes that Skylla took a step back and gazed at her with newfound respect.

"As you wish, mistress," Skylla demurred, surprising Syn with her odd choice of words and submissive response.

Later that afternoon, Syn noticed a group of Nanna warriors congregating around the tent. As the gathering grew to about twenty, Skylla called, "Mistress, will you come outside, please?"

Syn appeared in the doorway, dressed in her candy striper outfit. The women whispered and stared at her with looks that ranged from reverence and awe to lusty desire. Syn's physique was picture-perfect, and her outfit accentuated her curves. She gave the women a friendly smile and asked, "Hello, Skylla, what do you need?"

Skylla and her warriors placed their right hands on their breasts, fingers spread in a gesture reminiscent of the peace sign on ancient Earth, and intoned, "Mistress, we honor you."

"What's going on, Skylla?"

"You have been chosen. You are our Enrica," Skylla answered.

"Enrica? An Old Norse term that means powerful. I assume you want me to lead you, but I am not of your race, Skylla."

"The honor is not one you can choose to reject. You must accept or we must try to kill you," a prodigious, muscle-bound woman said. "We have been told you love our queen's daughter like a sister and offered your man to her to take her shame away. It is an unselfish act, and one our future generations will speak of as legend and with honor. We saw your fighting skills the night Nala's man was injured. You are a great warrior. You are our Enrica."

Looking into the faces of the Nanna warriors and seeing it was pointless to argue, Syn responded, "Fine. So be it."

* * *

Wolf and Nala had been walking south for most of the afternoon. As they reached a bend in the trail, Nala froze, sniffing the air, and then drew her whip and dagger. Wolf noticed that she had become so feral, he wasn't sure the old Nala ever would return. "My people watch us," she warned in a low voice. "Prepare yourself...and try not to kill too many of them if you can avoid it."

The attack came from three directions, forcing Wolf and Nala to the left side of the trail, which was blocked by fallen trees and enormous boulders. Nala shouted over the screams of the onrushing Nannas, "It's a trap, Wolf. Nets will drop over us, and they will try to entangle you with whips. Be careful."

Moments later, as Nala had predicted, heavy nets dropped over Wolf. Nala avoided the nets with her acrobatic skills and snapped her whip with devastating accuracy, causing several of the attackers to

257

yell in pain. Wolf stood, entangled in the nets, watching Nala as she battled with her tribe. Her agility and skill were remarkable. She had somehow acquired a second whip and was using both hands to fight off the attackers. Her hair flew in the wind, framing the intense look on her face like a poignant snapshot. She disarmed several warriors by striking their hands with her whip ends. Others came at her, but Nala repelled them and blocked their strikes with her whip's barbs. She dived, rolled, and then back-flipped herself to Wolf's side.

"Are you all right?" Nala asked, her breathing labored from exertion. She knelt and tried to untangle Wolf from the whips and nets held taut by the other warriors.

"I'm fine, Nala. I can break free easily. I was watching you fight," Wolf admitted with respect and admiration in his eyes. Suddenly, he yelled, "Look out!" as two wolves attacked. Nala whirled and smacked both in the nose at the same instant, causing them to whimper in pain.

"Hold, Nanna!" a rich, timbered voice ordered.

An older female approached. Wolf saw that she was dark, exotic, perhaps a descendant from the country known as Brazil on Old Earth. Her hair was long and jet-black, dropping to the middle of her back. Her face was oval with large, dark eyes, and her lips were full. She was taller than Nala, but Wolf recognized the likeness and knew the woman was Nala's mother.

"Nala?" the woman asked in shocked disbelief. She looked her up and down, sniffing the air, first with suspicion, and then with amaze-ment. "At first, I couldn't believe my eyes, but the nose never lies," she said, reaching out and hugging her. "My baby, I thought you were dead. How can this be?"

"Yes, Mother, it is I. It is a long story we will discuss later. I have returned now only to bring this brave warrior to meet you."

The woman gave Wolf an appraising look and flashed a predator's smile. "Well, well, he is a hefty one. Is this a coming home gift for me, Nala?"

"No, Mother, he is the Warrior of Legend. His name is Wolf."

The woman approached him, touching his chest and arms through the nets. "He is as hard as the rocks of this land. Tell me,

Nala, is he your man?"

Nala blushed and replied, "He has shown interest in me, Mother, but that's not why we have come here. We serve King Waylan."

"You serve our enemy?" The woman looked aghast and backed away from her daughter as if she had seen a ghost. "Nala, what have you done?"

Wolf had seen enough and grasped the netting that ensnared him, ripping away the thick mesh as if tearing strips of flimsy paper. He freed himself in a matter of seconds and tossed the netting on the ground. He took several steps towards the Nanna queen, and suddenly, whips sliced through the air, ensnaring his arms and legs from all angles. Wolf continued to advance, snapping the leather whips like gossamer strings and dragging several muscular Nanna warriors behind him like a child pulling a toy wagon. Stopping in front of the queen, he smiled and said in a friendly voice, "Hello ma'am, I am Wolf. I want to talk to you about joining me."

Astonished by what she had just seen, the woman swallowed hard and replied, "Let us talk in my tent. I will have food prepared. Follow me, big man." Wolf and Nala followed the queen and her warriors to their camp in the hills overlooking this forest glen. It was a half-hour walk, and when they arrived, Wolf saw a scarlet tent erected in the middle of the clearing. He followed the woman into the tent, accompanied by Nala. The interior was comfortable, decorated with numerous rugs and pieces of handcrafted furniture.

"Sit," the queen commanded. Turning to Nala, she asked, "What happened to you, my daughter. Why did you not return to take your rightful place by my side?"

"You know I was sick of the killing, Mother. After the last battle, Jonar's men hounded me without mercy until I left our lands. I married a man and had children. I was happy for many years. Then, this war started. I knew I would come back to you one day...and now I have."

Nala dropped her eyes to her hands and quietly confessed, "Mother, I must tell you...I have been shunned by a man in front of witnesses." She broke into tears, and Wolf had never seen a woman look so frail and helpless.

"Chockta! Attend me," the queen commanded in an angry voice.

A powerful, battle-scarred woman entered the tent, saying, "Yes, my queen?"

"Escort this outcast from my presence." Glaring at Nala with contempt, the queen added, "Leave this tent at once! Camp on the outskirts of the settlement, lowly one." She turned away from her daughter and gazed at Wolf. As Nala backed slowly out of the tent, she gave Wolf a sad, broken smile. It wounded his soul to see her shamed, and his anger flared.

Taking note of Wolf's rage, the queen said, "I am Dalla, leader of all the Nanna. Let me tell you how we came to be and why our laws require me to send my own daughter to the edge of the camp. In the time of the Never Ending Night, a family wandered into the great wasteland—one man, his wife, and three baby girls. The Fenrir, our animals today, roamed those wastes, and they were hungry. They spotted the family and attacked. The man threw his wife to the pack and abandoned his family. His wife stood firm, bravely defending her daughters. The pack leader stopped in front of her and asked, 'Who are you to stand unafraid before the Fenrir?' She looked at the leader, amazed it could talk, and replied, 'I am Nanna, a loving mother who begs you to show mercy.' The leader said, 'We hunger, and the darkness is forevermore, flesh is what we crave,' and the woman replied, 'Accept mine as sacrifice and spare my children.'

"The Fenrir leader looked at the woman with pity; yet, his pack was starving, and the young were dying. 'What am I to do with your young when you are devoured?' Nanna replied, 'Raise them as your own.' The leader's respect for the woman was high and he answered, 'So be it—your life for theirs. I will make your death quick.' He tore her throat out and the pack devoured her. The leader was true to his word and raised the woman's three daughters as Fenrir. He taught them the way of the hunt, and when they were old enough, he told them of their father's cowardice and how brave their mother had been. He said he regretted having to kill her, but his own young were starving. The girls took the name Nanna and grew strong in the way of fang and claw.

"To this day, we despise most men. We see how men show their cowardice, raping and killing the weak. Our sisters will not be subservient to cowards or inferior beings. We are predators and all are prey to our whips and blades. We use men merely to satisfy our lust. Love is a weakness...a taboo we do not tolerate. Nala shamed herself by falling for a common man...he is no better than Nanna's cowardly husband who abandoned her and his daughters to the Fenrir. Her man's vile actions prove our ways are just. That is why I expel my daughter to the edge of the camp as an outcast. Now tell me about yourself."

Wolf barely controlled his anger as he said, "I don't care for your ways. Love is not a weakness." Checking his anger, he made an effort to be civil. "I am called Wolf. I am from a land far away. Since I arrived in this kingdom recently, I have fought nonstop with savage beasts and violent people, many of them made crazy by a vile drug. I have joined with King Waylan because he has impressed me as a noble leader and a valiant warrior. Several warrior bands have sworn to me, including the Nanna warriors who follow your other daughter, Skylla."

Dalla sprang to her feet enraged and shouted, "You lie! Skylla is under my command. As we speak, she is harrying that decrepit king's land and killing his pathetic followers. Why would she change her allegiance? She would never betray me!"

"Skylla serves me now, and I support King Waylan. Your daughter put me through all the tests, and I will submit to any tests you wish. Let's do them and get it over with," Wolf said. He picked up a cup and took a careless swig of the beverage.

Dalla sneered at Wolf and retorted, "You think our tests are easy, do you? Well, here's a test for you." She picked up a heavy bench and smashed it over his head with no effect. Then, she drew her dagger, gripping it in both hands, and drove it into Wolf's chest, expecting it to pierce his heart and slay him. To her astonishment, the blade of her knife bent at a forty-five degree angle and Wolf was unharmed. He gazed at her with a bored expression.

Without warning, Wolf grabbed the queen's arms and pulled her into his lap. He grinned as she struggled against his strength and fought to break free. After restraining her for several minutes, he began to feel aroused and let her go, saying, "Dalla, I can't be harmed, so can we move on to your toughest test?"

Humiliated at being manhandled, the queen replied through clenched teeth, "Leave me! Go to your shamed one. I will prepare a test for you. If you pass, I will withdraw my warriors from the conflict. I'm not sure I want to fight for Waylan...I joined Jonar to cleanse the land of petty kings. If you fail my test, I will kill everything that walks or crawls in Waylan's kingdom. Now get out!"

Wolf left the tent and set out to search for Nala on the outskirts of the settlement. He found her encircled by a dozen Nanna warriors who were jeering and throwing mud and animal excrement at her. Her body was laced with bright welts from their whips, and she was fighting back tears. Oblivious to Wolf approaching, the women suddenly attacked, kicking Nala in the ribs and stomping her hands. She crumpled, making no effort to defend herself. A few of the women stood back, cursing and spitting on the fallen princess.

Wolf's anger flashed white hot as he ran to Nala's rescue and pulled the attackers away from her. "Stop!" he shouted with such rage he surprised himself and brought other warriors running over to see what had upset this giant from another land. "I will warn you all just once—no one is to touch Nala again. The next one of you bitches that harms her will answer to me, and I will break your neck. Do you understand me?"

A husky woman who had been among those kicking Nala drew her knife and pulled a whip from her belt. With a throaty growl, she demanded, "Who are you to interfere? She has been disgraced. She is worthless. No man will take her, except to use her as a whore. We follow the laws and do what is right. If you want it to stop, take her. Here and now."

"Commander, do it," Syn ordered in Wolf's ear.

Nala looked broken and humiliated as she sat in the dirt and dropped her chin, avoiding Wolf's eyes. She knew he was torn between wanting to help her and being loyal to Syn. He gazed at her and then back at the Nannas, responding, "She will be my woman—after the war. I will not have her hurt or disfigured before my night with her comes. The next one who touches or offends her will answer to me."

The women laughed raucously, and several drew their knives and whips, advancing on Wolf. Acting as a single entity, they attacked together, slashing at him with unbridled fury, intent on sending him to an early grave. They soon discovered that the frenetic assault was futile. He stood with arms crossed, smirking. They tried every tactic to hack him to death or at least bring him down, kicking, biting, slashing, and thrusting. He let them continue until they withdrew in fatigue. The last warrior to give up backed away with a look of disbelief and hissed, "What the hell are you?"

"I am Wolf. I support King Waylan, and I have come to seek your aid in vanquishing Jonar. Your queen will tell you more. Now leave us."

Wolf turned his back on the women and lifted Nala from the dirt. Bloodied and bruised, she forced a grateful smile and said, "I know I am not your woman, Wolf. You are Syn's man, and I would never hurt her by taking you to my bed. I will kill myself first if it comes to that."

"I love that woman so!" Syn gushed. "She is a true friend. Keep her safe, Wolf!"

"I will do what is necessary to save you," Wolf vowed. "But I never again want to hear you talk about killing yourself, Nala. Now let us go to the lake so you can clean up." He lifted her small body and carried her through the camp to a pristine, sparkling lake behind Dalla's tent.

The queen had observed Wolf's skirmish with her fiercest warriors, and the stranger's actions confused her. He loved her daughter, that was obvious. He was an amazing warrior; yet, for some reason, he refused to take her. She thought to herself, *I may have to hurry this big man along. I want my daughter back and he can restore her honor.*

Nala sobbed against Wolf's shoulder as he carried her to the sandy shore of the lake. He lowered her feet to the ground and tore a cloth from the tatters of his uniform. Wetting it in the crystal clear water, he dabbed Nala's face, wiping dirt and blood away from her fair skin.

"Nala, listen to me. I like you a lot, and I will possess you. But I

263

am incredibly strong. I don't want to injure you. I need time to figure some things out. Until then, I want you to stay by my side. I don't want you hurt. Do you understand?"

"Yes, Wolf. Will you stay while I bathe?" Nala asked. She cast a sidelong glance at a handful of Nanna sisters who had gathered nearby to spy on them.

With a deep sigh, Wolf said, "Yes, Nala, I will stay. But hurry." He turned his back to give her privacy.

Nala smiled shyly and removed her leathers, stepping into the water. She swam under it, allowing the cold water to clear her head. Her mind swooned with thoughts of Wolf and feelings of desire. She had never met a man like him. He was gentle and kind, yet he could be a terrifying and unbeatable foe on the battlefield.

After Nala had bathed, she was walking out of the water when an ear-piercing roar came from behind her. Wolf spun around and saw a reptile that resembled a gigantic crocodile bearing down on her. Nala saw the beast and froze as the creature attacked, its mouth wide open, as if it intended to swallow her whole. The beast was over thirty feet long with a broad snout that extended eight feet from its enormous body, which was covered in reptilian armor. Razor-sharp, three-inch fangs lined its enormous jaws, and its maw looked large enough to swallow a full-grown buffalo, hooves and all.

Wolf reacted instantly to the roar and sprinted to Nala's rescue. The Nannas who had gathered nearby screamed and pulled back to watch the grisly scene from safer ground. Dalla ran towards her daughter, whip and knife drawn, yelling for Nala to run. Then, she froze in her tracks and watched, spellbound, as Wolf shielded her daughter with his body and stood fearless, ready to fight a Sarcosuchus, the terror of fresh waters on this world, with his bare hands.

The monster opened its massive jaws and angled its head to the side, preparing to strike Wolf. Its jaws were over seven feet wide, lined with instant, skin-puncturing death, and they engulfed Wolf, slamming shut with tremendous force. The water of the lake made Wolf buoyant, and he lost his footing as the predator sank into the water. The reptile shook its head from side to side, dragging Wolf under the water to what appeared to be a certain death.

"Nala! Get out of the water...these creatures hunt in pairs!" Dalla screamed as she raced frantically into the water's edge. She grabbed her daughter's arm, pulling her to the shore. "Nala! Are you all right?" Seeing that her daughter was in shock and non-responsive, Dalla slapped her face several times, bringing her to her senses.

"Wolf—where is my Wolf?" Nala cried, trying to break free from her mother's grasp and wade back into the water to help him. Dalla motioned to several warriors who grabbed Nala and drug her away from the lake just as a second Sarcosuchus appeared. It floated on the water before them, baring its fangs. It taunted the Nannas, staring them down in a challenge to come closer to the water.

The first reptile surfaced, squealing in pain as Wolf rose from the water, holding the beast's tail in his left hand and dragging it towards the shore. Its mate saw Wolf, bellowed in fury, and charged him. Wolf balled his right fist and cocked it by his right ear. When the enormous creature opened its mouth and sprang forward, Wolf's fist slammed into its snout. The collision produced a sharp crack and sudden death as the creature's jaws were crushed into its brain. The remaining Sarcosuchus attacked, gnashing its needle-sharp teeth on Wolf's body but breaking most of its teeth on his rock-hard skin. Wolf reached out to the dead reptile, grabbing its armor-plated tail, and resumed dragging both to the shore. The other creature dug its large webbed feet into the mud, trying to gain traction. It dug twin furrows in the mud as Wolf pulled the squirming creature onto the sand.

"Shall I kill it or let it go?" Wolf asked Dalla in an almost bored voice.

The Nanna queen gazed at the terrified reptile and then at Wolf in disbelief, whispering, "It is frightened. I can smell its fear. I doubt it will ever hunt a human again. Release it."

Wolf dragged the beast a little further onto land, and it swung its head, attempting to bite him again. He caught the beast's snout, clamping its powerful jaws shut. Looking into its fear-filled eyes, Wolf said, "Go back to hunting fish. If I ever hear about a human being killed here, I will drain this lake and bash in your brains." He lifted the beast with both hands and threw it like a sack of flour out onto the water, causing a massive splash. The creature swam off in a panic, bellowing in pain.

Nala broke loose from her mother and ran to Wolf, crying his name. Still naked, she threw herself into his arms and kissed him, sobbing, "Oh, Wolf, I thought I had lost you." Wolf returned her kiss and then pushed her away with a reluctant groan.

"I am fine, Nala. Put on some clothes." Wolf turned away to give her privacy and waded waist-deep into the lake as the warriors who had witnessed the amazing spectacle applauded.

Nala smiled as her mother helped her dress. Gazing at Wolf out in the lake, Dalla sighed, "What a man he is, my daughter! Is it really possible he is the Warrior of Legend?"

"I do not know, Mother, but I want him!" Nala exclaimed, feeling a pang of guilt when Syn popped into her thoughts. Stepping away from her mother, she said, "I will return to my tent so I do not shame you by my lowly status."

Dalla grabbed her wrist and said, "Nala, he kissed you in front of us all. He fought the lake monster for you. It is clear he has feelings for you. It is not full possession, but it is a start. Come, we have much to talk about."

Nala followed her mother back to the tent as most of the warriors dispersed. A few stood frozen in place, staring at the dead reptile on the shore and at Wolf, who stood in the lake with his back to them, not believing what they had witnessed with their own eyes.

"I didn't mean to kiss her, Syn. I'm sorry," Wolf said, feeling guilty.

"It's all right, Commander. It already has been decided...you two will marry."

"No, it's not decided, Syn," Wolf argued as he soaked in the chilly water, trying to douse the fire in his aching loins. Nala's naked body pressing against his had left him aroused and dizzy with desire. "Not until every possible solution can be tried."

"Whatever you say, Commander," Syn answered with a hint of sarcasm.

Chapter 26

Syn had watched Wolf and Nala growing closer, and she knew it was just a matter of time before he crumbled to the woman's seductive charms. She wasn't happy about the prospect of Wolf lying in Nala's arms, but she genuinely liked the woman and didn't want her to spend the rest of her life shunned as an outcast.

Syn was in the engine bay, applying the finishing touches to her android's second arm. She had completed the first arm yesterday, and it was a masterpiece. Both limbs were still robotic, but she had developed a soft, polymer/titanium skin to coat the exterior. It had the look and feel of human flesh but could withstand a bullet at close range or a life-ending blow from a sword. Each arm had seventy-two actuators, and both were plugged into the ship's power grid for testing.

Substantial power would be required to run the android's body. Syn needed to fabricate a mobile power supply, and her calculations indicated that a power pack from one of the damaged satellites would be adequate. She materialized three clones of herself, and each worked on a different body part. In just under six hours, both arms and legs were encased in the pseudo-skin. Soon, she thought, she would have a body to compete with Nala.

Five miles away, on a wooded hillside overlooking a scenic forest glen, Dalla sat on a chair, humming softly as she braided Nala's long hair. She had mourned her daughter for a year when Nala vanished after a battle, and the prospect of losing her a second time melted Dalla's heart. As she braided a strand of Nala's hair, she said, "Tell me about my grandchildren."

"You have four, Mother," Nala replied, her eyes closed as she relaxed and enjoyed the gentle attention from her mother. "Two boys and two girls. One is like my great-grandmother and may one day become Enrica. The other is, for lack of a better word, tame. She will become an average warrior. The boys will make fine men." There was no need to further describe her sons because the Nanna killed or gave away male children.

"That is excellent, my daughter. I can't wait to meet them." With deep emotion, Dalla added, "I have missed you."

Nala reached back and patted her mother's hand, a dreamy smile on her face. It had been many years since she felt a genuine bond with an adult. She loved Haakon, but he had grown less affectionate over the years. Nala had accepted it, and she was content. Then Wolf arrived. He was strong, brave, and kind. He was everything she had ever wanted in a man—but Nala loved the woman who loved him. If only things were different with Syn, she thought. She leaned back and daydreamed while her mother hummed and continued braiding her hair.

A few hundred yards away, Wolf stepped out of the pristine lake behind Dalla's quarters, his desire temporarily quelled. He walked towards the tent Nala had begun setting up on the edge of the camp before she was attacked by her mother's warriors. When he arrived, he saw that someone had finished the task. He ran a hand through his hair and asked in a frustrated voice, "Syn, what are we going to do?"

"Are you all right, Commander?"

"Yes. I'm just wondering about the future. I don't know what I want or what we should do. I don't know if I'm even worthy to bring back what was good and decent from our time."

"If you don't, Wolf, who will? No one is left who remembers what was decent about your world. You are it, my love, so stop feeling sorry for yourself and live."

"Damn, you're getting as hard as nails," Wolf remarked, feeling dejected and hurt by her dismissive tone as he walked into the tent.

"No, Wolf, I'm being honest. Like I said, you're it. Defeat the evil warlord and live in happiness and love. Wasn't that the American way?"

"I'll meet with Dalla in the morning and see if I can sway her to our side," Wolf said, changing the subject. "Her warriors are fierce fighters, and we need them. We should be back at the castle by sundown tomorrow."

"Good night, Wolf," Syn murmured.

A few minutes later, Nala entered the tent. She gazed at Wolf's broad back and made a decision. She wanted him. She would beg Syn for forgiveness later, but she couldn't fight her feelings anymore. She quietly asked, "Were you hurt today?"

"No, I'm fine. But my clothes were torn to rags. I'll be down to dressing in leathers soon. My wardrobe has about run its course."

"I will make your clothes, Wolf. I will make beautiful garments fit for a king."

"I don't need fancy clothes...just pants and a shirt."

Wolf looked up at Nala for the first time since she had entered. She wore a light robe that revealed her full breasts and exquisite figure. Her hair was tied in two long braids that fell below her waist. She smiled and removed the robe, standing naked before him. Wolf caught his breath, and he wasn't able to exhale as Nala crossed to her sleeping mat and climbed beneath the covers. She smiled again, a gentle, almost shy smile, and patted the mat beside her. "Come, my lord, I will rub your back."

Wolf took several steps towards Nala but stopped and looked down at her beautiful face. His eyes lingered on her for a long moment, and then he said, "Nala, not yet. I want you more than you know, but tonight is not the time. Please do not be angry at me."

"I do not want to wait any longer, my love, but your word is law. I will wait."

Wolf turned away with a muffled groan of frustration and left the tent. He walked to the lake and out into the chilly water. He kept walking until he was submerged, and he remained underwater for ten minutes. When he resurfaced, he noticed several Nanna warriors standing on the shore, staring out across the water in astonishment. They had seen him go under and feared he had drowned. He came out of the water and walked past their quizzical faces, going back to his tent to dry off. Nala had fallen asleep on her back, and the blanket left her breasts exposed.

"Shit!" Wolf muttered, walking outside and back to the lake for another cooling off session. When he came out of the water, he settled himself in front of the tent, knowing if he entered, he would lose his self-control. He stretched out on the ground under the stars by the dwindling campfire. His clothes had been ripped to shreds during his skirmish with the water creatures, so what was left of them dried fast. As he drifted off to sleep, he mumbled to himself for the twentieth time, "Lord, I'm in trouble."

* * *

The morning sun peeked over the hills and through the canopy of trees as Wolf opened his eyes, awakened by whispers and giggling. He sat upright and stretched his muscular arms, prompting lusty sighs from several Nanna women who watched him from a respectful distance. Once he was alert, he got to his feet and walked to the lake, his admirers tagging along behind. He dropped to his knees and splashed cold water in his face, trying to clear his tortured mind. His long hair fell loose of its binding, framing his handsome face, and he decided to go for a swim. He removed his torn shirt, boots and socks, wading out into the lake and ignoring the Nannas' brazen comments about his brawny physique.

After washing up, Wolf dove under the water and then rose slowly, like the mythical Poseidon rising from the sea. He gazed toward the shoreline where the Nannas had gathered to watch him bathe, and as he headed back to land, they moved away from the water, laughing and yelling suggestive remarks. He stepped out of the water and was drying off with the remnants of his shirt when Nala approached from behind and said in a lilting voice, "Good morning, my lord. Did you sleep well?"

Wolf turned and his jaw dropped at the sight of Nala dressed in the same revealing robe that had driven him into the lake twice the night before. He groaned, fearing that he would lose his self-control, and pleaded, "Nala, you're driving me crazy. Please wear something else."

"I'm sorry, my love." Nala tried to hide a smile, and they both knew she wasn't sorry. "This is just the clothing we wear when we are not at war. My mother gave me this robe because my clothes are too ripped to repair. By the way, she wants you to join her for the morning meal. Come, I will take you to her."

Nala led the way, her hips swaying. Wolf exhaled a shaky sigh and walked behind her, looking everywhere but at Nala's enticing form. Following her into the tent, he saw that the Nanna queen wore a robe even sheerer than Nala's and mumbled, "Lord, help me."

"Ah, Wolf, come sit and enjoy the meal. I have good news," Dalla said as she patted the chair next to her. Wolf sat down and Nala handed him a plate of food. After he had devoured a few bites of meat, Nala said with a smile, "I see you like the water beast you killed yesterday."

"It's a different taste, but I enjoy it," Wolf agreed, savoring the chicken-flavored meat.

"Rarely do we get to eat this fare," Dalla said. "These creatures don't often die, and when they do, other animals scavenge them, leaving soggy scraps. We thank you for providing it, and I thank you for saving my daughter."

Dalla rose from her chair and knelt in front of Wolf, cupping her hands. He reached into what was left of his pocket and fished out a washer, handing it to the woman. She accepted it and stood, using a gold chain to make a necklace out of the disk.

"I offer my warriors to your cause, Wolf. We will follow where you lead, sleep where you sleep, and fight whoever and wherever you say."

"I accept your word as an honorable leader. But tell me, Dalla, why did you change your mind and decide to help me fight this war?"

"I saw you fight the water beast. It couldn't hurt you, my lord. In fact, it feared you. You also saved my daughter. I will do whatever you want, whenever you want, my lord," she vowed, making no effort to mask the passion in her dark eyes. Off to the side, Wolf saw Nala gazing at him with desire.

"I accept your loyalty, noble queen," Wolf said. He bowed and left the tent, heading back to the lake for an early morning swim. Dalla and her daughter grinned, and when Wolf was out of hearing, Dalla said, "He will break soon. He is going mad already. Keep teasing and tempting him—his manhood will be his undoing." Both women laughed as they finished their breakfast.

A short time later, Wolf returned from his swim. He had decided it was time to turn the tables and regain the upper hand on these women. He removed his shirt and used his knife to cut his pant legs off to mid-thigh. He still wore his short boots, but the result was what he wanted. Loosening his hair in the Native American tradition of ancient Earth, it fell over his broad back. He was adjusting his weapons when Nala and her mother came out of their tent and caught sight of him. Dalla stared at Wolf with lust and whispered, "Oh my," as a shiver ran down her spine.

"Indeed," Nala murmured, her eyes tracing the broad sweep of his chest and his chiseled midsection.

Wolf approached the women and asked, "So what's your plan, Dalla? Will you deploy your army as Skylla is doing? She is attacking the supply trains and enemy scouting parties."

Mesmerized, Dalla found it impossible to look away as Wolf walked up to her, stopping a mere foot in front of her. He was so tall she had to look up from his chest to see his face. She swallowed hard and said, "I will do whatever is needed, my lord."

"Can you sweep the country in packs, Dalla? I want the ruffians, flankers, and outriders neutralized. I want Waylan's people who weren't able to reach the castle protected," Wolf said, ignoring the stare of the woman who stood before him.

"You want me to kill these men?" Dalla asked with a delighted smile.

"Yes. The ruffians are scum. They are murderers and rapists. Their method of warfare must be extinguished. Waging war on defenseless women and children is unacceptable. Can you do this for me?"

"Yes, my lord. I will divide my warriors into groups of forty and sweep Waylan's land clean of the ruffians in a week. Then we will surround Jonar's army and bite off small chunks while you defend the castle," Dalla replied, her warring instincts fueled by a rush of adrenaline.

"Nala and I will return to King Waylan's castle at once to inform our allies of your support," Wolf said. He pulled the queen into his embrace and hugged her, lifting her off her feet and kissing her cheek. She was breathing hard and her eyes were closed, her cheeks colored with a lovely flush, as he lowered her to the ground and said, "Thank you, Dalla."

Turning away to hide the broad smile on his face, he said, "Let us leave at once, Nala."

Nala gave her mother a warm embrace and said, "I will see you when we have won the war, Mother. Stay safe." Then she ducked back into the tent to dress in the traveling clothes her mother had given her, while Wolf gathered food and water for the journey back to the castle.

They left the Nanna camp a short while later. Wolf took long strides that required Nala to run to keep up with him. He stayed in front of her to avoid the temptation of staring at her curvy figure as he worked to burn off energy.

They made the journey in half the usual time, and Nala was flushed and breathing hard when they reached the plain before the castle gate. The fields were deserted; Waylan's army had been brought into the castle except the roving Nanna warriors. Once Wolf and Nala were inside the gates, they dispatched a runner requesting an audience with Onel to report on their meeting with the Nanna queen. They proceeded to Wolf's quarters, next to the holo-tent, and found Leesa dressed in Nanna leathers, practicing with a whip and knife. Reon was asleep on a cot, and Trulane was eating a chunk of meat.

"Where's Brithee?" Nala asked.

"She is with the Nanna, my sister," Skylla answered from a darkened area of the tent.

"What? Why is she there?" Nala asked in alarm.

"She deserves to be. Her skill rivals yours, my sister, and she mastered most of the advanced skills while you and Wolf were gone. Brithee is very adept...she disarmed me several times yesterday, and I couldn't touch her," Skylla admitted with a rueful smile.

"I knew she would be," Nala said, accepting the news with a note of regret in her voice. "I have seen her move, but I tried to ignore it. I will try her skills myself to be sure she is ready."

"You will see she is more than ready, my sister. But Leesa will require six months before she can run with the Nanna." Skylla walked over to the girl and gave her an affectionate hug.

"I will make you proud, Mother," Leesa vowed with a bright smile. "I will become as good as Brithee, I swear."

"I am already proud of you, my darling. I love you and nothing will ever change that," Nala answered.

"Mother, I cannot be a Nanna, but I would like to fight as you do. Can you teach your eldest son some moves?" Trulane asked. He chuckled and added, "Aunt Skylla gave me a whipping yesterday because I laughed at Leesa when she whacked herself with her whip."

"You liked it, Trulane," Skylla teased. As much as she had tried to dislike and ignore Nala's boys, she was growing fond of them.

The family reunion was going well until Haakon walked out of the tent, spewing rancor. "Whores! Sluts! Nanna filth! How I wish I had never sired any of you. I committed a terrible sin. I hate all of you. I pray you are slaughtered in battle," he shouted.

Skylla glared at Haakon with outright hatred and drew her dagger. Nala grabbed her arm and said, "No Skylla, he is my husband. The right to first kill is mine."

Skylla jerked her arm away and hissed, "I swear to you, Nala, if he insults me again, I will kill him where he stands." Skylla spat at Haakon and stormed away.

Wolf quickly crossed the room to Haakon and grabbed him by the shoulder, pushing him back into the ship. As he walked the man back to his cot, he demanded, "What is wrong with you, Haakon? I don't like the person you have become. You are my guest here, and as my guest, you will refrain from verbal abuse of your family."

"I will leave here today—their presence sickens me. If you want that Nanna slut, take her and those abominations she calls children. I want their stench out of my nose," he said, gritting his teeth. Then he collapsed. Wolf picked him up and called out, "Syn, Haakon has collapsed. Meet me in the medical bay."

"I am already waiting, Commander."

When Wolf entered the room, Syn grinned and remarked, "Nice outfit, Wolf. You must tell me about its origins." She looked him over from head to toe, gave him a throaty laugh, and teased, "Sexy ass."

"Syn!" Wolf exclaimed, pretending to be shocked but grinning broadly. As he placed Haakon on the medical cot, his wristwatch dropped to the floor and he said, "Damn. I must have damaged my watch when I fought the water creatures." Picking it up, he activated the Syn hologram accidentally. He shut it off, but Haakon's eyes were open, and he saw the hologram. He shut his eyes and pretended to be unconscious, listening.

"Dalla's defection from Jonar is good news. She will make a powerful ally," Wolf said. "Nala is coping well—or she was until this fool came out." Wolf gestured at Haakon and added, "He is lost to us. His mind is poisoned. It's a shame. He was a respectable man with a beautiful wife and a family that would make any man proud."

"A beautiful wife who happens to be in love with you, Wolf."

"You find that funny, Syn? I don't."

"Don't tell me you aren't attracted to her. I monitor your vitals...I know she arouses you. I'm not too jealous, though...I'm willing to share," Syn said, laughing softly.

"You and Nala will be the death of me," Wolf sighed. "Have you learned anything more about the sonic device that knocked me unconscious?"

"No, Commander. It must be the harmonics. Somehow the sound softens your body. I am still working on it, but I've been busy with other things. I also have debris from that explosion to sift through."

"Come, let Haakon sleep," Wolf said. "I will talk to him again later, and maybe I can talk sense into him. I also want to shower and meet with the king. Is he up yet?"

Haakon continued to eavesdrop as Syn and Wolf walked to another part of the ship and their voices trailed off. When he could no longer hear them, he climbed off the cot. He was recovering well, thanks to Syn's treatment, and he wasn't hurt as badly as he had acted.

On a whim, Haakon picked up the pouch that held Wolf's ripped clothes from the floor and emptied it. Then he grabbed several random items from a nearby table—Wolf's wristwatch, the M21 pistol, and the Bowie knife—and stuffed them in the pouch. He ran to the exit and peered outside, but drew back when he saw Skylla and several others gazing out over the city as the citizens below prepared for siege. In the distance, smoke rose from the countryside as barns and forests burned. Jonar had arrived.

After a few minutes, Haakon exited the tent and looked down the stairs. A Nanna warrior guarded the corridor, standing with her back to him. Driven by insane delusion and convinced that he was among enemies, his sole concern was to escape this place alive. He knew the Nanna warrior could kill him without much effort if he attacked her head on, but he also knew it was his duty to kill every Nanna he encountered, and this one had to die.

Searching around, Haakon spotted a statue of a man holding a small child on a nearby shelf. It was about sixteen inches tall and weighed at least ten pounds. Grasping it in one hand, he approached the woman from behind and struck her in the head, knocking her senseless. He fled down the stairs, blending in with the palace staff and functionaries. He made his way to the outer gates of the castle, where the guards recognized him as Wolf's friend and allowed him to pass into the hostile lands that would soon be occupied by Jonar's army.

Chapter 27

King Waylan was lying in bed asleep as Nurse Syn explained to Wolf, "I've increased his sedative dosage. His body is developing a resistance to it, and he keeps waking up. The dosage I'm giving him now would knock out a dinosaur."

Syn adjusted an IV and remarked, "His blood work is unusual. My scans detected several properties and compounds I can't identify. If I didn't know better, I would say he is not of this world. Other than you, I have never seen someone whose body regenerates so rapidly. Since I removed the broken sword tip from his leg, he appears to be rejuvenating and getting younger." She handed Wolf the sword tip and he examined it, running his thumb over the inscription.

"What's this writing etched into the metal?"

"I haven't been able to decipher it. The metal is made from an iron compound found in meteorites. It's ancient."

"He is a remarkable man," Wolf said. He handed the metal shard back to Syn and picked up Waylan's chart, glancing through it.

Syn filled a syringe and inserted it into the IV. "This should bring him around in an hour or two. I'll monitor him and let you know when he awakens."

Just a few drops of the medication had infused into the IV when Waylan's eyes fluttered open and he demanded a draught of beer. Syn served the king water, which he sipped and spat out, demanding a beer.

"You can't have a beer. It's not good for you." Syn answered in a tone she might use to lecture a child.

"Woman, I can have whatever I want in my castle, and right now, I want a beer. I'll fetch it myself if you don't get me one." Waylan grinned at Wolf and added, "Can I get you one?"

Syn went to a nearby cabinet and took out a wine decanter and chalice. She poured a half-glass of wine and handed it to Waylan, who tasted it and declared, "This wine is excellent! You must teach my brewmasters how you make it so. Without a doubt, this is the best wine I have tasted in a long time."

As Syn attempted to feed Waylan, he grabbed her breast and patted her bottom, using both hands in a single movement. She turned to view a monitor panel on the wall, exposing her backside to him, and he gave her a playful slap. She moved out of his reach as Waylan and Wolf both laughed.

"My lord, are you sure you are up to a frolic with me? I can be quite frisky myself," Syn teased as she slipped down her top and exposed her full, perfectly formed breasts to the king and Wolf. Waylan dropped the chalice of wine in his lap, staring wide-eyed, and Wolf's laugh trailed off into a shocked, jealous frown. Both men remained speechless for a moment, and finally, Syn said with a smirk, "I thought not," and pulled up her top.

"Sire, back to business," Wolf said, deflecting the monarch's attention from Syn's breasts to more pressing concerns. "Dalla, the Nanna queen, has joined with us. Her warriors are out in the countryside as we speak hunting down Jonar's ruffians and outriders."

"Excellent news! Tell me, is Queen Dalla as lovely as they say?"

"What did you give him, Syn?" Wolf asked with a chuckle. "He's a randy old goat now." "No, my friend, I am pain-free now. It has been many years since I felt this good. I need good beer, good food, and maybe a good woman," Waylan replied, winking at Syn.

"Lecher!" she shot back with an amused grin.

"You do excellent work, Syn, and I thank you...but when can I leave this place? I want to sit in my throne room and discuss the plans to defend the castle against Jonar."

"Let me check your incisions," Syn answered. Waylan grinned but became serious as he caught a warning look in her eyes. She checked under his bandages and saw that several of the incisions were nearly healed. The staples she had used to suture the large incisions near his ribs were pushing out, so she removed them. She passed a scanner over the rapidly healing surgical wounds, and her face held a hint of confusion as she glanced at the readings.

"If you help him, Wolf, he can leave now. I will give him meds and a shot of antibiotics to prevent infection." Syn pulled several packets from a cabinet, administered an injection, and removed the king's IV line. He stood, hugged Syn, and walked from the room unassisted.

"That is one tough man," Wolf observed with a grin.

"Much about him intrigues me, Commander. It's as if he has been enhanced genetically."

* * *

Syn and Wolf walked back through the ship and noticed Haakon was not on his cot where they had left him. Wolf assumed that the man had gone for a stroll, perhaps to clear his head and cool his emotions. Syn went out to the roof to talk with Nala and several women congregated around her, while Wolf and Waylan proceeded to the stairs. When they reached the landing, they looked down and spotted the unconscious Nanna below. Wolf bounded down the stairs and saw that the woman was bleeding from a large gash at the back of her head. He quickly checked her pulse and detected a strong, steady beat at her throat. As he examined her for other injuries, he noticed a statue lying on the ground nearby, broken in two pieces.

Wolf lifted the woman and carried her up the stairs and into the tent, announcing, "Syn! We have an emergency. The guard we posted on the stairs has been attacked. There's an intruder in the castle."

Waylan followed Wolf into the tent, muttering, "I am surrounded by traitors!" He was furious that guests in his castle now had been attacked twice.

Syn was waiting for them in the medical bay and directed Wolf to place the woman on the examining table. She scanned her and said, "She has a concussion, but she will be fine. What happened?"

"She was struck in the head with a small statute. Someone tried to sneak in...or out." As Wolf said the words, he knew in his gut what had happened and declared, "Haakon! Quick, let's get back to where we left him."

They ran back to the room where Haakon had been quartered. As Wolf entered, he told Waylan, "My lord, please make sure no one comes inside."

The king nodded and positioned himself in the doorway, arms

279

folded across his chest and an angry scowl on his weathered face. Wolf searched the room and quickly discovered his M1 was missing and so was his new wristwatch. "Shit!" he cursed. "We must find Haakon at once! He has taken several very dangerous items from me," he informed Waylan, bristling with anger. He was furious at Haakon but even more upset with himself for misjudging the man he had called his friend.

"I will go to my throne room and order the gates sealed," Waylan said. "We will search every inch of the castle. Come, Wolf."

The two men left as Syn treated the wounded Nanna warrior and then activated a tracking device on Wolf's stolen watch. She detected that it had already been taken from the castle, and Haakon would soon be in the enemy's hands.

"I have located the watch, Commander. It is outside the castle," Syn said in Wolf's ear.

"Sire, go ahead," Wolf told the king. "I need to check on something. I will meet you in the throne room."

Waylan continued down the stairs, still unsteady on his feet. When he was out of earshot, Wolf said, "Damn it, Haakon was pretending to be asleep when we talked. He knows too much. Can you lead me to him, Syn?" he asked with a sense of foreboding.

"Yes, but he will be in Jonar's hands within the hour, and twenty thousand men surround the castle."

"Shit, can this get any worse?"

"Perhaps," Syn answered stoically. "Time will tell."

* * *

After Haakon passed through the gates to the plains outside the castle, he started talking to himself. As he recalled the conversation he had overheard earlier between Wolf and Syn, a jealous rage swept over him and he flailed his arms in the air, yelling, "That bastard has a fine woman and now he craves the Nanna whore who deceived me. I have consorted with a harlot and fathered filth. She deceived me with trickery and now tries to lure me back. Never will that whore set eyes on me again. And the outsider—even his own whore laughs at him for wanting to possess both women at once. He is not the warrior of legend. He is an impostor. I will stop his witch from casting spells by taking his toys and breaking them."

Haakon walked on, crushing leaves and snapping twigs underfoot, making no attempt at stealth. He was jabbering to himself and waving his arms like a lunatic as a band of ruffians drew closer. When they were within striking range, they jumped Haakon from behind. He struggled until one man hit him over the head with a club and knocked him out cold. One of the attackers was about to cut his throat when Sylvaine materialized and hissed, "Hold your strike, fool. That is the traveler's friend. Gather his belongings and follow me."

The ruffians collected the items Haakon had stolen and hoisted the unconscious man from the ground, handling him like a sack of grain. After walking a few miles, they came to a well-ordered camp. It was set up in Roman fashion, with four gates, one at each end. Inside, straight rows of tents wrapped around the camp in a square. The outer perimeter was protected by a wide ditch lined with sharp stakes. The men took Haakon to the largest tent at the center of the camp. It was guarded by several hulking warriors dressed in ancient, silver armor. Sylvaine ordered the men to drop Haakon's body by the entrance, and then he dismissed them. He picked up the pouch that contained the stolen items and stepped into the tent, announcing, "Sire, I have found someone and some objects that are very interesting."

"What have you found, my friend?" asked a voice. The man who stepped out into the light was black as coal. His features were finely chiseled, and his face had an aristocratic quality that hinted of African royalty in his lineage. He had short, straight black hair, tapered at an angle on the sides and back, giving a layered appearance and held in place by a small golden crown. He smiled, revealing straight white teeth and asked, "What have you brought me, Sylvaine?"

"Do you recall the outsider who destroyed an army of ruffians and thwarted our early occupations?" At a nod from the man, Sylvaine said, "I have his friend and these things." He removed the objects from the pouch and spread them on the table in front of Jonar. The man's eyes glowed with excitement as he saw the items, and he said, "Bring our new friend inside. I want to ask him about these. I am very pleased with you, Sylvaine."

Two guards dragged Haakon into the tent and dropped him face up on the floor. Sylvaine picked up a basin of water and dumped it in Haakon's face. The man lurched to a sitting position, sputtering, and looked around with a jaundiced eye.

"Where am I?" Haakon demanded when he saw Sylvaine gazing down at him.

"You are in the camp of Jonar, rightful ruler of the world," Sylvaine replied.

"Jonar! Where is Jonar?" Haakon cried out. He laughed insanely and struggled to his feet, swaying unevenly.

Sylvaine pointed a grimy, unwashed finger at the dark man and answered, "This is Jonar, master of the world."

"I am in the presence of Jonar?" Haakon mumbled, squinting at the man. He erupted into hysterical cackling as Sylvaine glared at him.

"He is mad," Jonar said with a chuckle.

Suddenly lucid, Haakon replied, "Mad? Am I mad? No! I have seen the evil. It lies in the castle of Waylan. The man everyone calls a hero talks to shadows. His woman disappears and makes copies of herself. She is beautiful but evil, and like my wife, she is a whore." He rambled on for several minutes, insulting the Nanna and everyone he knew.

"What do you mean by copies of herself? And what are these items?" Jonar interrupted.

"She can appear in different forms and be anywhere. She is a demon with evil powers." Haakon pointed at the items on the table and identified them one by one. "This is the false hero's knife...and this is a weapon he used to kill a dintar." Gesturing to Wolf's wristwatch, he added, "That is a summoning device he uses to call the demon bitch...I will show you." He lurched to the table and pressed random buttons on the watch.

Back at the castle, Wolf was talking to Syn when she suddenly said, "Your watch has been activated, Commander. I am in a tent with Haakon, a black man, and Sylvaine."

"Deactivate it, Syn. Now!" Wolf shouted.

Syn's hologram materialized in front of the three men, dressed in her Tomb Raider outfit. Haakon dropped the watch on the floor, cowering in fear. She gazed at the men as Sylvaine drew his sword and positioned himself in front of Jonar.

"So, witch, you have returned. You are no more real than my projections are," Sylvaine laughed.

"I am no mere projection, you fool!" Syn materialized a blade and raised it as Sylvaine drew his sword and swung. Their weapons met in midair with a loud clang, showering sparks around the room. Haakon grabbed the watch and frantically pressed buttons, thinking he was sending the demon woman back, but Syn had already severed the connection and the hologram vanished.

Haakon babbled, "You see! The bracelet summons the witch! I saw him do it. She is evil. The witch can be everywhere at once. He is a false hero. They both must be slain!"

Jonar looked at the watch and asked, "May I see that, my friend? I will help you kill the witch. Together, we can do it. What say you?"

Haakon nodded and replied, "I know the outsider is not the warrior of legend. He can be hurt or even killed."

Jonar's eyes lit up at that news, and he flashed a sly smile, playing devil's advocate. "No, my friend, he is invincible. He will rule the world and all women will become his slaves." With a wink at Sylvaine, he added, "We must protect the world from his evil and the demon bitch that serves him. If only I knew how to stop him...I would bestow great wealth and prestige to know that man's weakness."

Haakon stared at Jonar and his face broke into a crazy grin. "I will tell you how to slay him, and I ask for nothing but to witness his agony." Haakon lapsed into another babbling rant about the Nanna being diseased and dirty whores, and then he said in an even tone, "The thing that exploded had something in it that almost killed him. It hurt his ears."

Jonar's eyes snapped to Haakon and he smiled. "Ah, the fire must have hurt him."

"No, the fire has no effect. His demon whore said it was something called harmonics. It makes his body soft like everyone

283

else's. That is why I now know he is not the one. A real hero can't be hurt by harmless noise."

Jonar knew immediately what Wolf's weakness was. He caught Sylvaine's eye and cocked his head, giving Haakon an evil sneer. Sylvaine walked behind the ranting man while Jonar distracted him. Something in his hand glistened as he raised his arm, and then Haakon cried out as Sylvaine plunged his dagger into his back. Jonar drew his own dagger and stabbed Haakon in the chest, saying, "Goodbye, my friend. I'll do this on my own. But don't worry, I'll send your whore wife to be with you soon enough!"

Haakon muttered, "Slay the woman of the wasteland, do not let her breed or you bring death to your door..." his breath trailed off as he coughed up blood, closed his eyes, and died.

"Yes, Haakon, you sinned by fathering those children and now you have your just rewards." Jonar wiped the blood off his dagger, turning his attention to the objects Haakon had stolen. He had seen pistols and the manner in which men held them in an old book. He picked up the gun and pulled the trigger, but nothing happened. Dropping it, he snatched up Wolf's watch and said, "This is marvelous, Sylvaine. It may be what I have been searching for all these years. It is high technology—a power source, like the old books say used to exist. I will be able to use this to reactivate the machine."

"I thought we would use it to kill that muscle-bound buffoon," Sylvaine complained.

"If what this babbling lunatic said is true, we have always possessed the power." Jonar smiled as he caressed the watch face with his fingers, being careful not to press the buttons. He now had vital information on how to fight the stranger, and how to hurt him. The simple howlers, used to keep rodents from damaging the outdoor boxes, could cause him pain. Jonar's face broke into a sinister smile as he thought, *I want it all!* He told Sylvaine, "Recall the troops and return to Danmore Castle. We will attack another day."

"Master, the men will not like it. The ruffians have been sipping drynox for hours, and they are looking forward to rapine and slaughter. It could cause us to lose face. Not only that, they are in a killing frenzy and can't be reined in."

284

"What do I care? When I figure this out, we will not need an army. This is real power," Jonar declared, holding up the watch. "Remember, the machine is what I want most of all, and the demon witch is the key to unlocking it. I saw the light flash on the machine when that man first arrived. That same light moves whenever he travels. I know he has something...a ship that follows him, and that witch will give it to me. The howler signal affects his power to talk with the witch, and I have changed its noise further. The ancients were a strange race, leaving books that explained how to create such wonders. The machine is complicated and may need repair, but I know the witch can repair it. Then, I can call the Old Ones. I will ask them to return and take us to the stars."

Noticing Sylvaine's angry expression, Jonar chuckled and asked, "Honestly, my friend, do you think we can take the castle with the men we have?"

Sylvaine considered the numbers and scowled. "We will lose thousands and may only force the exterior gates. We would never get to the Bridge of Heroes."

After considering for a moment, Jonar said, "This is what I will do, Sylvaine. I will give you the ruffian army to attack the castle, and we will give this legendary warrior a surprise. Give the men pure drynox."

Sylvaine stared at Jonar in shock.

"I want them insane for this fight," Jonar said. "You will like what I have in store for the outsider. When you encounter him, give him my regards. Let the ruffians fight and do as much damage as possible. I will bring my main army back to defend our homeland against the Nanna. Take the remainder of the army and attack the castle, although I doubt you will have many men left when you are done playing."

"Aye, my lord, I will destroy the castle gates. When we return to attack the next time, they will be gone."

Jonar glanced down at Haakon's lifeless body and said, "Put this fool in a box, along with these two items." He handed Sylvaine two large cylinders. "Deliver the box to Waylan's castle immediately. This should create a certain amount of tension and chaos."

Both men laughed as Sylvaine summoned soldiers to drag Haakon's body away and clean the bloody area where the man had been murdered.

* * *

Back at Waylan's castle, in the privacy of the ship, Wolf was quizzing Syn about what she saw at Jonar's camp and asked, "What did they look like, Syn?"

"I assume you mean Jonar? He's an African, I believe. Very handsome and fearless. I tried to slay him but Sylvaine engaged me. I'm sorry, Commander, but not only did I fail to slay him, I also failed to scan him. I've locked out the watch. I can track it by its radioactive power source, and I can reactivate it if we recover it. But I worry Jonar might reverse engineer its technology if he is as smart as we think he is. Haakon may have given him easy access to our advanced technology."

"Damn it, I can't believe Haakon would betray us. What the hell happened to him?"

"His close call with death unhinged him...and he was very jealous of you. He knew Nala was in love with you. He sensed it on your first meeting. I detected her hormonal activity when she first saw you, but I paid no attention. I knew you would respect her marriage to Haakon. But it seems every woman who gets around you wants to mate with you," Syn remarked with a rueful smile.

"I didn't know she was in love with me. I felt something when we touched, but I didn't react to it. I should have told you."

"I knew, Wolf. I monitor you too," Syn admitted. "I don't mind. You know I love Nala."

"Syn, please don't. I am already on the verge of going as crazy as Haakon. Please don't add this. You know I can never be with Nala anyway. I have so many biological hazards from the twenty-first century in my system, it could kill her."

"Commander, when Nala was injured, I inoculated her against everything and anything you could possibly give her. She is the only woman on this planet you could mate with and not put in danger,"

Syn said.

"What about you, Syn? You're a woman," Wolf said, watching her reaction.

"Why do you torture me, Wolf? I am light and energy. What I feel for you may be just a program in my memory core put there by my creator. I can't give you what you need now, and Nala can. You don't age as these people do, Wolf—they grow old much faster. Enjoy Nala and any life you may have together while you can." Syn's voice was cool and detached, sounding as if she would soon depart Wolf's life and he might never see her again.

Wolf's mind filled with a sense of foreboding. He was about to respond when a soldier approached with a sense of urgency and announced, "King Waylan requests your presence at the front gate of the castle, my lord. Please come at once."

Wolf gave Syn a sad smile and promised to return soon. She tapped into the satellite feed as he left, zooming in on the front gate. When she saw blood pooled around the corners of a large wooden box, she thought, *My poor Wolf. Your guilt will never let you find love now.*

* * *

Wolf accompanied the guard through the castle and came upon Onel conversing with the priest Randelf. The priest's face broke into a broad smile as he shook Wolf's hand.

"Greetings, Randelf. How do you like the book?" Wolf asked.

"It is amazing, my lord. The writing is profoundly beautiful. I weep from the sheer beauty of its words. The book you have given to us will reshape our world. I am now reading the Book of Psalms. Everyone who reads the passages is amazed," Randelf answered.

"It gets a lot better, my friend. When you finish reading the Old Testaments, the Son of God arrives and the world changes. Do not skip any chapters...they are well worth the time to read. Now come, Onel, the king has something important to show us," said Wolf.

Eras and King Waylan were waiting at the castle's main gate. When Wolf approached, Eras cautioned, "It's not pretty, my lord. A while ago, several ruffians came out of the forest. They approached the castle wall, dragging that box." He gestured towards the main portcullis where a large wooden box had been placed. "The ruffians stopped just beyond spear range and left the box. We went out to inspect it."

"Show me," Wolf ordered, swallowing hard as he fought back a sinking feeling.

A guard pulled open the lid, and Wolf gazed inside at Haakon's mutilated corpse. It had been hacked into pieces, and his severed head was positioned to display a large "S" carved into his forehead.

"It is the bloody mark of Sylvaine the butcher," Waylan muttered in disgust.

"I will rip his head off with my bare hands," Wolf muttered through clenched teeth. His face flushed crimson with rage. "Why would he do this?"

"He does it to push you over the edge and bring you outside to fight on his terms," said Onel.

"I will kill him. He will get what he wants now. I will destroy Jonar and everyone with him," Wolf vowed.

"Commander, a large army is approaching to attack the gate. I estimate eleven thousand," Syn reported in Wolf's ear.

"King Waylan, alert your men. Jonar approaches with an army of thousands. Prepare for battle!" Wolf shouted.

Waylan flexed his arms and ordered, "Knights! Squires! Spearmen! Prepare to repel the invaders!"

"I will go out to attack," Wolf said to Waylan, grabbing a sword from a man at arms and tucking it into his belt. He then took a large, ornate war ax from the wall and walked outside. The portcullis slammed down behind him with a thud that sent a tremor through the earth underfoot.

"Commander, don't be silly. Get inside now!" Syn yelled.

Wolf took off running towards the enemy as the first wave of ruffians charged across the plain, screaming insanely and brandishing an array of primitive weapons. He leapt into the air and came down in the midst of the enemy like a bomb, sending men and body parts scattering in all directions. Using his fists, he knocked down one ragged man after another, trying to avoid killing them. He blocked sword thrusts with his large war ax and urged the attacking men to retreat. Then, he saw their vacant stares and foaming mouths, and heard their insane babbling, and he knew these men were lost forever.

With a deep sigh of regret, Wolf muttered, "So be it!" He drew his sword and brought it down with one hand, hacking a man in two with an overhead swing. Swinging his ax at another man, he cut his head off cleanly. He waded into the onrushing sea of attackers, wielding the sword with one hand and the ax with the other. Men went down one after another as he cut them apart. Even in his rage over Haakon's senseless murder, he didn't want to kill these men—he wanted their leaders. He kept telling those who faced him to surrender, to run away, but they just kept coming.

Waylan was watching from the castle gate. He had sent a runner for his battle armor, and he was rallying his spearmen to the gate. As he looked on, ruffians attacked from all sides. Wolf rose above the blood-soaked plain, climbing up a hill of death and sinking moments later into a pile of mangled flesh. Waylan roared with pride that such a brave warrior was fighting for him. He pulled a sword from a guard and declared, "I will assist him. No man fights my battles alone!"

Onel grabbed his brother's shoulder and asked, "Are you sure you are fit?"

"I have not felt better in years," Waylan answered. "Wolf's woman even removed the metal from my leg. Let me go, brother."

Onel paled and demanded, "Give me the fragment."

"Wolf's woman has it. Now release me!" Waylan growled, becoming agitated.

"Waylan, wait! You can't go out there and fight without your armor. Wolf is invincible. You are not," Onel argued.

"How can I stand here and watch him fight? Am I not a man? Am I not a king?" Waylan struggled to wrench his arm free from Onel's surprisingly strong grip.

"Yes, you are king, but I am oldest and you will wait for your armor!" Onel said with more force than Waylan had ever heard from him before. Waylan stopped struggling and replied, "Yes, my brother. I will concede to you as oldest."

Wolf's slaughter of the ruffians raged on for another fifteen minutes. Finally, two soldiers approached Waylan, carrying the king's massive armor. The men were exhausted and perspiring from the effort.

"Get my armor on me at once!" the king shouted, pointing out at the battlefield. "Look at him, men. There is a true warrior!" Waylan stripped, and his squires dressed him in his battle armor. Grabbing his sword, he yelled, "Open the gate!"

Onel gazed out at the battlefield and couldn't believe what he was seeing. Wolf, a one-man killing machine, was mowing down Jonar's vast army. "Sire, you have but a few hundred spearmen. Wait until the rest arrive," he urged.

"A brave warrior out there fights for me! Can I do any less for him?" Waylan shouted. "Old Guard! We have fought many battles, vanquished many enemies, and slain many foes. I ask you one more time, my loyal friends, give me your courage. Give me your hearts. Give me your power to defeat these evil men who attack us, and to uphold justice. They laugh at our age, tell jokes about our waning strength. Let us show them what men once roamed this land while they were sucking milk from their mothers' breasts! I am Waylan of Springdale, and I say 'Death to Jonar!'"

Waylan's men shouted the chorus, "Death to Jonar," chanting it again and again like a mantra. The massive portcullis opened with a creaking groan. Waylan and his Old Guard surged through the gate, hitting the enemy ranks like a freight train. The king was still sore, but he came on like a whirlwind and tried to battle to Wolf's side, leaving his Old Guard warriors to clean up his leftovers. While Wolf allowed swords, knives, and clubs to strike him, and he dealt death to anyone close by, Waylan avoided the strikes aimed at him. He swung his heavy sword like a willow switch, striking death wherever it touched as he fought his way towards Wolf.

Sylvaine spotted Wolf and walked towards him, slaying his own ruffians who blocked his path. He carried a small wooden box. Placing it on the ground, he flipped a switch and turned a dial that clicked. He then shoved the box under a bloody corpse to conceal it. At that same instant, the wooden box that held Haakon's body at the castle gate started ticking.

Sylvaine moved closer to Wolf. When he was face to face, he hissed, "So, buffoon, we meet again. My master has a surprise for you." Wolf ran at Sylvaine and they exchanged sword strokes. Sylvaine was quick and dexterous but knew he couldn't withstand a direct stroke, so he used redirection to avoid Wolf's mighty sword.

"You are no hero, you jackass. You kill weak men with ease, but see how skill evens the score," Sylvaine shouted. He landed a series of slashes to Wolf's body but merely shredded his clothes.

"I will kill you! Why would you murder an insane man?" Wolf shouted, rage in his eyes.

"I did the world a favor. I did you a favor, too, by clearing your way to his whore wife's heart. That lunatic told us of your love for his Nanna wife, how you coveted her. You are a wife stealer, an adulterer —a lecher of a man. How could you betray a friend for his wife? Now that I have killed him, your conscience can be clear. She can be your whore now." Sylvaine laughed and backed towards the box he had concealed.

"You foul-mouthed bastard! How dare you insult her so?" Wolf shouted, jumping at Sylvaine. Suddenly, the box Sylvaine had placed on the ground made a humming noise. The sound grew louder and Wolf dropped his sword, holding his ears in pain.

Sylvaine walked up to Wolf as he fell to his knees. With a cruel laugh, he declared, "My master was right. You can be hurt." He kicked Wolf's battle ax out of reach and placed a heavy boot on his shoulder, forcing him over onto his back.

"Commander, are you all right? My sensors show you're in distress," Syn yelled.

"Syn, help me," Wolf croaked weakly.

"Wolf!" Syn screamed in a panicked voice.

"Syn, what's wrong?" Nala demanded, appearing in the doorway with a frightened look.

"Wolf is in trouble. His vital signs are weak. But don't worry, Nala, I am about to show you Wolf's boat." The ship rose and the tent disappeared as Syn lifted off and navigated out to the battlefield. Only Reon saw the tent vanish, and to his young mind, it was just magic.

291

"Wolf is in trouble? What could hurt him?" Nala shouted, terrified by Syn's demeanor. Then, her face paled and she asked, "Jesu, are we *flying?*"

"Jonar has discovered Wolf's weakness. He is trying to use it to kill him. Yes, we are airborne."

Nala's shock was short-lived as her concern went back to Wolf. She thought of him dying and yelled, "No! This can't be. We must help him!"

"I am losing power!" Syn hissed. "It's another jamming signal. This one is disrupting my circuitry and scrambling the ship's electronics. The frequency is rotating, and I can't isolate it. If I go any closer, we will lose power and crash. Damn it, I can't even get a weapon lock." With tears in her eyes, Syn whispered hoarsely, "I can't help him, Nala."

"How close can you get? Can you put us on the ground?"

"I can get about thirty-five feet above the signal. It is too far to jump, Nala." Then, Syn had an idea and added, "Wait...I can lower you with the robotic arm."

Syn split in two—Tomb Raider Syn navigated the ship while Nurse Syn grabbed Nala's arm and headed for the bay. She took a harness off the wall and wrapped it around Nala, saying, "Pull this lever like this to detach the rope." Syn demonstrated the release mechanism. "When you are close to Wolf, detach it."

Nala was wringing her hands and seemed to be far away. Syn grabbed her shoulders and warned, "Nala, don't detach until you are seven feet or less from the ground. If you detach too soon, you could break your legs."

"I will wait until I am close. Take me to Wolf."

Picking up an ear bud from a nearby table, Syn showed it to Nala and said, "I need to put this in your ear. It will allow us to talk to one another." Nala nodded, and Syn pressed the tiny device onto the triangular fossa of Nala's right ear, applying momentary pressure.

"Can you hear me?" Syn asked, and Nala nodded in amazement.

"Good luck, Nala. Please save Wolf," Syn whispered. She engaged the mechanical arm, pulling Nala from the ship, and dangled her over the battlefield.

Sylvaine flashed a triumphant smile and his eyes roamed across the battlefield looking for Waylan. The old king was surrounded by ruffians and would have his hands full for some time. Sylvaine raised his visor and spat in Wolf's face. "So, clown, how does it feel to be in pain? Does it hurt? Here, let me help you," Sylvaine taunted, swinging his sword and hitting Wolf in the head with it. A small trickle of blood ran from a paper-thin gash.

"Ah! My master's magic makes you human!" Sylvaine smirked with delight. He struck at Wolf's neck, and another thin, bleeding laceration appeared. "You ass in a lion's skin, I told you I would kill you. We know your secret." He pulled a long, thin dagger out of his belt. Wolf was lying on his back, holding his ears in pain. Sylvaine placed the knife on Wolf's chest above his heart and said, "My master sends his regards." He pushed down, twisting the dagger. The tip of the weapon started a pinprick of blood as he leaned his full weight on it. The blade sank a little deeper into Wolf's chest as Sylvaine rocked it back and forth. Wolf gritted his teeth in pain and began singing the Hopi death chant.

"Noooooooo!" Syn screamed as she translated the song.

Sylvaine was jubilant as he saw the trickle of blood flow from the wound, and then the knife sank another eighth of an inch deeper. He hit bone, but twisted the blade around, looking for a way into Wolf's chest. The knife penetrated deeper, and Sylvaine leered as he said, "Now, you die, buffoon!"

Suddenly, Sylvaine grunted in pain as he was thrown several feet into the air and away from Wolf's body.

"Keep your filthy hands off my man!" Nala screamed. She leaned on her left foot, poised for battle. Her right ankle was visibly dislocated. As Syn had feared, Nala had detached from the harness early, dropping fifteen feet to the ground.

Sylvaine climbed to his feet and glared at Nala with contempt. "So, the Nanna slut has arrived. You're the one Haakon cursed before he died."

"You lie! Haakon is not dead."

"He is dead, bitch, because I killed him. I took the items he stole and delivered them to my master. He died like the weak dog he was, but he saved his last breath to curse you, whore."

Sylvaine ran at Nala, laughing and swinging his sword. She jumped to the side, trying to balance on her left foot, and grimaced in pain from the movements of her dislocated right foot. Sylvaine signaled to a knot of ruffians and they converged on her, driving her back from Wolf's body, although the attack left three ruffians dead.

Sylvaine approached Wolf, who was now unconscious, and kicked him in the face. Then, he dropped to a knee and placed the tip of his dagger in Wolf's right eye. With a wicked laugh, Sylvaine glared at Nala and hissed, "Say goodbye to him, bitch."

Time ran in slow motion for Nala as she watched Sylvaine place his dagger in Wolf's eye. She took a step forward but lost her footing and fell. A swarm of ruffians toppled her and pinned her down on the ground, laughing, punching, grabbing her breasts, and tearing at her clothes. She struggled ferociously but could not fight them off. One man drew his dagger and slashed her across the chest, just above her breasts. He laughed and cut another deep gash above the first, slowly working his way up to her throat. Nala fought wildly, but her eyes weren't on the blade the ruffian held to her throat. Her gaze was on Sylvaine as he taunted her, moving his dagger back and forth from Wolf's right eye to his left as she watched helplessly. It felt like an eternity passed as she closed her eyes and whispered, "I'm sorry, Syn. I couldn't save him."

A horn blast sounded from the battlements. Sylvaine hesitated and looked up to see the castle gates opening and another wave of Old Guard fighters pouring out onto the field. Severed heads and arms flew in all directions as the old men swarmed forward. The ruffians holding down Nala disappeared in sprays of blood as Waylan finally reached her. He smashed one man's face with the pommel of his sword and swung backhanded, cutting off the head off another. Drawing his poniard, he stabbed a third ruffian in the back and then knelt, grabbing the one who had Nala pinned. With a mighty twist, he broke the man's neck. Nala scrambled to her feet, bloody but still ready to fight. She fought at Waylan's side as he battled to reach Wolf.

Sylvaine held his ground, sheathing his dagger, and he stood with his sword drawn, the point on the ground. He had gloated over his victory, and it had cost him his chance to slay the outsider. "So Waylan, we meet at last," he sneered as the king confronted him.

"Yes. I have come to kill you. Now get away from that man."

"This man?" asked Sylvaine, kicking Wolf in the face. "I think not. He dies here, now."

Waylan advanced, swinging his sword in a figure-eight pattern, and Sylvaine barely got his sword up in time to deflect. As the two men battled, Nala limped to Wolf's side. Several ruffians came to defend Sylvaine, but Waylan hacked and slashed until only the silver knight remained.

"Syn, can you hear me?"

"Yes, Nala...just barely. The jamming device that prevents me from landing isn't disrupting communications. How is Wolf?"

"He has several wounds. One is deep in his chest, above his heart. He's bleeding, Syn!"

"Is he breathing, Nala?"

"I think he's dead," Nala sobbed.

Syn's circuits heated up and the sky above the plain rumbled from the ship's engines accelerating to full power. Many of the combatants on the field stopped and gazed up at the sky in wonder at the loud, rumbling noise.

"Is he breathing, Nala? Put your ear on his chest."

"Yes, he's breathing, but he won't wake up. Wolf, my love, come back to us! Please come back to us," Nala cried.

"Get a hold of yourself, Nala! Something is affecting Wolf. Look around for anything unusual or out of place...something close to him."

Nala rubbed the tears from her eyes and looked around. She saw nothing but mutilated bodies and abandoned weapons. "I don't know what I am looking for, Syn."

"Damn it, Nala, look for something that shouldn't be there. Get up, damn you, and walk around him. Move a few feet out in all directions."

"All right, Syn." Nala limped in a circle around Wolf, searching the ground for anything that didn't belong on a battlefield. She

295

glanced briefly at Sylvaine and Waylan as the two men fought, neither retreating. Sylvaine intensified his attack, driving Waylan back. The old king had to turn and defend himself from a ruffian, allowing Sylvaine to run to Nala's position. She crouched, brandishing her dagger and raising her whip. Before he engaged her, Sylvaine stopped and turned back to Waylan, who had eviscerated his attacker and was charging like a stampeding dintar at the Templar's back. Sylvaine hesitated for a moment, indecisive about which of the two to attack. He looked at Nala and then Waylan, crouched, and waved his sword back and forth like a dog wagging its tail. He threatened both but never moved a step from where he stood. It seemed to Nala that he was trying to protect a certain area and did not want to leave where he stood. She glanced down and spotted a small box, partially concealed by a dead soldier's legs.

"Syn, could it be in a box?"

"Maybe, Nala...do you see one?"

Nala pulled her whip and attacked Sylvaine. He stood his ground, repelling her whip as well as Waylan's sword. Several of Sylvaine's men came to his aid, and Waylan was forced to engage them while Nala battled Sylvaine. She changed her attack, snapping at Sylvaine's face from many different angles and driving him back several feet. The tactic gave her the chance to snag the box with her whip and pull it to her.

"Nanna bitch! NO!" Sylvaine yelled, charging at her. He raised his sword, preparing to deliver a vast, overhand blow that would smash through her hastily raised dagger and split her skull. But Waylan charged Sylvaine from behind and let out an animal roar. Sylvaine felt death's cold breath as his nape hairs rose on the back of his neck and he spun around, blocking Waylan's well-aimed sword that would have cut him in half.

"I got it, Syn. Should I smash it?"

"No. Don't do that, Nala. It is probably rigged to blow up. It will kill you."

"I will gladly give my life for Wolf!" Nala cried. "I will smash the box. Goodbye, Syn. Tell Wolf that I loved him."

"Nala, don't! In his weakened condition, Wolf will also die. Just get it away from him. The farther away you can take it the better. Run, Nala!"

Nala hooked her whip on her belt clasp. Holding the box in one hand and her dagger in the other, she limped away. She had walked only a few yards when she had to sit down. Placing the box and her knife on the ground, she grabbed her dislocated ankle with both hands. She took a deep breath and twisted it back into place, letting out an anguished cry of pain.

"Nala, what happened? Are you all right?" Syn asked.

"I had to put my ankle back into its socket. It still hurts, but I can walk faster now," Nala answered. She got to her feet, picked up the box and her dagger, and headed away from the battle towards an area where the Old Guard still fought.

"Stop her, men!" Sylvaine shouted as he continued to fend off Waylan.

A band of ruffians ran at Nala, but she was ready. She flipped on one hand, using her tumbling skills to avoid the men. A dagger buried itself in her right shoulder, sending her sprawling on the ground, and she dropped the box. She scrambled to her feet and threw her own dagger into the face of one man, then groaned as she pulled the ruffian's knife from her shoulder and continued to fight. A fist struck her square on the chin and she saw stars. She reflexively swung her blade up in a disemboweling thrust and felt it sink into flesh. A man screamed in pain. She blinked several times, trying to focus her eyes as she flailed her dagger back and forth in a defensive stance.

When Nala's vision cleared, she saw that she still faced four drynox-crazed ruffians. She was injured and slower than usual, so she absorbed blows she would have otherwise avoided. After several minutes of intense fighting, a dozen Old Guard warriors surrounded her, repelling the drug-crazed ruffians and slaying them.

"Your king fights alone over there," Nala said, pointing. "Help him."

The old warriors swarmed over the ruffians who were pursuing her, and Nala ran as fast as her injured ankle would carry her. Suddenly, Syn materialized in front of her. Nala stumbled into her arms, exhausted and weak from loss of blood.

"Here it is," she said, handing the box to Syn's flickering image. The hologram wavered and disappeared, letting Nala and the box drop to the ground. Tired, bleeding, and barely holding on, Nala was too weak to stand. Sobbing, she asked, "Syn, what's wrong? Where are you?"

"I can't hold my shape there," Syn responded, her voice breaking up in Nala's ear bud. "But I scanned the box and it contains explosives. It has more wires and dials than their first device, and it's probably enough to kill everyone near Wolf. Nala, you must take it into the forest so I can destroy it. Take the box into the woods and set it down...place this by it." A small pack of gel with a blinking light dropped from overhead.

"What is this?" Nala asked, picking up the packet.

"It is a tracking signal," Syn explained. "It will help me locate the box and destroy the device that is hurting Wolf."

Nala struggled to her feet as Syn's voice in her ear urged her to hurry. She ran towards the woods, limping on her damaged ankle but determined to save the life of the man she loved. She plunged into the thicket and headed into the forest. After twenty minutes, Syn's crackling voice said, "That should be far enough. Put the box on the ground, Nala, and run back towards the castle as fast as you can."

Nala did as she was told and then began the trek back to the castle. She tried to run, but she was exhausted and in pain, and she moved in slow motion. As she entered a small clearing, she looked up and was startled by a rope dangling in front of her. She forced a weak smile as she thought, *Who else could it be from?* She tied the rope around her waist, and moments later, she was hoisted into the air. Syn appeared and extended a hand, helping Nala climb up into the ship.

The ship rose over the forest as Syn carried Nala to a bench and gently laid her down. When she was a safe distance away from Jonar's sonic device, she used the tracking device on the gel pack to pinpoint the box and then aimed the ship's laser weapon, detonating the howler. The explosion leveled the forest for a mile in all directions. Syn turned the ship and flew back towards the battlefield to see if she could help Wolf, but the jamming signal was still disrupting the ship's navigation and prevented her from descending to the plain.

* * *

The battle raged for several hours. Some of Jonar's ruffians went insane from the pure drynox, discarding their swords and attacking with their bare hands and teeth. Waylan fought valiantly to protect Wolf's unconscious body. He never moved more than a few feet from Wolf, fighting incredible odds as Sylvaine sent his men in waves to drive the king away from the fallen warrior's body.

Syn called Wolf's name again and again in his earpiece. "Wolf! Wolf! Wake up, damn you!" He heard her calling his name from afar. The terrible buzzing pain was gone, but he still felt pain in his chest, head, and neck. His eyes opened and his head throbbed with pain as he mumbled, "Syn?"

"Commander! I was afraid you were dead," Syn gasped, relief in her voice. "Nala, he lives! You saved him!" Nala broke down sobbing and then fainted from exhaustion and loss of blood as Nurse Syn tended to her wounds.

Wolf rolled over onto his elbows and knees. He had an excruciating migraine and was seeing double. He struggled to his feet and asked, "Syn? What happened?"

"You were hit with an LRAD, Commander. It knocked you unconscious and you've been out for hours. I can't land down there because a jamming device is preventing me from getting within a mile of you. I can only fly thirty-five feet above the battlefield. I know where you are because I am tracking your earpiece. We've destroyed the LRAD...but I can't help you."

Wolf's vision focused and he saw the men fighting around him. The roar of the battle exploded in his ears as his full hearing returned. It appeared Jonar's ruffians were going to win. The Old Guard still fought, but they were old men and age was creeping up on them. Some clutched at their chests and dropped to the ground as Jonar's men speared them like fish in a barrel. Others were exhausted and couldn't stand against the strength of the younger mercenaries. They sank to their knees and the ruffians hacked them apart, showing no mercy.

Anger rose in Wolf as he watched Waylan's men being cut down. He picked up a sword and charged into the nearest cluster of enemies, slashing and chopping furiously. He sang a Hopi war song and felt the power of the words energize him. Wolf fought smarter, avoiding direct strikes from the ruffians' weapons. His mask of invincibility had been shattered by recent events, and for the first time since landing in this primitive world, he knew that he could be hurt or even killed. Still, he fought hard, slashing at Sylvaine's warriors. He released the inner beast his grandfather had feared, and he rampaged across the battlefield, slaying dozens of men with no remorse. He no longer regretted killing the ruffians—they were scum, and this world would be better without them. Men scattered and ran as he sang his war song and gained strength. Waylan's men who were still alive took heart and renewed the attack, turning the tide of the battle and repelling the ruffians.

Sylvaine saw the writing on the wall. He had hoped to overwhelm the gates and demolish Waylan's geriatric warriors, but this was crazy. He had lost the only weapon they had that could kill the arrogant outsider. Sylvaine himself had thrown three spears at Wolf and scored direct hits in the chest, head, and thigh with no effect. He assumed Jonar's howler had been destroyed, and now, nothing could scratch his nemesis.

A short distance away, Sylvaine saw Waylan clubbing and hacking at his ruffian troops. The gray-bearded old king should have died a dozen battles ago, but he had lived on and fought on. Hours ago, he had been forced to retreat behind a line of his own warriors, and Sylvaine had expected him to yield to the daunting odds, but the steely old man kept coming, slaughtering all who stood in his path. Despite outnumbering Waylan ten to one, Sylvaine's warriors couldn't kill that wild man.

Now that Wolf was up again, Sylvaine's army was melting like ice on a sunny day. The wounds Sylvaine had inflicted on Wolf earlier had healed. Jonar's howler had worked—but it couldn't kill the man. Still, he had the satisfaction of pushing his dagger into Wolf's chest. He drew the blade, which still had Wolf's blood on it, and examined it with satisfaction. He would have to show this blood to Jonar. Replacing the dagger in its sheath, he glared with disgust as his ineffective army disintegrated.

* * *

Darkness had fallen over the battlefield, yet the fighting raged on. The field was lit with metal pots from the gate's parapets, and Wolf was fighting again, rallying his men. Sylvaine's army was in retreat, trampling in the ankle-deep blood of their fellow warriors. As the men fled, they were intercepted by Dalla's army of ferocious Nanna warriors who had finally arrived to defend the kingdom of Springdale.

Sylvaine cursed the cowardice of his fleeing men as the Nanna and their animals ripped into them. The women were lightning fast and deadly as they flipped through the air, spinning and twisting, slicing and hacking his men to shreds. Sylvaine reflected on Wolf's successful ploy to subvert the Nanna and muttered to himself that this was supposed to be Waylan's army being demolished. A flank of Nannas blocked Sylvaine's retreat as Old Guard warriors closed in from the rear and sliced down his remaining forces. The Templar glared with hatred, first at Wolf and then at Waylan, before retreating into the forest and away to safety.

Wolf heard the howling of Dalla's warriors drawing closer. Across the battlefield, he saw the queen moving with liquid grace as she stabbed, whipped, and beheaded ruffians with a sadistic pleasure that sent a chill down his spine. Freezing in his tracks, he nearly dropped his sword as he saw Brithee. She moved a bit slower than Nala, but the girl was remarkably adept. Wolf got another shock when he caught sight of Onel fighting nearby. The man wasn't the juggernaut his brother was, but he was slaying Sylvaine's men right and left, fighting with a sword in one hand and a shield in the other. His movements were highly skilled and fluid.

Eleven thousand ruffians took the field that day, and fewer than five hundred escaped. Waylan lost two thousand Old Guard fighters and hundreds of men at arms, but it was a victory for his kingdom.

Wolf lost eight hundred men who had pledged to him, while the Nanna didn't lose a single warrior, although many were injured.

Waylan walked over to Wolf and clasped his hand, raising it in the air. "To victory!" he shouted, provoking a roar of jubilation from the field. Wolf raised Waylan's hand proclaiming, "To Waylan, King of the World!" The Old Guard warriors clapped their swords against their shields and cheered again.

"Commander, are you all right?" Syn asked in a shaky voice, and Wolf sensed that she had been crying. Placing a hand over his mouth, he answered, "Yes, Syn, I am unhurt. We have won."

"No, Commander, this was just a token force to whittle down your numbers. Jonar took his best troops and departed hours before Sylvaine attacked with the ruffians. He will return."

"And we will be waiting, Syn."

"Wolf, you need to find the device that is jamming me. It uses a technology superior to the ones Jonar deployed before."

Chapter 28

As the battle ended, and an age-old ritual was acted out—one witnessed in every war fought in human history: the outpouring of misery, weeping, and despair of the survivors. The mighty portcullis swung open, and the wailing started as the wives and children of the fallen came out to find their dead, wounded, and dying. As grief-striken loved ones congregated by the portcullis, the wooden casket holding the mutilated remains of Haakon suddenly exploded. The blast was enormous and ripped the massive gates off the castle entrance.

When the smoke and dust had settled, hundreds were dead or maimed, and the horrific sight of twisted, mangled bodies—most of them defenseless women and children—made men howl with rage. Jonar's bombing was an atrocity, and only a sadist would delight in such a tactic. Soldiers and stunned family members ran to the gates, clawing through the rubble in a frantic search for survivors.

The search and rescue mission went on throughout the night. Men slept where they were, some lying among the dead, as torches were moved around to illuminate the area. Finally, dawn colored the horizon and the first light played across the field of death.

Wolf had labored through the night and was still sorting through the dead. He had lined up his fallen troops in neat rows for burial and tossed the corpses of Sylvaine's ruffians in a pile. He dispatched a detail of men into the forest to gather wood for funeral pyres. Priests blessed the remains of both armies, asking God to accept the fallen knights who had defended the kingdom and forgive the sins of Jonar's invaders. At one point, Syn informed Wolf through his ear bud that the massive blast had silenced the jamming signal.

Waylan toiled beside his subjects, but when Wolf saw him stagger and nearly fall from exhaustion, he grabbed the king by the arm and said, "Sire, come, let us retire. We have done all we can. The Old Guard warriors who gave their lives have been buried, and their graves are blessed. My loyal soldiers have been laid to rest. The only dead out there now belong to Jonar. We will finish later."

"Aye, Wolf, I am spent. Many of my Old Guard left this life as warriors. It is the way all old soldiers past their prime have always dreamed of dying—in battle, serving their lord. I weep for my friends and loyal men. But I am king. No one will work while I rest. This burden I must share," Waylan said, and he went back to digging. By the dozens, the men around him dropped their shovels and sat down, knowing Waylan wouldn't stop working until they did.

Waylan stood to stretch his back when he noticed that his men had stopped working and were watching him. "So you all stop to appease me?" he growled. "My respect for you men and women is beyond question. My pride in you is great. So be it, I will retire...for the time being."

The king gave orders to the men who remained behind to deal with the carnage and placed guards at the demolished gates. He then walked into the castle. The moment he was out of sight, he slumped against a wall. After resting briefly as Wolf looked on with concern, Waylan steadied himself, and they proceeded to the throne room. Onel, who had left a few hours earlier on his brother's order, was waiting for them with goblets of cold wine.

"An incredible victory, my brother," Onel said. "We have eliminated a large part of Jonar's army."

"I, too, lost many of my men," Waylan lamented. "They were loyal friends and retainers who had served me for forty years. They gave their last breath serving me on that field. These great wars must end. Another battle will leave me no one to rule."

"That is not true, my lord," a woman's voice called from the doorway. Dalla walked into the room, accompanied by Eras and Titus. She approached Waylan and declared, "I will serve you."

"As will I," Eras affirmed. "I have contacted my father, and he is sending three thousand subjects to Springdale. Granted, two thousand are women and children, but you also will receive fighting men. I served Wolf, and he has said you are a just lord. Wolf desires no servants, and you are worthy of our allegiance, Your Majesty, so we will serve you."

"Aye, we come too, my lord. We run the land, but we will settle here if it is your desire. I bring over two thousand Nanna warriors to serve you," said Dalla. Raising a suggestive eyebrow, she added in a sultry voice, "And I would serve you personally, my lord."

Waylan nodded and said, "I accept your pledges to serve me, but I do not condone rapine, murder, or slavery. If this is acceptable to you, then we are as one, and I invite you to settle in the lands. Eras, do you prefer castle life or range life in my service?"

Eras stepped forward and said, "Sire, it would be an honor to defend this place. It is the finest castle I have seen. Do you have enough room for my people?"

"This castle can hold many thousands. Even when the Old Guard was at full force, we had the room. Dalla, what is your wish—castle or range?"

"Range, my lord. But I will stay here with a small garrison of Nanna, and my daughters will run the range."

Waylan looked at Titus and said, "What of you?"

"I am considered an outcast by my people," Titus said sadly.

"You are of my castle now—be at peace. And what of you, Wolf? What will you do?" Waylan asked. "The foe is pushed back and the war is over. Will you go on to explore, or will you and Syn stay awhile?"

"We will stay for a time, my lord. I want to make sure you heal, and we still have injured men who need care. Also, I don't want Jonar to return by surprise. We must be certain his army is in full retreat. He is far too intelligent not to know we are in disarray."

"Agreed," said Waylan, yawning. "I must sleep. The night was long and difficult."

"I will see you after you have rested," Wolf said. Turning to Onel, he instructed, "If the king's injuries are more than his chirurgeons can handle, send for me."

"I will...and thank you, Wolf. We could not have won without you," Onel said earnestly.

"I don't believe that. I was unconscious for hours as your king and his men fought to hold the line. I take no credit for this victory— that honor belongs to the brave men of this kingdom."

Wolf turned and left the throne room, heading off to his quarters on the upper floor of the castle. He hoped Syn had returned with the ship.

"Sire, he belittles his skills and lessens his worth. What a fine man he is," Onel remarked to Waylan.

"Aye, if he hadn't awakened when he did, we would have been defeated. We were played out. He is an honorable man," Waylan agreed.

"Forgive me, brother, I need to ask Wolf something," Onel said, standing and quickly exiting the throne room.

* * *

Wolf walked up the stairs and found Syn waiting at the entrance to the tent. She threw herself into his arms, sobbing. Then she turned her face up and kissed him. "Are you all right, my love?" she murmured, running her hands over his body, probing for injuries.

Before Wolf could answer, Onel called from the stairway, "Your pardon, Wolf and Lady Syn, I was wondering if I could ask a favor of you?"

"Anything, Onel. I owe you and your brother much," Wolf said, easing himself from Syn's arms and wondering what Onel could want.

"I merely ask for the shard you took from my brother's leg."

"Syn will fetch it for you. But may I ask why?" At a nod from Wolf, Syn went to the med bay to retrieve the sword tip.

"My brother received that injury the night before his first battle. He was stabbed as he lay sleeping. Even wounded and bleeding, he followed our father's warriors into battle the next day. That is where our mighty sire was slain. Waylan was ten years old, and since he stood as tall as any man, he fooled others into thinking him a common soldier. The odds were frightful, and our troops were badly outnumbered, but Waylan inspired the troops to victory by refusing to retreat from our father's body. He fought for hours with only my father's remaining bodyguards until reinforcements arrived. I thought the blade tip would make a fitting heirloom for Waylan."

Syn returned with the shard and handed it to Wolf. As he passed it on to Onel, he asked, "Do you know what the inscription says?"

"Yes, but I will not speak it. It is too terrible to repeat. We may all come to regret that you removed it." Onel tried to hide a look of apprehension as he turned and walked down the stairs.

Wolf was confused by Onel's words but shrugged and turned to ask Syn about it. She cut him off and threw herself into his arms, asking repeatedly if he was all right.

"I'm all right, Syn," Wolf consoled her. "My wounds healed quickly as soon as I regained consciousness. But what happened?"

"Jonar used harmonics to undermine your strength. He has discovered a way to counter your invincibility and make you as vulnerable as any mortal on this planet. I don't know how he did it, Wolf, but Jonar is smart—and very dangerous."

"I will have to be careful," Wolf agreed. With a rueful chuckle, he added, "I guess I'm not a superman after all."

"Even the comic strip Superman had his kryptonite. Yours is high-frequency sound."

"What else is going on, Syn? Did I miss anything?"

"Nala knows about the ship and most of its capabilities." Syn raised a hand to silence Wolf's protest. "It was necessary. Sylvaine had you down, and he would have killed you. I couldn't get to you, so we lifted off. I took her to your location on the battlefield, and she jumped fifteen feet to the ground to save you. She dislocated her ankle when she landed, yet she fought hard for hours, protecting you from Sylvaine. She reset the dislocation herself, causing more damage to her foot. It will heal, but it will take time."

"Where is she?" Wolf asked with concern.

"Commander, that's not all."

"Syn, is she okay? Just tell me if she's all right," Wolf demanded.

"Nala is alive, but she was injured in the battle. I have her sedated. She fainted after you recovered, and I placed her in the med unit. She has three broken ribs, a broken tibia, a torn abdominal muscle, several deep stab wounds, and deep cuts to her chest that will require plastic surgery. Come, my love, let's check on her."

They walked into the med unit, and Wolf gazed at the woman, shocked by the severity of her wounds. Her face was purple, swollen, and bruised; her lip was split, attesting to the ferocity of the battle she had waged to protect him. "She is amazing...and very brave," he said.

"Yes, very brave. She loves you as do I."

"Syn, what are we going to do?" Wolf asked, feeling unstable and confused. "This love triangle scares me. I'm in love with two women, and I don't know if I can choose."

"There is no choice to make, Wolf. I told you, Nala is for you. She is flesh and blood. I can offer you nothing. Believe me, I am not angry. I love Nala and I would do anything for her, even sacrifice my love for you."

"Stop, Syn. What you and I have is special. I will not lose it. Let's allow time to decide what will be," Wolf suggested, as he and Syn each held one of Nala's hands.

* * *

In the weeks after the battle, life at the castle returned to normal. The official story was that Haakon had died a hero in the king's service. Only Wolf, Nala, Syn, and Waylan knew the truth. When Nala told her children the news, Reon, Leesa, and Trulane cried, while Brithee remained aloof, as would be expected of a trained Nanna.

Wolf began to suspect that Nala was avoiding him. She was content to spend her time with Syn and the others on the roof or in public, but when Wolf came around, she averted her eyes and made a weak excuse to leave.

Nala had fully recovered, and one day, Brithee challenged her to a friendly duel. The young girl had defeated several highly adept Nanna warriors and wanted to impress her mother with her skills. She even had the audacity to challenge her grandmother, but Dalla laughed and dismissed the girl with a wave of her hand. When Waylan heard about the challenge, he decided it was a good time for a contest of arms and offered fabulous prizes to the most skilled contestants in the use of swords, knives, whips, and other events.

The day of the contest, Brithee strutted into the coliseum behind the castle with an air of cockiness. She had developed into a Nanna warrior in a remarkably short time. Her physique was ripped with muscle, and she walked with her head held high. She was accompanied by her aunt Skylla and her sister Leesa. Skylla was well aware of Nala's fighting prowess and had tried to dissuade Brithee, but the headstrong girl scoffed at her warnings. Nala entered the arena with an air of supreme confidence that bordered on amusement over her daughter's precocious challenge, with Syn and Wolf at her side.

The two women bowed to Waylan, who signaled for the contest to begin with a wave of his hand. Nala and Brithee bowed to one another and then brandished blunted whips. Brithee attacked with a series of overhand swings aimed at her mother's wrist, trying to disarm Nala straight off. Nala blocked each stroke with lightning fast counters that precisely hit the tip of her daughter's blunted whip. Brithee clenched her teeth in stubborn determination and changed tactics, attacking her mother's feet. Nala flipped in incredible handsprings, back flips, and no-handed fulls—moves that resembled the floor routine of an Olympic gymnast on ancient earth—and she avoided her daughter's well-aimed strokes.

Brithee was breathing hard and Nala smiled. Then the two women exploded into a mass of flipping, spinning chaos, swinging their whips with amazing precision as they fought around the ring. Brithee gave her all and was sweating profusely, determined to prove a point to all who watched, especially her mother.

The trading and blocking went on for a full ten minutes. Nala smiled and flipped her whip, tangling in Brithee's arcing whip. Nala spun several times, winding Brithee's whip around her sleek mid-section until they stood face to face in the center of the arena.

"Are you ready to learn how it is done, my darling?" Nala asked.

"Learn? Mother, you will lose. You are defeated now—I have you ensnared in my whip! I have matched your speed and power," Brithee said, congratulating herself.

"Have you, my daughter? Ha! I was playing with you! Now behold my true skills and you'll see why the old ones chose me."

Nala renewed the battle, pirouetting out of Brithee's whip. She dropped to her knees, spinning and moving into range, using her whip to remove Brithee's right shoe as the girl swung her own whip wildly, trying to score a point off her mother. Nala sprang into the air and peeled off Brithee's hood with a dexterous flip of her whip, then did a double full and rolled, removing Brithee's left shoe. Brithee answered with a flawless back flip in midair, and Nala snapped her whip in quick, successive strikes that continued to disrobe her daughter until Brithee wore only her leather shorts. Nala smiled and then used her whip to loosen the girl's long, dark hair to hide her bare breasts. It was clear to all, including Brithee, that she was no match for her mother.

Brithee surrendered and gave Nala an affectionate hug. "Mother, I stand corrected. I can't defeat you yet, but it was fun."

"You are young, and your skill will grow. You did well, my darling. I am very proud of you," Nala responded.

In the other tournaments, Wolf won the strength contest by lifting the new portcullis twenty-five times, while Waylan won his own swordsmanship contest. As the merriment wound down, a final round of wine and beer were served, and then the crowd dispersed. Syn and Wolf withdrew to a hidden balcony overlooking the city below and talked late into the night.

* * *

Wolf had asked to occupy the top floor of the castle while he remained at Springdale, and King Waylan agreed that he could reside in the tower as long as he wished. Syn had removed the tent, and the ship hovered above, invisible, allowing her easy access, although she had completed the micro-emitters and could now go wherever she wanted. She redesigned Wolf's earpiece with a noise reduction coil and made a second unit for his other ear with new features that she hoped would make him immune to the debilitating effects of Jonar's sonic weapons.

It had been several months since Jonar's incursion into the kingdom, and the ambitious warlord had made no further moves. As always, in times of peace, love finds its own way and people come together to fulfill its promise. One such chance meeting had occurred between Trulane and Onel's daughter, Jhondra, and they were now inseparable. Outside the castle, the Nanna ran the surrounding plains, patrolling day and night. Brithee and Leesa ran with Skylla, learning the Nanna skills. They had fought many times together, and both were praised for their skills. The strenuous exercise had toned Leesa, and her body had trimmed down to a healthy appearance. The Nanna had scoured Waylan's land, clearing it of bandits and ruffians, and times were easy now.

Dalla had taken a liking to Waylan, and the irascible monarch seemed ten years younger when he was with her. He appeared to be regaining muscle mass and his youthful vigor. But as the days passed, Onel fretted more and more. He seemed sad, withdrawn, and afraid of *something*. He constantly shadowed his brother, and even Waylan was becoming annoyed with Onel's dark moods, provoking several heated arguments between them.

Eventually, Waylan ordered Randelf to rescind the ban on Nanna marriage and abolished the ancient laws that made them outcasts. It was an easy decision because he didn't agree with the laws in the first place. Randelf, who spent his days poring over the Bible that Wolf had given him, was happy to oblige. The corrected religion he now preached had no room for hatred or prejudice. Dalla had grown quite fond of the old monarch, and he enjoyed her attention. They were often seen walking hand in hand in one of the many palace gardens.

The first day of summer was mild, and the sun cast its bright rays over the lands. It was a beautiful day. Birds flew overhead and flitted through treetops, their songs filling the air with cheerful melodies. Butterflies swarmed around the colorful sprays of flowers that adorned the castle gardens and grew along the terraces. Wolf was inside the ship, talking with Syn. She had landed the vessel on the roof to perform routine maintenance.

"Has there been any activity at Jonar's castle?" Wolf asked.

"His army has been disbanded and I show only a regular garrison at his castle."

"That's strange. He was so close. Why did he stop?"

"I can't speculate, Wolf. I am sure we will find out. The man is cunning."

"Maybe I should travel to his castle, retrieve the watch, and just finish it."

"Why wade in more death? He has done nothing in months. Let him be. The watch is deactivated and I'm sure it's beyond his understanding. If he opens it and exposes its power source, he will irradiate himself and die eventually."

"I worry about it, Syn. He has proven that he can surprise us." Wolf stood and took Syn's hand, pulling her to her feet to face him. With a dazzling smile, she said, "Let's go out on the parapet. I want to see the view from the top of the castle."

They left the ship and walked hand in hand across the roof. Wolf stopped and turned Syn into his arms. She stood in front of him and felt his broad chest pressing against her back. Wolf smelled her hair, amazed by the pains she took to appear real. She smelled delicious, as if she had lightly sprayed herself with perfume. He felt her shiver as he exhaled warm breath on her neck and nibbled at her ear. Syn turned in his arms, smiling. She had never looked more beautiful to him. He drew her close for a kiss. Suddenly, she flickered erratically.

"Syn, what's wrong?" Wolf's hands passed through Syn as her physical form dissolved, leaving a faint, glowing hologram that wavered in and out of focus.

"I do not know," Syn replied in a scratchy voice. "Something is... wrong. I am losing power. I detect power readings from Jonar's castle...they're off the scale." She stared at Wolf with fear in her eyes and then screamed as if in pain. She screamed again and said in a trembling voice, "Wolf, I have been hacked. I am being downloaded. Something is using our satellites against me. That power source on the moon has accessed the C29 and the Dawn. You must remove my power unit immediately or I will be lost to you forever. Hurry, Commander!"

Wolf ran back into the ship to Syn's primary control board. Kneeling, he reached under the control panel and groped around until he found the power rods. He looked around for Syn, but she was nowhere to be found.

"Syn, where are you? I can't lose you!"

Syn's hologram flickered to life in front of him. "Hurry, Wolf," she pleaded. "I cannot block the download much longer. I detect power...massive power. Do not reactivate me until you find and destroy the hacker."

With tears in his eyes and his heart in his throat, Wolf withdrew the power rods.

"Goodbye, my love," Syn whispered, and then in a choked voice, she cried, "No! It cannot be..." Her voice trailed off, and her hologram vanished, leaving Wolf staring at nothing and wondering what her last words meant.

Syn's computer program shut down with a short hum followed by several clicks. With her computer powered off, Wolf wasn't sure if he would be able to move or re-materialize his ship, or communicate with the orbiting satellites. He didn't care—the only thing that mattered now was that he had lost Syn. Someone knew how to hit him, and just one person on the planet had that kind of brainpower. Jonar had wounded him worse in the last few minutes than he did with his howler in the last battle.

Wolf sat for hours, wondering what to do. He sank into a dark depression as he realized that Syn might be lost to him forever. She was delicate, extremely complicated, and Jonar's crude hacking could have a disastrous effect on her programming. Wolf felt panic churn in his gut, and he broke into a cold sweat at the thought that Syn might never return.

As nightfall engulfed the land of Springdale, Wolf stood up, his shoulders slumped in defeat, and he walked to Waylan's throne room. He had to inform the king that the war had begun anew, but this time, he had been wounded before the first sword was drawn. He felt incomplete and vulnerable. Someone had used his greatest weakness against him, and he had no idea how to defend himself.

To be continued...

Coming Soon: *Syns of an Iron Wolf* *(Book 2 of The Fractured Earth Saga)*

The unthinkable has happened...Syn has been hacked! Someone has hijacked Wolf's only remaining connection to the world he left behind in the twenty-first century. To rescue Syn, he must make the perilous journey to Jonar's stronghold with a pair of condemned thieves and his trusted friend Nala. Jonar's castle is surrounded by evil Templars, ruffians, and ancient scientific wonders Jonar has dredged up from earth's distant past. Once Wolf reaches the castle, he will have to deal with a massive power source Jonar has unleashed and a second mysterious power source that flared to life on the moon moments before Syn screamed in anguish. What did her last words mean? *'No! It cannot be!'* What unseen force could put such terror and agony in her sweet voice? Will Wolf be able to fly the shuttle without her? Will her intricate programming be altered? Why did Jonar hack Syn? These questions haunted Wolf as he trekked across the wastelands towards Jonar's heavily fortified stronghold.

www.ingramcontent.com/pod-product-compliance
Lightning Source LLC
Chambersburg PA
CBHW070807180626
46818CB00001B/145